LOVE ABANDONED

Honorable Intentions, Book 2

by Rose Phillips

DRAGONBLADE PUBLISHING, INC.

ARE YOU SIGNED UP FOR DRAGONBLADE'S BLOG?

You'll get the latest news and information on exclusive giveaways, exclusive excerpts, coming releases, sales, free books, cover reveals and more.

Check out our complete list of authors, too!

No spam, no junk. That's a promise!

Sign Up Here

www.dragonbladepublishing.com

Dearest Reader;

Thank you for your support of a small press. At Dragonblade Publishing, we strive to bring you the highest quality Historical Romance from some of the best authors in the business. Without your support, there is no 'us', so we sincerely hope you adore these stories and find some new favorite authors along the way.

Happy Reading!

CEO, Dragonblade Publishing

**Additional Dragonblade books by
Author Rose Phillips**

Honorable Intentions Series
Love Denied (Book 1)
Love Abandoned (Book 2)

From thee, the pleasure of the fleeting year!
What freezings have I felt, what dark days seen!
What old December's bareness everywhere!
And yet this time remov'd was summer's time,
The teeming autumn, big with rich increase,
Bearing the wanton burthen of the prime,
Like widow'd wombs after their lords' decease:
Yet this abundant issue seem'd to me
But hope of orphans and unfather'd fruit;
For summer and his pleasures wait on thee,
And thou away, the very birds are mute;
Or if they sing, 'tis with so dull a cheer
That leaves look pale, dreading the winter's near.

—Shakespeare, "Sonnet 97"

PROLOGUE

Hear my soul speak:
The very instant that I saw you, did
My heart fly to your service; there resides,
To make me a slave to it.

—Shakespeare, *The Tempest*

1808

THREE YEARS, AND Elizabeth was as bewitching as the day he'd married her. As beguiling as the first day they'd met. Richard would ravish her where she stood were it not for the room full of guests. And it would be hours before they could retire, so he might as well rein in his lustful aspirations and turn his attention elsewhere. What a rubbish idea this anniversary gathering had turned out to be. Even worse, it had been his rubbish idea.

Richard had been in town for far too long, chasing down business investments when he'd rather be chasing down Elizabeth. But the estate could not sustain itself indefinitely, and it was time to expand his fortunes. One day an heir would be grateful for his forethought. Hopefully, the manor would be full of children to support. Children. He'd far prefer slipping away and trying to create one than this standing around talking about inconsequential trivia. Unfortunately, he'd thought an anniversary celebration would be cheering for Elizabeth. The lack of children had been wearing on them both.

"Still gawking at your wife after all these years?" Bentley slapped Richard on the back jovially. "You almost make me consider marriage."

Richard cast his glance sideways at his old school chum and raised an eyebrow. "Is there something…or someone…I should know about?"

"I said 'almost,' my friend. You know me better than that. Too many skirts in the wilderness, waiting to be tamed, for me to put myself in a cage."

"Once a rake, always a rake? Don't be so certain. Someday you'll find your Lady Bentley, and she'll cast her spell over you as mine has done to me. And you'll be glad of it."

Bentley guffawed, drawing the attention of some of the guests and of Elizabeth. Richard smiled at her and held her stare. Her pale cheeks flushed a soft pink, but she did not look away. "If you'll excuse me, Bentley?" he said and walked toward her.

Lovely gathering. Such a wonderful evening. Good to see you, Lord Thornwood. The voices swirled around him, but he had eyes only for Elizabeth. "Lady Thornwood," he said, interrupting old Mrs. Farnsworth, who was wearing far more ribbons and bows than a fresh debutante. "May I see you in private for a moment?"

Elizabeth's cheeks deepened to scarlet, but she nodded and set her hand on his arm.

"If you'll excuse us, Mrs. Farnsworth," he said, not waiting for her response. More platitudes followed them out of the room.

"Is there something I can do for you, my lord?" Hastings asked, two footmen in tow behind him, each carrying several decanters of wine.

"No, Hastings, we're fine." Richard tilted his head back toward the room. "Make sure glasses are full and no one is in need of anything. And set the food out a little early."

"Yes, my lord."

No one would complain with an overflowing glass in hand and a full stomach. They would not be missed. He'd been delayed and had arrived along with guests, and he couldn't wait another minute to hold her in his arms.

"Richard?"

"Shh," he said. "Let me whisk you away."

Her smile lit the hallway, and she leaned into him as they walked silently along the corridor. Although it would afford them definitive privacy, as no one would dare enter it, he chose not to stop at his study. The saloon next door to it had been opened to the large drawing room, which put the revelers far too close for comfort.

He released an audible sigh of relief when they made it to the library without encountering any strays. Richard pulled Elizabeth inside, begrudgingly letting her go to firmly close the doors. He turned around and leaned back on them, drinking her in. She stood there, looking shy and confident at the same time. Her blonde hair was piled on top of her head, but she'd left wisps caressing her long, slender neck. Only two gilt lamps had been lit, and they were behind her. Her lovely shape was well illuminated with the backlighting, but he could not see her eyes. It didn't matter. He knew them by heart and was confident they mirrored the love she would see in his.

Richard opened his arms in invitation. She smiled and stepped into them, and he embraced her. Her heart beat against his own. This was home. "I missed you," he whispered.

"I missed you too," she said and tilted her face to look at him.

He could resist no longer. He took possession of her mouth, hoping his kiss would tell her more adequately than words the truth of his longing for her. They parted, both panting breathlessly.

"Richard," she finally managed, touching her lips as she spoke his name. "The guests will see…"

He glanced out the windows at the night. It was a miserable one, windy and rainy. No one would be strolling the gardens. He told her so.

She smiled tentatively and touched her lips again. "No, that's not what I meant. They will see the evidence. You know how easily I bruise."

"Did I hurt you, my love?" He cursed himself for being an uncontrolled lecher, tugged her close, and kissed her forehead. "I would never willingly do so. You know that, don't you?" He pulled back so he could see her face.

"Of course I do." This time her smile was mischievous. "Hurt me again."

And wolfishly, he did. This time, when he finally let her go, he wondered how either of them were going to be able to return to the soiree. They would be fodder for endless gossip. He could hear them now disdaining a married couple who were actually in love.

"Come sit with me, and we'll give ourselves some time to recompose." He touched her swollen lips, and she kissed his fingers. "Elizabeth," he growled in warning. His blood would never cool if she continued to look at him like that. He led her to the sofa and pulled her down beside him. "It is good to see the rose in your cheeks. You were exceptionally pale when I arrived, and I worried this gathering had put too much of a strain on you. I do apologize. It was a thick-witted idea."

"Not at all, my dearest. A husband who remembers an anniversary is special. One who wishes to celebrate it is a rare find."

He kissed her cheek, feeling as young and in love as when they'd first met five years ago. He'd been able to claim her as his own now for three years, and the glow that warmed him at the mere thought of her did not dull. She entwined her fingers in his.

"And we have much to celebrate," she said quietly. She shifted their hands to her midriff and clasped them with her other hand, holding them tightly to her stomach. "Much to celebrate."

Richard's heart skipped a beat. Could it be? Dare he hope? "You are...? We are...?"

She nodded, her eyes shimmering in the dull light. "We are,

Lord Thornwood. Finally."

He pulled her close, biting back the emotion clogging his throat, making it impossible to speak. It was all he'd dreamed of in his young years. To hear the voices of other children ringing off these old walls. And now it was going to happen. His children. Her children. *Their* children. "Thank you," he finally managed to whisper into her hair.

"Oh, Richard," she whispered back. "This is only the beginning."

CHAPTER ONE

For my part, I may speak it to my shame,
I have a truant been to chivalry.

—Shakespeare, *Henry IV*

1813

ELIZABETH SURVEYED THE room. Her feet were tired, her back ached, and she longed for the quiet of Thornwood Manor. The little appeal London ever held was long gone. But appearances were appearances, so here she was making hers. It would be easier if Richard were equally compelled to keep up the facade. She scanned the room again. He'd assured her he would attend. Where was he?

"*Bella*, why so glum? It's a grand crush, no?"

Elizabeth turned to Sophia. Sophia was the opposite of everything she was—curves to Elizabeth's edges, color to her blandness, daring to her reserve—and she was her best friend for all those reasons. Elizabeth loved Sophia's joie de vivre and relished her company because of it.

"It's a lovely gathering, as usual, but I tire of them. I fear London, and its mob, hold little charm for me."

"On a dreary January night, what else is there to do? You have grown rusty in the country and need oiled, *mia amica*.

Dance. You must dance."

"I'm not sure I remember how," Elizabeth said, rather than complaining about her aches and pains. She'd no wish to dampen Sophia's spirit.

"It is like riding a horse," Sophia said, waving a hand in dismissal. "But never mind. All the good gossip in these dull days comes from what happens at the Argyll Rooms. It is most important to be seen." Sophia quickly fluttered her fan under her chin. "And to see." She smiled wickedly. "Help me pick out a man. An attractive one with big, broad shoulders and healthy teeth. It is awful, no, when they are sculpted like granite, then smile and…" She shuddered dramatically.

Elizabeth laughed. Sophia was a widow and took full advantage of the freedoms that came with such a status. She did not disguise her enjoyment of male company and was often seen with a different one for each event of the week. Elizabeth was convinced Sophia delighted in the scandalous rumors and whispered gossip as much as she did the men.

"I'll help you find one so long as we move. I've been standing in one spot far too long and need to stretch my limbs."

"Certainly, *amica* mine, let us take a stroll." Sophia scooped her arm through Elizabeth's.

Immediately, fresh blood flowed through Elizabeth's ankle and down to her pinched toes. She'd chosen her favorite slippers not only because they matched the ribbon of her sash but because she associated fond memories with them. However, as with many of her shoes now, they were far too tight. Her feet had widened since the birth of Sebastian. Her entire body would have permanently widened after his birth had she not been so ill. Small blessings, she supposed and made a mental note to finally make the time to purchase a new set of cerulean slippers.

Sophia stopped. "What is your opinion of the gentleman dancing with the Countess of Cholmondeleye? He is handsome, no?"

Elizabeth looked to where one of tonight's patronesses was

deep in conversation with an unarguably fine-looking gentleman. "But the duke is married, and you do not engage the affections of a man who is taken. Or so you always say."

Sophia laughed. "I was checking to see if you were paying attention. You seem elsewhere this evening."

"My feet can assure you I am right here," she said, wincing as they continued their promenade past the columns, navigating around groups deep in conversation while avoiding the dancers to her right. She eyed the ladies sitting comfortably on the side benches, watching the country dance and twittering behind their fans.

"Lady Thornwood. Countess Tessaro."

They acknowledged everyone who addressed them as they walked by but did not stop for conversation. Elizabeth continued to watch for Richard but was not truly surprised to see no sign of him. Sophia politely turned from all eager potential suitors. Instead, she seemed to prefer to hunt for her own prey.

"Oh, that one might have done, but look at his stockings. One has a run, and the heels of his shoes are scuffed." Sophia shook her head in mock disgust. "And that one? His blond hair is *bello*, but those ears? Like an *elefante*. I believe they are held up by his cravat."

Elizabeth guffawed out loud and quickly raised her fan to hide it, lest someone think she was laughing at them. That would not do at all. Sophia might like to be the center of attention, but Elizabeth did not. On their second turn around the room, three ladies abandoned their places for the dance floor.

"Oh, please, Sophia," Elizabeth said and sunk onto the padded red velvet bench. Sophia obligingly sat beside her. It was all Elizabeth could do to resist the urge to slide out of her slippers.

"Thank goodness I found you. No easy task in this crush."

"Lady Walford," Elizabeth said at the same time Sophia exuberantly exclaimed, "Catherine!" to the lovely woman who gracefully eased herself onto the last vacant spot.

Lady Walford smiled at them both. "Please, call me Catherine," she said to Elizabeth. "We are well past formalities." She glanced around the ballroom. "Even here. Although, one need not shout my Christian name," she said teasingly to Sophia.

"But I adore that you're here." Sophia jumped from her seat and brushed a kiss to each of Catherine's cheeks, which flushed charmingly. "It has been impossible to pry you away from that husband of yours. My only hope to see you was to take the dreadful ride to Woodfield Park when I returned to the country."

Catherine brushed her gloved hand across her midriff, and Elizabeth stiffened. Of course, she should have noticed immediately. Catherine's cheeks were rounder and her bosom more plentiful. Her hand had briefly accentuated a bump, one that had disappeared back under the folds of her high-waisted dress.

"Congratulations," Elizabeth said politely, suppressing the emotions tumbling uncontrollably. Elation, fear, sadness. She'd felt them all with her second child and would do it all again if God were willing. But it seemed he was not. Nor was Richard. He would need to come within closer proximity to her for that to happen. She quickly examined the room again, then returned her attention to Catherine. "I had no idea. Sophia said not a word."

"It was not my news to share, *mia amica*. And you said I could not keep a secret," Sophia said, tapping Elizabeth's shoulder playfully with her fan before turning back to Catherine. "So when will you begin your confinement?"

Catherine shrugged daintily. "In truth, I wish I already had. I am not well trained for these grand events, and now I find everything tiring. But Nicholas assures me our stay will be brief. And he enticed me with the promise of shopping for the baby. And for myself." She glanced down at herself before continuing. "I will need more forgiving dresses before long."

"You are *perfetta, mia amica. Bellissima.*" Sophia pinched her fingertips together, touched them to her lips, and kissed them, then opened her hand as though throwing the kiss into the air. "Do you not agree, Elizabeth? Is she not beautiful?"

"You are truly lovely, as you've always been." Elizabeth's

rampant feelings were now firmly under control. She knew Catherine, squarely in the thrall of love, saw the baby as a symbol, a promise of endless possibilities for the future. As Elizabeth had when she'd carried William. And again with Sebastian. She hoped, for Catherine's sake, the years ahead lived up to her every dream. Elizabeth would not wish her own past two years on anyone.

"And where is the handsome papa?" Sophia asked, glancing around the room, then returning her gaze to Catherine and raising an eyebrow. "And is he accompanied by friends? An Adonis who might be smitten by my womanly charms?" Sophia laughed and tugged at her dress, pulling the neckline lower than its already daring plunge.

"Sophia, behave," Catherine said, laughing along with her. "As a matter of fact, he is with someone else who is also charming and good-looking. But I believe he will be immune to your charms as he is married to an absolute pearl."

Sophia slumped theatrically back in her chair. "The best ones are always taken."

"They are," Catherine said in commiseration. "Oh look, here they come now."

Elizabeth followed Catherine's gaze. Lord Walford, with eyes only for Catherine, walked straight toward them like he was once again leading a battalion. At his side, looking more leisurely in form but keeping stride while acknowledging greetings, was the perfect gentleman. Her husband. Richard.

RICHARD THORNWOOD HAD waited an insufferable amount of time outside of the Argyll Rooms. Insufferable both because of the tedium of acknowledging each attendee as they went in and because he was going to eventually have to go in himself. He'd always found the games within these walls shallow and tedious, and the older he got, the less patience he had for them. But he'd seen the hope in Elizabeth's eyes and had not been willing to dash it, so he'd begrudgingly conceded to the evening. At least this dance was being held as a benefit. His money would not be wasted for sheer vanity alone.

Why Walford insisted they meet here, he'd no idea. It would have been better to have met him elsewhere afterward. Unfortunately, Richard had gotten tied up in chambers and had not been able to escort Elizabeth himself. He'd scribbled a hasty note to her and sent Bentley in his stead. It had been an irksome rush to get home and change. He'd told Walford he'd catch him outside but had since decided the street was no place to talk. Of course, Walford didn't know he'd changed his mind, so Richard had been waiting impatiently in the cold for him.

He looked up at the tall, bland building. Richard couldn't possibly have the conversation he needed to have with Walford inside either. He sighed heavily. Elizabeth, no doubt resplendently beautiful, was waiting expectantly for him. This evening was proving to hold more artifice than he could manage.

"Thornwood!" Walford shouted as he came around the corner.

Richard dipped his chin in greeting, stuffing his impatience down. Walford could not possibly know how important it was for him to see him in private. He'd been deliberately vague, not anxious to put the meeting's purpose in writing.

"Good to see you, old friend." Walford thrust out his hand, and Richard shook it vigorously. "I was surprised to get your note but quite pleased. We haven't talked since…"

Walford let the sentence drift. Their last meeting had been somewhat awkward, with family secrets oozing from the wood panels. Though, it had been an unusual and exciting distraction too. He'd never been party to capturing a culprit before. Would he be again now? Were there culprits in the game of war or merely players?

"Thank you for coming. Although, I did assume we would

meet at the club."

Walford grinned. "Yes, I thought you might. But Catherine has priority claim on me, and she wanted to see the countesses before we dash back to the countryside. It's why she came earlier rather than wait for me to finish my business with the company."

"Right. Congratulations on your purchase. It's good you are so forward-thinking. Trade is frightfully lucrative right now, and I can't see it changing for the foreseeable future."

"I'll take you to see some of the ships. Top of the line workmanship." Walford glanced at the dwindling crowd. "We'd better go in. We've kept our ladies waiting far too long as it is. And Catherine will have my hide if we do not dance at least once."

Richard fought the sharp pang of envy. He knew the look on Walford's face. He'd worn it once himself. How could he possibly resent the man for being in love? Walford had been to hell and back on the continent, only to return to the loss of his only brother. He had a right to some happiness. Richard genuinely hoped life did not rob Walford of it as it had him.

The warmth of the assembly room was a stark contrast to the cold outside. The pungent smell of too many sweating bodies swirled with the heat. His gut churned, and he resisted the urge to run a finger under his cravat and pull it from his neck. He also fought the urge to look where he was headed, for he knew Elizabeth might be watching him. Instead, he focused on responding to those who greeted him even though he cared not a whit who was here. Elizabeth was the only person he cared about, but he forbade himself to dwell on her. Being in her presence was sometimes almost unbearable.

"My ladies," Walford said smoothly but was obviously only addressing his own. His wife smiled sweetly in return.

"My ladies," Richard echoed, quietly taking each of them in, setting his eyes on Elizabeth last. His gut turned. He could see the hurt in those blue eyes and the shadows under them no paint could conceal. He'd done that to her. She looked away, and he stiffened his shoulders. What was done was done. But it would not happen again.

"Lady Tessaro, if I may?" The Duke of Salinger held out his hand to the countess, without so much as a glance at Richard or Walford. Walford raised an eyebrow at Richard and was biting back a smirk. The duke was a pompous, dreadful bore and far too old for the countess, but if she regarded him as such, it didn't show.

"Of course, Your Grace. It would be my pleasure," she said pleasantly and rose to her feet. "Surely you will all join us?"

The question was directed at Richard, and in fact, it was patently not a question but an order. The woman never followed etiquette and expected others to flaunt it as well.

"With pleasure. Lady Walford?" Walford held out his hand, and his wife took it, her eyes only for him.

It appeared Walford took direction well and had no issue dancing with his own wife before making an effort with others. Strains of the next dance were beginning, wafting through the air from the far side of the room where the orchestra assembled on a stage. It would be beastly to leave Elizabeth to sit while her friends were on the floor. He, too, held out his hand. "Lady Thornwood?"

She seemed to hesitate before placing her hand in his, and even with the glove as a barrier, it sparked a heated reaction in his body. God give him strength.

RICHARD LET GO of her hand to take his place in the line on the other side. Elizabeth slipped in beside Catherine. Sophia and the duke, having more superior ranks, were positioned closer to the lead of the line. Catherine smiled at her but quickly returned her attention back to her husband. Lord Walford was grinning lasciviously back at his wife, and Richard, in contrast, seemed to want to look anywhere but at his.

Despite his disinterest, Elizabeth remained attracted to him. She didn't want to be. Life would be so much easier if she weren't, but she could not lie to herself. She yearned for him daily and wished nothing more than to return to the early days of their marriage. When he'd touched her hand a moment ago, she was certain a frisson sparked between them. She was sure he'd felt it too, but he'd dropped her hand as quickly as he'd taken it.

The line moved, and she shifted, continuing to eye Richard. She didn't often see him in knee breeches anymore. Of course, she didn't often see him at all. He spent more time in London than he did in the country. While she respected his excuse of attending to parliamentary and business matters, being left to rusticate in the country had become tedious. His Christmas visit had been short and altogether unsatisfying. He'd spent more time with the boys and the horses than he had with her. Each time she'd tried to broach discussion of their relationship, he'd excuse himself for estate business.

She had spontaneously decided to join him in town. She'd hoped the surprise might ignite a flame. Instead, he'd awkwardly greeted their arrival and turned his attention to the children. She had been hard-pressed to get a commitment from him to join her here this evening, and only the threat of gossip had secured an agreement. At least the pressure of societal judgment held some sway, because apparently she held none.

They stepped toward one another and, hands held high, pressed palm to palm before turning and walking through the row of people. The assembly might believe he looked at her, but she knew the truth. He looked through her, his eyes a painted still life. Elizabeth's heart plummeted to her stomach. Did he care so little for her now that he could not bear the sight of her? They separated at the end of the line and took their places opposite each other.

The music, lively and cheerful, helped her maintain a smile, though her cheeks hurt with the effort. Laughter surrounded her. Hopeful young women in playful conversation with potential suitors. Matrons deep in dreaming about how they could manipulate the marriage mart in favor of their children, strategizing for the season to come. Their husbands, no doubt, sharing some ribald story and keeping an eye on their pocket watches, calculating when they could safely sneak out to their gambling. The noise enveloped her, smothering her, and suddenly she couldn't breathe. She stumbled out of line, desperately looking around for an empty spot on the benches.

"Elizabeth," Richard said quietly in her ear, grabbing her elbow and steadying her. "Are you unwell?"

She looked at him. Her Richard was back. His eyes no longer vacant, she saw genuine concern in them. She could breathe again. She inhaled deeply, and slowly exhaled, before daring to answer. "I believe I was overwhelmed by the heat."

Richard's eyes narrowed solicitously, and he led her to a darkened corner under the far balcony where, blessedly, the bench was empty. "Sit," he commanded.

She did as told, grateful to get off her feet again. She'd not registered how much her toes hurt until this minute. She bent over, slid out of her slippers, and gasped. Her lovely stockings were ruined.

"Elizabeth," Richard said and fell to one knee. He grabbed her right foot. "Bloody hell," he muttered under his breath.

Bloody was the correct word, for her stocking was red with it. "Richard," she squeaked as he reached under her skirt and untied her garter.

"Hush," he said, so softly and tenderly she was momentarily disoriented. She glanced around. They were partially tucked in the corner, and no one seemed interested in them. He gently unrolled the stocking, and she winced as he pulled it off. Her large toenail was torn at a haphazard angle, the missing piece nowhere to be seen. In all likelihood, it remained in the stocking, not that she wished to check and verify that.

Richard grimaced and repeated the procedure with the other leg, although the revelations there were much less dramatic, only broken blisters mingling with fresh ones. He looked at her and frowned. "Dear God, Elizabeth, your feet must sting like the devil. Why would you wear these? Why would you bear it?" He dangled the offending slippers.

Elizabeth bit her bottom lip, fighting tears. How could she tell him it was because they were her favorite? She'd worn them when they'd first danced. She'd worn them when he had proposed to her, on one knee much like now, charmingly explaining how life with him was her only choice for, he'd declared, he would die without her. And how could she tell him they no longer fit because carrying their children had flattened her feet into ducks' feet? She shrugged a shoulder and said nothing.

Richard shook his head and stood. "Wait here."

She watched him disappear into the throng of people before glancing at her feet. They were a proper mess. But Richard's touch lingered, and she could not regret that. Nor the caring in his eyes. This was not the way she meant to entice him back to her, but she'd take whatever she could get.

"Oh my," Catherine said as she came around the corner and spied Elizabeth's feet. "They must hurt terribly." She took a seat and put her hand on Elizabeth's. "Whyever didn't you say something?"

Elizabeth didn't answer the question for Catherine either. Only Sophia knew about the detachment between her and Richard, and it was Elizabeth's desire to keep it that way. "Where is Richard?" she asked.

"He's sent Nicholas to get the carriage, and he and Bentley are checking to see if there is a more discreet exit to use. Although"—Catherine looked pointedly around at the matrons who were now taking notice—"I suspect you will be in tomorrow's *Morning Chronicle*, regardless of how discreet Richard is." She grinned. "And I can say I saw it all. We don't have this kind of excitement in our corner of the country."

Elizabeth smiled back, genuinely this time. "Nor in mine,"

she said, picturing Richard's fingers as they'd gently unrolled her stockings.

"The carriage will be at the side door. You can take the back stairway," Nicholas said to Richard as they arrived from opposite directions.

"Thank you, Walford."

"I'll come with you," Catherine announced, jumping lithely to her feet, her condition not yet encumbering her movements. "You'll need someone to administer to those," she said, pointing at Elizabeth's feet.

Elizabeth fought disappointment, but how could she turn Lady Walford away when she was being all that was kind?

"No need," Richard said. "Enjoy the remainder of the evening." He bent over and slid an arm under Elizabeth's legs. "Put your arm around my neck."

Her heart pounded as Richard picked her up. She caught the knowing smiles on the Walfords' faces, and the smirks on those standing by, as Richard elbowed his way through the crowd, toward the stairwell at the back of the building. Let them smile. Let them smirk. Let them write all about it in the broadsheets. Tonight, she was exactly where she wanted to be. In Richard's arms.

CHAPTER TWO

From a little spark may burst a flame.

—Dante Alighieri, *Paradiso*

T HE CROWD PARTED as Richard pushed his way through the room. He did make an effort not to jostle everyone, but he couldn't avoid bumping a few people. He muttered insincere apologies while cursing internally. There had to be more here than was safe. There ought to be laws against such congestion. They chattered around him, like a gaggle of geese unexpectedly interrupted. He did not doubt by morning they would have worn themselves out over the drama, but the paper would pick at it like a raven at a carcass. Let them. All he cared about was getting Elizabeth home and having her wounds attended.

Her face pressed to his chest, she hid from curious eyes. Richard did not doubt she was mortified by the scene they were causing. At the door, a footman stood with his coat and Elizabeth's wrap.

"Lord Bentley…said you might…like…these," the man said, wheezing uncontrollably. He must have sprinted across the room and down the stairs.

"Yes, thank you." Richard eyed the closed door. It would be considerate to let the footman catch his breath, but he'd not be able to hold Elizabeth and open it. "Do get the door, would you?"

The man quickly complied, and Richard stepped out into the bracing night air. The promised carriage was there, his man standing at the ready. "My lord," Simon gasped and stepped forward to take Elizabeth.

"No." Richard held Elizabeth possessively. "Grab our garb, and let's get Lady Thornwood home."

Simon placed their garments on the seat and waited at the ready. It was awkward getting in with her in his arms, but he didn't let her go. He fell back onto the bench with a harrumph, his breathing labored, and Simon closed the door. The carriage rocked as Simon climbed onto his box, and seconds later, it rattled along the road. Elizabeth's shoulders lifted and dropped in rapid succession, and his heart sank. He'd caused further pain. But she let out the most unladylike snort, and he realized she was laughing.

He scooped her chin with a finger, lifting her head so he could see her face, and even in the dim light, it was clear she was fully amused. It was Elizabeth as he'd known her, before life events had extinguished her joy, and his heart melted a little. "You minx," he said. "You think this funny? Your feet are a mess. You'll not be able to stand on them for days."

"Oh, do tell, Doctor Thornwood. Off my feet? Resting in bed?" she asked playfully, her arm still around his neck, her smile inviting.

His heart skipped a beat. Doctor's orders. Off your feet. Bed rest. The memories came rushing in, flooding him with a fear he never wanted to experience again.

"Richard?" Her voice was no longer playful. Was she remembering too, or did she sense the momentous shift in him? He couldn't do this. He lifted her gently onto the bench across from him and looked away from her crestfallen face. He needed more distance than the carriage could provide. He knocked on the roof, and the carriage stopped.

"Elizabeth," he said with a nod in her direction before he stepped out onto the street. He hated to abandon her, was an absolute swine for doing it, but do it he must. "Simon, see that Lady Thornwood is carried to her rooms and attended to."

He didn't wait for an answer. He turned and walked down the nearest side street, a casual stride when all he wanted to do was run. Run from it all. From decisions made. From the memories of the past. From the disappointment on Elizabeth's face.

STUNNED WAS AN understatement. Elizabeth was dumbfounded. There'd been a connection, their old connection, she was sure of it. It was as though time had slipped away and they'd once again been the couple they had been. She knew she was not wrong. She'd seen the care and concern in his eyes, felt it in the security of his arms. She'd heard his deep inhale into her hair. He'd relished her scent as she'd savored his.

Did he feel spurned by her laughter? Impossible. The situation had been entirely ridiculous and their exit fodder for the stage, but it had also been a grand gesture. She dared to imagine it was one of love. But when he'd grunted as he'd fallen onto the bench, her knight in shining armor puffing and trembling with her weight, it had all become too much. A caricature of them had flashed through her mind, and she'd been overwhelmed by the humor in it all. And her laughter had been freeing. Perhaps too much so.

It had been years since she'd felt disencumbered enough to tease, to insinuate an invitation to her bed. Was that what had turned him? Was the thought so distasteful he must run at the suggestion of it? Her heart sank to its familiar place in the pit of her stomach. Was there truly no hope for them? She grabbed her wrap from where it had been set and pulled it over her shoulders. No, she could not accept it. She would not accept it. There was a spark of interest. She would hold on to the memory of it as though it was a small ember glowing warmly inside her chest.

The carriage slowed to a stop, and Simon opened the door.

"My lady, can you stand?"

"Of course I can." She moved to do so, wincing as pain lanced her feet. With Simon supporting her elbow, she shuffled toward the first step. The front door opened, and Gordon stood gaping. Her maid bobbed behind him, then shoved him out of her way, her face creasing with concern.

"It's nothing, Lucy, I assure you," Elizabeth said, although at the moment it did throb like something. She wasn't sure she could make it up all the stairs to her rooms.

"Gordon, fetch Marcus," Simon ordered, before turning back to her. "Marcus will carry you in," he said, softening his tone for her, adding as Elizabeth was about to object, "His Lordship demanded it."

Elizabeth was not about to make a scene in front of the servants, so she waited until Richard's valet arrived. She allowed Marcus to scoop her up, stiffening at the awkwardness of being in another man's arms, even if the man was barely out of childhood. He carried her effortlessly up the front steps, where Hastings now stood ready.

"My lady, I am sorry to hear of your injury," he said.

"Thank you, but I believe I shall live."

Hastings was a fixture. Richard had inherited him, along with his title, long before Elizabeth had become part of the Thornwood world. He was a consummate professional, the soul of discretion, and—Lucy told her—a tyrant with the staff. All good traits in a butler.

Hastings led the way, not pausing to see how Marcus was doing. Marcus was doing remarkably well, despite the stairs and having to traipse with her all the way to the back of the house. He set her gently on the settee. He remained calm and in full control of his breathing. Such was the gift of youth. It was a definite contrast to Richard's winded collapse onto the carriage bench. She smiled to herself. In all fairness, Richard would be thirty this coming summer. Which was not old, but nor was it young. Elizabeth sighed. Would that they could turn back the clock and begin again. What could she do differently to ensure he was here by her side instead of darting through the dark streets, away from her?

Several footmen arrived carrying an ironstone footbath and several urns of water. They set them at her feet and stood nearby waiting for instructions, which Lucy was not adverse to issuing. Efficient, as always, she'd arrived with a basket full of medical supplies in hand.

"One hot and half of the cold, if you please." Lucy watched as they poured. When they were through, she turned her attention to Elizabeth's feet.

"Out with you all," Hastings said. "Gordon, you wait outside the door for further direction." He looked at Elizabeth, his brow furrowed. "My lady, have you need of anything, please have Lucy let Gordon know."

"Thank you, Hastings," she said and looked away, biting back a yelp of pain as Lucy guided first one foot, then the other into the water. The door clicked, and she knew they were finally alone. She let out a long hiss as Lucy swirled the water around her feet.

"My lady, however did you do this? I warned you those slippers were too snug, but I did not imagine they'd cause such damage."

Elizabeth said nothing. The night's harm was the accumulated result of wearing too many shoes that no longer fit properly. Her leather half boots had gotten wet when she'd been out at the park with William. They had chafed her feet and pulled at the nail. The slipper had merely finished it off.

Why did she insist on wearing them? It was not as though she could not afford new pairs. While many around her changed their wardrobes based on the whims of a handful of women who, each year, decided what was fashionable, she'd held steadfastly to her clothes from several seasons ago. Had she been too low-spirited to bother, or was she trying to hold on to happier times?

Lucy eased Elizabeth's feet out of the water and set them on a drying towel. She covered them with another square of linen before going to the door. Gordon made no eye contact as he grabbed the basin. Settled, with the pain lessening, Elizabeth became increasingly aware of the awkwardness of the situation, feeling exposed even though her feet were hidden from sight. Of course, Gordon had already seen them bared. As had Hastings, Marcus, and the other footmen. For that matter, the entire assembly at the Argyll Rooms had had a good look at them and her stockingless legs. Now that the rush of activity had passed, she fully grasped the spectacle she'd made of herself. She flopped back on the sofa and groaned.

"Oh, my lady, do they hurt so much?"

"Not as much as my pride, Lucy. Not as much as my pride." Elizabeth stared at the ceiling while Lucy applied salve and carefully wrapped her feet. When she was through, she helped Elizabeth up. "I'm fine, Lucy. Do go get me a warm cup of milk, though, and dismiss Gordon. I'll need nothing further from him tonight."

She waited for Lucy to leave before attempting a tentative step. A little unsteadily, though walking was doable, she hobbled through the sitting room and into her bedroom. Later, after she'd slipped into her night rail and Lucy had taken down, brushed, and capped her hair, Elizabeth lay again on her back, staring at the blackened ceiling. In her mind's eye, she could see its vine-and-leaf cornice wrapping around, no beginning, no end. Which also seemed to be where she was with Richard.

When had this distance begun? She couldn't remember, but she knew he'd not been drawn to her since Sebastian's birth, and that was soon to be two years. In fairness, she'd been ill for a long time afterward, so relations hadn't been possible. But his total disinterest? When had he lost his desire for her company, never mind her body?

All she knew was it must end. She'd thought she was well on

her way tonight to breaking the stalemate, then he'd bolted. But not before she'd seen the spark. A spark she had every intention of fanning until it was a flame burning hot. She didn't know how, but she was determined to have him back in her life...and in her bed.

CHAPTER THREE

To me alone there came a thought of grief:
A timely utterance gave that thought relief,
And I again am strong.

—Wordsworth, "Ode: Intimations of Immortality from
Recollections of Early Childhood"

RICHARD CAME IN through the back, from the mews, and stomped his feet.

Hastings stepped out of his rooms. "Good ride, my lord?"

"It was," Richard said, handing his hat to Hastings. Hastings set it on the side table, then assisted Richard with the removal of his driving coat. It was a chilly morning, which was exactly what he'd needed to clear his head following a sleepless night. After sending Elizabeth on her way, he'd wandered to White's, hoping Walford would end his evening there, but after several hours of waiting, Richard had surrendered. It was clear Walford was not going to leave his wife's side, and Richard couldn't blame him. There was a time when Richard had felt the same way about spending time with Elizabeth.

The late hour provided for a quiet return, with only Hastings and Marcus waiting up for him. He dismissed them both and headed upstairs. Although he'd been assured Elizabeth had long gone to bed, he walked quietly past her bedroom and into his own across the hall, relieved when the only thing that followed him into his room was the sound of the door closing. He was blurry-eyed weary but could not go to bed. So he stood at the window, with a brandy in hand, staring vacantly into the darkness until the early-morning, when the collier's cart rattled to a stop and the man hopped off to shovel coal into the vault. Only then did Richard stretch out on the coverlet, still fully dressed.

The morning sun woke him a short time afterward, and there was no more sleep to be had. He rang for Marcus, had a quick wash and shave, and headed out, hoping he could leave the turmoil of his endless introspection behind with a brisk ride. Apparently not. His brain was a befuddled, swirling mess. He needed to speak with Walford. At least Walford might be able to help him sort out the odd situation he'd found himself in with Miss Paisley. He strode through the hall, to the library. The early-morning noise on the streets was more prevalent at the front of the house, and he found it oddly comforting. He'd been quietly alone with his thoughts for too many hours. He penned a quick note to Walford and stepped back into the hall, heading back the way he'd come.

Hastings stepped out of the kitchen. "My lord, your breakfast will be in the tea room shortly."

"Thank you, Hastings. Do see this finds Lord Walford's hands as soon as possible."

"Yes, my lord."

Richard took the stairs to the tea room. Adjacent to the ball-room, he liked to use it as a breakfast room instead of the large dining room on the ground floor. Growing up, he'd had too many lonely dinners at the big table at Thornwood Manor to want to replicate the experience in his adult life. He preferred the intimacy afforded in the smaller room.

At the top of the stairs, he glanced into the ballroom. He could not remember the last time they'd hosted an evening of dance. He recalled one after William was born, but there had not been one since Sebastian had arrived. He could not see ever hosting one again. He ran a hand through his hair. *Devil it all.* What was he doing standing here lamenting lost socials? He'd hated the blasted things even when Elizabeth had stood by his side.

He entered the tea room and sat at the table where his place was already set. The simple rosewood table was a stark contrast to the ornate mahogany one downstairs. A domineering piece of furniture, it sat twenty-four. Here, they could seat eight comfortably, which was plenty for overnight guests. Which they never had anymore. He didn't wish anyone to get a glimpse of the reality of their situation, and Elizabeth seemed in full agreement, as she had not requested any company.

Several footmen arrived with silver platters and set them on the sideboard. Hastings followed close on their heels, grabbed a cup for Richard, and tidily poured from the urn. The bitter aroma of coffee mixed with the tantalizing smell of eggs and liver, and Richard's stomach growled. "Prepare me a plate," he said, too drained to get up and look for himself. He knew he'd like whatever was there. No simple bread and jams for him. He enjoyed an old-fashioned meal, and neither of his cooks ever disappointed.

Hastings and a single footman stood by as he ate, topping his coffee not once but twice. Richard focused on the food with single-mindedness, not wanting to think at least for a few minutes. When he finally set his silverware aside, his plate was cleared and a paper was set in its place.

"More coffee, my lord?"

"Half a cup, thank you."

Hastings poured the coffee and left the room, leaving the footman to stand guard. "You may go too," Richard said, and turned to the paper.

He scanned the first page and, finding little of interest in the advertisements, moved on to politics. Some committee notes of no interest, and little information regarding the happenings on the peninsula. Definitely nothing to shine a light on his current predicament.

The third page was of more interest. An announcement regarding the expansion to Walford's shipbuilding warehouse. Richard must give credit where credit was due. Walford moved fast and definitively. Richard, too, wanted to dip his toes in those waters. When this mess was cleared up, he'd talk with Walford about it.

He returned his attention to the paper. The crime section seemed to be growing daily. Fourteen Luddites were to be hanged Saturday. He sympathized with their loss of livelihood, but surely they understood the recklessness in their ongoing destructions? Agree or disagree, the Frame-Breaking Act was very specific and clear about consequences, and the law was the law. They must find a better way to express their discontent.

He usually skipped the town gossip, but he could not this morning. The incident last night jumped out at him from the column. He read it and grunted. It should be of no surprise they'd made the paper after the display he'd put on. What had he been thinking? He hadn't been, was all there was to it.

"Richard."

He looked up. Elizabeth, dressed in a pale-blue morning dress that matched her eyes, her golden hair piled loosely on her head, looked as beautiful as the day he'd met her. His body responded as he stood up, and he hoped the evidence did not show.

"Elizabeth," he said, grabbing the paper and setting it at her place. "Enjoy your repast. I'm going to see the children. I'll be out for the remainder of the day." He pulled the cord to let Hastings know he was needed, and like the coward he was, ducked out the door before she could respond.

ELIZABETH TOOK A seat, fighting the overwhelming despair that she was losing the fight to get Richard back. She glanced at the paper, quickly surveying the Mirror of Fashion column, not at all surprised to see a reference to the scene at the Argyll Rooms.

Lady T and Lord T created a stir at the Argyll Rooms last night. Ripples began when they danced with one another, alongside Lady W and Lord W. (Although, the latter must be forgiven as they had been parted and are compensating for lost time.) A torrent of gasps resounded at the baring of Lady T's feet. Lord T's subsequent stampede, through ladies and gentlemen alike, was equally outrageous. However, the most scandalous part of the drama was witnessing a husband and wife so in love. Do let us hope it does not become the norm.

Elizabeth smiled. *A husband and wife so in love.* If that was what they'd seen, then there was a chance she was right. For all his reticence, Richard did love her. Was it possible she'd only lost a battle and would yet win the war? Hastings tapped lightly before entering the room, a pot of fresh steaming coffee in hand.

"A beautiful day ahead, my lady," he said as he poured.

"Indeed, Hastings, I believe it may be," she said, looking at the paper and smiling.

CHAPTER FOUR

Whereof what's past is prologue; what to come,
In yours and my discharge.

—Shakespeare, *The Tempest*

RICHARD HAD CONSIDERED a tavern. It seemed appropriate for a covert meeting. He'd changed his mind, coming to the conclusion there were too many ears in such an establishment and no guarantee some of those ears might not also use their mouths to spread what they overheard. He had no idea how sensitive his information was. Or legitimate. So it was back to White's. The unusual time of their meeting might be noted, but one could, at least, rely on discretion. And at this hour, they would be sure to find a quiet corner.

The bow window sat empty. Brummel and his sycophants were probably still abed, getting their beauty sleep before their next showing. Richard could not grasp the fascination the town had with the man. He found Brummel insipid and vacuous. Worse, the man was grating, sitting in the window with his fawning toadies. What kind of man concluded that such self-centered idleness was how one should spend his days? Had Brummel nothing more of value to offer the world than the latest turn of his collar or curl of his hair?

Richard left his coat, gloves, and hat with the doorman, who assured him Walford had arrived and was waiting for him upstairs. At the top of the stairs, raucous laughter burst from the back cardroom. Doubtless some of the men he'd seen last night were still in there, continuing to throw away far too much good coin and, most likely, coin some of them didn't have to spare.

He shook his head and turned toward the coffee room at the front of the building. The space was large, and there were only a few gentlemen about, all sitting in front of the windows that overlooked the street below. Walford had positioned himself on the opposite side of the room to them. Even better, he sat by the fireplace. He stood when he spied Richard.

"Thornwood," he said as they shook hands. "Do sit. Coffee?"

"No, thank you." Richard took the large chair beside Walford so they might speak quietly. The leather was heated by the fire, and he sunk back into its warmth, the chill from the wind easing from his body.

"Anything at all?"

Richard shook his head, and Walford waved away the servant who was crossing toward them.

"And how is Lady Thornwood this morning?"

Damn and blast! He hadn't even inquired as to her situation. She had truly married an insensitive boor. "She was on her own two feet" was all he said to Walford, which was at least the truth. How much those feet hurt, he'd no idea.

"Glad to hear it. Now to the business at hand." Walford sat back in his chair, angling himself so he could comfortably watch Richard. Richard almost squirmed under his scrutiny. As a military captain, Walford must have been damned commanding.

"I have some information I need verified. Military, not political."

"Interesting." Walford tilted his head. "And why me? You must have many contacts who can provide any confirmation you seek."

"It's delicate and needs discretion. It involves my mistress."

Walford sat straighter. "So the rumors are true? I know many do keep one, but I would not have thought it of you, Thornwood. I would not."

"What? No," Richard said as it dawned on him what Walford was insinuating. "What rumors?"

"That you keep a mistress. That she's why you are in London far more than at your estates, because you prefer her company to your wife's. I give little credence to gossip, and after what I saw between you and Lady Thornwood last evening, I am even more surprised."

Richard was not offended by Walford's bluntness. It was why he'd always liked the man. He shook his head. The damn geese gaggled about everything, and fabricated fantasies when they had nothing new to peck at. "Let me rephrase my sentence. It involves my ex-mistress. From my youth. Before I even met Elizabeth."

Walford relaxed back into the chair, raising an eyebrow. "But she is back in your life again?"

"No. Yes. Maybe." Richard ran a hand over his hair. Luckily, he'd smoothed it back and tied a queue at his nape; otherwise, he might run his fingers through it and look like the madman he felt he was becoming.

"She accosted me in the street, saying she needed my help and I'd appreciate hers. Said she had valuable information for the government. Information regarding the war on the peninsula. Slid me this as proof of her veracity." Richard pulled the paper out of his inside pocket. "Told me the information was not public knowledge and that, should I check, I would find it accurate."

Walford took the paper and unfolded it, reading quietly, his face expressionless. He glanced up thoughtfully before returning his attention to the missive. When he was done, he folded it and set it on his lap. "This claims to be Colonel Scovell's deciphered code, apparently sent to Frenada last month regarding the French holding their lines."

"So it's true?" Richard had hoped Walford would dismiss it out of hand, but if the worried lines on his forehead were any indication, that wasn't going to happen.

"I don't know. But I did hear rumors Scovell had cracked a cipher out of Paris last year. So the fact his name is linked with this information is revealing. Good Lord, if this *is* true, she has access to operational intelligence."

Richard raised his hand, and a footman crossed the room immediately. "A brandy, please." He looked to Walford, who shook his head. "Just the one."

When the servant was out of earshot, Walford spoke again. "Who is she, Thornwood, and what does she want?"

This was not a road Richard wanted to walk down, but it seemed he must. "Patricia Paisley, but I have no idea if it's her real name." He sighed heavily. "I met her when we left Eton. Eighteen and free of that damned school. My uncle continued to manage estate affairs sufficiently, and I wasn't ready to head home and wear the mantle of my role, nor would I have been allowed to fully do so had I been so inclined. I came to London instead."

Those years seemed so long ago. A lifetime. He'd been reeling from the death of his mother. She'd been all he'd had throughout the years. Her brother, Richard's official guardian alongside his mother, had had his own business to attend to and, therefore, administered Thornwood Manor from a distance. His mother and their steward, Bosley, had been exceedingly capable on their own.

Richard had never really known his father, the man having died when Richard was five. As such, he'd been schooled to be responsible to the title, and he'd accepted it without question. So it was not a shirking of responsibility. He'd not wanted to return to the empty manor house. Eton had provided no comfort, even in those months after his mother's death. It had been oppressive, and some of the masters harsh. If he'd not had friends like Walford and Bentley, he'd have been truly miserable. They'd taught him to laugh, at least a little.

"You went back to hearth and home, but I ran from mine."

Richard decided he might as well share the entire story. Last summer, Walford had trusted him with his own secrets. Richard must now entrust his own private tale.

"I met Patricia at a soiree. A decadent…" Richard hesitated, then forged forward. "A salacious and illicit gathering. The bawdy houses had lent some of their girls to enhance the evening. She sat with me, and one thing led to another, and we were in a back room. In retrospect, I believe she worked hard to catch my attention. And catch it she did. Pleasures of the flesh are addictive at that age, but I could not see myself frequenting a brothel to see her. So I put her up in a set of rooms. She was truly lovely, and we enjoyed many nights together.

"Two years later I saw Elizabeth on the other side of a ball-room, and I knew she was mine. I left and immediately broke it off with Patricia. I wanted nothing to taint my chances. I didn't meet Elizabeth officially until weeks later. I've not seen Patricia since, until…" Richard thrust his chin toward the paper sitting on Walford's lap.

"So she turns up out of the blue after…?"

"Almost ten years," Richard provided.

"After ten years," Walford repeated, his brow crinkling. "To what end?"

"Money. This was offered as proof she truly has secrets to offer. She said future installments would cost."

Walford whistled out a long breath. "A spy. Or knows one. One who wants to profit from what they know instead of assisting the war effort."

"So it would seem."

They both fell silent as the footman returned with Richard's brandy. He swirled the dark liquid and inhaled deeply, but he did not take a sip. "But why share with me? I have no great position in politics. No military connections."

Walford raised that imperial eyebrow again.

"Well, except you, of course. But you weren't around when I was with Patricia, so she'd not know about you."

"I would hazard to guess she had no one else to turn to. Or she trusts you. Liaisons can create strong bonds, and I assume you left her kindly."

"I did. And with substantial coin. Although, she did not look the better for it when I saw her."

"It is not an easy life, and if one does not manage it well, money can sift through hands quickly." Walford pressed his fingertips together and stared at Richard. "But there are plenty of better-connected men with coin, so that cannot be the reason. Two years is a lot of time with a man. Enough time to weigh his integrity and his loyalty. Many a gentleman would easily turn from sullying their hands with such subversive activities. She must think you won't." Walford picked up the paper. "If this is verified, how *do* you feel about gathering more information?"

Richard finally took a drink, letting the warmth fire his body, as he contemplated his response. He'd been wrestling with that very question since Patricia had slipped the paper into his hands. "How are we doing on the continent? The reports have been vague."

Walford shrugged. "It's difficult to know from the outside, but from what I hear, there have been some serious setbacks. Lives lost. Plans diverted. I'll not pretend insider information is not of great assistance in decisions. I know Wellesley is very receptive to vetted intelligence reports."

Richard took another sip. "Find out if there is truth in her missive, and I'll consider my choices."

"Will do," Walford said. "I'll head over to the Home Office directly." He stood. "Catherine is hosting a small fete this evening. She's making the most of her stay in London and enjoying making me squirm with all her plans." He laughed, unashamedly content with his wife's maneuverings. "Please join us." He thrust out a hand, and Richard shook it. "I'll share what I find out," he added more seriously.

Richard nodded and watched Walford stride from the room. He tossed back the remainder of his brandy. *Hell and the devil confound it.* It was bad enough he had to sort through this intrigue; now he must spend another evening in Elizabeth's company. He knew the latter was going to be the more difficult to endure.

CHAPTER FIVE

Friendship is constant in all other things
Save in the office and affairs of love.

—Shakespeare, *Much Ado about Nothing*

"Y OU'RE LIMPING," CATHERINE noted, staring at Elizabeth's feet.

"It's not so bad. The right one is bound in soft cotton. But it makes my boot much tighter." Elizabeth hadn't wanted to miss the shopping expedition, especially for baby linens. They'd had such fun picking out lace to trim gowns, and those tiny bows were worth enduring a bit of pain to see.

"New shoes," Sophia declared, waving to her man, who followed at a discreet distance, carrying packages. Luckily, he had big hands, for Sophia had made more than her fair share of purchases. He disappeared around the corner, and Sophia turned her attention back to Elizabeth. "Soft ones, *mia amica.*"

"Oh, I don't want anyone to see my feet! They are terribly wretched and"—she lowered her voice—"big and wide."

"Soft, big jester shoes," Sophia said merrily, and Catherine hit her lightly on the arm before joining in the laughter. Elizabeth couldn't help but smile.

Sophia's carriage pulled to the side, and her man jumped off the hind bench and opened the door, assisting each of them into it. "Wood's," Sophia said before he closed the door. The carriage rocked as her man joined the driver, and they rattled out onto the road.

It was a biting day outside, typical for the time of year, but the carriage exuded warmth from her friends. Sophia always had a way of brightening the dullest of times, and although Elizabeth did not know Catherine as well as she did Sophia, she was enjoying her positive companionship. She was especially relishing living vicariously through Catherine's current situation, the joyous memories of her own first confinement rushing back with every gush from Catherine.

"Tomorrow, I'd like to go to Papworth's," Catherine said. "The nursery needs refreshing. I don't believe it's been touched since Nicholas and Daniel were in leading strings. It's too somber. I don't want our child spending time in such antiquated darkness."

"You should send someone to do that," Sophia said, brushing at her pelisse.

"But I am not here long enough to arrange such things. Besides, I am quite capable of choosing wall hangings myself." Catherine looked to Elizabeth for confirmation, then back to Sophia.

Sophia looked up and shrugged. "Papworth's it is." The carriage began to slow. "Oh, here we are."

The carriage stopped, and the door opened. They each alighted and stood in front of the shop. They chatted amiably until Sophia's man opened the door, and they went inside.

"My ladies." An elderly gentleman bowed elegantly. "Please, do come in."

Sophia wasted no time in describing Elizabeth's needs, and Elizabeth soon found herself sitting on a chair, the man's bald pate all she could see of him as he measured her feet. He politely refrained from commenting on their condition. She selected a style and some fabric and gave him direction for delivery, ensuring she was willing to return should they not fit properly.

Which was a distinct possibility considering he was working with wrapped feet.

"*Bella*, you need shoes *rapidamente*," Sophia said, her back to Elizabeth as she and Catherine perused the shoes on display in the front window.

"I will make these a top priority," the gentleman said, not looking up from where he was making notations.

"How about these?" Sophia turned from the window, a pair of blue satin slippers in hand.

The shopkeeper glanced up, scooted around the counter, and took the shoes from her, shaking his head. "It is better to have custom-made. These are far too big, my lady."

Sophia grinned. "Perfect," she said, touching them as she looked at Elizabeth. "And soft." Catherine giggled, and Elizabeth joined in. She had her promised jester shoes.

Sophia invited them to join her at her townhouse for refreshments, but they both declined.

"*Mie bellezze*, you disappoint me," she said with a perfect pout. "I will have to accept calls. So many cards this morning." She waved her hand in front of her face as though she was too hot and smiled mischievously. "Shall I pick one of them to bring tonight?"

"Oh, do," Catherine said as she got out of the carriage. She turned around and stuck her head back in, looking directly at Elizabeth. "You *are* coming tonight? I know it was last minute, but you must join us."

Elizabeth hesitated. She'd left the invitation for Richard to see, but she doubted he would agree to attend. "I have not talked to Richard about it."

Sophia made a dismissive sound, and Catherine smiled.

"I will see to it that Nicholas ensures his compliance."

Compliance. From Richard? *The best of luck with that.*

Elizabeth hugged Sebastian to her chest. She'd not been able to nurse him herself, but she'd insisted on holding him every day so he'd feel the bonds of her love. However, today he was not in the mood to snuggle. He squirmed and wiggled, babbling incessantly, some of the words recognizable, most of them not. She sighed as she put him on the floor. William had been able to articulate words clearly at a far younger age than Sebastian, who still only garbled basic words. And he would soon be two. She must consult with the doctor regarding how to best precipitate improved speech for him. Not that Sebastian cared. He happily toddled, fell, and rolled onto his back, laughing. He was such a joyous child.

"My lady." Hannah stood in the doorway, William's hand in hers. "The young master is awake now, should you have time."

Elizabeth held open her arms. William ran across the room, and she wrapped her arms around him, hugging him tightly before pulling back. "Hannah tells me you have had a busy day. Too busy to see your mama?"

At almost four years old, William was a miniature of his father and equally serious. "No, Mama, I have time for you." He frowned, his brow furrowing so much like Richard's did when he was focused on something. "I was…tired…no…I was…ex…extausted."

Elizabeth smiled. "Exhausted, William. No *t* sound." He repeated the word several times until he said it correctly. "Perfect. Now do sit and tell me why."

Hannah sat on the floor, occupying Sebastian while William told her of his ride in the square, speaking as though he'd ridden a great wild stallion rather than been walked by lead on a leased pony. He further regaled her with tales of his sword fight with young Sir Edwin. He was elaborating on the final battle when his attention was drawn to the door.

"Papa," he said, jumping to his feet.

"William," Richard said warmly, not looking at Elizabeth. "How was your ride today?"

William reviewed his ride with Richard as he'd done with her, but Richard did not seem to see the humor in it as she had.

"Did you brush the pony afterward?" Richard asked.

William shook his head. "No, Papa," he said quietly. "But it is not mine."

"You are the one who rode it. See that you do next time. Pleasures come at a price, and one must take care of those who provide it."

"Yes, Papa." William was crestfallen. He so hated to disappoint his father, but Elizabeth knew Richard was correct. Responsibility must be engrained at a young age. Especially in William. He would one day inherit not only the title and the estate but every person and animal within it.

Richard looked pointedly at Hannah, who jumped to her feet and scooped up Sebastian. She stepped to William and touched his shoulder, guiding him forward toward the door.

"I will take you riding on my horse one morning this week," Richard said to William, leaning in and kissing the top of Sebastian's head before letting them pass by.

"Yes, Papa!"

She could not see William's face, but she could hear the pleasure in his voice. She smiled. Richard may have faults as a husband, but he was a good father.

"It is late for time with the children, is it not?" he asked formally, stepping into the room, the nearest lamp lighting one side of his face and shadowing the other. It was a foreboding look to match his now rigid stance.

She shook off an unwanted dark premonition, searching deep inside for the renewed sense of optimism she'd had last night and again this morning.

"I, too, had a busy day," she said as cheerfully as she could muster. "I needed to rest. Sebastian requires my full attention and energy now that he is walking." She debated telling him about her concerns for Sebastian's speech but decided she would wait to see what the doctor said when they returned to the country. She trusted Dr. Redding implicitly. He had saved her life.

"Your feet?" His face was still shadowed, his voice neutral, but at least he was expressing concern.

"They are fine, thank you."

"Then why are you not in your chambers, preparing for this evening?"

"This evening?" Richard had not been in all day, so he could not know about the invitation to tonight's fete.

"Lord and Lady Walford's?" he said as though he was prompting her memory.

She sat straighter. "We are going?"

"Of course we are. Walford insisted."

Elizabeth fought to keep her shoulders from slumping. So it was not for her sake they were attending. It was because of Lord Walford. Catherine had kept her promise to urge her husband to convince Richard.

"I'll see you downstairs in an hour," he said and pivoted, leaving without another word.

She stared at the spot where Richard had stood, biting back tears. She'd known wooing Richard back was going to be difficult. They had drifted apart for almost two years, and the chasm created by their separation was expansive. She refused to believe it was impossible to cross. They were going out *together*. It was a start, and she was determined to make the most of it.

CHAPTER SIX

Who could refrain,
That had a heart to love, and in that heart
Courage to make 's love known?

—Shakespeare, *Macbeth*

ELIZABETH WAS HER usual punctual self and appeared downstairs on the hour. Resplendent in a blue much richer than her morning gown's, her hair piled high, with enticing tendrils licking her delicate neck, she looked regal and far too delicious. He had to take her pelisse from Hastings and help her into it in order to distract his far-too-attentive body. It didn't help that the scent of her stirred more memories, tantalizing ones. He left Hastings to finish assisting her and strolled into the library. If he hadn't taken an opportunity to adjust himself, it would have been deuced uncomfortable walking to the carriage.

He draped a fur over Elizabeth's lap and sat across from her on the bench, continuing to fight lecherous fancies, until he spied her slippers. Her feet were wedged awkwardly in her pattens, which looked as though they were too large. Which they must be. He had held those feet in his hands last evening, and they were nothing to match the size of those shoes.

"Are your feet so swollen?" he asked. Even in the dim lamp-light, he could see her faint blush.

"My right one remains tender. I suspect the nail will take some time to grow in," she said, looking at her feet and not at him.

"Then you must buy some more while you wait," he said, oddly irritated as he looked at her shoes. Did she assume he would begrudge her purchasing temporary shoes? "Those are quite…" He hesitated, realizing how insulting he sounded.

"Clownish?" she supplied, wiggling her feet. "Should I add red triangles to my cheeks and rouge my lips?"

He was taken off guard by her quiet giggle, and when he looked up, his eyes were drawn to those lips she so casually referenced. Merriment danced in her slight smile, but sinful pleasure was promised by those sweet bows. His blood heated, and he was once again uncomfortable, but he could not look away from her lips. "I was going to say ridiculous." He shook his head, attempting to redirect his wayward mind, and met her gaze. "Wherever did you get them?"

"Wood's. Sophia picked them out. I've ordered a new pair, but they won't be ready for a few days." She wiggled her feet again. "For all their buffoonery, they are extraordinarily comfortable."

The carriage slowed in front of Walford's place, and they got out. Richard held Elizabeth's elbow firmly lest she lose her footing and cause further damage. He'd not considered her feet when he'd agreed to attend the gathering. It was thoughtless of him. He could have met Walford later in the evening, or even tomorrow. Admittedly, he was anxious to hear what Walford had found.

Elizabeth's pattens clicked across the walk and up the front stairs. She was surprisingly graceful even in her cumbersome shoes. Although, why he should be surprised, he didn't know. She was consistently elegant in everything she did, including her dealings with him. He did not deserve her.

The butler greeted them, and two footmen assisted them in removing their outerwear.

"Do hurry," Walford called from the mezzanine above. "I am desperately outnumbered this evening." His wife stepped in beside him and tapped him playfully on the shoulder before waving to them and pulling him away.

Richard curled Elizabeth's hand into the crook of his arm, and they took the stairs slowly. To everyone else, this would look like a normal occurrence, but out of necessity, he usually avoided physical contact with Elizabeth. However, she needed him this evening, and he found himself relishing it tremendously. As he had when he'd carried her last night. He could get through the evening as long as he remembered not to engage beyond a simple touch. It should be easy enough to do if he kept his focus on tonight's meeting with Walford instead of on the warmth of her hand on his arm.

Lady Walford greeted them effusively, waving a servant over with a selection of beverages. Elizabeth chose a lemonade and Richard a sherry. Walford had not exaggerated. The women did outnumber the men. An oddity, but from what he'd seen of Lady Walford, she did not stand on precedent and ceremony. For that matter, nor did Walford.

He was pleased to see Mr. Randall, who was currently deep in conversation with a man Richard did not recognize. He would have to catch him later. There was much to discuss since they'd last seen each other at the Walfords' wedding dinner. From the other side of the room, Walford looked over the head of a petite matron and mouthed, "Help me." Richard grinned at him and excused himself from the ladies.

"Pardon me," Richard said to the woman, who up close, was much older than he'd surmised at first glance. She squinted at him, and Walford discreetly cupped his ear. Richard leaned in closer and spoke louder. "May I borrow Lord Walford for a moment?"

"You may," she said, smiling, her teeth more yellow than her sallow face. Her jewelry and clothing spoke of another era and also of money.

"Bless you," Walford said under his breath as they crossed the room. "Catherine's great-great-aunt six times removed on her mother's side or some such thing. Deaf as a post but pretends she can hear. It would be comical were it not so taxing."

They stepped into the hall and headed to the back of the house. Walford opened a door on the right, and they passed through. He closed the door behind him. "Not exactly your study, my friend, but it will do." Walford looked at Richard's hand, still clutching the sherry. "Put that damn thing down. I'll pour us a brandy."

Richard set his glass on a side table and took a seat across from the desk as Walford got them drinks. The study was small but serviceable, although its bookshelves were woefully lacking in anything substantial.

"You lease, I presume?" he asked, more to make conversation than out of actual interest.

"Yes," Walford said, pressing the brandy into Richard's hand before taking his place behind the desk. "My sire was not fond of London after Mother died. He let our house go and rented when he was here for parliament. Catherine and I aren't much for town either, I'm afraid. So it makes more sense for us to lease."

"I had expected your man Fredericks at the door."

"I leave all staff at Woodfield for my sire and hire for when we're here. Which is seldom. But enough about my domestic situation. Curious?"

Richard leaned forward in his chair. "Beyond curious. What did you find?"

"She was on the mark, Thornwood."

"By God, how can that be?" It all seemed preposterous. At the same time, he'd known it when she'd handed it to him. Part of Patricia's appeal had always been her lack of artifice. He could not fathom how she'd become embroiled in passing intelligence information.

"The Home Office conferred with the Foreign Office, and they concur it is Scovell's cipher. They can't conceive of how she managed to get her hands on such important information. Both sectors are beside themselves."

"One can imagine," Richard said, sitting back in his chair.

"They want you to pursue this." Walford lowered his voice. "To see what else she has. They will supply the coin."

"Why me? They have men to do this sort of thing, don't they? Trained men." Richard had hoped to authenticate the information and pass on the contact.

"For the same reason we assume she chose you. She trusts you."

"Damn and blast." Richard had decided to bow out of any further involvement, but he knew Walford was right. Still, he was torn. To participate in spying? It was an ignoble thing to do. Besides, he had an estate to run and a partly advanced business proposal, one he hoped to extend to Walford when his end of the deal was sealed. "And what did you tell them?"

"That I'd ask you."

Richard ran a hand through his hair. "Your thoughts?"

"About intelligence gathering or your participating in it?" Walford grinned, although his eyes remained serious.

"Both."

"Wellesley is adamant about the use of intelligence, both operational and strategic. It has saved many lives. Although, on occasion it has cost them too. There are sometimes misleading reports. It is why the accuracy of this one stunned them." Walford took a sip of his brandy. "From a personal standpoint, intelligence reports ensured Marmont and Soult were unable to combine forces at Badajoz. I might not be here today had they managed it."

Richard rested his glass on his knee, conflicted. On one hand, he'd no desire to become embroiled in spying. On the other hand, there were men like Walford out there, fighting on the peninsula. Their very lives might depend on information.

A light tap sounded at the door, and Lady Walford poked her head in. "Nicholas, I need you."

The change in Walford's expression was instant as they both jumped to their feet.

"Are you unwell?" Walford was across the room in seconds.

"What? Oh no, my love. I am fine." She ran her hand over her midriff. "We are fine. It's time for dinner."

He'd not known Lady Walford was with child. He recalled the excitement when Elizabeth had told him about William. How right the world was back then. The look on Walford's face was too much to bear. The last two years had been too much to bear. Richard swallowed the lump in his throat and waited until the door had closed behind Lady Walford. "I'll do it."

Walford looked surprised. "You're certain? It's safer here than on the continent, but it does not come without some dangers."

Richard nodded slowly. "I'm certain. For king and home."

To have something to keep him physically from home. To keep his thoughts *of* home at bay. But he kept that part of the decision to himself.

CHAPTER SEVEN

You are my true and honorable wife,
As dear to me as are the ruddy drops
That visit my sad heart.

—Shakespeare, *Julius Caesar*

ELIZABETH WAS KEENLY aware of Richard's thigh pressed along hers. He was preoccupied with His Grace and, doubtless, was oblivious to the fact he was creating such a stir within her. Being held in his arms at the Argyll Rooms, his hands touching her legs as he rolled down her stockings, and now this intimacy were too much after such disinterested distance. She burned at the memory of the pleasure his touch could bring. She shook her head as though she could dislodge the images. Her imagination was far too wanton and inappropriate for the setting.

She turned to her left. "Mr. Haydon, I have heard much praise regarding your talent. I do hope to see your work someday."

"Thank you, Lady Thornwood. It would be my great pleasure to share some pieces with you. If you'd like, we could arrange a showing while you are in London."

"That would be lovely," she said, distracted by his shiny pate glowing under the chandelier.

He must be younger than Richard, yet this poor man's hair

receded, whereas Richard's was gloriously thick. She loved to run her fingers through it and pull his head down for scorching kisses. Richard was an outstanding kisser. Not that she had any to compare them too, but none could possibly be any more enjoyable. How had she wandered back down the same dissolute path?

She cleared her throat. "Are you working on anything currently?"

She tried to focus as he described his vision for his next painting—Christ, crowds, Jerusalem—but she could not bring her rampant imaginings under control. "I look forward to seeing it," she said when it was clear he was done elaborating.

He looked at her quizzically. "Yes, well as I say, I am ruminating at this point. When I will put brush to canvas, I don't know. I will wait for my muse."

"Of course," Elizabeth responded, grateful servants had arrived with another course and she could turn her attention to her food. Where were her manners? She prided herself on her etiquette, but it had been sorely lacking in her conversation with Mr. Haydon. She picked at her glazed carrots and strove to do better.

"May I?" Richard dutifully held the porcelain platter toward her.

"Yes, please."

He speared a fillet onto her plate, set the dish down, and grabbed a matching sauce boat before pouring a puddle of white sauce on the fish. She followed his glance around the room, knowing he was ensuring all the women had been served, before he served himself a much more generous helping. Richard had always had a healthy appetite.

He waited for her to begin before lifting his own fork. The routine was so familiar and so foreign of late, her heart ached a little. But she would not allow herself more than a melancholy moment, not when Richard was so close and so relaxed. She cut a piece of fish and enjoyed its rich flavor as she surveyed the room.

Catherine had eschewed head-of-table protocol. She'd placed herself and Lord Walford, as well as all their guests, to either side of the table, leaving the ends vacant. When watching her and Nicholas together, Elizabeth had no difficulty discerning why Catherine chose to put husbands and wives beside one another. Catherine didn't want to be apart from her own husband for a moment. And no wonder. He'd been gone for four years, and they had overcome such a difficult beginning to their marriage.

Across the table, Sophia was engaging the Duke of Salinger's attention. A side glance told her Sophia had also managed to engage Mr. Haydon's. Stunning in her signature scarlet, Sophia wore her neckline daringly low, and Elizabeth suspected that was what was captivating Mr. Haydon as much as Sophia's beauty. She felt sympathy for the companion to his left, whose name she'd forgotten but who must feel neglected. Or relieved. One never knew when strangers were put together.

Lord Bentley, too, could not seem to keep his eyes from Sophia, even with his dinner companion yelling in his ear. Catherine's aunt loudly prattled on about the food, not seeming to notice that Lord Bentley was distracted and spared her no glance. Elizabeth returned her attention to Catherine. Hanging on her husband's every word, she positively glowed—in an entirely different way than Mr. Haydon's head. Elizabeth lowered her gaze so no one would see the smirk that threatened at the comparison of the two.

"Do you wish to share what has brought on that mischievous smile?" Richard asked quietly.

"I but amuse myself with my own thoughts," she said, turning to Richard and, with some difficulty, swallowing the last piece of fish. His hazel eyes were flecked with gold in the light, and a smile teased the corner of his mouth.

"A penny for them? I'll pay a full shilling if you also bring back that smile."

She hadn't realized she'd dropped her smile. "I may save sharing my thoughts for the carriage, my lord." She couldn't possibly tell him what she'd been thinking with everyone about. Someone might overhear.

"Fair enough," he said, turning, as he must, to Mrs. Randall on his other side.

Elizabeth had never more regretted the formalities of a dinner party. When had she last seen him so relaxed in her company? She sighed and turned her attention back to Mr. Haydon, judiciously avoiding gazing at his forehead as he droned on.

RICHARD HAD NO idea why he was so at ease with Elizabeth this evening. Maybe it was because he now had a way to keep himself busy? In fact, two methods of distraction. First, this business with intelligence gathering. Second, Mr. Randall was looking to increase his shipping business and was seeking partnership. Randall was also amenable to purchasing ships from Walford should Richard be inclined to invest. A beneficial deal all around.

"My turn," someone squawked, and all heads swiveled to the far end of the table. Richard leaned in to see past Elizabeth in time to witness Catherine's aunt swat Bentley's shoulder. "I'll have your attention, young sir!"

Bentley turned beet red. Richard worried the man was apoplectic until he registered what had caused the outburst and realized Bentley was genuinely mortified at being caught gaping. His Grace glared across the table at him.

The countess's musical laughter broke the tension. She tsked at Bentley and laughed again. "Do respect your elders, Lord Bentley," she teased.

Richard wasn't sure if she was referencing Catherine's aunt, herself, or the duke. For Countess Tessaro was several years older than Bentley, and the duke was a good double hers. His Grace seemed an odd choice of partner for a woman so vibrant and independent, but he'd seen stranger matches. And Sophia flitted from man to man, so possibly there was nothing to make of it at all.

Walford pushed from his chair and stood. "Thank you all for joining us tonight. It's a special time in our home, and we appreciate you sharing it with us." He smiled down at Catherine and held out his hand. "No, don't get up. Simply hold it," he said.

"Stuff and nonsense." Catherine got to her feet. "I am not an invalid…yet." Her cheeks were rosy as she smiled at him fondly.

"Tonight we officially announce our very poorly kept secret. A new little lord—" Catherine tapped his arm and wagged a finger, and he grinned. "—or lady will grace the halls of Wood-field in the spring."

There were claps and cheers around the table, and Walford raised his glass. "To the future. And to the women who make it happen."

Richard raised his Madeira and cheered along with everyone, although a slight pang perforated the joy he should feel for them. A future world with Elizabeth in it was exactly what he wanted. He'd continue to do whatever he must to ensure that was the case.

ALTHOUGH THE SELECTION of sweets set out on the table looked positively delicious, Elizabeth could not eat another bite. She gazed at them ruefully. Poached pears and trifle and a tier of small cakes—some glazed, some plain—were all enticing, but she would need to loosen her stays were she to consume one more thing. She was relieved when Catherine announced the end of the meal. The return to the drawing room was a welcome stretch for her body. She suspected she was not the only one who had overstuffed herself, as several groans were emitted as the ladies climbed the stairs.

Sarah Randall spoke quietly with Catherine while she busied

herself with the tea, so Elizabeth sat beside Sophia on the elegant settee.

"Oh, the poor thing," Sophia said in a pseudo whisper. "I do hope she has better prospects than this evening has brought her."

Elizabeth followed Sophia's gaze. "Oh dear. I've forgotten her name."

"Margaret. She's the daughter of Nicholas's man, Mr. Langdon. She lives with them at Woodfield now."

"I had no idea." She was a lovely girl and a patient one, as her face showed only serenity as Catherine's aunt shouted at her. "Should we rescue her?"

Sophia waved the suggestion away. "She must earn her dues like the rest of us. Besides, we would get stuck with Signora I'll-Have-Your-Attention-Young-Sir." Sophia's laughter sprinkled throughout the room as Lady Setherington entered. She came directly toward them and sat on the nearest chair.

"Oh, do tell, what is so funny?" she asked, looking from Elizabeth to Sophia and back again.

"The signora's chastisement," Sophia said. "It was delightful. Did you see Lord Bentley's color?" She laughed again as the final three ladies entered the drawing room. They sat snugged together on the sofa opposite Elizabeth. "Good evening," Sophia said amiably. "I trust you are enjoying yourselves."

"I most definitely am, Lady Tessaro," Lady Adsworth said. "But my girls are not so amused as I am by the company."

"Mama!" the two of them said in unison, their matching faces shocked.

"Shush. We are among friends, are we not?" She addressed the question to Sophia but was looking pointedly at Elizabeth.

"Of course," Elizabeth said. Elizabeth had only a passing acquaintance with Lady Adsworth. Her husband had passed away five years ago, and she'd been broken by his loss. She'd remained in the country until recently. The twins would have their season next year.

"They were hopeful for more young men, but as I told them,

we are only in town for a short time to practice our social skills. I fear, I did not do well by them these past few years."

"*Hai fatto bene*, Mary," Sophia said quietly. "*Hai fatto bene*. Do you not agree she has done well, Elizabeth? Look how graceful they are." She looked at the girls, who were blushing prettily. "I can give you His Grace if you'd like. You may practice on him."

Simultaneously, the girls scrunched their faces and shook their heads, and Sophia laughed again. "Go play me something on the pianoforte. Something *felice*…happy!" The girls headed over to the far corner of the room.

"Oh, that's lovely," Catherine said as music filled the room. Sarah passed out the cups, and Catherine poured the tea. The other two ladies joined them, with Catherine's aunt taking the hostess's chair. "Auntie," Catherine said, unruffled, as she handed her a full cup.

"She'd take the regent's seat, given the chance," Sophia said, not even pretending to whisper this time.

"Now, Sophia, you must abide by the advice you gave Bentley," Elizabeth whispered, fighting a smile.

"I must confess I have an ulterior motive for having you join us this evening, Elizabeth," Catherine said. "Oh, you look alarmed. Don't be."

Elizabeth would not describe her reaction as such, but she was certainly uncomfortable with the focus on her.

"Sophia has told us about your project, and we want to help. Lady Adsworth, Lady Setherington, and dear Auntie. And of course, Sophia."

Elizabeth looked to Sophia, who smiled triumphantly.

"We have dug into our pin money. We have solicited from our friends and will continue to until you have sufficient funds to see to the building of your orphanage and the maintenance of it as well."

Tears sprung to Elizabeth's eyes. In the village, she'd discovered several children being housed in homes that already had too many of their own. She'd also found two waifs clinging to each other, hiding near the parish, when she'd been strolling the grounds. Parson Brown was temporarily providing for them with her funds. He said it was an unfortunate sign of the times and likely more would be destitute as machinery took over the jobs of men and women.

She had talked to Sophia about her dream of building an orphanage. She'd already had an architect draw the plans. But she'd not found the courage to ask Richard about the funds. Business was his world, not hers, and he'd been so unapproachable. Now she need not rely on him for it.

"I don't know what to say." She sniffed back tears.

"Say thank you, *mia amica*." Sophia put her arms around Elizabeth's shoulders and pulled her in for a hug. "Her auntie is rich as Croesus. Ask for much," she whispered as she brushed Elizabeth's cheek with a kiss.

"Thank you," Elizabeth said, laughing and crying at the same time. "From the bottom of my heart, thank you."

The girls stopped playing and cheered along with the others before beginning a quiet piece. But there was nothing subdued about Elizabeth's mood. How could there be when she had such extraordinary, caring people in her life?

Before Elizabeth had fully recovered from the overwhelming emotions washing over her, the men arrived. The duke led the way, followed by Lord Walford and the others. Richard was last to turn up. He looked directly at her and raised an eyebrow. She smiled hesitantly, and he smiled back. Her heart skipped a beat. Yes, she thought as she wiped her eyes one last time, good people surrounded her, but even better, there was a chance she had her husband back.

CHAPTER EIGHT

Love is a smoke made with the fume of sighs;
Being purged, a fire sparkling in lovers' eyes.

—Shakespeare, *Romeo and Juliet*

H E WAITED UNTIL the carriage pulled away before asking Elizabeth about her evening.

"It was far better than I anticipated," she said with a smile.

"Then may I ask what your tears were about?" Despite her smile, it had been clear when he'd walked into the drawing room that she'd been crying.

Her eyebrows drew together, and he could almost see her mind weighing sharing the truth with him. He might be treading into feminine territory and it was something reserved for ladies' discussion only. "You need not share if it makes you uncomfortable. My apologies for prying."

"No, I want to tell you. I should have told you long before now, but…"

She let the word drift. There was no need for her to finish the sentence. He knew he was absent far too much. Worse, he knew he would be again.

"Go on," he said.

"I have plans for an orphanage in the village. There is a growing need."

He tilted his head questioningly. "And that brought you to tears?"

"The ladies have offered to help finance it."

He leaned back on the bench, digesting the last bit of information. "Why would you not come to me with such a project?" She winced at his tone, and he damned himself, but it was galling she'd gone to others.

"I tried." Her voice was meek, but she lifted her chin defiantly. "Several times."

The wind went out of his sails. He did not doubt she had. "It is a worthy endeavor."

"I believe it is." She, too, leaned back against her seat. "You're not angry?"

"About the orphanage? Of course not. We are only as good as the deeds we do." He glanced out the window as they rounded the corner a little too sharply. Almost home. "I would like to contribute, if I may."

"Oh, Richard, that would be splendid."

The carriage pulled off to the side, cutting short any further conversation. Simon opened the door and assisted them out, Hastings and their London head footman, Clarkson, at the ready in the doorway. He handed over his great coat to Clarkson and waited for Elizabeth to shed her pelisse and pattens. He crooked his elbow, and Elizabeth tucked her hand in it.

He looked at her ridiculous slippers. "Would you like me to carry you up?"

"Yes, but I won't ask it of you," she said teasingly.

"Thank goodness. I barely made it out of the Argyll Rooms."

She leaned into him, laughing. He couldn't remember the last time he'd been comfortable in her company.

"I, too, have news," he said as they crested the top of the stairs and headed down the hall toward their rooms. "I am investing in Randall's trading company. We have not hammered out the details, but he wishes to expand his fleet and has agreed to a partnership."

"That's wonderful, Richard. I'm so very pleased for you."

They stopped at her door, and he hesitated. It had been a good night, the best he'd enjoyed in a long time. Perhaps they could make a better life than what they had. The candle flickered in the wall sconce, and her eyes sparkled along with it. He sensed her invitation, although she didn't say a word.

He leaned into her, the floral smell of her hair intoxicating. His body ached for her, but his mind forbade it. They might be able to manage a decent life together but not beyond that door. The thought of losing control and carelessly making love made his stomach roll with unease. He kissed the top of her head and stepped back.

"Good night, Elizabeth." Richard turned and crossed to his room without looking back. He did not relax until he had closed his own door. He pulled the bell, signaling Marcus to come give him a hand, and poured himself a brandy. He was proud of his restraint. He pulled at his neck scarf in irritation. Then why was he so bloody disappointed?

ELIZABETH WATCHED RICHARD disappear into his room before entering her own and leaning back against her closed door. She blew out a long breath, disappointment warring with triumph. Richard had considered kissing her, truly kissing her. She could see it in his eyes when his gaze had lingered on her mouth. Even the simple brush of his lips across her head had been exhilarating after the years of abstinence. Even though he'd bolted again, she'd felt his draw to her. A baby step though it might be, it was a move forward.

She turned and opened the door back into the hallway, catching Lucy off guard.

"Oh, I'm sorry, my lady. I was about to knock," Lucy said, wide-eyed. "Would you like me to assist?" she asked, glancing past Elizabeth into the room. Hastings must have cautioned her, since Lucy would normally have no reason to think Richard was in there.

"Yes, please. I'll be back shortly."

Elizabeth took the back stairs to the second floor, noticing her aching feet for the first time in hours. She limped toward the front of the house, quietly approaching the nursery. The governess's room on the left remained empty, although it would not be long before she must seek one for William. She stepped into the doorway of the larger bedroom on the right. Hannah stirred and sat up.

"No need, Hannah. Go back to sleep."

A pale light washed the room. Sebastian snored lightly, his cheeks reflecting the fullness of tonight's moon. He'd kicked off his quilt, and his chubby legs were akimbo. She straightened them and snugged the quilt tight, leaning in to kiss his forehead.

She turned from the crib to William. Tucked into his bed, hands underneath his cheek, he lay on his side, looking so much like his father. The familiar pang of regret nudged at her heart. In all likelihood, this nursery would see no more children.

"Elizabeth?"

She turned and put a finger to her lips, her melancholy chased away by the sight of Richard framed in the doorway. He placed his finger to his lips, too, and stepped into the room beside her.

"He is so like you," she whispered. "In looks and manners."

"And he's so like you," Richard whispered, turning to the crib. "Your hair, your eyes. Your laugh."

Sebastian kicked at his cover and freed a leg. Yes, Elizabeth thought, as restless as me too, but she didn't say it. She kissed Sebastian once again but left him as he was. Let him have his liberty. Richard stoked the coals before they left the room, ensuring there would be enough warmth.

They descended the stairs together in amicable silence and, with quiet good-nights to each other, parted at her room. This time, she was content to go to bed. For the first time in a long time, she believed everything could be right in her world again.

CHAPTER NINE

In what have I offended you? What cause
Hath my behavior given to your displeasure,
That thus you should proceed to put me off,
And take your good grace from me?

—Shakespeare, Henry VIII

IT HAD BEEN a beastly uncomfortable night. Not only had he struggled with his desire for Elizabeth, but he'd also tried to solve how he could somehow share a life with her *and* resist temptation. The ease of her company throughout the evening had made it seem doable, but the fire raging through his body had made a lie of the thought. He'd been no closer to a resolution when the first light of morning chased the shadows from his room.

His morning ride had not cleared his mind any further. He should be dwelling on his new business adventure. On the goings-on in the House of Lords. On the damned intelligence Patricia had given him. Anything but Elizabeth and her beguiling smile and enticing body.

Richard went directly to the study and, as directed, sent an anonymous missive to the address Patricia had provided. A bawdy house, for goodness' sake. He'd given the woman plenty of coin and advice on investment when they'd parted, so he could not comprehend how she'd fallen so low once again. She was smart and should have been able to do much better. Richard also sent a note to Walford to let him know he was making contact with the woman.

Afterward, he reviewed the notes sent from his steward. Bosley indicated the fencing in the east pasture was in need of repair and the stable roof was leaking. He wrote directions and included the need to consider the impending orphanage. News of such an altruistic endeavor would make Bosley blanch. He was stringent with the purse strings, believing all moneys should be channeled directly into Thornwood Manor and be used solely for its gain. Richard smiled. He liked that Elizabeth's heart reached out beyond the walls of the estate.

The smell of bacon wafted into the study, and he set aside his work. He stepped into the hall and followed the footmen carrying silver chafing dishes. He'd never been patient when it came to food, especially when he was hungry. Which was constantly. Elizabeth had used to tease him about having a tapeworm.

Hastings met him at the top of the stairs. "The young lord would like to join you for breakfast this morning. He asked directly, and Miss Hannah said he did so in the most gentlemanly manner."

Breakfast with William might be just the thing to take his mind off…well…off everything. "Send him down," he said and turned toward the breakfast room.

He'd taken his first sip of coffee when William appeared at the door, Gordon standing a pace behind him.

"Come in, son, come in. Set a place right there, would you?"

Hastings tilted his head at Gordon, who hastily gathered flatware and a plate and set it in front of the chair diagonal to Richard's seat.

"Good morning, William," Richard said, oddly pleased his son had requested to join him. He'd only vague memories of his own sire so had no foundation for a father-son relationship. At William's birth, Richard had determined he'd be present for him as much as possible. His absences now complicated matters, but he did work to make up for it when they were together.

"Good morning, Papa," William said, smiling. "I trust you slept well?"

Richard almost spit out his mouthful of coffee. The boy may look like him, but those words were his mother's. Only recently breeched, William was already a little gentleman. He now understood why Elizabeth had wanted the boy out of gowns a bit early. He did not doubt she long ago saw the young man blossoming in the child, while he'd only recognized it in this moment.

"I did. And you?" he asked equally formally.

"Yes, sir, I did." William fell quiet as Gordon slid a plate in front of him and a cup of hot chocolate.

"Do you not eat meat?" Richard asked as his own plate piled high with bacon, kidney, and eggs was set before him. William's slice of bread and poached eggs seemed measly in comparison.

"I do but not in the morning. Mama says meat is too much for my system so early in the day."

"Indeed," Richard said, not knowing if it was true or not but trusting Elizabeth's judgment in all things child-rearing. They ate together cordially, Richard asking a few questions and William responding, but generally the clicking of flatware was the main sound breaking the quiet.

When the table was cleared, Richard eyed the folded paper to his right longingly, but William did not move. It was obvious he had something on his mind.

"Did you wish to speak with me about something?"

"Indeed," William said in perfect mimicry of Richard's own words. Perhaps his son was not wise for his age but was a simple parrot instead. Richard bit back a smile behind his cup and waited patiently for William to continue.

"I would like my very own pony, sir. For when we return home, sir. I would care for it and groom it as I should."

Richard set his cup on the table and wiped his mouth. It was a reasonable request. The boy had a good seat on the small pony they'd leased. He was calm and steady when the groom led him around. But there'd be less supervision in the country, more opportunity to ride freely. If the boy was anything like he'd been as a child, he would sneak rides in without accompaniment. He didn't know how Elizabeth would feel about it. She was incredibly cautious with the boys, worrying all the time. It was understandable, considering the circumstances, and he would not do anything to increase her anxieties.

"I am not sure, William." The boy's expression did not change, but his eyes glazed with tears. "It is not a definitive no. I must take some time to consider it and talk with your mother."

William struggled with his emotions and spoke when he had them firmly under control. "But Mama said I should speak to you. That it was your decision."

"Did she?"

"I did."

They both swung their heads toward Elizabeth and gasped, although Richard was sure William's noise was because he'd been startled, whereas his was a direct reaction to her ethereal beauty. Her face pale against her indigo frock, her hair down and shining almost white in the morning sunlight, she looked more angelic than earthly. He shook his head, knowing he must not succumb to such romantic notions, but he could not take his eyes off her. She was truly breathtaking.

"Forgive my manners," Richard said, clearing his throat and getting to his feet. William followed suit.

She waved away his apology and took a seat across from William's chair, to Richard's right. "You may both sit, please."

He waited until Hastings had poured a chocolate for Elizabeth before continuing, his thoughts now back on track.

"What is your opinion regarding a pony for William? At Thornwood Manor. Or should we talk about this later?"

William sat straighter but didn't say a word. A sensible lad. Surely it was not too soon for his own pony?

"I will worry regardless of what age William is, so I leave it to your discretion. I trust you to make the right decision. Besides, you were once a boy, whereas I have never been one." She smiled at William, who appeared far too tense and focused to smile back. "So you bring a perspective I do not have."

He didn't get his own pony until he was five, but like William, he'd been seated on leased ponies at a young age. Quite young, as he had no memory of ever not being on a pony or a horse. He'd made a point of William's ongoing exposure to the full stable of horses at Thornwood Manor and had taken the boy on rides with him in the park with great success. There was truly nothing like riding. It was a pastime he thoroughly enjoyed.

"When I return to the country, we will choose the right one."

William flew from his chair and threw his arms around Richard. "Oh, Papa, thank you!"

"It's Papa again now, is it, not sir?" he teased, ruffling his hair. "Thank your mother. She is the one brave enough to let you have one of your own."

William ran over to his mother and repeated his exuberant performance. She hugged him back and kissed each cheek. Richard enjoyed the child in the boy as much as the man. Elizabeth was doing a fine job.

"Why don't you share the news with Sebastian and Hannah?" she said, laughing as he ran from the room without a glance backward.

"Manners are a fleeting thing," Richard said, signaling for more coffee.

"As they should be when you're not yet four. His birthday is next month. I must plan a gathering. Will we be in London?"

It was a simple question, but he had no answer. For many reasons, he could not tell her about this business with Patricia, and he had no idea how long it would take to play out. And *we*? How long could he manage to stay under the same roof and not fall to her charms?

"For you, my lord." A footman stood with a note on a tray.

Grateful for the interruption, he waved him in and unfolded it.

Mrs. Tate's Parlor at seven o'clock. Alone. 10 guineas.

"Please excuse me," Richard said, pushing from his chair. He needed to speak with Walford. He also needed to escape her inquiring gaze. He glanced back from the doorway. "I'll not be available this evening."

He didn't wait to see her face, fearing she'd have the same glazed eyes as their son had earlier. Richard fled down the hall, cursing himself for the coward he knew himself to be.

CHAPTER TEN

Why do not words, and kiss, and solemn pledge;
And nature that is kind in woman's breast,
And reason that in man is wise and good,
And fear of him who is a righteous judge;
Why do not these prevail for human life,
To keep two hearts together, that began
Their spring-time with one love, and that have need
Of mutual pity and forgiveness, sweet
To grant, or be received.

—Wordsworth, *The Excursion*

ELIZABETH WAITED FOR Hastings to pour the lemonade before continuing. "I am unbelievably grateful for your generosity."

Catherine, pretty in a moss-colored gown draped with a delicate creamy lace, shook her head. "Your generosity is to be admired, not ours. The village is fortunate to have such a charitable benefactor."

"I must agree, *bella*," Sophia said, picking up a piece of cake and eyeing it appreciatively. "There is much poverty, but many choose not to see it. You look at it, and you do something to help. That is special." She broke off a piece of cake and popped it into her mouth, moaning dramatically. "It is so good, no?"

Dust motes danced in the late-afternoon sun, and Elizabeth noted the fading of the upper section of the drapes. The damask paper hanging, too, was showing its age. She'd spent little time in the townhouse these past few years, and it was past time to do some updating. She would speak with Mrs. Fernsby about it and see if they could get something underway before Elizabeth returned to the country. She could not live without the housekeeper, so she would need to find someone else to supervise the work. She asked the ladies.

"I would loan you mine, but she is indispensable. I know nothing about running a house, but don't tell her that." Sophia grinned and took another bite of her cake.

"The woman we hired for our stay is doing a superb job. Nicholas has suggested we steal her back to the country with us, but Fredericks's nose would be out of joint. Woodfield has managed without a housekeeper for so long it hardly matters. Besides, Lord Woodfield would have an apoplectic fit should we make such a decision without his input. And he's only coming around to behaving decently. I'd hate to poke the old lion again." Catherine absently ran her hand over her stomach and smiled. "All that to say I shall talk with the housekeeper about her plans, if you'd like. You may want to keep her on permanently and leave your efficient Mrs. Fernsby in the country."

"Oh, she'd like that, I'd think. Although, I should check with Richard to hear his thoughts." Mrs. Fernsby had been inherited, along with Hastings, when Richard's father passed away. She had been the only woman in his life, after his mother had died, until Elizabeth had come along. He was the one who insisted the staff travel with them, although he did keep a skeleton staff in London for when he came alone. Which had been far too often of late.

"I must not linger too long," Sophia said, putting her plate on the side table and relaxing back into the sofa, not looking at all in a hurry. "His Grace has asked me to join him at Carlton House. He is sending a carriage at eight o'clock."

Elizabeth glanced at the clock on the mantel. "It is nearing five. Should you not be on your way?"

"Yes," Sophia said, leaning forward and snatching another piece of cake. She sat back, balancing the small plate on her lap. "I should, but…" She grinned before taking a large bite of the cake, holding a finger up to indicate she needed a moment before finishing.

Catherine laughed and shook her head, and Elizabeth enjoyed the levity.

"I am in need of three hours for my toilette," Sophia continued after a sip of lemonade. "If I leave now, I might be ready at the assigned time. *His* chosen time. That I cannot allow."

Her laugh was delightful, and they both joined in. Elizabeth had always admired Sophia's independent spirit and wondered at her choice of the duke as a partner. "You cannot be considering the duke, Sophia? Would it not be like wedding your father?"

Sophia shuddered theatrically. "That will haunt me all night, you evil woman. I should insist you both join me this evening as a bulwark to his advances."

"I cannot save you, my friend," Catherine said. "Last night was fatiguing, and I am all for an evening at home. I'll most likely go to bed early. It was my plan to snuggle with Nicholas, but he has some urgent business to attend to and does not know when he'll be home."

"How odd. Richard, too, is occupied this evening. Do you think they might be together?" It was a pleasanter thought than some of the things Elizabeth had been imagining.

"I don't know. They did huddle together in the library last evening, so they may be up to something." Catherine shrugged. "Nicholas did not expand, and I did not ask him to. I was too grateful for a reprieve from the world. Although, truth be told, I am enjoying my time here far more than I anticipated. I may extend it if I don't increase too quickly."

"Oh, lovely," Elizabeth said. "I do enjoy your company, and I've not had much female companionship of late."

"Catherine I must excuse, but *bella*, there is nothing to prevent you from joining me." Sophia said it as if the deal was sealed.

"Oh no. I, too, prefer the quiet tonight. Besides, my feet, remember?" Elizabeth waggled her oversize slippers at Sophia.

Sophia sighed heavily and sat forward. "Yes, they do already have jesters at court, don't they?"

Laughter again filled the room as Sophia stood. Catherine got to her feet as well. "I must leave too. I find myself tiring more easily as of late."

"I remember it well," Elizabeth said, walking to the door and ringing the bell. "I do thank you for joining me this afternoon. It has been a pleasure."

Their light chatter filled the entrance as their carriages were brought around. Afterward, Elizabeth wandered around the empty house, unsure of how to fill her time. She took a seat by the window in the drawing room and picked up her embroidery. She stared at it but didn't raise the needle. After the gaiety of her friends' company, the silence was stifling.

"Can I bring you anything, my lady?"

"No, thank you, Hastings. I believe I'll go up and see the boys. I am sure William would like to discuss the pony situation for the hundredth time."

She took the stairs slowly, the familiar loneliness more acute after the promise of yesterday. Baby steps, she reminded herself. Baby steps.

CHAPTER ELEVEN

A mistress never is nor can be a friend. While you agree, you are lovers; and, when it is over, any thing but friends.

—Byron, *The Works of Lord Byron: Letters and Journals*

WALFORD SAT BACK in his chair, pressing his fingers together contemplatively. Richard had given him the note earlier and had waited not so patiently for him to return from the Home Office. He'd wanted to accompany Walford, but Walford hadn't thought it wise at this point. Richard rubbed his forehead, not for the first time baffled by the entire situation. That he was participating in some sort of espionage seemed ludicrous, yet here he was.

"I know you are willing to do this, Thornwood. Lord knows the undersecretary would like you to go through with it. But Beckett's unable to provide a field agent on this short of notice, and I'm not at all comfortable with you doing it alone," Walford said. "The problem is if I go with you, she might not be forthcoming."

"I'm sure I'll be safe enough. As safe as a man can be in a brothel, since I'll have my clothes on," Richard joked, trying to lighten the growing tension. He did believe he'd be safe, but it was an odd game they played, and he didn't know the rules.

"Yes, safe enough, I suppose." He either missed Richard's jest or chose to ignore it. "Still, there's always the possibility that you're not." Walford grunted, tugging on his bottom lip pensively, then slapped his palms on the arms of his chair. "I see no way around it but for me to go too. You must have some sort of backup." Walford waved a servant over. "A pencil and stationery. And coffee." He looked at Richard. "It could prove to be a long night."

When the servant dropped the paper by, Walford leaned forward. "I took the liberty of strolling past Mrs. Tate's on my return." He drew a rough square to represent the brothel. "There are several doorways I can tuck myself into. Here." He tapped the page, smudging the graphite. "And here." He scratched an *x* on the square. "You must go in through the door on the right and leave by the same door. Do not let her convince you otherwise." He drew several more lines. "These are the alleys. Too many for me to watch. We don't know if she has accomplices, and I'll not have you surprised by an attack.

"When you come out, you stroll my way and duck into the doorway, here, with me. We'll wait a minute to see if you're followed, and if all is clear, you'll stay and watch the front. I'll head around back. I doubt she'll be allowed to use the front door, so your job will be to note who goes in. If she comes out the back, I'll see where she goes."

"Should I push her for her source?" Richard asked, relieved that Walford had taken charge of the situation but concerned he was taking on far more risk than Richard was himself.

"Gently probe, but don't scare her. If she has genuine intelligence, the Home Office wants to open the line of communication. They can use all the help they can get on the peninsula. It seems Wellesley's regular lines have been drying up lately, and he is preparing his spring campaign."

"And what of you? What if there are accomplices out back?" Richard had not meant to drag Walford into anything dangerous. Of course, it had not been his intention to put himself in jeopardy either.

Walford grinned. "You forget I sullied my hands for four years on the continent. I can take care of myself. Besides, I've no intention of tangling with anyone."

"Be sure keeping an eye out is all you do. You have a child on the way now. A responsibility."

Walford's grin grew bigger. "That I do." He stood, grabbed the paper, and tossed it on the fire. "I shall head home for a few hours with my current favorite responsibility. I'll be in position before you arrive. Don't look my way," he said and winked before walking away.

Richard chuckled. He couldn't blame Walford for considering him an amateur sleuth. Stealth and secrets were not a part of his world. Politics. Law. Investments. Those were his specialties, his areas of expertise and comfort. Spying was entirely ungentlemanly but, he had to admit, rather titillating. He'd felt a strange wave of excitement when Walford was outlining the plan.

He had hours ahead of him and did not want to return to the house. How could he with this evening hanging over his head? But he'd already been sitting for hours and was restless. Richard stood and stretched, shaking his sleeping foot until it began to tingle awake. He stared at it. He knew exactly what he could do to pass some time. He headed down the stairs and out the door, waiting while a footman found him a hackney coach.

"To Wood's." Richard climbed in cheerfully, exceptionally pleased with himself.

RICHARD STEPPED FROM the coach and pulled his collar tighter. The night was typical of January, cold and wet with a thick fog curling around the few lampposts that dotted the street, muting the already dim lighting. All the better to keep Walford hidden, although the dampness was devilishly miserable for standing around in. He resisted glancing in Walford's direction despite that the temptation was strong.

He waited as another hackney stopped in front of the building, and two young men fell out, laughing boisterously, holding each other up. A bit early to be in their cups, but Richard supposed such were the foibles of youth. It was the very same weakness that had led him to Patricia in the first place and, ultimately, his current situation. They rapped on the door. A doorman opened it immediately, and the two tumbled in. Richard caught a glimpse of a gaudy entrance hall before the door closed again.

Well, there was nothing for it but to put the game in motion. He crossed the road and knocked on the door. The doorman opened it, quickly surveyed Richard, and stood back with a slight bow, letting Richard in. Richard took off his hat and brushed at the droplets before handing it to the man. "Lord Thornwood," he said authoritatively.

"My lord," the man said, bowing more deeply this time. "Welcome." He pulled a bell cord, and two footmen arrived immediately, assisting Richard in removing his outerwear before leading him through the house. They stopped at a drawing room in the back.

"Do sit down, my lord."

Richard stepped into the room. A sad attempt at an *Arabian Nights* theme, it had seen better days. Frayed silks draped faded daybeds; chipped chair legs bolstered lumpy chairs. He walked across a carpet that had had its share of wear and chose the sturdiest-looking chair to sit on. The stale smell of booze mingled with cigars and the distinct odor of sweat. He swallowed a rise of bile. What had he gotten himself into?

"Lord Thornwood. What a pleasure it is to have you grace my fair establishment." The woman was not altogether unpleasing, but she was as faded as the room. He wasn't sure he'd ever seen a woman so well endowed, but for certain he was *seeing* one now. She'd barely managed to contain her ample bosom, and he worried it might spill out if she were to bend over. She smiled seductively, and he realized she'd misinterpreted his stare for interest, not astonishment.

He cleared his throat and looked at the carpet. He'd expected Patricia to be readily available and was not sure if he should ask directly about her or not. A footman returned with a tray, setting it on the table beside the chair. The woman sashayed across the room and sat across from him. When she leaned to pour, he looked away, not wanting to see the entirety of her assets. Her laugh was as subtle as her attire as she handed him a glass.

"Our finest port, reserved for our finest gentlemen," she said as she examined him, measuring his worth. "Forgive my manners, my lord. Mrs. Tate at your service. What is it you'd like this evening?"

It would appear she was unaware of his reason for being there, so he presumed he'd better not mention Patricia lest he reveal something he should not.

"It's early, so you can have your pick. Light, dark. Small, big. Young, old. Name your type, and I am sure we can find someone to fit your fancy."

His cheeks burned, and she laughed and poured herself a drink. *Hell and the devil.* He'd not thought this through.

"Are you looking for more exotic pleasures?" Mrs. Tate eyed him over her drink. "More than one girl? Some toys?"

"One would be sufficient," he managed to say, rejecting the images she was painting and pulling himself together. "Preferably a redhead. Voluptuous, not rail thin." He tried to recall any other attributes to narrow the field to Patricia. "Oh, lightly freckled is fine but not too freckled. I prefer pale skin." It was absolute poppycock. He had nothing against freckles, but he knew they were a common feature among redheads, and Patricia only had a smattering of them across her nose.

She looked at him quizzically, but if she speculated about his specificity, she didn't say. "Let me see what I can do." She took her port with her as she left.

Richard took a sip from the plain cut-glass tumbler, surprised at the quality of the drink. It was far superior to the decor. Again, he wondered how Patricia had managed to sink so low. He knew she'd been supplied by a brothel the night he'd met her, but it was not something he'd dwelled upon at the time. He'd never even asked her about it. Or about her life at all. He'd set her up, and that was that. The discourteousness of his actions lumped into a guilty ball in his gut.

Mrs. Tate stepped back into the room with two footmen. "Lord Thornwood. One or all. Your choice."

She clapped her hands, and the two men walked across the room and pulled back a drape on the far wall, revealing another entrance to the room. He made a quick mental note of its existence as one of the servants opened the door and a statuesque redhead stepped into view. Draped in a white cloth, she stood like Venus, her smile sensual and enticing. He shook his head, feeling oddly remorseful for her disappointment. He'd not come here to offend anyone. More, he'd not come here to gawk at women, although he needed to pretend he was doing so.

Another took her place. Small and waiflike, he hoped she was not as young as she looked. She looked no older than sixteen years and, definitely, could not have been long out of the schoolroom. He shook his head both in refusal and at his speculations. These women had never been inside a schoolroom. If they had, they'd not have landed in such a situation. Where were the men in their lives? Their fathers? Their brothers? Why had he never considered their unfortunate circumstances before? He'd never set foot in a brothel until this evening. He thought of Elizabeth and her orphanage. There were so many in need.

Mrs. Tate cleared her throat loudly, regaining Richard's attention. "I have but one redhead left. Saved the best for last," she said, clapping again.

Patricia stepped into the entrance, and Richard swallowed what would have been an audible sigh of relief. Her red hair cascaded over her shoulders, but it did nothing to hide her body. She stood rod stiff, staring straight ahead. Her frock was sheer, leaving nothing to the imagination, but it was not her body drawing his attention. It was her bland expression and the lack of recognition in her eyes.

"Yes," he said but did not take his eyes off her. If she was glad of his choice, she gave no indication.

"Patricia," Mrs. Tate snapped. "Some manners, if you please." Patricia didn't move. "You may entertain *Lord* Thornwood in the blue room."

Patricia turned and walked away. Richard jumped to his feet and followed. "That woman is going to get what's coming to her one—" was all he caught of Mrs. Tate's angry rant before the door closed behind him.

THE BLUE ROOM was aptly named. It contained every shade of blue known to man with no consideration for respite from the color. Richard turned and closed the door, seeking to lock it, but there was nothing with which to do so. He turned around as Patricia threw herself on the bed. She lay faceup, her arm covering her face, and her shoulders shook.

"Did you see her face?" she said, and Richard was relieved to hear the laughter in her voice, not the anguish he'd expected. "Old battle-ax thinks she runs me. Me!" Patricia sat up and patted the bed. "Oh, do come sit with me, Thornwood. I'll not bite. Not unless you want me to," she said slyly, laughter still twinkling in her eyes.

"I believe I'll stand, thank you," he said, focusing on her face and not her body. A body he had once had great familiarity with but that no longer held any appeal. Not because she was not beautiful. The quick glimpse through the sheer fabric had proven she'd retained all her charms. But his only interest here was the information she purportedly had for him.

She waved a hand, a flare of impatience darkening her eyes

before she tamed her expression. "Suit yourself, but your legs may tire."

"I'll be but a minute. Give me what I've come for, and I'll be on my way."

Patricia put a finger to lips. "The walls have ears sometimes," she said, lowering her voice. "You must stay awhile. Otherwise, it will look suspicious. I cannot raise any alarms."

He'd not considered lingering. He'd intended to be in and out as quickly as possible.

"Besides, they'd think you a young buck with no control. To shoot your bolt and leave would not do for your manly reputation, now would it?"

Richard flinched at her implied vulgarity. Patricia had always been free in her speech but never crass. The ten years had definitely wrought some changes in her. But she was right. He must act the part of a man in need. He grabbed the single chair by the fireplace, moved it closer to the bed, and sat.

"Coward," she said, but she smiled, and he saw the old Patricia despite the creases beginning to line her face and the smudges of blue-black under her eyes. She looked weary.

"May I ask how you became part of—"

She put a finger to her lips again and scowled. He raised his brow at her audacity. Did she take him for a fool who would say it aloud?

"This latest endeavor," he finished, crossing his arms and giving a stare for a stare.

"No, you may not," she said with quiet confidence. "It would not be safe for either one of us."

He waved a hand around the room. "And this? May I ask how you came to be here?"

She shrugged a shoulder, and again, he caught a glimpse of the Patricia he once knew. Timid and sure, cocky and tentative. She'd always presented an alluring dichotomy. "A girl's gotta eat," she said. "I've only had one generous protector in my life."

"If you are referring to me, I do believe I left you with

enough money and advice so you'd need not return to…" He could not call it by name. Patricia had never been a harlot to him. He'd actually been fond of her.

"What would a woman like me know of investments and such?"

"You should have come to me," he said, wishing he could turn back time and do things differently. What that would be, he didn't know. But he'd had no wish to see her so fallen. There must have been something he could have done?

"You had fallen in love, Thornwood. How was I to come to you, if you would no longer come to me willingly? You were generous in your departure. It is my failings that see me here, not yours." She flicked her hair over her shoulders. "Besides, I have come to you now, haven't I?"

She shifted off the bed and turned around, exposing her backside to him as she fumbled under the mattress. Richard turned his head and stared at the painting on the wall. He was out of his depth, an intruder. He was sure she was trying to entice him, but he was definitely not tempted. Not even a little bit titillated. His desire was reserved for only one woman. A woman who would be appalled if she knew where he was right now.

"I knew the old hag would put a lord in this room," she said as she turned around. "It's her best, you know," she added with a bitter laugh. "Here."

She thrust out a folded paper, and Richard took it, tucking it inside his jacket without looking at it. Patricia flipped her hand over, palm up, and raised her eyebrows expectantly. Richard pulled out a small bag, the irony of its blue velvet not lost on him, and handed it over. She took it, weighing it in her hands thoughtfully, but she did not untie the strings.

"Don't you want to check it?" he asked.

She laughed. "I trust you. It is not in your nature to deceive."

Richard pulled out his pocket watch. "I believe my manhood would remain intact should I leave now."

"Unless you want me to check to ensure your manhood is as

it should be," she said, switching to a seductive purr.

He stepped back from her approach, and she stopped, her smile oddly sad. "A girl can dream," she said and stepped quickly to him, pulling his face close. She quickly rubbed her lips across his cheek and pulled at his hair before he could stop her. "There," she said, wiping at the corner of her mouth where her rouged lips had smudged. "Now you look like you've been doing more than talking."

She patted his pocket. "There will be more where this came from. For a price. I'll be in touch."

Patricia walked to the bed and threw a pillow on the floor, tugged at the coverlet, and poured a small amount of liquid from the water glass onto the bedding. She pulled the cord, tossed off her gown, and sprawled on the bed. Richard averted his eyes, grateful it was only seconds before a footman knocked and opened the door.

"This way, my lord."

Richard followed him through the dimly lit hallway, his heart heavy with regret for a life that should have turned out so much better.

⟫⟫⟩⟨⟨⟨

"I BELIEVE I shall," Richard said, accepting a second cognac from the servant. The first had chased the chill from his bones. He'd passed the paper to Walford before taking up his own position in the shadowed doorway across from the brothel. He'd not seen Walford since. He didn't know if Walford continued to wait out back of the building or whether he'd gone to deliver the information. Richard had waited in the cold for a good hour, and when it became clear Patricia had either gone out another door or remained inside entertaining customers, he'd headed to the club to wait for Walford.

"Ugh," Bentley said as he folded his long body into the chair opposite Richard. He was dressed too formally for a night of cards in the back rooms. "Another blasted ball," he said, raising his hand to garner a footman's attention. "Another night being thrown to the wolves…er…ladies."

Richard chuckled. "You've nobody to blame but yourself. You're twenty-nine. Far past time for you to have chosen a wife and settled down."

Bentley brushed off an imaginary crumb on his lapel before responding. "Why settle for a single flower when one can have a bouquet?" he asked, taking the glass of port from the waiter. "Besides, you and Walford picked the roses. There is only goutweed left."

"Ah, but goutweed has a delicate, sweet-smelling flower. Don't discount it," Richard countered.

"That may be. But it is boringly common and damned prolific." He threw back his port, and Richard laughed.

"Too many mamas throwing their treasures at you, Bentley?" Walford asked, sliding smoothly into the chair beside Bentley. "Thornwood," he said, dipping his head toward Richard in acknowledgment. "How fare you gentlemen this evening?"

Looking none the worse for his night out in the cold, Walford was as superior an actor as Patricia. Her impassivity when she'd been brought into the receiving room had been worthy of the stage. He'd believed it. Now Walford showed no sign at all of what they'd been up to. Richard would keep his own self in check and ensure he did not let the game be known either.

"I was commiserating with Bentley over the woes of bachelorhood," Richard said, and Bentley moaned melodramatically.

"May I suggest marriage?" Walford said. "I highly recommend it."

"I already proposed it as a solution, and he wants none of it. Apparently, we have taken the best off the market."

"I can't argue with that." Walford took his glass off the servant's tray and raised it in the air. "To our wives and the good fortune they tolerate us."

Bentley snorted disdainfully. He finished off his port and got to his feet. "Off to sacrifice my self-respect once again," he said, bowing slightly.

"The gentleman doth protest too much, methinks," Walford said, smiling over his glass.

Bentley grinned. "To marry or not to marry—that is the question."

"Frailty, thy name is Bentley," Richard said to Bentley's departing back, and Walford burst out laughing.

When he was out of sight, Walford put down his glass, his mood abruptly shifting to one of solemnity. He leaned in closer, and Richard followed his lead. The room was loud, most chairs filled in contrast to earlier, so it would be difficult to be overheard, but it made good sense to err on the side of caution.

"It's in code. They've called in an expert, but they recognize the cipher so are convinced it's a genuine missive."

Richard sat back and shook his head. However had Patricia become involved in this? And who was her source? He put the questions to Walford.

"The Home Office would like an answer as well. Unfortunately, you may not be through with this, although the decision rests entirely with you." Walford lowered his voice further. "They've asked you to continue. I provided them no assurances."

Richard ran a hand through his hair. It was not a question of wanting to, for he had no desire to put himself in tonight's situation again. He'd thought of Elizabeth as he'd sat waiting and how appalled she'd be if she knew where he'd been this evening, what he'd been doing. He was a gentleman, not a spy, and he said as much to Walford.

"I know it, Thornwood. And I'd not encourage you to consider it, were it not for their insistence the woman might be vital to the spring campaign on the continent. It could save lives," he added, his expression darkening.

Richard didn't know what memories had been prompted, nor what demons haunted him, but he did know Walford—Captain

Sinclair in those days—had lost many men to battle on the peninsula. Richard imagined it carved a permanent mark on one's soul. "I'll give it thorough consideration," he said, worried he'd already headed down a path with no end.

"If it's any comfort, there was no movement out back, unless you count the privy. It will not be remembered as one of my favorite reconnaissance missions. Some things cannot be unseen." Walford grimaced and shivered dramatically.

Richard appreciated Walford's attempt at levity, but he couldn't shake the feeling that if he didn't back away from the situation now, he wouldn't be able to at all.

"Well, home to that lovely wife of mine Bentley so envies me," Walford said, coming to his feet. "Oh, almost forgot." Walford reached into his pocket and pulled out a small bag. "Reimbursement. Beckett must have worked hard to get it. The Home Office almost squeaks its purses are so seldom opened. I'll let you know when I hear something."

Richard tucked the money away, sat back down, and grabbed the newspaper. The words blurred into a single blot as he contemplated his decision. He wasn't sure he truly had a choice. If lives could be saved, was it not his moral obligation?

He rolled his neck from side to side. His head hurt, and he'd like nothing more than to crawl into his bed. Instead, he turned to the second page. He'd no interest in catching up on the debates in parliament, but he could not go home until Elizabeth was long to bed. How could he possibly face her tonight?

CHAPTER TWELVE

There's rosemary, that's for remembrance; pray,
love, remember.

—Shakespeare, *Hamlet*

RICHARD WAS AVOIDING her again. He hadn't returned to the aloofness of the past two years. Elizabeth would have surrendered—packed everything and removed to the estate—were that the case. Since Thursday, he'd been polite but hesitant, almost on edge, when they saw each other. Which did not happen for more than a few minutes before he'd dash from the town house, escaping to who knew where. For he certainly did not share his whereabouts with her.

She thought they'd made progress. A week ago, he'd held her in his arms and gallantly pushed his way through the crowded assembly room. And the night of Catherine's soiree, they'd been relaxed together. Their growing connection had seemed a guarantee when they'd stood side by side in the nursery that night. She'd been so pleased to find him with William the next morning. But he'd received a message and left abruptly.

Elizabeth had tried to wait up that night but had surrendered before midnight. She'd lain awake until the clock rang out twice, and there still had been no sound indicating he'd returned. She'd awoken late the next morning. Lucy had assured her he'd returned safely, but he was already gone by the time she was dressed and presentable. Now, five days later, here she sat, alone again at the breakfast table, contemplating what was in the missive he'd received.

He'd not been the same since. She had never pried into his affairs before, but the temptation now was great. What had drawn him away, and why did it continue to impact on his presence? Or was she merely hoping his absence was due to external affairs and not from his disappointment in their relationship? It was too discouraging a notion to entertain.

Richard had always been kept busy chasing business concerns, and he was keenly involved in parliament. He enjoyed a good debate and was an advocate for laws and bills that supported a growing economy and the betterment of all citizens. He used to talk to her of the necessity for money to flow, not just among the wealthy but downward as well. He believed the country would flourish if more people were lifted up. He'd always had a social conscience, and she loved him for it.

That he was occupied with these things was not new. But he'd never been secretive about any of his business matters, nor his political opinions or causes. She'd scanned the paper each day but could see nothing that would demand his unending attention.

Conceivably, it could be the business dealings with Mr. Randall. She knew little about the new alliance, although she could not fathom why it would keep him from home so much. So it came back to avoidance. Of her. But what had she done to cause such a rapid reversal in his behavior? She sighed heavily. Men. She'd never understand them.

"Excuse me, my lady. A Mr. Wood is here with your shoes."

"Show him to the small drawing room, Hastings." Elizabeth set aside her chocolate and stood, checking to ensure there were no crumbs on her gown. She was surprised Mr. Wood had come himself. It was, after all, a single pair of shoes. As comfortable as they'd been, she'd be glad to shed the blue slippers. It was only her toe wrapped now, so the new ones should do nicely until it was fully healed. She sighed. Other shoes may soon fit again, but she knew she'd no longer be able to wear her favorite pair.

She strolled through the ballroom to the front of the house. Mr. Wood bowed politely when she came in, as did the young man by his side. Neither of them drew Elizabeth's attention.

"I'm at a loss for words," she said, not able to make sense of what she was seeing. "I ordered but one pair." There were at least ten paper-wrapped packages.

"You did," Mr. Wood said. "But Lord Thornwood ordered more. He has kept us very busy." He threw his shoulders back, standing taller, his chest puffing out and his smile beaming with pride.

Richard? Richard had gone to the shoemaker? For her?

"Do sit down, my lady. I would see that each of these fit to your liking. The earl insisted upon your comfort."

Elizabeth obeyed, too taken aback to speak. Each time she despaired of ever breaching Richard's defenses, something happened to renew her optimism.

There were twelve sets in all, with only two needing adjustments. But it was the last pair that left her dumbfounded. They were exact replicas of the ones she'd been wearing at the ball when her toenail had torn.

"His Lordship said I should give you this pair last, and he wanted you to have this as well."

Wood handed her a note and turned to wrap the pairs he needed to take back and modify. She unfolded the paper.

They hold a special memory for me too. For I once saw them on bended knee. R.

The note blurred, and Elizabeth smiled through her tears. That he remembered his proposal seemed a small miracle. That he recalled what she'd worn? It was a greater gift than the shoes. She need look no further for assurances her marriage was salvageable. The evidence was here in his words. All she needed was a plan to turn words into deed.

➤➤➤❮❮❮❮

"HERE," RICHARD SAID, sliding the purse onto the bedside table. "This is for you. You need not share it with whoever it is you are garnering your secrets."

He'd decided to accept reimbursement from Beckett and pass it on to Patricia. It was all he could come up with to help her out, at least a little. On their second meeting, he'd offered to move her out. Get her set up somewhere, temporarily, until she found a sponsor.

"And if I don't? Will you support me until my hair is gray and beyond?" she'd asked.

It had been a fair enough question, and he'd paused, debating it, thoughts of Elizabeth and how she would feel mingling with this obstinate sense of obligation.

"I didn't think so. I don't want your charity, Thornwood." Patricia had haughtily tossed her long red locks over her shoulder and held his gaze. "Besides, I may have a new sponsor soon."

"Hopefully it will tide you over until you secure a protector," he'd said when she'd peeked into the purse.

Now, on his third visit, he'd grown even more weary of her circumstance. He'd become a man with her tutelage, and although he'd made an effort to do right by her when they'd parted, he felt he owed her for it. He worried this information gathering would end badly for her.

"Don't look so pensive, Thornwood. You need not worry about me," she said, as though she'd read his mind. She seductively ran a hand along her scantily clad body. "My charms have always seen me through."

He headed to the door.

"Thornwood."

He turned. Her smile gone, her hand clutching the purse, she sat up and swung her legs over the bed. "I do thank you for this. You have always been nothing but kind to me."

Richard left, paying Mrs. Tate the fee before heading to White's. Patricia's voice haunted him all the way. There had to be a better way than this for her to survive. He chewed it over as he sipped his cognac, waiting for Walford.

"You could lose your manly bits out there tonight. Snap them right off," Walford said as he dropped into the chair across from Richard. "Why is town always chillier than the country?"

"Any sign of anyone?" Richard asked, not interested in discussing the weather in London or anywhere else.

Walford shook his head. "No untoward movement at all." He plucked a cognac from the servant's tray and took a long sip before continuing. "And that's it for me. I'm out. The Home Office wants me to distance myself from it all. Apparently I'm too obvious an intermediary for you. The second bit of information got them all fired about not jeopardizing this line of communication in any way. They've finally assigned an agent. Two, as a matter of fact."

Richard's mood diminished. He'd hoped this would be a short run, but it would seem he must continue. And without Walford. "I'll miss your reliable companionship."

"As long as I'm in London, there's no reason we can't run in our usual social circles together. It's the frequency and consistency of these meetings they worry will somehow interfere." Walford shook his head slowly, clearly not in agreement with their assessment of the situation. "You'll be in better hands. These men are trained. They're also going to watch Mrs. Tate's fine establishment, cataloging comings and goings. As well, they'll have your back during visits. One will get my privy duty. Lucky sod." Walford grinned, then grew serious again. "There'll be an agent out front ensuring you exit after each visit. Much safer. Which may be their greater concern. It would not do for a peer to come to harm at their direction."

Richard nodded, although he'd not perceived any threat to date. He reached into his jacket, and Walford raised his hand, signaling him to stop. "Not to me anymore. It will go to the agent. Who, for whatever reason, must remain unknown."

"How the devil do I pass it on to an unknown person?" Richard said, becoming increasingly irritated by it all. He should never have agreed to any of it.

Walford chuckled. "I know. But apparently it is imperative for the safety of both you and the agent that you not know who it is. You are to put the information at the back of the first book on the first shelf in the first case."

Richard looked at the shelves lining the far wall. "First on left or right?"

"Left. Both the case and the shelf," Walford said, eyeing him over his cognac.

"First shelf top or bottom?"

"Bottom."

"What if someone else finds it?"

"When do you see anyone touch these books?" Walford laughed, catching Richard off guard. He could see no amusement in the situation.

"Apparently, most books grabbed randomly are the ones at eye level. The first shelf is far below that. And no one in this room would admit to reading this one, never mind be seen holding it in public." Walford's face again lit with merriment. A stark contrast to Richard's mood.

"The book is a woman's novel. *Love in Excess* by Eliza Haywood," Walford said, leaning forward in his chair. "Relax. I'd wager the agent is in the room already and will watch you do it. He'll preempt anyone getting it."

Richard ran a hand through his hair and surveyed the room. He recognized most faces. Was the agent someone he knew? He shook his head. "Confound it all. Soon I'll be cloaked with a hidden dagger like some damn melodrama."

Walford guffawed, and some of Richard's tension eased.

"Do you know when the next exchange will occur?" Walford asked.

"Patricia doesn't seem to know when she'll get information.

She said she'd contact me when she had something further."

"Good. Perhaps before she does, these agents will deduce who is giving her this material, and you will be freed of the obligation."

"It would be of some relief," Richard said, knowing it was an understatement. His head was spinning. He'd wanted a distraction from Elizabeth, but this was insanity. Nights at a brothel with a half-naked woman, men skulking in the dark, hiding information in a book. He was not built for intrigue.

"While I am left out of the game now, I shall be around to assist should you need it. Catherine has decided to linger in town for longer than planned. She does so enjoy your wife's company. And the countess's. A daunting trio, don't you agree."

Richard smiled with relief. He'd escaped quickly each day and had hoped Elizabeth was keeping busy, so was pleased to hear that friendship had been warming her days. He'd not liked picturing her lonely in town any more than he'd liked imagining her rambling around the manor alone.

"Please indulge Catherine and join us for some of the entertainments she is queuing up. It was a long four years when I was gone to the continent, and confinement will bring renewed quiet and waiting. I'd have her not dwell on her upcoming isolation yet."

Richard remembered their own trepidation and exhilaration with William. He also remembered the dread of loss with Sebastian. He would not begrudge them this time of joy with no burden of worry. Or guilt. Besides, a few evenings in Elizabeth's company, shielded by amiable friends, might be exactly what he needed. "I look forward to it."

"Good," Walford said, getting to his feet. "I'll leave you to your task. Do keep your dagger out of sight," he said with a laugh and a wave before leaving.

"Will do," Richard said with a sigh, sizing up the bookcase. When to do the deed and how to ensure discretion? At least he had something to contemplate, and more than enough time to execute the task, while he prolonged returning home.

CHAPTER THIRTEEN

And his unkindness may defeat my life,
But never taint my love.

—Shakespeare, *Othello*

Elizabeth was surprised by the note Richard had left in the breakfast room. He was off to the chambers at Westminster but would return in time to escort her to the Rawleys' ball. She wondered how he'd managed it, as she had not responded to the invitation when it had arrived at the beginning of the month. There had seemed little point.

Regardless, she was pleased about the unexpected turn of events. She hadn't fully fleshed out a plan of seduction, but she knew intuitively she must take it slowly. Rebuild their relationship first. She looked at the shoes lining her wardrobe floor and smiled. Her heart was bursting with hope.

She took the stairs to the nursery. Hannah put a finger to her lips as Elizabeth walked in and pointed to the puddle of cloth that was Sebastian fast asleep on the floor.

Hannah stepped closer and whispered, "He's had a reckless morning, my lady, barreling about the room as though he'd only that minute discovered his legs. I barely managed to keep up with him. I didn't have the heart to disturb him."

His blond hair the only thing visible, he was motionless. If it weren't for his soft snores, she might have panicked. He appeared comfortable where he lay. "That is fine, Hannah. I will take William for some air, and you may catch your breath."

William sat with his back to her. Hannah startled him when she tapped him on the shoulder, and Elizabeth wondered what had been so engrossing. Hannah whispered in his ear, and he turned around, glancing over his shoulder. He jumped to his feet and ran to her, a book firmly grasped in his hands.

"Mama!" he said excitedly, and Elizabeth put a finger to her lips and led him from the room.

"What is it you are reading, dearest?"

William held out the book proudly. "Horses."

She took the book from his hand and bit back a smile. *The Art of Animal Husbandry.* "Horses?" she asked.

"Yes, Mama," he said, snatching the book back. He flipped through the pages before stopping and tapping one triumphantly. "Horses."

It was a black-and-white plate of three horses, fortunately in repose. "Horses indeed," she said. "And what have you learned about them?" she asked, closing the book.

"They are big and like to stand together. They gallop fast. And they truly enjoy boys riding them."

"It tells you all that in this book?"

He smiled sheepishly. "I knew it already, Mama."

"I'm not the least bit surprised," she said as they took the final step to the ground floor. "Let us put this book back in the library and see if we can find one with more horse pictures for you to gather your information. One with a pony or two."

They perused the shelves to no avail. He knew his letters and could read many words, but most of the books in the library were beyond his abilities, and she couldn't find any with plates of horses. She would ask Richard for a suggestion. He was far more familiar than she with the town house library.

If William was disappointed, he didn't show it. He excitedly donned his coat for a walk, chattering about how he had groomed the pony this morning as well as one of the horses. "It is hard for me to reach, so Simon got me a box to stand on. And, Mama?"

"Yes, William?" she responded as they stepped out into the afternoon sunshine, with Gordon following protectively a few feet behind.

"I always groom the pony, even if it isn't mine. I hadn't that day because Edwin was waiting for me. You always say not to keep someone waiting." He looked up at her with glazed eyes. "I won't be so neglectful again."

Her eyes watered too. "I know you won't. I will let your father know how it came to pass."

He cheered instantly and talked incessantly as they strolled in the grounds across from the town house. Mostly about horses. And his father. It would seem Richard was a preoccupation for both of them. Did he know his good opinion could make or break his son's day? And hers?

RICHARD HADN'T RETURNED when Elizabeth had come upstairs to ready for the ball, but Lucy informed her he'd recently arrived and was now in his chambers. Elizabeth rolled her shoulders to loosen the tension. Richard was a man of his word, so she should not have worried so. He would not have left the note if he didn't intend to honor it.

Elizabeth selected a white satin gown with a sheer silk over-dress. It was embroidered with delicate lilac flowers that matched the sash. It had used to be a favorite of Richard's. Lucy snugged her stays, pushing her breasts up and on display. Elizabeth's instinct was to cover herself more modestly with the addition of a fichu. However, if seduction was to be her focus, she must make herself as appealing as possible. It would not do to look too matronly, although that was exactly how she'd been feeling these last two years.

Lucy had done a lovely job with her hair. Piled high, she had woven in a string of pearls and neatly tucked in feathers dyed to match the sash and embroidery. Even though the evening was cold, Elizabeth had Lucy remove the long undersleeve, leaving the dress with the short puffed Bishop-style sleeves. It was a private ball, but formality was still an expectation regardless of the weather. Besides, the shorter sleeves were far more elegant and her long gloves would stave off a chill. Her shawl would also keep her warm. Or dancing would. With Richard, she hoped. He'd broken protocol once. It would be divine if he would do so again. She smiled in anticipation as she pulled on her gloves.

"You look right beautiful, my lady," Lucy said as she clasped a set of pearls around Elizabeth's neck.

"Thank you, Lucy. I'll wear the new white satin slippers."

"Yes, my lady," Lucy said, going into the dressing room to get them.

Elizabeth stared at herself in the mirror, pleased with her reflection. She had gone to great effort with her looks this evening, even adding some kohl to her eyes and touches of rouge to her cheeks and lips. The longcase clock on the landing chimed. It was time to see if her preparations would have any effect.

CHAPTER FOURTEEN

*You cannot conceive how I ache to be with you: how I would die
for one hour.*

—Keats, Love Letter to Fanny Brawne

MARCUS FINISHED THE last tuck of Richard's neck scarf and stepped back to admire his handiwork. A simple fold would have sufficed as far as Richard was concerned, but Marcus was imperious when it came to evening fashion. He held out a white waistcoat, and Richard slipped his arms into it, fastening the thread-wrapped buttons himself.

"The blue or the black, my lord?" Marcus dangled the two coats by their collars.

"Whatever you suggest, Marcus. Let's get on with it. I'll not keep Lady Thornwood waiting."

"Of course, my lord. I would normally suggest the navy with your pale breeches, but I have it on good authority that this evening you will look much more striking in the black when beside the countess."

Richard shrugged into the jacket. It had been a tedious night waiting at the club, and it had been followed by a frustrating day in chambers. They'd argued in circles over the establishment of a permanent paid police force in London and had been no further ahead when the day ended than when the session had begun. It was exasperating but not surprising. It had been that way since he'd first attended parliament. In actuality, the battle for such an extensive trained force had been fought and lost many times before he'd even become a standing member.

The longcase clock sounded, and Marcus knelt and held Richard's black leather shoes steady as he slipped into them. He'd been on his feet much of the day, and the shoes fit overly snug. How had Elizabeth borne the pain in her feet? He'd not seen her, but Hastings had mentioned Wood had been and gone. He smiled. Richard hoped he'd gotten something right this dreary week.

He stepped into the hall. A light shone beneath Elizabeth's door, and he could hear the slight murmur of voices. At least he was not late. He headed to the library to wait for her.

"Would you care for anything, my lord?"

"No, thank you, Hastings. I don't believe we'll be lingering this evening. Have the carriage brought around."

Richard stared back out the window. A single oil lamp flickered dully at the entrance to the square across the road. It illuminated little, so blackness gaped beyond it and all around. A man stepped into its dim light, and Richard stiffened until he heard him shout the weather. A watchman doing his rounds. Having spent several nights near the boundary of the west end, he was grateful for their safe corner of London. The residents here had financially encouraged the parish to hire younger, abler watchmen. As a result, they'd not seen the break-ins and thefts some of his peers had encountered. It brought him comfort to know Elizabeth and the boys were well watched when he was not around.

He didn't hear Elizabeth's footfalls, but he saw her reflected in the window, and his heart fluttered like a young buck's. He turned and smiled, taking her in. She was wearing one of his favorite ensembles. The lavender of her shawl did full justice to her eyes, which were alluringly lined this evening. Richard admonished himself instantly. Surely he could spend an evening with his wife and not lust after her every look, her every movement.

"You look wonderfully handsome this evening, Lord Thornwood," Elizabeth said, returning his smile.

"And you are a marvel, Lady Thornwood," he said and meant it. "Age seems to pass you by."

She flushed becomingly and stepped fully into the room. He glanced at her feet, pleased to see a new set of slippers. When he returned his gaze to her face, her blush deepened, as did her smile.

"Thank you for the gift, Richard. You truly surprised me."

"Then it was worth the effort," he said, stepping up to her and brushing a kiss across her forehead. "I must confess, choosing fabrics for a woman's footwear was a daunting endeavor. Mr. Wood was immensely helpful."

She smelled of flowers and fresh fields. His mind flashed to life before the boys were born, to happier moments at Thornwood Manor. A particular rendezvous in the woods rushed through his mind and coursed through his body. He took a step back. They were memories best left in the far recesses of time.

"Your carriage, my lord."

He crooked his elbow. Elizabeth placed her gloved hand on his arm, and they strolled into the entrance hall. He draped a soft velvet mantle over her shoulders and left her to fasten it at her neck, before turning and allowing Clarkson to assist him with his great coat. He tugged on his gloves, then assisted her down the steps and into the carriage before sitting across from her on the bench.

He watched her as Gordon placed a brass foot warmer in front of her. Her loveliness simply did not fade. If anything, she grew more beautiful. And elegant. She sat regally while Gordon adjusted the box for her comfort. When he was done, he closed the door and tapped the carriage. It jolted as it pulled onto the road. Elizabeth tugged her mantle closed.

"Are you cold?" he asked, grabbing the fur before she could

answer. He leaned across and covered her lap, his hand burning where he touched her thigh. Richard sat back abruptly. He wanted nothing more than to sit beside her. To hold her. To do more than warm her body.

Hell and the devil confound it. He must observe the formalities if they were to have any relationship at all. He rubbed a hand over his face and averted his eyes, wishing the curtains were open for distraction. Would he never be free of her lure, of this aching draw toward her?

IT HAPPENED AGAIN, and Elizabeth could not understand it. She had not imagined their connection, nor the interest in his lingering gaze. Yet he'd abruptly turned it off. They spoke pleasantries, and he was as polite—and as distant—as he would be to a stranger. She wanted to stamp her feet in frustration, to shout at him and demand an explanation. But the distance between them had only started to shorten, and she could not risk it. Instead, she remained equally civil and took his hand as she exited the carriage.

Coaches lined the street, and the queue was long. It took almost ten minutes to gain admittance to the townhome. They had talked amiably with Lord and Lady Anderson, who were ahead of them in line, and it helped prevent Elizabeth from fretting about Richard. She had seen no sign of the Walfords or Sophia. Hopefully they were well and good inside, out of the damp cold.

Rawley's townhome was in keeping with the size of their own, although the Rawleys could enlarge their ballroom by opening it up to the large front drawing room, whereas theirs was not directly adjacent. Of course, it was all irrelevant. They'd not held such a large gathering in years, and if her progress in the carriage was any indication, there would be none in their future either. She sighed heavily.

"Are you still chilled?" Richard asked, leaning in closer.

His solicitous demeanor baffled her already boggled senses. The warmth had returned to his eyes. She could make no sense of it. Was it for public consumption? Richard deplored being the focus of gossip. It was why nobody, except Sophia, knew about the long drought in their relationship.

"Thornwood." Lord Rawley clasped Richard's shoulder enthusiastically. "Good debate today. Good debate."

"Lady Thornwood." Lady Rawley greeted Elizabeth smoothly, inviting her to the waiting room to freshen up.

Elizabeth glanced at Richard, who was lingering in conversation with Lord Rawley. She caught his eye, and he nodded, so she followed the maid to an anteroom outside the ballroom. Plush in red-and-yellow velvet, the room was crammed with women lounging on settees, pruning in mirrors, and clustered in standing groups. The maid slipped off Elizabeth's mantle and pattens and disappeared with them. Elizabeth met Sophia's eyes at the same time Sophia spotted her. She turned from the group of ladies she was talking with and called out Elizabeth's name, waving her over.

"*Mia amica,*" she said affectionately, kissing each of Elizabeth's cheeks. "I am happy to see you. You have come with your wayward husband, no?"

Warmth flushed Elizabeth's cheeks. Absent, yes. Distant and disinterested, yes. But she could never consider the possibility of wayward. Not Richard.

"I tease when I should not," Sophia said quietly, rubbing a hand on Elizabeth's arm in apology.

"I am too sensitive," Elizabeth said. "And who is attending you this evening?"

Sophia sighed dramatically. "It is the duke again. People will begin to talk, I know, but I needed his sway for your invitations this evening." She delicately shrugged and smiled. "With Catherine unexpectedly deciding to stay, we are scrambling to find entertainment she will enjoy. And you, my friend, have ignored too many of your invites." Sophia clicked her tongue in a tsk. "Now that Lord Thornwood is more amenable to gatherings, you will consider not being so neglectful?"

Elizabeth flushed again but for a different reason this time. It was exactly what she hoped, except she also desired he be more amenable to some private activities as well.

"I have been given my signal. I must away. The duke is opening the ball with Lady Rawley, and I must partner with Lord Rawley. Wish me luck." She leaned in to Elizabeth's ear. "He has the feet of a duck and the grace of a *pinguino*," she whispered and laughed joyously as she swung around and walked regally from the room.

Elizabeth lingered, letting the crowd dissipate. When it had thinned, she checked her hair and face in the mirror and left the waiting room. Richard was talking with Lord and Lady Walford, his lean frame relaxed compared to his rigidity in the coach. Catherine spied her and smiled invitingly.

"Wonderful! We may go in now," Catherine said to Lord Walford before turning back to Elizabeth. "They're opening with a minuet. I know it's terribly out of fashion, but it's so elegant to watch."

"For a time, but it gets dull standing around, don't you think?" Elizabeth had had enough lingering for a lifetime.

"It is a private ball, not court, *mia amica*. We can have more than one couple at a time, no?" Catherine said in perfect imitation of Sophia's accent, then giggled. "Sophia told me those who know it may dance the second set." She nudged Lord Walford, and he smiled indulgently.

Richard smiled at Elizabeth and raised his arm as though they behaved with such ease regularly. His gaze was still warm and inviting. If he was acting, he was doing a fine job. She placed her hand on his forearm, and they turned to the ballroom.

The small orchestra finished warming up, and a general hush fell over the crowd. The Duke of Salinger strolled gracefully across the gleaming wooden floor and bowed to Lady Rawley, who in turn curtsied. Together they walked to the dance floor, then separated. The first notes of the violin lightly brushed the air, and a quiver of excitement raced around the large room as His Grace and Lady Rawley bowed to their audience before turning to each other and bowing again.

Together or apart, they danced beautifully, their lines curved, their steps sure. The duke danced as a young man would, showing no sign of his age, and Lady Rawley, although voluminous and visibly top-heavy, moved with exquisite grace. They were a pleasure to watch. The first dance of the set finished, and Sophia and Lord Rawley joined the couple. The ballroom manager circulated, inviting a few others to join the second dance of the set, with the specific direction to keep to the far end of the ballroom, away from the foursome.

"Oh, Nicholas, can we?" Catherine said, looking up to her husband from where she sat.

"Well, you can, darling, but it is beyond me. I would prefer to disappoint you than shame you."

Elizabeth caught Catherine's crestfallen face before she recovered and smiled. Catherine would soon be sequestered in the country, growing rounder and more awkward with each day. There were not many dances left for her this season.

"Richard, why don't you escort Catherine to the floor?" She turned to look at Catherine. "He is an outstanding dance partner."

"You don't mind?"

"Not at all." Elizabeth smiled encouragingly at both Catherine and Richard.

Richard waved to the manager and got his nod of approval, then he politely held out his hand for Catherine. Elizabeth watched them walk away, Richard leaning in to hear what Catherine was saying and Catherine sashaying in that manner that slowly builds as one increases. If anyone did not yet recognize she was with child, it would not be long before it became blatantly obvious.

"That was kind of you," Lord Walford said. "I do appreciate

it. A seat?" he asked, indicating she should take the chair Catherine had vacated.

"I shall stand, thank you. I sit far too much. As for kindness, I believe it is more a sense of kinship. I have had two children and remember well the lonely days of confinement as the time grew nearer and I could not even find the strength to entertain female guests."

Lord Walford grew pale. "Forgive me. I did not grow up with women. It is that uncomfortable? That unbearable? Or that dangerous—"

"No," she said, realizing she had stirred anxiety in him. "My apologies. I meant only that a child steals nourishment from its mother even before it enters this world. And I needed to preserve my energy for what lay ahead. There is no more danger in the later months than the earlier ones." She did not add the true risk was in the birthing. It was something no one could control, so there was no need to bring it up.

He nodded but did not truly look relieved. "I could not imagine a life without her," he said quietly as he watched her dance.

"And there is no reason you should. Forgive my thoughtlessness. I have two boys, and I would not trade a single minute with them. Catherine will feel the same way. As will you, Nicholas." She deliberately switched to his Christian name, something they only did at private gatherings. But she had initiated such an intimate topic, and it seemed right to comfort him as a close friend.

He rolled his shoulders. "I bow to your experience."

The last notes of the orchestra floated across the room, and his smile renewed in full as he watched his wife walk toward him. Elizabeth turned her attention to Richard. Darkly handsome in his midnight tails, his hair tied at the base of his neck, he looked part scholar, part rake, and fully patrician, as he bowed to Catherine and handed her to Lord Walford.

The next dance was called. Richard turned to Elizabeth and held out his hand. Before she could place hers in it, Sophia stepped in and placed her hand in his.

"Yes, my lord, I would adore a dance with you," Sophia said.

Richard, the consummate gentleman, did not withdraw his, but he looked quizzically between Elizabeth and Sophia.

"I'm sorry, *mia amica*, you must save me," Sophia said, whispering loudly into Elizabeth's ear. "I have promised the next set to the duke. If I dance this one with him as His Grace wishes, the whole world will decide there is an understanding between us."

"I heard that," Catherine said. "I thought you didn't care about what the world thinks."

Elizabeth laughed despite her own disappointment.

"I don't," Sophia said. "But the duke will think so too. And that I cannot have…yet." She smiled wickedly. "So I will dance with your safe, handsome husband first, *va bene?*"

Elizabeth shooed them onto the floor, pleased when Richard mouthed "sorry" before turning his back to her.

"Nicholas, I must catch my breath. Besides, it would not do to dance too much together. We'd find ourselves in the papers like a certain Lady T." Catherine giggled playfully. "Why don't you and Elizabeth dance?"

"It would be my pleasure."

Elizabeth gratefully took his hand and allowed him to lead her to the same group Richard and Sophia had joined. Sophia was flirting shamelessly, but it did not bother Elizabeth. It was Sophia's way and perfectly harmless. Besides, Richard would never consider such a liaison. As if he knew what she was thinking, he caught her eye and smiled. Her spirits buoyed. She would not let him away for the next set. Her body tingled. It was the waltz.

THE FIDDLE SCRAPED, and they bowed to one another. The dance was more energetic than the previous one, but it did not slow the countess. She quipped lightly as they came together further down the line. Richard was not flattered by her attention, nor should he be. She bantered with every male she partnered with. The countess was an incorrigible coquette. He might find it irritating were it not for the fact Sophia had long ago proven herself a caring woman of substance. She had stayed by Elizabeth's side during those hard days and long nights. He would forever be indebted to her.

Elizabeth smiled affectionately each time the progression put them together. When they touched hands and circled one another, his heart raced from more than the energy he was exerting. Each time they parted for the next movement, he was disappointed. He liked the feeling of her hand in his.

The first dance came to an end, and they paused for a brief rest before the second dance of the set.

"I would enjoy a promenade, Lord Thornwood, if I may."

"Of course," Richard said smoothly, although he would prefer to stay near Elizabeth. He escorted the countess to the side of the room, and they began their stroll, her hand placed lightly on his arm.

"It is *buona* to see you and Elizabeth at entertainments," Sophia said quietly. "She has been missing gatherings."

Richard stared straight ahead. There had been no chastisement in her words, but he'd felt the countess's censure nonetheless. He knew it was well deserved, but it rankled anyway. Before he could formulate a response, they paused to speak with the Rawleys. The countess's expression was unperturbed. It was conceivable his own guilt led him to presume she was passing judgment.

Sophia enthused about the dancing, the music, the company, before they moved on. "It is a dangerous game you play."

Richard almost came to a halt, but there were too many eyes upon them. It wasn't just the stark contrast in her tone, from gushing to grim; it was her choice of words. She could not possibly be aware of the game of espionage he played.

"You hold out promise by attending such events, but you are absent at home. It leads one to wonder why. Deception is difficult to sustain and always comes to no good end. I'll not have my friend hurt." Her smile was beguiling, but her eyes flashed a warning.

Richard cracked his neck, the tension easing. She knew nothing of his intrigue. "I fear you are correct about my absence." There was no sense in denying it. Sophia was Elizabeth's confidante, and he was glad of it. Elizabeth had been through much, and he had not been able to help her through it. How could he, when he was the root of her misery?

"You are wrong in assuming I deceive her," he added, for he could honestly say he had never strayed nor desired to. Even Patricia's offers, a woman whose pleasures he'd used to thoroughly enjoy, held no appeal. "I would not see her hurt either."

She tilted her head quizzically, as if debating saying more, but she merely smiled. "I am happy to hear it."

They'd come full circle as the next dance was called, and they rejoined the others. Elizabeth raised an eyebrow at him in the manner she did when she was ready to tease him, and he smiled. Yes, there was a promise in accompanying her to these events, and he would strive to fulfill it. He was determined to become a better husband in every way but one.

"MY LORD, I do hope I am up to scrutiny. It is my first waltz." Elizabeth batted her eyelashes flirtatiously at Richard as he led her to the floor. It truly was her first waltz in the newer style.

"I regret that it is your first, my lady, but I know you will be a sublime partner. You always are."

Richard's words filled her with the rush of anticipation. She turned to him, hoping he could see how much they meant to her. Hoping he could see how much *he* meant to her. He held her gaze as he placed his right hand around her waist and encouraged her to do the same with her left. She could not remember the last time she had touched him so intimately, and here she was doing it in public.

"Now place your hand, thus, on my arm. Your blush is charming, but look around. No one is watching, and all couples are embraced in such a way."

She glanced around to find he did not exaggerate. The room was filled with couples, and those not dancing appeared disinterested or otherwise engaged.

"I have not seen it done at public balls."

She had heard much about it and had hoped to view it at the assembly hall, but she'd seen only the waltz of her youth, which was far from this physical familiarity.

"They have too many rules at those dances for my liking," Richard said, turning to the left.

"I thought you a stickler for rules," she said teasingly, enjoying the weight of his hand on her arm and the warmth of his other one at her waist.

"For laws. And yes, I'll agree, some rules. But arbitrary ones by self-appointed rule makers? I've no patience for them and ignore the most baffling of them."

"So are rules meant to be broken?"

Elizabeth could see the twinkle in his eye before he responded.

"I believe they are, but do not tell our sons that."

She laughed as he swirled her. His hand at her waist guiding her, the polished floor was like ice as she glided smoothly along with his every movement. A whirlwind of color surrounded them as couples turned. She returned her gaze to Richard's face, ready to tease again, but did not. She saw her hope reflected in his eyes, and her heart skipped a beat.

Holding her gaze, Richard tugged her a bit closer, and her body hummed in response. They whirled again and again, until Elizabeth was giddy with joy. This was the Richard she remembered. The Richard she had longed for. She could not remember the last time she'd been this happy.

CHAPTER FIFTEEN

O for a Life of Sensations rather than of Thoughts!

—Keats, Letter to Benjamin Bailey

RICHARD WATCHED ELIZABETH from the other side of the table. She was daintily selecting from the wide assortment of food while conversing with Lady Walford, who was piling far more onto her plate than Elizabeth. Elizabeth had also been ravenous, when she'd carried William. He'd ring for food for her at all hours of the day and night. It had not been so with Sebastian. They should have seen the warning signs.

He pushed the memory away. Tonight there was renewed companionability, and that was what he needed to focus on. She looked up and smiled at him, and it was easy to smile back. She was lovely, and she was still his even though he'd been a lout for far too long. He must find a way to navigate this new amiability without allowing it to blossom further. She popped a grape in her mouth. Richard stared at her lips as she chewed, the act far more sensual than it should be. He averted his stare and headed to the cardroom. It would be no small task keeping their relationship in check.

Richard found Bentley hiding in the back room and joined him for a few rounds of piquet.

Some time later, Walford found them. "Catherine has eaten

her fill and says she cannot possibly dance any more. So we are off to our beds."

Richard looked at the clock on the mantel and stood. "Almost two. I'd happily head home too."

Walford slapped Richard's back. "I suspect you may be in luck. Your wife has expressed her envy at our early departure. Something about missing country hours."

"Lighten my purse, then abandon me to the matrons," Bentley said, shaking his head.

Richard looked at him and grinned. "You can afford the few shillings, my friend. As for the matrons and their young misses, it is not only the clock on the mantel ticking. Ticktock. Your time as a bachelor is almost up."

Walford laughed as they shook hands with the scowling Bentley, ribbing him a bit more before going in search of their wives.

An hour later, Richard and Elizabeth were climbing the stairs to their rooms. Elizabeth had filled the coach ride with small talk, mostly gossip about who had danced with whom and why. Richard was not at all interested in any of it, but he'd enjoyed the sound of her lively chatter and the glimmer in her eyes. If a night at a ball could bring back the spark of the old Elizabeth, he must endeavor to attend more of them.

They stopped at her door, and he could feel her hesitation. It was a mirror of his own. "It was a wonderful night," she said quietly.

"It was." He cleared his throat. "We must attend more events."

"Oh, Richard," she said on a sigh, touching his cheek.

He placed his hand on her gloved one and held it there, the yearning in her eyes reaching into the well of his own desires. Longings he must ignore. He brushed a kiss across her cheek, and before he could withdraw, she raised her other hand and directed the kiss toward her mouth.

When their lips met, she tasted him, moaning softly. The

sound was fuel on the embers that had been threatening to ignite all evening. He lost himself to the kiss. He pulled her close and took control, demanding more. She opened for him, and he savored the familiar feel and taste of her, wanting to swallow her whole. She nestled closer. Her heat burned through her gown and his jacket and seared his flesh. His whole body responded, fully enflamed and ready to go. She gasped for breath, and sanity splashed cold on his fevered intentions.

He took a step back.

"Richard?" she asked, panting heavily.

"It's late," he said, hating the confusion that dampened the light in her eyes. He wanted their agreeable friendship back. He could not have her like this, but he could have her in his life. "I am going to look at ponies tomorrow afternoon. Would you join me?"

"Of course," she said, biting her bottom lip.

"Then good night." Richard turned away, unable to face her disappointment. He entered his room without looking behind him and leaned back against the closed door.

However was he to remain in proximity and manage his desires? He had no idea, but he knew he must. He would not risk losing her again.

CHAPTER SIXTEEN

And therefore is Love said to be a child,
Because in choice he is so oft beguiled.

—Shakespeare, *A Midsummer Night's Dream*

ELIZABETH HAD SPENT the night fretting about her impulsivity. It was unlike her to be so rash, so bold, but she'd been overcome by his nearness. She couldn't bring herself to regret experiencing his response. It had been delicious and encouraging. Although it was clear she must tread slowly, she was more determined than ever to entice him back into the marriage bed. In the meantime, she would enjoy their newfound amity.

She'd chosen to wear the only new dress she'd had made since Sebastian was born. A long-sleeved woolen walking dress with a shorter hem than her older ones, it should make for ease as they strolled. She didn't know where they were going to view the ponies, but she was certain it must involve stables. Lucy tied the laces on Elizabeth's new half boots. Dark-brown leather, they matched well with the meadow green of her frock. Richard had done a wonderful job with his selections.

Elizabeth slipped into her matching pelisse and tied the ribbon on her bonnet before tugging on short gloves. A last check in the mirror proved satisfactory. A ripple of excitement made her smile. She was going to spend the afternoon with her husband.

No friends. No dancing. No children. Just the two of them. She felt like skipping down the stairs. Of course, she did not.

"What are you up to, my dearest?" she asked William, who stood with Gordon on the landing.

"Mr. Hastings said I can wind the clock with him today." He beamed with anticipation and pride.

"Well, aren't you the lucky one?" Richard said, coming down the stairs, as dapper in his daywear as in his night.

"I am, sir. But I must wait until you're gone. So that's what I'm doing. Waiting."

"Indeed," Richard said, the corner of his lips twitching as he fought a smile. "Then we'd best be off so you may get the deed done."

"Yes, Papa!"

William bounced on the balls of his feet, his enthusiasm getting the better of him, and Richard ruffled his hair before offering Elizabeth his elbow.

"My lady," he said, leaning closer as they descended. "His eagerness for us to depart leaves me unsure. I don't know whether to be amused or take offense."

Elizabeth laughed, and Richard chuckled. Hastings stood by as Clarkson helped Richard into his greatcoat.

"It seems you rank over me this afternoon, Hastings. My son anxiously awaits you."

Hastings glanced up the stairs and smiled. "Yes, my lord. It is a task he enjoys. He has many questions about the inner workings."

"He has many questions about many things," Elizabeth said, recalling the animal husbandry book. She shared the tale with Richard as they exited and got into the carriage. "I looked on the shelves, but I couldn't find something more accessible or appropriate."

Richard appeared contemplative as he tapped the roof and sat back on the bench across from her. She would have preferred he sit beside her, but at least he wasn't gazing out the window blankly.

"I cannot think of any offhand, other than the Weatherbys *General Stud Book*, but it would be even—forgive my pun—less fruitful than the animal husbandry one."

She laughed again, delighted to see him so relaxed as he grinned, clearly taken with his own joke. His conversation continued to be light and amusing, and far too soon, they pulled in front of a livery stable. Richard helped her out of the carriage as a young boy ran inside. Richard held her securely as they walked along the wooden ramp that bridged the way through double stone arches. The dark entrance led to a small courtyard surrounded by stables.

A rather small man stepped out from the far side and hurried toward them. He looked surprised as he whisked off his cap and bowed.

"My lord," he said, then turned to her and repeated his actions. "My lady." He straightened and addressed Richard again. "Is there a problem with your stable, my lord?

Richard waved his hand in dismissal. "Not at all, Bennet. Not at all. We are looking to purchase a pony for my son. Lord Rawley tells me he has two here to be sold."

Bennet jammed his cap back on his head, looking relieved that Richard was not there with complaints. "I'll bring them out. It's not fit in the stalls for a lady."

Elizabeth looked around at the stalls lining the courtyard. She knew their two carriage horses and the pony were leased, but she'd never been party to the arrangements. Richard always brought his own mount to London. He detested long coach rides and preferred to ride more quickly astride his horse. She'd fast grown used to his sunrise rides in the early days of their marriage, although she could sometimes convince him to forfeit one for other pleasurable activities. She smiled at the memory.

"I knew you would enjoy choosing William's pony," Richard said, catching her smile and misinterpreting it. "Although, I do believe poor Bennet is not accustomed to seeing a woman in here."

"He did seem somewhat uncomfortable."

"I'm certain you would find a horse repository interesting. You would enjoy the thrill of an auction. But we wouldn't manage to get so much as a toe inside Tattersall's or Aldridge's."

"And I thought you didn't care for rules," she teased. "Especially…" She put a finger to her lips and tapped them as though pondering a great issue. "Let me get this right"—she lowered her voice to mimic his baritone timbre—"arbitrary ones by self-appointed rule makers?"

"You minx," he said on a laugh. "Your mind is a receptacle where everything is neatly stored for future use. Unfortunately, I'd be pulled apart limb by limb if I dared attempt to bring you to one."

"Ah, yes, the secret lives of men," she said, and his playful countenance disappeared as though a magician had snapped his fingers and worked his magic. Her stomach turned slightly. What had she done now?

"My lord," Bennet said, leading a rich-chestnut-colored pony with white stockings. It stopped when he did. The young boy she'd seen earlier led a dun-colored pony. It shifted restlessly when the boy came to a stop.

Bennet reviewed their age, height and abilities, and Richard watched as Bennet put the ponies through their paces. Afterward, Richard walked around each pony, running his hands firmly along their necks and flanks. He rubbed his hand on each leg, pausing at their knees and lower legs, before inspecting each hoof. They both remained placid during his administrations, even when he checked their mouths.

When he was through, he looked at her. "I can find no flaw with either of them. Your choice." His smile was back, and it was as though nothing had occurred. Did the problem lie with her? Did she anticipate the worst and look for a brooding mood when there was none?

"They are both lovely. The one on the right shifts a bit when unattended, as though restless. The chestnut has not moved at all. It bodes well for little boys, does it not?" Envisioning William on its back at Thornwood Manor, galloping freely in the fields, did provoke some anxiety.

"She has a right good disposition, my lady. A steady temperament," said Bennet, nodding in agreement.

"Then the chestnut it is," Richard said. "Twelve guineas."

Bennet dipped his chin. The boy took the leads and walked both horses back into the stable.

"And another for your loss of lease, Bennet. You can retrieve your pony when you bring the chestnut," Richard said, shaking the man's hand.

"Yes, my lord."

Richard raised his elbow. "Shall we, Lady Thornwood?"

He was every inch the relaxed gentleman again. Elizabeth set her hand on his arm, dismissing her previous concerns. She had far too active an imagination. She beamed at him. She didn't want the day to end.

⫸⫷

"Are we to home now?" Elizabeth asked as they took their seats in the carriage.

For the second time in two days, he could see disappointment on her face. Last night he could do nothing about it, but today he could. He'd intended to return to the town house, but there was nothing pressing on his schedule. There'd been no word from Patricia, and he'd argued his stance in parliament without reception or a promise of more debate. It was clear there would be no consideration for a permanent police force and the city would have to continue to rely on inept watchmen and the overworked Bow Street Runners.

He tapped the roof, and the carriage immediately stopped. The streets were busy, and it had not fully pulled into the stream of conveyances.

"Where would you like to go?" His question was rewarded with a brightening in her eyes.

"Oh, Richard, truly?" When he nodded, she smiled and clapped her hands. "I'd so love a pastry. Gunter's?"

He groaned.

"Not Gunter's? Or not pastry?"

"I'm all for pastry, Elizabeth. It's the gossiping crowd at Gunter's I cannot abide. Our names have been bandied about enough of late."

She could not argue, for she was as weary of gossips as he apparently was. "It will be far too busy anyway. I forget we are no longer in the country. I believe I would find the crush in full season unbearable now, although there was a time the bustle was part of the pleasure."

His memories drifted back to those days, and he had an idea. "I know the perfect place." He opened the door, stepped out, and gave direction to Simon.

"I remember it well," Simon said, grinning.

Richard returned to his seat and tugged the door closed.

"You are looking smug," Elizabeth said as they pulled away, her happy demeanor now returned in full.

"I am feeling smug." He smiled. "I'm impressed with your observation about the pony," he said, trying to change the subject. He didn't want to discuss their destination and ruin the surprise.

"I am not simply another pretty face," she said lightheartedly.

"I would never describe you as such. You are an uncommon beauty, Elizabeth."

She blushed becomingly but did not look away. Her eyes darkened, and he knew she was responding to his compliment as his body was responding to her presence. Richard wanted to slide in next to her and do wicked things until she screamed with release. *Hell and the devil.* He'd been spending too much time in brothels. He shifted uncomfortably and broke their gaze, grateful the carriage was slowing down.

He cleared his throat as Simon opened the door. Richard stepped out and took a deep breath of cool air before assisting Elizabeth. Her knowing look and the heat from her gloved hand did nothing to aid him in distracting his manhood's attention.

"Oh, Richard," she said, and her eyes glazed with tears. "You remembered."

"How could I forget?" he said, presenting his arm. "It was the only time I had you to myself."

The small tea shop was tucked down a side street. Popular with merchants, its pastries were exceptional, but that was not why they'd used to come here. Elizabeth's mother had refused to allow her to join Richard without a chaperone. Except when they'd met others at Gunter's, there'd been a constant shadow dogging their courtship. So they contrived a plan. He would pick her up, ostensibly to join others at Gunter's. They would instead come here, where they could talk privately. They'd hold hands under the table, an indescribable thrill at the time.

"It was a wonder we were never caught out," she said, her eyes clearing and the familiar mischievous look sparkling in the sunlight.

"I suspect she knew," he said, "although I have no proof."

"Do you?" Elizabeth smiled sadly. "I do hope so. I'd like to think she's smiling down, pleased with herself for being the biggest trickster of the three of us."

He opened the door to the shop, and a bell tinkled. No one looked their way except the mobcap-wearing maid behind the counter. She brushed at her apron, came around, and after glancing out the window, she curtsied, no doubt spotting the emblem on the carriage.

"The table in the back corner, if we may," Richard said.

"Of course, my lord."

Richard shook from his greatcoat and offered to take Elizabeth's pelisse.

"It is a bit chill in here. I'll keep it on."

He hung his coat and hat on the nearby peg and sat across from her at the small table. The maid returned with a tray of pastries to choose from and listed several more that were in back. Elizabeth chose a plum cake, while he ordered several of the savory pastries and a fruit tart. He hadn't noted until this moment that he was bordering on famished.

They waited patiently for the tea, chatting as if the last two years had never happened. Richard was glad for it. He'd missed her conversation as much as he missed her body.

"William will be pleased with his new pony. Should I guide him in naming her?" Elizabeth asked.

"I suspect he needs no guidance. The boy is well rounded and articulate already."

Elizabeth frowned. "Sebastian's speech concerns me. His vocabulary is so limited. William was much further along at his age."

Richard reached across the table and covered her hand with his. "You worry far too much. Sebastian has no need to talk."

Her frown deepened, and she tilted her head in question.

"He has William to do it for him," he explained. "William often jumps in before Sebastian gets a chance to form a thought, never mind a word. I will speak with him about it, if you'd like."

"No, I shall speak with him. And I'll have a word with Hannah as well. I'm afraid if you do it, he will think he has disappointed you again."

Richard listened while she explained why William had not groomed the pony the other day, surprised his words had weighed so heavily on the boy. He, too, must remember to think before he spoke. The tea arrived, and he reluctantly pulled his hand from hers.

"You look lovely." He'd noticed her frock at once. With its soft green shade, the blue of her eyes, and her white-blonde hair, she was a walking pastoral painting—grass, sky, clouds. It seemed an apt comparison. She was *his* world. His stomach churned, and he set the pastry back on the plate. He could not imagine a world without her in it, but he'd been forced to. Never again.

"Why do you not have more new dresses?" he asked, attempting to redirect his thoughts.

"I haven't had the need."

Her tone of voice was schooled politeness, but he heard the hurt. Guilt clogged his throat, and he coughed to clear it. "The new style suits you. I'd have you buy more."

Her face went from downheartedness to happiness in the blink of an eye. A slight blush rouged her cheeks, and she smiled. "I'd enjoy some new gowns."

They stayed to lighter topics for the remainder of their meal. The sun was ebbing when they stepped back outside.

"The boys will be wondering where I am," she commented when they were back in the carriage. "Would you visit with me when we get home?"

Richard hated that she was tentative with her question. He'd done that to her. Made her unsure of her place in her own home. In their relationship. He wanted to sweep her off her feet and tell her how much he loved her, drive away those doubts. But he could not, for as much as he wished he were captain of his body, last night proved him wrong. Elizabeth must know the danger; still, she tempted him at every turn. He didn't want to spurn her, yet he didn't know how to tell her that the fear of losing her swallowed him whole. Perhaps if they could manage to find some normalcy in their days, he could find the words about the terror that filled his dreams at night.

"Let's do better than a nursery visit. Let's have William join us for dinner this evening in the large dining room. It will be good practice for him."

Elizabeth had shone throughout the afternoon, but now she positively glowed. Richard was inordinately proud of himself as they arrived at the town house. Clarkson greeted them and assisted with outerwear.

"I'll be up shortly," Richard said and stood watching her enticing backside as she mounted the stairs. She smiled flirtatiously over her shoulder before disappearing from sight. *Little minx.* He caught himself and silently chastised his errant mind. His mind could not stray there.

He strode to his study, intending to pen a note to Bosley about increasing Elizabeth's pin money in case she was hesitant to ask Richard for more. He'd like to encourage her to more freely spoil herself. He stopped short when he saw the envelope on the tray on his desk.

"My lord," Hastings said from the doorway, "my apologies for not catching you on your way in. A message has been delivered."

"Yes, I see that," Richard said irritably.

"The boy said it was urgent."

"Thank you, Hastings. That will be all." Richard ripped open the envelope and quickly read the contents. "Damn and blast," he growled to the empty room. Why had he allowed himself to become embroiled in this escapade? There was nothing for it but to forge ahead, but... *Devil confound it all.*

He climbed the stairs slowly. He'd debated taking the coward's route and leaving a note, but after today, he could not bring himself to be so horribly dismissive. Elizabeth sat in the rocking chair with Sebastian on her knee, listening to William share his day's activities. He watched for a few minutes, his heart longing for the tranquility of a simple family life, unfettered by the threat of loss, untethered from this espionage folly.

Sebastian spotted him first, pointing and babbling incoherently, but Richard was certain he heard Papa mangled in there somewhere. William stood immediately, waiting for an invitation, which Richard willingly gave by holding out his arms. William ran to them, and he scooped him up for a big hug before putting him back down.

"Papa, Mama says I can dine with you this evening."

It seemed he would be disappointing two people this night. "I'm afraid there has been a change of plans, and I won't be in this evening after all."

William's face crumbled, and Richard could see tears in his eyes, but like his mother always did, he bit his bottom lip to hold them in.

"I do apologize," he said to William, but he was looking at Elizabeth. She was not biting her lip, nor were her eyes glazed. Her brow furrowed in question, and his brain scrambled for an answer. He certainly could not tell her the truth. "Walford has an urgent situation with his company and seeks my assistance." He would need to tell the man of his lie.

"Then by all means, you must go," Elizabeth said, her face brightening. "William, you may dine with your Mama this evening."

Cheered, William returned to his mother's side. Richard stepped into the room and kissed each of them on the cheek before excusing himself, feeling like the biggest fraud. These covert meetings were bound to create havoc, but resorting to blatant lying did not sit well with him. How long before the shadows of doubt darkened her thoughts and he managed to permanently extinguish the light in Elizabeth's eyes?

CHAPTER SEVENTEEN

Desperate remorse swallows the present in a quenchless rage.

—William Blake, *Vala, or The Four Zoas*

RICHARD SAT WOODENLY in the now familiar back parlor, refusing to fidget, although restlessness was making him edgy. If it weren't for the lives that might be saved, he'd be done with this business and focusing on his own. And Elizabeth. He'd followed Walford's contact instructions and sent a message to a man named Miller, indicating he would be at his usual place this evening. Richard assumed the man was out front, although he'd seen no evidence of it. There must be a way for them to untangle this mess through their surveillance.

"My lord," Mrs. Tate said smoothly as she glided across the parlor to the decanter on the side table. "Some port?"

"Not this evening. I'd like to see Miss Patricia."

Her back stiffened, and she poured a glass anyway before turning around. "I trust you don't mind if I do?"

"Not at all."

She took his measure as she sipped, and he wondered at her game. Her dress was more conservative this evening, although by no means discreet. He did not think she was making a play for him again. So if not that, then what?

"May I?" she asked, waving at the settee across from his chair.

"Please do." His patience was wearing thin, but he'd not let it show. He wanted to get in and back out without complications and, with a little luck, return to the house in time to bid Elizabeth good night.

Mrs. Tate draped herself provocatively across the settee, pulling her feet up and leaning forward so her assets were once again on full display. He remained unconvinced her goal was seduction. He waited as she took another sip.

"I must confess I'm quite surprised you have come to frequent my humble abode. Pleased, mind you, but puzzled by it."

"It was recommended. And I find myself…" Richard hesitated, seeking the right word. "…satisfied."

"Oh, do tell," she said.

He'd not anticipated an inquisition nor had he time for one. He raised a commanding eyebrow at her to no apparent effect.

"We don't get many noblemen here, my lord. I'm curious about how it truly came to pass that you found us." She coyly wrapped one of the draped silks around her hand as though she was only vaguely interested in his answer.

"I would see Miss Patricia now," he said, standing.

"She is busy tidying up from her last gentleman." Mrs. Tate pushed herself to a decent sitting position. "No need for you to have someone's leftovers, my lord. Let me offer you some other enticement."

Damn. He'd not considered the owner would try to switch off Patricia.

"Someone younger? Unsullied by others?" Her voice was slow and inviting, but her eyes were sharp as a harrier hawk's as she waited for his response.

"I've no interest in any other. It is not my inclination to frequent such establishments nor risk relations with multiple women." He'd decided an honest rebuttal was the safest route.

"Which brings us full circle, doesn't it, my lord? If it is not your inclination, why have you come?" She stood and faced him.

Richard was stymied by her boldness and had no immediate

answer. "If you cannot provide what I need, I shall look else-where." He turned to leave.

"My Lord Thornwood, I would not deny you anything," she said, cooing soothingly. "You will find Patricia in the blue room, as usual."

He did not look back at her. Instead, he followed the footman who opened the door and closed it after he stepped in. Patricia lay with her back to him. Even in the dim light, he could see she'd lost weight, and he regretted the sight of the sharp bones of her shoulders and her spinal column.

"Patricia," Richard said quietly, stepping closer to the bed. She rolled over, and he swallowed a curse. The right side of her face was mottled with bruises and the corner of her lips swollen twice its size. "Patricia," he said again and sat on the edge of the bed. He pushed strands of hair off her face. "Who did this to you?"

"Your news is tucked behind the paper hanging behind the dressing table," she said, ignoring his question. "Get it now, in case we are checked."

He did as she directed and moved across the room, easily shifting the small table. He ran his hand along the seam of the flocked blue paper until he detected a slight ridge. With the tips of his fingers, he eased the document carefully from its place.

"There are two today," she said, watching him from the bed.

He ran his fingers farther along the wall and withdrew the second sheet. He patted the crisp paper back into place as best he could, moved the table back, and returned to Patricia's side, the documents safely tucked in his pocket. He pulled a chair nearer the bed.

"I'd know who did this," he said gently, although anger burned through his veins. What kind of man laid hands on a woman who offered only pleasure?

"Mrs. Tate thinks I'm holding back coin, that men are paying me personally for extra favors. That *you* are giving me money on the side," she said, not bothering to sit up. "Refuses to give me my part of the fees. Says it's for my room and food. She searched every room I've done business in. Tore this one apart."

Richard ran a hand through his hair. This was not a world he knew. Nor did he want to. But here he was, and he hadn't a clue what to do about it.

"Luckily, I had no secrets yesterday. And your extra money is where no one will get it. The old bat is not going to outsmart me," she said, wincing when she smiled.

"I'll have her before the magistrate," he said, his anger firing at the sight of her pain.

Patricia touched his arm. "On what charges? Providing room and board? Beating a whore? Thornwood," she continued when he was about to protest, "you are not unaware of the reality of this life I lead. The law does not care about women like me. I will finish with Mrs. Tate my way."

She was right. He had no solution to offer. He went to grab the money for her, and she stayed his hand with hers.

"No. One of her men waits to search the room after each customer. I cannot hide it, and it will prove her suspicions. Keep it. Or do some good with it to ease that overburdened conscience of yours."

He left her and headed straight down the corridor to Mrs. Tate's office, where he usually paid his debt. She looked up at him when he walked in without being announced. "You were exceptionally quick—"

"You touch her again, and I will have this place shut down," he said, his voice cold as frost.

Mrs. Tate sat back in her chair. "I don't know what you're talking about," she said, looking genuinely surprised. "It is a drawback of the trade, I'm afraid. Not all visitors are gentlemen." She tilted her head. "I did not touch a hair on the woman's head."

Richard was at a loss for words. Which woman was lying? "You are withholding her coin," he said, looking for confirmation of Patricia's side of the story.

"Is that what she told you?" Her laugh tinkled musically in

stark contrast to his dark mood. "I house and feed all the girls in this establishment. I clothe them. I keep them off the streets. It costs money. Sometimes there's a little left over. Sometimes there's not." She shrugged and shoved his bill toward the ink, holding out a quill.

He ignored the quill, refusing to put his name in writing, and dug in his purse for the fee. Anger percolated through his body, but he was unable to discern the truth in what had happened. To what end would Patricia lie about who beat her?

"I did try to steer you toward someone else, Lord Thornwood. The woman is nothing but trouble. Next time, you may want to take my advice."

He turned on his heel and left. Next time. He looked at the shadowed doorways across the street, hoping the agents were doing their jobs and there would be no damned next time.

CHAPTER EIGHTEEN

The music in my heart I bore,
Long after it was heard no more.

—Wordsworth, "The Solitary Reaper"

ELIZABETH HAD NOT spent the evening moping. While disappointed, she was also filled with hope. She'd had a remarkable day with Richard, much like their early days. Except where once they'd dreamed of living their lives together and of children to come, yesterday they'd talked of their lives and their sons. He'd allowed her leeway to choose William's pony and had recalled their secret rendezvous at the tea shop.

William had chattered happily throughout dinner and made no reference to his father's absence. She'd decided to dine, as usual, in the tea room. She hadn't wanted to sit in the large dining room with silence gaping around them, making her day seem small. For it was not small. She may have convinced herself she was content with tiny steps, but the big step yesterday had been an incredible lift to her spirits.

She'd sent a footman to see if a fitting could be arranged tomorrow, and he had returned with a lovely note from Madame Moreau saying, of course, she could make time. So Elizabeth had written notes to Sophia and Catherine to see if they'd like to join her. She could use some advice in choosing fabrics and styles.

She'd been somewhat discouraged when Richard had not returned by the time she'd headed for bed, but she'd already received both Catherine's and Sophia's replies, and that had cheered her greatly.

Richard had already come and gone when she arose for breakfast. He'd left no note, although Hastings indicated he'd gone to chambers. It made good sense, since he'd missed a session yesterday. She was glad to have the company of her two friends today.

"Countess Tessaro has arrived," Hastings said, interrupting her perusal of the books in the library, still on the lookout for something for William. "She sent her man in. She awaits in her coach."

Clarkson assisted Elizabeth, and Gordon walked her out to the street before helping her into the carriage. Sophia kissed each cheek before Elizabeth sat beside Catherine, who unlike the brash countess, more conservatively pressed her hand in welcome. Sophia refused to adhere to English rules of engagement. She said they were too cold for a hot-blooded woman.

"Thank you for joining me. It has been so long I am not sure I am capable on my own."

Catherine looked her up and down. "Your frock and pelisse are lovely and cannot be so old."

Elizabeth had worn her walking dress from yesterday so the modiste would see a style that suited her. "It is my only new one in some years, and I had it made by a seamstress in the village. Not so overwhelming as Madame Moreau's."

Sophia laughed. "Madame Moreau's is like drinking from a fountain. So much, eh…" She looked at the ceiling, then snapped her fingers. "*Materiale,*" she said triumphantly. "The easiest of words are the hardest to find sometimes. *Mi sento stupido,*" she said, shaking her head in mock exasperation with herself. "I agree your dress is the most becoming I have seen you wear for some time."

"Richard noticed it too. He has encouraged me to indulge."

She was still heartened that he had noticed and approved.

Sophia raised her eyebrows but only commented that he had good taste.

"I must confess to selfish reasons, once again, for joining you." Catherine ran a hand over her midriff. "I would like some more liberal but beautiful dresses before I leave. I know it's foolish. No one will see me at Woodfield, but…"

Sophia leaned forward and waggled her finger at Catherine. "You have earned your pleasures, *mia amica*. You must always indulge yourself. And that *magnifico* husband of yours. It will be worth seeing his pleasure, no?"

"That is it exactly. You always know how to put into words what I cannot express myself," Catherine said, blushing prettily.

"It is because I am a woman of the world," Sophia said. "I am like the big cat in a menagerie, and you are but a kitten."

"And what am I?" Elizabeth asked, enjoying the lively repartee.

Sophia pursed her lips and narrowed her eyes, contemplating the question. "I believe you, too, are a cat. Maybe the beautiful leopard? You never change your spots, but you have changed your strategy and are ready to pounce."

Elizabeth laughed along with her friends, but inside she quaked with excitement. Sophia was far too astute. Getting Richard back in her bed would advance their refreshed friendship to a new level, and she was determined to make it happen sooner rather than later.

Sophia entertained them with stories about the gala she'd attended at Carlton House, and before long, they were standing in front of Madame Moreau's. Several doors down from the fashionable and always busy Madame Devy's, it was an elegant shop with a large room in back that housed more fabric and several workers. A young maid greeted them with a curtsy and ushered them into one of the two small front rooms. Fashion plates were strewn on the table, and Sophia grabbed a few before sitting beside Catherine on a lush burgundy settee. Elizabeth sat on the edge of one of two chairs, too eager to relax.

"*Mesdames*," Madame Moreau said as she sailed into the salon and curtsied. Tall and elegant, she was a walking advertisement for the design and quality of her clothing. "It is a pleasure to see you," she said in her thick French accent. "Countess Tessaro, it has been far too long."

"*Sì,*" Sophia said. "But I have needed nothing from you."

Something flashed between the two women, but Elizabeth could not say exactly what. She had an odd sense she was missing something. But whatever it was, it was gone quickly.

Madame Moreau turned to Elizabeth. "It is good to see you again, Lady Thornwood. I feared you had abandoned me."

"Oh no," Elizabeth said, feeling a little guilty. "I have been hiding in the country and have had no need for a new wardrobe."

"I do," Catherine peeped, waving her hand before running it over her midsection. "Desperately."

"I see my chemise has done its work," Madame Moreau said with a smile. "Congratulations, Mrs...." Doubt clouded her expression. "Sinclair?"

"Lady Walford now," Catherine said proudly, her cheeks flushed becomingly.

"Ah, yes, of course. I am so sorry. Your soldier, he did not—"

"Oh no!" Catherine said. "He *is* my soldier. He came home."

"He is Lord Walford now," Sophia said.

Madame Moreau nodded, although she clearly did not follow that Walford had come into a title. It had been, after all, entirely unexpected, even by Catherine.

"What's in a name? That which we call a soldier. By any other name would be as sweet." Catherine giggled, but her mangling of Shakespeare further confused Madame Moreau, which made them all laugh.

Madame Moreau waited patiently before steering them back to the business at hand. "What is it you would like today?"

After they outlined their needs, she disappeared in back before returning with a bolt of muslin. "I must refit you, Lady

Thornwood, for you have grown *mince*," she said, holding her finger and thumb close together. "And you as well, Lady Walford, as you will grow." She held her finger and thumb far apart, and they all laughed again.

The next few hours passed quickly. They were served champagne and small cakes while they pored over fashion plates. The selection of fabric was overwhelming—muslins, crepes, gossamer satins, velvets. Elizabeth often deferred to Sophia's opinion.

"Do you have no Chinese silk?" Sophia asked.

"*Mais oui*," Madame Moreau said. "They are in the back. I will get them."

"No need. I will come see for myself and pick the best to show Lady Thornwood." Sophia stood and stretched gracefully. "Too much sitting. I must give my body a stroll," she said to Catherine and Elizabeth before trailing Madame Moreau into the back room.

Catherine stifled a yawn. "Oh, do forgive me. It was a late night."

"I trust all is well with Lord Walford's business," Elizabeth said.

"Should it not be?" Catherine asked, her face scrunching in puzzlement.

"I apologize. I may have overstepped my bounds. It's just when Richard rushed out to meet Lord Walford last evening, he indicated it was urgent."

Catherine shook her head, looking genuinely confused. "But Nicholas did not meet with your husband. We were at my aunt's for a small dinner and stayed far too late playing whist."

Elizabeth's stomach turned over, and she fought to maintain her composure. Richard had lied to her. Why? "Perhaps I have misrepresented the situation," she said calmly.

Catherine leaned forward and touched Elizabeth's arm. "It is possible they are meeting today."

Which of course did not resolve why he'd misled her last night. Elizabeth hated seeing the concern in Catherine's eyes. She had seen it on too many faces these past two years. Why was it every step forward led to two steps backward?

"If you'll excuse me," she said to Catherine, "I'll go see what is keeping Sophia."

Elizabeth heard the voices from the back corner of the room, behind a table piled high with fabrics. Hushed but heated, they argued in French. She'd had no idea Sophia spoke French fluently enough to hold her own with the Frenchwoman.

"*Pas pour toi. Je le fais pour Gaston!*"

"*Merde!*" Sophia said and stepped out from behind the table, stopping at the sight of Elizabeth.

Heat rushed to Elizabeth's face. "I'm sorry. I did not mean to intrude." She stumbled over her words. She'd never seen Sophia like this.

Sophia's glare softened, and she smiled, walking quickly to Elizabeth and taking both hands. "No, *mia amica*, it is I who should apologize. I so wanted the golden Chinese silk for you, but Madame insists it is for another customer. She cannot be budged."

They strolled back to the front where Catherine was standing, ready to leave. "I find myself needing a rest," she said apologetically.

"Of course, *mia bella*. Let us go and leave Madame Moreau to work her magic."

On the way home, Catherine and Elizabeth sat quietly while Sophia chatted gaily. Too gaily. Although she could not imagine what it was, Elizabeth was sure Sophia was hiding something. But then, everybody had their secrets, she supposed. Elizabeth sighed. At least it was clear Sophia had not lied to her about anything relevant to Elizabeth's life. That, apparently, was Richard's forte. And she was resolved to find out why.

CHAPTER NINETEEN

On that best portion of a good man's life,
His little, nameless, unremembered, acts
Of kindness and of love.

—Wordsworth, "Lines Written a Few Miles above
Tintern Abbey, on Revisiting the Banks of the Wye
during a Tour, July 13, 1798"

RICHARD HAD BEEN pleased to find Elizabeth gone when he'd returned to the town house. He'd stayed at Westminster for the review of happenings on the continent but had left immediately afterward. He was still disgruntled about their dismissal of his arguments the other day. Truthfully, he was irritable about pretty much everything at the moment, including his inability to get some sleep last night.

What happened to Patricia weighed heavily on him. It was no life. He'd begun to form a speech for the House of Lords, insisting upon laws and regulations for brothels. Although illegal, they were hidden in plain sight, so why not mandate acceptable treatment? A tax that could potentially be fed back into the system to provide a better environment for the workers?

He'd seen the folly in it immediately. Half the peers in attendance frequented such houses. Well, houses with higher standards, but nevertheless, they would not be eager for the government to interfere in their bed sport. And since the call for a permanent police force continued to fall on deaf ears, there would be no enforcement. Any law or regulation would be in word only. It would serve no purpose.

Besides, how could he argue for better protection for prostitutes and not draw attention to the very intrigue that had brought their plight to his attention? Or even worse, tie himself irredeemably to that world? He could not do that to his family. To Elizabeth. There must be some other solution.

Richard looked through his correspondence. A letter from the bank confirmed a draft to E. D. Narrows, the architect for Elizabeth's orphanage. He stared at it for a long time. Elizabeth had intuitively figured out what he had not. If change could not happen from the top down, then it must occur from the bottom up. He thought of children begging on the street or slyly dipping into pockets, the ones flogging papers or gathering horse manure to sell to the gardeners. What if Patricia had been lifted at a young age? If given such a chance, would her life have taken a different course?

Elizabeth's goal was likely to be far more effective than his wasting his time arguing in parliament. Besides, debate regarding the war monopolized the time on the floor, and he'd be hard-pressed to even be provided the opportunity. Rightfully so, he imagined. Their country was in jeopardy. Lives were at stake. As much as he was uncomfortable with his role for the Home Office, he was doing his part for those men on the continent. He could do no more for the cause on the peninsula, but he could do more here.

He stood, stretched, and walked to the bell cord, feeling a bit lighter. A coffee was in order, and something to eat. His correspondence awaited him. He'd take care of it first. Afterward he'd decide how best to proceed. The idea of working with Elizabeth on her project was not simply morally satisfying. With such a focus, he could be near her without any threat of intimacy. A frisson of anticipation rippled through him. Damn his body for recognizing him for the liar he was.

>>><<<

"H E'S IN HIS study, my lady," Hastings said as he took Elizabeth's bonnet and pelisse and handed them to Clarkson.

"Thank you," she said and marched down the hall to his study. She tapped on the door and waited for his voice before entering, then stepped into the room and caught her breath. Richard sat in dishabille, his jacket discarded, his top button undone, and his neck scarf tossed on the desk. He'd been running his hands through his hair, something he often did when he was lost in contemplation.

He glanced up at the sound of her and immediately got to his feet. Her body hummed in reaction to his dishevelment. She wanted to walk over and complete the task of undressing for him. All her anger dissipated, and heat pooled in regions she'd best not think on or she'd not be able to speak.

"Elizabeth," he said, looking down at himself. "My apologies for my untidy state." He walked toward her and held out his hand. "I did not know you were home."

His hand seared hers, and a quiver ran through her. Her body was such a traitor.

"Do sit down."

He waited for her to sit, then offered her a sherry, which she declined. She needed to regain focus.

"Then I shan't either. I am rather full anyway." He motioned toward the right corner of his desk, where an empty plate and cup sat. "I trust your expedition was fruitful?"

He didn't look like someone hiding anything. She couldn't detect deceit in his eyes nor a lie in his smile. Her shoulders relaxed a little. She'd never had a penchant for drama and would not create any now. But she would not avoid the truth either. She would know, for better or worse, what was going on. Best to get straight to the point.

"I have a proposal for you," he said, his satisfied smile derailing her intention. "It involves William. You wish to celebrate his birthday?"

"I do," she said, her heart accelerating at the growing twinkle in his eyes. "We didn't honor his breeching. I would have him commemorate this next stage of his life. His birthday seemed a logical choice. It is, after all, a day I shall never forget."

"Nor I," Richard said softly. "One of my happiest in memory."

Elizabeth swallowed the lump in her throat, unable to speak. She had almost ruined this moment of sharing by coming in primed for a confrontation.

"I suggest we hold a grand picnic in his honor." He sat back, awaiting her response.

"But the weather this time of year, Richard, it is not predictable," Elizabeth was surprised he was taking such a keen interest. He'd not concerned himself with details of such matters in years.

He grinned, seeming pleased with himself. "I agree. We shall use the ballroom and set it as though we are outside. Some canopies, some blankets for the children. All the food suited to a true picnic. What do you think?"

"It's a marvelous idea," Elizabeth said, instantly envisioning it. "We could add some foliage and an arbor or two."

"Splendid. I knew your creative mind would not be left wanting. I leave everything to you. There is one other aspect I'd like you to consider, although I am confident you will be amenable." He leaned forward and propped his elbows on the desk. "I'd like it to be a benefit. For your orphanage. As a matter of fact, when your orphanage is complete, I would like us to select another area of need and provide for it."

"Oh, Richard," she said, and this time, she did not fight her tears. They were tears of happiness, for the children who would be helped and for the man who was indicating he would be by her side to see it happen. He handed her his handkerchief, and she wiped at her eyes. They were also tears of relief. A man bent on betraying her could not make such a promise. Could he?

CHAPTER TWENTY

Come not within the measure of my wrath.

—Shakespeare, *Two Gentlemen of Verona*

RICHARD WAS GLAD for Walford's note. It had been a week since he'd slid Patricia's last missives into the copy of *Love in Excess*, and he'd heard nothing about it. Nor had she contacted him again. He was concerned for her well-being, but he'd no excuse to go check on her. He could only hope Mrs. Tate would not lay another hand on her after his threat. The memory of that confrontation rattled him. When had he become a man who threatened anyone, never mind a woman? *Hell and the devil.* When had he become a man who worried about prostitutes? He urged his horse into a gallop as though he could outdistance his thoughts.

He reined in at the end of the run, all the better for the fresh air and the firm, determined beast underneath him. He wished he were in the country where he could truly have full rein, but at least there was this short pass on Rotten Row, and with few people about, it was somewhat freeing. He nudged to the left and headed toward the walnut grove before stopping at the halfway mark to wait for Walford. It seemed an odd place for a rendez-vous, but he wasn't complaining. He enjoyed taking in the air, and it seemed less in the city here. Richard wished he could head back to the estate and enjoy some peace and quiet.

It wasn't long before Walford arrived. After greetings, they both dismounted and led their horses off the path. They strolled along the grass, exchanging pleasantries as though they hadn't a care in the world, until the handful of people about were well out of earshot.

"The last piece of information caused an uproar. It indicated the French have anticipated planned battalion movement," Walford said, getting straight to the point. "Spring is on the horizon, and they can afford no such exposure to their plans." They entered the woods and were soon out of sight of others. "The agent from Home Office would like to speak with you directly."

"About damned time," Richard said. The whole clandestine aspect of how they'd been dealing with the information was ridiculous. "When?"

"Now," Walford said, pointing his chin toward the pond, next to which a man now stood where seconds before he had not.

They approached, and Walford introduced Richard. The man thrust out his hand. "Lord Thornwood, good to finally meet you."

"Mr. Miller," Richard said, shaking his hand and taking his measure. He was unassuming. Dressed for riding as both Walford and himself, he wore clothes of a quality cut. The man's dark eyes were alert as he did his own quick survey of Richard.

"We appreciate what you have done for the effort," Mr. Miller said, and Richard tipped his head in acknowledgment. "But it is past time for us to find her source. Did you tell him?" He looked at Walford.

"Not all of it. Only about the French knowing Wellesley's planned movements."

Mr. Miller's already serious demeanor darkened. "The second sheet was a replica of a letter from Wellesley himself. A letter only recently received by the Home Office regarding a move to the Port of Corunna. It details the need for supplies and for closer proximity for intelligence communication from London, much like what you've been aiding to provide."

"I'm not sure I follow," said Richard, although he had an inkling of the implication.

Miller stared at Richard as though contemplating him. He took his hat off and ran a hand through the few strands of hair splayed across his head. He exhaled audibly as he put his hat back on, seeming to come to a decision.

"My lord, you must keep this in the strictest of confidence." Miller waited for Richard's assurance before continuing. "Sir Murray has indicated the letter went straight from Wellesley's hands to their agent, whom they trust implicitly. Yet somewhere between the initial transaction and our office, a replica was made."

"By God, a traitor in the Home Office?" Richard could now appreciate the upheaval his last delivery had caused.

"It's a possibility," Walford said, shaking his head as though he could not believe it.

"A possibility, yes," Mr. Miller agreed. "Murray is double-checking on his end and will thoroughly cross-examine his agent on his return. We're concerned whoever your woman is dealing with might be playing both sides of the fence."

"Not *my woman*," Richard said, balking at the reference.

"My apologies," Mr. Miller said, although he hardly looked apologetic. "Of course not. We were going to bring her in, but we don't want to scare him off. We decided to see what you could find out first. Whoever the informant is, he has gained some valuable information, and it's aiding Wellesley in the field. We don't want to lose that. But we're not sure what game he is truly playing. Did he only share the letter to prove how clever he was? Or has he shared the letter, and more, with our enemies? It is imperative we find him."

Richard's head was reeling. This was to be a simple exchange, one that might help save lives. Now he was to interrogate Patricia? He was convinced she would give him no more than she had at any time he'd attempted to question her. So what was he to do? Beat her as Mrs. Tate had done? He shuddered in disgust.

"She is not very forthcoming," he said. "I doubt I'll discover anything."

"A month of hard labor at Bridewell might loosen her tongue."

"Bloody hell," Walford said.

Richard fought rising fury. "Are you threatening me, Miller?" he asked through gritted teeth.

"Not at all, Lord Thornwood. I'm threatening Miss Paisley. We'll give you a week." Mr. Miller turned and walked into the walnut grove.

"I had no idea that was what was on their minds, Thornwood. I merely received a note to meet Miller here, and I assumed they were going to impress upon you how important your role has been. Perhaps entice you to continue." Walford looked as furious as Richard felt.

"For the first time in my life, I know what it feels like to want to put my fist in a man's face."

"I would have held him for you."

Richard looked sharply at Walford and saw the boy at Eton who had often promised to do exactly that same thing for him if he'd ever had a need. They both burst into laughter. They laughed far too long and too hard, and it felt damned good to rid himself of the rage.

"I have little choice but to try to gain the information," Richard said as they walked their horses back to the woods. "Do I?"

Walford eyed him and shrugged a shoulder. "There's always a choice. You can walk away from it all. The woman has set herself up for trouble, not you."

Richard contemplated it for a moment. If it had not been him, it would have been someone else. Walford was right, of course. He had not led her down this path.

"Has she never let any clue drop? No word of who or of comings and goings? Nothing?"

"She is not a woman of many words. Other than about the services she provides. She likes to talk about those." Walford raised his eyebrows, and Richard scowled at him. "Don't you dare ask it. I did not and would not partake in anything at a whorehouse, with Patricia or anyone else. I would never dishonor my wife."

"Speaking of your wife," Walford said. "You have been caught out in a lie. I presume it was for one of your assignations."

Richard stopped, his stomach clenching like he'd been kicked. *Damn and blast*, he'd neglected to tell Walford he'd used him as an excuse to abandon Elizabeth and William.

"Relax, old friend," Walford said, clasping his shoulder. "I covered for you. While the ladies were in the drawing room with their tea, you came over and discussed some urgent business with me. At her aunt's place, not our house."

"Thank you," Richard said as they both mounted their horses. "I am no good at these covert operations. Too many secrets for my taste." The word *secret* twigged a memory: *"Luckily, I had no secrets yesterday."* How had he missed it? "Walford, I believe we can narrow the time frame of the informant."

Walford promised to take the information directly to the Home Office, where they could check the agents' notes on the comings and goings at the brothel. A bit more optimistic about being able to end his role in this little espionage ring, Richard nudged his horse back toward Rotten Row. One more ride to clear his head before returning to the town house and the only responsibility he wanted to have—his family.

CHAPTER TWENTY-ONE

The eye—it cannot choose but see;
We cannot bid the ear be still;
Our bodies feel, where'er they be,
Against, or with our will.

—Wordsworth, "Expostulation and Reply"

ELIZABETH HAD ENJOYED planning the picnic. Sophia and Catherine had helped write the invitations and rush them out. She'd worked on a small well-chosen guest list, but Sophia would have none of it. She'd declared she had no intention of spending an afternoon with mamas and their babies. To which Catherine had responded by pointing at her midriff, and Elizabeth had pointed at herself. They'd laughed uncontrollably until their stomachs hurt.

Sophia had a point though. This was an ideal opportunity to raise funds for the orphanage, and she should not waste it. Elizabeth had held her own in terms of William's friends. It was his celebration, after all. But they'd carefully drafted a list of guests who were more than capable of contributing to the cause.

"These are brilliant," Catherine declared, holding a small wooden fish by the tail and waving it in the air to dry. "It has been great fun painting them."

"They were Richard's idea. He said it wasn't a picnic without fishing." Richard had not been around a tremendous amount this past week, but when he was, he'd been very attentive and most helpful. He'd had the fish made and affixed loops of twine to their heads to hook with a rod. "We'll have to decide where to set the water barrel."

"Out of the way so no one gets a hook in the eye," said Sophia as she wound another vine through the arbor. "I have ordered fresh flowers for the morning. Ensure one of your servants tucks them in among this foliage."

"Oh, that will be lovely. Thank you, Sophia. And you, Catherine. I could not have managed this so quickly on my own."

"The haste was imperative, no?" Sophia joined them at the table. "Entertainments in town will soon be increasing, as will the demand on wallets." She picked up a fish, stared at it, then set it back down again. "Tomorrow this room will be swimming with people, not just fish. We must...*usa una lancia.*"

"I trust you mean spear their purses, not their persons," Elizabeth said with a laugh.

"But of course," Sophia said, smiling naughtily. "Although there are one or two I might be inclined to poke a few times."

"Sophia!" Catherine leaned forward conspiratorially. "Who?"

Sophia gossiped wickedly about a few ladies while Elizabeth and Catherine finished painting the last of the fish.

"I bet Nicholas tries his hands at this," Catherine said when they were done. "We should put a cup beside it and make the men pay."

"I believe we should always make men pay," Sophia said, smiling sweetly.

"Oh, that reminds me, Elizabeth, I hope I didn't cause any friction between you and Richard. It seems I was wrong. Richard did come to see Nicholas. Apparently, I was in the drawing room when their meeting occurred."

The tiny knot in Elizabeth's stomach unraveled. Richard had not lied to her. Which in turn meant their time together this week had been genuine. She smiled at Catherine but did not miss

Sophia's arched eyebrow. Elizabeth was about to ask her what was running through that fertile mind of hers when a commotion arose outside the ballroom. Hastings entered looking flustered.

"My lady, pardon me for interrupting. There are birds. So many birds." He flapped his hands around the room as though he was seeing them fly through the air.

"Birds?" they all said in unison.

"Birds," he repeated as the door opened behind him and Catherine's aunt sailed into the room, far spryer than she'd appeared at the Walfords' dinner party.

"Auntie!" Catherine said, rising and going to her. "What are you doing here?"

"Contributing," she said, clapping her hands.

Elizabeth gasped. Servants poured into the room, each carrying a birdcage. Some of the more elaborate cages were so large it took two servants to carry them.

"I have emptied my aviary. There must be birdsong at a picnic."

They looked at each other and were unable to contain themselves. Catherine's aunt looked both delighted with herself and confused at their laughter.

Catherine walked over to her and kissed her cheek. "You are my favorite auntie," she said loudly against her ear.

"I am your only auntie," she said curtly, but she beamed, betraying her pleasure.

Elizabeth looked around the room at all the cages. Of course, there must be birdsong. Why had she not thought of it? A picnic must also have courting and romance. And love. Ah, yes, there must be love.

In that moment, she was decided. Tonight was the night.

RICHARD TRIED TO ignore the noise outside his study, but in the end, he could not. He stepped into the hallway to see what all the fuss was about as the last of what seemed like a brigade of servants took the stairs, each carrying a birdcage. He stared after them for a moment, debating if he should follow, but decided it was best he not know what was going on and returned to the sanctity of his study.

He'd not liked being given an ultimatum as though he were some civil servant to be ordered about. It rankled him thinking about it, and he'd a good mind to go over to the Home Office himself to tell them exactly where they could put this assignment. But it wouldn't keep Patricia out of Bridewell. And therein lay the crux.

What to do now? After his confrontation with Mrs. Tate, he couldn't easily return to the brothel and insist on seeing Patricia. He couldn't risk drawing more attention to her. And demand of Patricia that she reveal her source? He knew her too well not to recognize that path would lead nowhere. She must have her guard down, so subtlety was key. Unfortunately, there was little time for that.

A week. *The devil confound it.* How was he to convince her to expose her source in such a short amount of time? Especially since he'd no choice but to wait for her to summon him, and who knew when that would be? His only hope was the Home Office could deduce the informant for themselves now that he'd narrowed the time for them. It was, after all, their job, not his. He ran a hand through his hair, shaking his head in frustration. He was not built for subterfuge.

The infernal comings and goings in the entranceway made it difficult to hold a thought. When he'd suggested the picnic, he'd no idea he'd be put in this untenable position. Even though time was of the essence, he hoped Patricia did not contact him before the entertainment was through. It had been a gift to share time with Elizabeth these past days and to see the light fully return to her eyes. He didn't want to do anything to compromise it.

He decided some fresh air would clear his mind, and he might manage to see a different course of action, or formulate some sort of plan to coerce Patricia's confidence. He shrugged on his jacket and stepped into the hall as the women were descending the stairs.

He bowed politely. "My ladies," he said, although he had eyes for only one of them.

"Oh, Richard, you should see all the birds," Elizabeth said, laughing. "It's quite fantastical. It sounds like a forest in the ballroom."

She glowed with excitement, and his body stirred with memories. He'd used to make her shine like that. Wanted to do so again. Wanted to do more than he should. Which was the root of the struggle that warred within him. He mustn't forget why he needed to take control of the demands of his body and allow only his heart to be satisfied.

"You take good care of them!" Catherine's aunt shouted, drawing his attention back to the small gathering. Catherine mouthed "sorry" at him as she steered the woman toward the entrance.

Sophia held his gaze, and he shifted uncomfortably. What did she see in him, and why did it unnerve him? She could know nothing of his nocturnal activities.

"I can't concentrate," he said, breaking her stare and turning his attention back to Elizabeth. "I'm going to take in some air."

"You'll be back in time to introduce William to his new pony? It's in the stable, and I'm going to put a big bow around her neck."

He hated the wariness behind her smile, although he understood it. He had worked hard to place it there. "Yes, I will be back in plenty of time."

"William is excited to join us for dinner tonight," she said. "I've arranged for his favorite dishes."

He hesitated. What if Patricia contacted him? Would it be better to make excuses now than at the last moment? Which would provide the least disappointment? He glanced at Sophia, whose right eyebrow rose imperiously. She was commanding him without saying a word. *Damn and blast the woman's arrogance.* But she was on the side of right.

"I look forward to it," he said, excusing himself and heading to the back of the house and out to the mews, putting as much distance as possible between the women and the guilt that threatened to suffocate him. Why was life so beastly complicated?

CHAPTER TWENTY-TWO

Whether we be young or old,
Our destiny, our being's heart and home,
Is with infinitude, and only there;
With hope it is, hope that can never die,
Effort, and expectation, and desire,
And something evermore about to be.

—Wordsworth, *The Prelude*

"OH, PAPA, SHE'S a beauty. Thank you."

Richard ruffled William's hair, looking over his head at Elizabeth and smiling. "You can thank your mother. She chose her. She has exquisite taste."

Elizabeth flushed at the compliment, a small trill running through her body as his gaze lingered. She was exhausted from preparations for tomorrow's picnic and had considered abandoning her plans of seduction. Now she was glad she had not.

She'd dressed for the evening in one of the new gowns that had arrived this morning amidst all the chaos in the ballroom. Madame Moreau had rushed to complete three. More would arrive next week, but she was glad Sophia had insisted this one be part of the first delivery. The soft silk draped becomingly, and the imperial blue suited her coloring. She'd selected a diamond-and-sapphire necklace to draw attention to the daringly low neckline.

Her hair was swept up with matching sapphire pins. She'd had Lucy pull tendrils to soften her look. From the look in Richard's eyes, the effort had been worth it.

"Thank you, Mama. Can I ride her now?" William asked, pulling her attention away from Richard.

"It's too late," Richard said, interceding before Elizabeth could respond. "Besides, she's only just arrived. Imagine how she must feel in a strange stable. Give her time to adjust. We'll take her out Sunday."

"I believe she will like Horatio, don't you agree?" William asked. The mews was small with only four stables, and Horatio towered next to the new pony.

"I certainly hope so," Richard responded. "They will be spending a lot of time together."

"Do you think horses talk to one another?" William made an odd sound, followed by an equally peculiar whinny. "That's 'Hello, I'm Horatio,'" he translated. "And 'Hello, I'm…'" His voice trailed off, and his face scrunched in consternation. "I do not know her name."

"It is for you to decide. It's an important task, so do not rush it. She must live with it all the days of her life. As will you," Richard said.

"Why did you choose the name Horatio, Papa?"

"Because Horatio was a stalwart friend to Hamlet."

"Who's Hamlet?"

Richard chuckled. "That is a tale for another day. For now you must concentrate on a name for your pony. Let us head in for our meal."

Elizabeth had enjoyed watching Richard with William, but when he placed his hand at the small of her back to guide her across the square, to the door, her whole being centered on the heat it generated, not only where he touched but throughout her body. Oh yes, she was definitely glad she had not changed her plans.

RICHARD WAS HAVING difficulty concentrating on his son, who chattered away, oblivious to the undercurrent of tension in his father. He signaled Hastings to fill his glass again, hoping to dampen the rising desire. A seeming impossibility when Elizabeth looked delectable enough to devour right here on the table. And whether she knew it or not, he could not discern, but her smile was an invitation to the pleasures he knew lay beneath that damned stunning gown. *The devil confound it.* He tossed back the sherry and signaled for more.

"Can you name a horse a color?" William asked, setting his fork on his plate and looking seriously at Richard.

"You can name a horse whatever you want. But a color does not reveal much, does it?" Except for the blue of that dress. It revealed almost everything. Richard shifted uncomfortably and took another sip of sherry.

"I believe your father is telling you to take time to determine what you want your new pony to be for you. A worker? A friend? Strong? Fast? Gentle? What qualities do you hope your pony has? When you're on top of her, what do you want from her?"

Richard choked on his sherry. "Excuse me," he said, wiping his mouth and clearing his throat. "It went down the wrong way." Elizabeth raised her brow and took a sip, then ran her tongue over her top lip. The little minx. She knew exactly what she was doing to him. It would be amusing if it weren't so damn frightening. And enticing.

William continued to ruminate over names, only becoming distracted when sweets arrived. He was quiet, eating six small cakes as though he had not eaten three courses of dinner. Elizabeth laughed, and William looked at her and grinned as he popped another bite in.

"He seems to have inherited your bottomless pit. Oh no, don't," she said as Richard grabbed a cake. "I have arranged a special dessert for us this evening." She turned to William. "My dearest, you have a big day tomorrow. You must get some rest. Gordon, please walk William to the nursery."

William dutifully kissed Elizabeth on the cheek and paused before Richard. "I hope she's not lonely," he said solemnly.

"I'll see she isn't," Richard said and looked up, catching the shadow of sadness that drifted across Elizabeth's face. Was she relating this to her own situation, as he was?

Satisfied, William held out his hand. "Thank you, Papa."

Richard pulled him in for a hug. "Off to bed," he said. "Dream of your new pony and her name."

Gordon offered his hand to William, but he did not take it. "I've eaten a proper meal in the dining room, Gordon. I'm not a little boy anymore."

Richard smiled as the two exited the room, then turned his attention back to Elizabeth. "And what is this special dessert you have arranged?" he said, riveted to the mischief twinkling in her eyes.

"You shall soon see," she said, pushing from the table. "Follow me."

He trailed her out of the dining room and past his study. She threw a glance at him over her shoulder before climbing the stairs. The dress clung to her, revealing her long legs and her alluring backside. Richard groaned and adjusted himself. It was going to be a long night.

CHAPTER TWENTY-THREE

Some Cupid kills with arrows, some with traps.

—Shakespeare, *Much Ado About Nothing*

Elizabeth could feel Richard's eyes on her as she took the stairs, deliberately leading the way so he might be tempted by what he saw. If the hum of her body was any indication, it was a good beginning to her plans. She resisted turning around until she was at the landing. When she did, she had to stop herself from smiling at the expression on his face. Oh yes, a very good start indeed.

The servants had followed her directions perfectly, and the far corner of the ballroom looked magical. The canopy was set, its perimeter lit by small lanterns creating a dreamlike glow. Beneath it a large cloth was spread with a dozen or more cushions artfully arranged around their final course of the evening. Also, as instructed, there was not a servant to be seen. They had been expressly told to disappear for the remainder of the evening. She wanted absolute freedom with Richard.

Richard cleared his throat as he stepped up beside her and took in the room. "It looks enchanting," he said. "Elizabeth, I can't—"

She quickly put a finger to his lips. She didn't want to hear what he couldn't do. She forbade herself to consider for a single second that she would fail this evening. "Can I not have one night of enchantment? Only the two of us? Sharing dessert and spirits?"

He contemplated her quietly. "My apologies," he said. "Of course."

Richard held out his hand, and she placed hers in it, the warmth of his as comforting as it was exciting. They walked quietly across the dark room, carefully navigating the various cages and children's event setups. He assisted her to the floor before taking a seat himself on the other side of the basket of food. Elizabeth refused to be disappointed. She'd woo him to her side yet.

"I didn't know what your preference would be," she said, indicating the silver tray with various decanters and glasses. "Port? Sherry? Brandy?" She'd asked for those three, but there was a fourth, and in the dim light, she could not tell what it was. She extracted the glass stopper and smelled the last decanter. "Madeira…maybe?"

He smiled and held out his hand for the decanter. He swirled it and sniffed. "Claret," he said. "You've never had a good nose." He chuckled, reaching across and tapping her nose lightly with his finger. "But it is a cute one."

She warmed at his compliment, disappointed when he quickly withdrew his finger and turned his focus to the decanters. "I believe I'd enjoy a brandy."

"Shall I too?" she asked, overcome with a sense of daring. She'd never had it, although Sophia frequently drank it. But Sophia often did things Elizabeth would never consider.

Richard poured a second glass and handed it to her. She sniffed it, recoiling at its strong scent. Richard laughed and raised his glass. "To a successful picnic," he said and took a sip. "I see Hastings has tapped into my finest cask."

"I asked him for the best of everything. I trust that was acceptable?" Elizabeth asked, worried she'd overstepped her bounds.

He smiled encouragingly, and she took a large sip of the

brandy and choked, coughing uncontrollably. Richard was by her side immediately, rubbing circles on her back until the spasms subsided. She looked at him through tears brought on by the eruption and smiled apologetically.

"Perhaps a sherry might be preferable," he said, taking the glass from her and setting it down on the tray.

"Perhaps," she echoed as he poured her a stout glass. He handed her the sherry and settled back beside her. She was thrilled he did not return to his place across from her. A small shudder of excitement rolled through her as his thigh pressed against hers.

"And what delights await?" Richard asked, and her head snapped in his direction. "In the basket, Elizabeth," he said, his calm voice belying the ruddiness creeping into his cheeks.

"Exotic treats to tease your palate," she said, pleased he was not unaffected by their proximity. She lifted the linen from the basket and withdrew the two plates. Cook had done well. She set the plate of sweets nearer Richard and the one with fruit in front of her.

"Pineapple? However did you manage that?" Richard asked as he snagged a plum cake.

"I have my sources," she said. It was gratifying that he recognized the effort she'd gone through. "The grapes were far harder to procure. The oranges Catherine got from her aunt's orangery."

"Along with the birds, which"—he glanced around the large room—"are surprisingly quiet." He sniffed the air. "Although, they are very much present."

"Oh dear," Elizabeth said, noticing the subtle smell for the first time. "I must have the cages cleaned in the morning. And air out the room."

Richard laughed. "It makes the picnic authentic. Not everything out of doors is a rose." He grabbed an orange and bit into the rind, looking at her as he did so. "Although, I see before me the most beautiful of flowers."

Elizabeth was giddy with his playfulness, but giddiness quickly turned to need when he held her gaze as he dug his finger into his bite mark and slowly peeled the orange. She swallowed and waited, afraid to ruin the moment. He broke off a piece and held it out, but when she went to take it, he shook his head.

"Let me." He pressed the soft flesh of the orange against her lips, and she opened for it, imagining she was opening for him, as she longed to do. She wasn't sure if he groaned when she did, but the heat gathering between her legs was both tantalizing and a torment, and she knew she would have him this night. There was no other recourse.

The orange was sweet, and she relished its taste, touching her fingers to her lips, lingering where he'd touched.

"Bloody hell," Richard said under his breath, but she heard it and resisted a triumphant smile. He threw back his brandy and grabbed the decanter, pouring himself another. He took her sherry and replaced it with her original glass of brandy. "Here," he said, handing her another slice of orange. "Take a bite of the orange, then a sip of the brandy."

She raised the glass to her lips.

"A small sip," he cautioned with the hint of a smile.

Elizabeth did as he instructed. The strong spirit was smoothed by the sweetness of the orange, the combined flavor filling her mouth and warming her body as it flowed down her throat and heated her stomach. "Oh," she said, enjoying the sensation.

"Oh," he said, shifting and looking off into the darkness before returning his gaze to hers. "It is always best to savor in small increments. It is a richer experience."

His hazel eyes were dark in the dim light, but she didn't need to see them fully to feel the fevered intention from his body. She could throw herself on him now, such was the depth of her own need. Tumble with him like a streetwalker. Would he enjoy that? She took another bite of her slice of orange and a sip of brandy, licking her lips to catch the sweet juice that escaped. This time his groan was audible.

He tossed back his entire glass of brandy and grasped the decanter. He hesitated, set it down, and pulled her close. His kiss was not tentative. Nor was it gentle. It was a siege. She was a fortress, and he had breached her defenses. Or was it the other way around? She moaned when his tongue met hers, the taste of him far more satisfying than the sweetest of oranges. He devoured her, and she savored him. When he pulled back, she was both satisfied and bereft.

"Oh, Richard," she said on a happy sigh and tugged at his jacket, wanting him pressed against her once again.

"Oh, Richard." Her voice echoed back at her, and they both stiffened. "Oh, Richard." It rang out again in perfect imitation of hers.

Richard got to his feet, and Elizabeth followed suit, her heart pounding. He glanced around the room but stood stock-still listening. Their breathing filled the air. Her skin prickled when she heard breathing echo from the far side of the room. Richard clearly heard it too, as he grabbed a lantern and moved cautiously toward the sound. She followed close behind.

"Oh, Richard."

Richard took several strides and, holding the light high, whipped the linen off the birdcage. The parrot looked at him and cocked its head, its imitation of their breathing filling the space. "Oh, Richard," it said again in Elizabeth's voice.

"What the devil?" The bird stared back at Richard, unperturbed.

Elizabeth could not squash a bubble of laughter, and when Richard heard it, he joined her. They both laughed until Elizabeth was on the verge of crying, all the emotion of the evening channeling through her. She knew the moment she'd been dreaming of had been within reach but was now lost. As if sensing her grief, Richard pulled her close and hugged her snugly.

"This was a lovely evening. Thank you." He kissed the top of her head. "It's a big day tomorrow," he said, repeating her words to William. "You must get some rest."

She watched him stroll through the ballroom and into the hall that led to his bedroom. And hers. Which had used to be theirs. She longed for it to be so again. She sighed and slowly followed, swallowing her disappointment. Tonight she'd won a battle. She would regroup, strategize, and be prepared for the next skirmish. The war was not lost. Not by a long shot.

CHAPTER TWENTY-FOUR

She gave me eyes, she gave me ears;
And humble cares, and delicate fears;
A heart, the fountain of sweet tears;
And love, and thought, and joy.

—Wordsworth, "The Sparrow's Nest"

RICHARD PAUSED AND looked at the bird in the early-morning light. It cocked its head to the side but said nothing. The damned parrot had saved him from himself last night. Saved Elizabeth from him. Her yearning had been palpable, and he'd longed to satisfy her needs. He'd been sorely tempted. Had the bird not interrupted, he wasn't sure he would have turned away from the invitation in Elizabeth's eyes and the promise from her body.

"Thank you," he said.

The parrot shifted its feet and hopped to the far side of its perch, but it did not take its eyes off Richard, who was waiting for its response. *Hell and the devil.* He was talking to birds now.

"My lord, flowers are arriving. Are they all to come in here?"

"Yes, they are, Clarkson. Thank you."

Richard turned at the sound of Elizabeth's voice. She smiled tentatively, looking ethereal in the morning sun, a bandeau wrapped around her head like a halo. He smiled back, and she came closer. His heart tightened in regret.

"Did you sleep well?" he asked, although he knew the answer. The light bruising under her eyes told him she had slept as little as he had.

"I had much on my mind," she said, holding his gaze momentarily before sweeping her hand around the room. "There are many details to attend to before guests arrive."

"I am sure you have it fully in check. I will make myself scarce so as not to be underfoot."

Elizabeth's forehead creased with concern, but she said nothing.

"I will return in plenty of time to greet the guests. I promise." He turned before she could respond, for he would not leave were she to ask him to stay, but he needed to distance himself from her and regain some modicum of self-control.

As he descended, servants flowed upward carrying great bouquets. The floral scent filling the air did not help matters at all. Elizabeth smelled of flowers. Tasted of honey. And like a bee to a posy, he was irrevocably drawn to her.

Several hours, and thanks to Bentley's encouragement, many a sherry later, Richard returned to the town house. Marcus helped him quickly change and ready himself for the event, and he congratulated himself when he stepped into the ballroom before any guests had arrived. Elizabeth was fiddling with flowers in the arbor, her back to him, wearing another new gown. This one clung as delightfully as the one she'd worn yesterday, but whereas her dress last night was the blue of an evening sky, this one captured the shade of the pink roses at the estate.

Elizabeth straightened and turned toward him, a smile lighting her face. Richard swallowed. She was truly the rose, not the dress. A perfect flower. The hours apart, and the drink, had done nothing to dampen his desire. He wanted to steal her away to the bedroom and explore the garden of treasures promised beneath that gown.

"You're here," she said, walking toward him.

"As promised," he said, taking the hand she offered, grateful she was oblivious to his wayward thoughts.

"As promised," she echoed, stepping close. "Thank you." She leaned in and brushed a kiss across his cheek, her floral scent as arousing as her breasts pressed against his chest.

"Oh, I do hope I'm not interrupting," Sophia said. "I told Hastings I was hired help today and would see myself up." She smiled wickedly, glancing back and forth between the two of them. "I should have shouted in advance, no?"

Richard stepped back, his cheeks burning. "Countess Tessaro," he said, bowing slightly.

"Oh, do stop with that, Richard. Being caught in dalliance with your wife calls for far less formality."

Elizabeth giggled, and he smiled. Sophia always cut a swath through conventions. It seemed to be a point of pride with her. She quickly kissed Elizabeth and leaned in to do the same with him.

"I see my chastisements have had some good effect," she whispered before giving him a kiss on both cheeks and stepping back, looking smug.

Richard would allow her sense of accomplishment to stand, for he was relieved to know her warnings were fully in relation to Elizabeth and had nothing to do with the damned intrigue he was entwined in. Besides, Sophia cared for Elizabeth as though they were sisters. He'd not begrudge her that protective instinct.

Servants marched through the room like small battalions, placing vases of flowers on the linens strewn strategically around the room. Gordon and Clarkson struggled up the stairs with a large harp, a small, harried man, presumably the musician, trailing behind them, muttering directions and gasping intermittently as though they would damage it.

"Oh, good," Elizabeth said. "I thought he might have abandoned us. I feared we would have to sing for entertainment."

"That would be a terrible thing, no? We sound like two magpies in the garden," Sophia said, making a face.

"You both are as delightful to listen to as these songbirds," Richard said, although he absolutely agreed with her comparison.

"Oh, you do have a gilded tongue, my lord," Elizabeth said, tucking her arm in his. "Let me show you around the room now that we can see it much better."

Her reference to last night both worried him and titillated him, as did his convenient view of her décolletage. The sweet mounds of pale flesh he'd dreamed about last night. He cleared his throat and tried to focus on her tour.

"On this floor we have games for both children and adults to enjoy. Bilbocatch, spillikin, taw, and your inspired idea of fishing. After the children have had a turn, they'll go to the nursery floor to enjoy blindman's bluff and have their own picnic. William doesn't know it, but we've set up a teeter-totter as well. I do hope they don't hurt themselves. The floor is unforgiving if one falls off."

Richard was having the damnedest of a time focusing on anything Elizabeth said. Sophia wandered about directing multitudes of servants, and the harpist shrilled orders six feet from them, and even with that racket, all Richard could do was lust after his wife. He must stop this obsession. It could come to no good end.

"Do you not agree? Is that not a coup?" Elizabeth asked.

"I'm sorry, my love..." He silently cursed himself for letting the endearment slip out. He'd worked so hard these last two years to create distance. But her eyes lit as though the sun was shining directly on her, and he found he could not truly regret it. Tomorrow would be time enough to rebuild the safety of a wall between them. He would let her have this day.

"Shuttlecock," she said, poking his forearm. "I'll try not to take offense that I must repeat myself." She smiled, the joy in her eyes belying her rebuke. "The anteroom off the drawing room has been cleared for shuttlecock. For the ladies only, of course." She leaned against his arm playfully. "You men are brutes and would probably do damage."

"My ladies, my lord, the first coaches are arriving," Clarkson announced, then disappeared quickly back down the stairs.

Richard walked to the landing with Elizabeth. "Please join us," he called to Sophia.

"*Sì, signore.*" Sophia sailed across the room to stand with them and greet their guests. "Incoming money," Sophia said with a grin. "Time to put on a grand show."

Sophia had no idea how close to the mark those last words were. Richard took a steadying breath. This day. He could give her this day.

ELIZABETH WAS HAVING difficulty concentrating on her role as hostess. *My love.* When was the last time she'd heard him say those words? She couldn't remember, but she knew she wanted to hear them again. The turnout was spectacular, and the room was bursting at its seams. The ticket to the picnic wasn't the only opportunity to raise funds. Large bowls sat by each game for voluntary donations, and they were filling surprisingly quickly. She commented on it to Richard, who had returned to her side after joining the gentlemen for a drink.

"You can thank Bentley."

"Bentley?" Elizabeth asked, looking up at Richard as she slipped her hand through his proffered arm.

"Bentley," he repeated. "He has encouraged wagers between the men on the games and insisted the victor donate his winnings to the orphanage."

"Gambling, Richard? Here at my picnic with ladies and children?" She wasn't sure whether to reprimand for such a breach of etiquette or laugh at the audacity of it all.

"All for a good cause, my love, all for a good cause," he said, patting her hand.

And there it was again. *My love.* She beamed at him, hoping he could see how much his words meant to her. He cleared his throat and steered her toward the fishing barrel. The children had recently retreated to the nursery, leaving the games for the adults. Bentley was teaching Lady Adsworth's daughter—which one Elizabeth didn't know, as they looked alike to her—how to cast the line successfully.

"He does realize she is not yet out, doesn't he?" Elizabeth quietly asked Richard.

"I would imagine that is precisely why he is giving her his attention. He's avoiding the mamas who have eligible daughters. His parents are pushing him toward a decision, and he is resistant."

"Ah, I see. I wonder how we will feel about it when the time comes for William and Sebastian," she said, a slight melancholy sifting through her happiness as she imagined the boys full-grown.

Richard leaned in and quickly kissed the top of her head. "Let us get through today before we marry them off, shall we?"

She smiled at him. "You are correct, of course. I must get the baskets out now."

He bowed, and she left, certain his eyes were upon her. A shiver of excitement ran through her, and she wished she could empty the room and pick up where they'd left off last evening. She could still taste him, still feel the urgency in his kiss.

She paused in front of the parrot, tempted to stick her tongue out at it. It had cut short her triumph. It squawked, and she scrunched her nose and narrowed her eyes, hoping it could see her frustration with it. The bird shifted on its perch. When she walked away, it felt like the bird was also staring at her. She glanced over her shoulder. Richard had disappeared. It seemed it was only the bird watching her.

She directed Hastings to distribute the picnic baskets, and she strolled around the room, encouraging people to leave the games and enjoy a repast. Sophia joined her, linking her arm in Elizabeth's.

"It is the event of the season so far, *bella*," she said. "Look at all the happy faces. And the money." Sophia put her hand in the bowl by the fishing barrel, scooped a handful of coin, and let it drop again, the tinkling barely heard above the din in the room.

"A kiss in broad daylight. It is so beneath their standing."

The voice cut through the noise in the room, as though the birdsong and harp, the laughter and chatter, had died away. Elizabeth didn't know the context, but she instinctively knew it was in relation to her. As must Sophia, as she had stiffened and grown silent.

"I'd understood she'd been put out to pasture. A broodmare. The heir and the spare. Her job was done."

Elizabeth didn't recognize the second voice any more than the first. She was tempted to turn around, but she was rooted to the spot. Sophia apparently had no such qualms. She spun on her heel.

"*Voi vecchiette*" was all Elizabeth heard before she moved in the opposite direction. If Sophia was beginning her conversation by calling them old ladies, Elizabeth did not want to be witness to it. Besides, she was mortified. Not only because they'd said such things but because it was exactly what she'd thought too.

She was about to make her escape to recompose herself, when the insistent sound of metal on glass drew her attention. As did the stream of hired footmen coming through the door with trays of fluted glasses and bottles of champagne. As the bottles were delivered to the groups sitting around their baskets, the clinking grew. People continued to tap until there was quite a din. Richard walked to the middle of the room and held out his hand toward her.

"Go to him, *mia amica*," Sophia said quietly in her ear. "Do not let bitter old women bother you. They are jealous. There is no *amore* in their lives. This is your day. Seize it." She gently pushed Elizabeth in the small of her back.

Elizabeth took a tentative step, and Richard smiled invitingly. Maybe they were right. Maybe she had been put out to pasture.

But she'd refused to stay there. He was here now, and so was she. Let them have their malicious tête-à-tête. If she had Richard back, what did she care of their opinion? She threw her shoulders back, walked purposefully to his side, and placed her hand in his. He raised his other hand, and the room grew quieter.

"I would like to thank all of you for joining us here today. We are both so pleased you have made the effort on such short notice." He smiled down at her before returning his attention to the crowd. "We are also delighted you have allowed us to fleece…"

Elizabeth slapped his arm playfully, and everyone laughed.

"I mean, delighted you have been so generous. Elizabeth is the driving force behind today's events and the worthy cause your donations will benefit."

A blush warmed her cheeks, and joy lifted her flailing spirits. This was life as it had been, as she'd imagined it could be again. He squeezed her hand and smiled at her again, and her elation expanded until she was sure her chest could not hold all the happiness in her heart.

"And before we uncork and let you return to your meals, I have some good news not even Elizabeth is aware of, as I only received it myself this morning."

Except for the birds chirping, there was not a sound. "Ground for the orphanage will be broken next month. The timber has been ordered, and the workmen will be ready to begin by mid-March."

"Oh, Richard," Elizabeth said, and instantly the parrot mimicked it. All heads swung in its direction, and laughter erupted as folks registered who had imitated her. Richard looked at her, and she was sure it was the memory of their kiss last night that darkened his eyes. He held her gaze for a melting minute, then lifted his hand, signaling all the footmen who were standing at the ready beside each group.

Cork stoppers popped around the room, and once Richard and Elizabeth had their glasses, he raised his. "To Lady Thornwood and her good deeds," he said, and cheers erupted. He watched her over his glass, slowly lowering it without taking a drink. "And to her beauty and grace, for it is infinite," he said quietly.

A shiver ran up Elizabeth's spine, and long-neglected parts of her heated with need. She should be circulating and thanking people, but all she wanted to do was drag Richard to their rooms and begin where they'd left off last night. She sighed and regretfully broke his stare. How long, she wondered, before she could politely push people out the door?

Chapter Twenty-Five

But my five wits nor my five senses can
Dissuade one foolish heart from serving thee,
Who leaves unswayed the likeness of a man,
Thy proud heart's slave and vassal wretch to be.

—Shakespeare, "Sonnet 141"

"MY LORD?" HASTINGS offered more champagne, and Richard held his glass out obligingly. He'd lost count of how many he'd had, but knew it was not enough. He took a large gulp, wishing he could wash away this incessant draw to Elizabeth. It was dangerous.

She sat with Sophia and Catherine in the far corner. He couldn't hear their laughter from where he stood, but it was written on their faces. Sophia had become fast friends with Elizabeth when she'd moved to a nearby estate shortly after they were married, but Catherine was a newer addition. He was glad of it. She needed the company of women, and he needed her distracted.

"Well done, Thornwood," Walford said, slapping him on the back. "I'll not ask how you got your hands on so much champagne, but I daresay it'll be noted in the papers." He swept an arm around the room. "This was bloody brilliant. It will definitely make the gossip merry-go-round tomorrow."

"And you know I live for that," Richard said and rolled his eyes. "Although, Elizabeth and her project might enjoy some benefit from it, I suppose."

"Not to change the subject, but it will. Any news?" Walford lifted his glass to his lips, seeming relaxed, as though this was a casual conversation. He was far better at dissembling than Richard.

"In a day? I'm not a damn miracle worker."

"Goodness, man, no need to snap," Walford said, eyebrows raised in surprise.

"My apologies. I want done with this business, yet there seems no end in sight." He threw back the remainder of his champagne. "Surely I can have one day free of it?"

"It is I who should apologize. You are right, of course. It's been an unexpected burden for you. I ask only out of concern. And also because Catherine is growing tired and would like to return to Woodfield. We will be leaving town this week."

Even though he'd known it was inevitable, it was a punch thrown at his already battered spirit with regard to this mess. He'd dragged Walford into this and been glad of his assistance. More, he'd been relieved to have a confidante and an ally. When Walford left London, he'd have neither. "I envy you" was all he said.

"I've outrun them all so far," Bentley said, stepping up to them and swaying slightly on his feet. "No filly has managed to pen me in."

He gave an exaggerated wink and chuckled, clearly amused with himself. Richard grasped his arm and steadied him.

"What?" Bentley brushed at Richard's hand, but Richard held tight. "You two look a little intense for"—he paused, covered his mouth with his free hand, and hiccuped—"a picnic."

"I do believe it's time for me to take my leave. And you, my friend," Walford said to Bentley. "Let's go gather my wife, and we'll drop you off on our way home."

Bentley grinned foolishly. "The great escape, aye? I knew I

could count on you. Is Miss Langdon to go home too?"

Walford raised an eyebrow at Bentley, and Bentley guffawed.

"Don't even think it. Only want to make sure you don't leave the poor girl behind with this…lot," Bentley said, stumbling over the word *lot* three times before completing his sentence.

Richard grabbed a full glass from a passing footman and watched as Walford guided Bentley toward the ladies. One in the throes of love and the other doing his damnedest to avoid any entanglement. It struck him that the men represented the two sides warring within him. And he knew which side must win.

⤐⤐⤐⫷⫷⫷

"*BATTI IL FERRO finché è caldo*," Sophia said, stepping up beside Elizabeth and startling her.

She'd been watching Richard escort the last of their guests down the stairs. Truth be told, she was imagining what lay beneath that jacket and those trousers. "*Batti il* what?" she said, blushing with embarrassment even though she knew Sophia could not possibly know what was on her mind.

"Strike the iron while it is hot," Sophia said, raising her fan and flapping it wildly as though she was suffering great heat. "I see the way he looks at you this day, *mia amica*, and you him. You must fan those embers."

So much for Sophia not knowing the depraved path Elizabeth's mind had wandered down. She was certain her face must be crimson now. Sophia laughed and kissed each cheek before Elizabeth could form a dignified response.

"You are far too *innocente* for a married woman." Sophia patted Elizabeth's cheek, the soft silk of her glove cool on her face. "Leave your purity at the bedroom door tonight. Show him it is not only your cheeks that burn."

"Countess, would you join us for a drink?" Richard asked, nearing the landing. The question was directed at Sophia, but his eyes were on Elizabeth.

"The duke awaits." Sophia sighed dramatically. "He promised to stay away today if I joined him tonight at the theater. And I did so want this day with my friends."

Elizabeth said her goodbyes and turned from the stairs as Richard escorted Sophia to the door. The room was a mess. Contents of baskets strewn across linens, glasses scattered about, flowers plucked and tossed like confetti. She sniffed the air.

"A hound on the hunt?" Richard asked, leaning against the balustrade.

Elizabeth laughed lightly. "Can you not smell it? I suspect it will become terribly fetid."

"We'll have the cages cleaned tonight, and I will arrange for return delivery in the morning."

"I would appreciate that. Thank you."

He pushed from the rail and walked to her, and her heart pounded against her chest.

"Have you eaten?" he asked, his hazel eyes soft with concern.

"Very little. And you?"

He shook his head. He sent a footman to retrieve Hastings, who was downstairs ensuring the smooth departure of Sophia's carriage.

"Thank you, Richard," Elizabeth said, waving her hand around the room. "For all this. Your support has meant everything."

He tilted his head and studied her. "You didn't believe you'd find a champion in me?"

She shook her head and raised her shoulders, not knowing what to say, for until recently, she'd believed he cared not a whit about anything she did.

"My lord?" Hastings crested the stairs, trying to hide his labored breathing, but his heaving chest gave him away. Poor Hastings. She'd had him running around for days.

Richard gave instructions for setting the room back to rights, as well as for the return of the birds. "And we'll have our picnic in the breakfast room," he added.

Elizabeth's heart sank. The breakfast room was not conducive to her plans. She did not wish to sit formally across from him. They'd had enough distance to last a lifetime.

"May we have it in our private sitting room?" she asked.

Richard stared at her for a moment, his lips pursed in seeming discomfiture, and Elizabeth braced for rejection.

Finally, he nodded at Hastings. "Of course," he said, smiling at her. "It is your day."

Relief coursed through Elizabeth's body, quickly replaced by cautious anticipation. Step one accomplished. She hoped the other stages of her plan of seduction were far less stressful.

RICHARD POURED HIMSELF a brandy, feeling as unsteady as Bentley looked when he'd left. Except it wasn't the alcohol making Richard's hand shake as he set the decanter on the tray. It was his delectable wife sitting on the sofa behind him. He knew it had been a bad decision to come to their private rooms together, yet he'd found he could not deny her. Although she didn't know it, he had vowed to give her this day, and he would honor his promise. He poured her a glass of champagne and turned to her, hoping neither his trepidation nor his desire showed.

She had eased out of her slippers, and one stockinged foot peeked out from where she had tucked her legs underneath her gown. She leaned forward and took her glass, and Richard bit back a moan at the full display of her cleavage. He settled in the chair opposite lest he be tempted to take her right where she sat.

"Any idea of the funds raised?" she asked, trailing a finger along her glass, a droplet of condensation hovering at its base before slipping free onto her chest. Would that he could be that drop. He looked to the side table, the sconce, the fire, anywhere but there. Elizabeth cleared her throat, and heat washed across his face. Was she drawing attention to his stare or his attempted withdrawal?

He took a sip of brandy to hide his embarrassment. "I will give you a total tomorrow. Walford collected the coin from wagers and the game donations in the bowls. They've been put in the safe but not counted. Combined with the tickets, it should be substantial."

"We must deduct some of the cost of the picnic," she said, setting her glass down.

"A gift from me."

"Oh, Richard!"

Elizabeth unfurled and threw herself across the small space into his arms, catching him off guard. He clutched her with his arms so she would not topple off as she peppered him with kisses. He was both aroused and amused and was thoroughly enjoying the weight of her body on his. A tap at the door broke her exuberant assault, and he lifted her from him. She fell back onto the sofa, laughing softly.

"Enter," he said, not taking his eyes off her beaming face. It was deeply satisfying to see her happy.

Hastings entered with two footmen Richard didn't recognize. There'd been a plethora hired for the party, which had not only ensured a seamless event but also boded well for a quick cleanup of the ballroom. They moved a table in front of the sofa and covered it with linen.

"Shall I unpack the basket, my lord?" Hastings asked, discreetly averting his glance from Elizabeth, who had quickly tucked her feet under her skirts but could not so easily fix her disheveled hair.

"I'll do it," Elizabeth said. "Another bottle of champagne, and you need not worry about us for the remainder of the evening."

Richard raised an eyebrow at her and was rewarded with an impish smile. He sipped his brandy, waiting as servants ran in and out, setting dishes and flatware, distributing several of the large bouquets Sophia had provided, and placing lanterns around the room. When the champagne chilling on shaved ice arrived, Hastings bid them good night and left the room.

Richard took in the space. "It seems the picnic has come to us."

"Indeed it has," Elizabeth said, smiling coyly.

Warning bells went off, but he ignored them. It had been far too long since he'd enjoyed such intimacy with Elizabeth. He would relish it for a time and excuse himself when they were through with their meal.

"Come sit." Elizabeth patted the seat beside her. "It is far easier to eat side by side."

As much as his mind screamed no, her invitation was like a siren song, and he followed its call.

RICHARD SAT BESIDE Elizabeth, his spine stiff as a board as he leaned forward pensively. She assumed they must both relearn how to be physically comfortable in each other's presence. Although, she'd been entirely at home on his lap when she'd bombarded him with truly appreciative kisses, and she was sure he'd not been adverse to her sudden burst of gratitude. She smiled to herself. It was a bit like getting Sebastian to walk— encouraging movement in small but enthusiastic increments.

She tugged the linen off the basket. "Oh, I do believe you shall be pleased," she said, rifling through the contents. Cook had conspired with her, ensuring she provided all Richard's favorites. "Pork loin, roast beef, pigeon pie, eggs, bread, gingerbread cakes." She set them out on the table as she named them. "Oh," she said, digging in again. "And cheese and grapes. Note not a vegetable in sight."

He chuckled. "Horrid things, vegetables." His shoulders relaxed a little as he sat back on the sofa.

Elizabeth prepared a plate for him, aware of his eyes upon

her. She wanted to lure him in as she did it, but there was truly nothing enticing about preparing a plate of food. Or so she thought, until she turned toward him. His eyes had darkened with a promise she'd not seen in over two years. She hoped it was not a fancy of her imagination.

He took the plate from her and held her gaze for a moment before finally dropping it and devoting his attention to food. She almost laughed out loud. Food would always supplant her in his life. She suspected food would supplant everything in his life. He glanced at her and smiled in a way so reminiscent of William when he'd been caught doing something he shouldn't but knew wasn't really that bad. God, but she loved the men in her life.

She'd eaten a little bit with Catherine and Sophia, although it had been difficult to swallow at times as Sophia regaled them with the trials and tribulations of the duke's pursuit. She wished she had Sophia's freedom, toying with men as though there were no consequences, laughing at their antics as though they held no sway over her. She looked at Richard. He had the power to destroy her. She'd given it to him freely, not knowing he would come dangerously close to using it. She shook her head. They'd changed course. He would not be here tonight had they not.

Richard set his plate on the table, and she picked up the cluster of grapes. Time for the next stage of her plan. She slowly pulled a single grape from the bunch and looked at him. He watched her, and her body tingled with anticipation. She put the grape in her mouth and opened her mouth slightly so he could see her pop it. She chewed excruciatingly slowly and pronouncedly swallowed, then chased the taste across her lips with her tongue. He groaned audibly. She thought of the fish in the barrel in the ballroom and smiled. Hook. Line. And sinker.

RICHARD SHIFTED UNCOMFORTABLY. He'd adjust himself, though

not only did he not wish to appear crass, but he also didn't want to draw attention to the erection pressing against his pants. Elizabeth held far too much power as it was. If she knew she had him dangling at the end of the line, she might try to reel him in. And that would not do.

"Walford tells me they will be withdrawing to the country next week," he said, sitting back again against the sofa. He took a sip of his brandy and a bite of the gingerbread cake. The marrying of the two flavors would normally be exquisite, but tonight the only deliciousness he wanted to taste was his wife. *Hell and the devil confound it.* His mind was absolutely beastly tonight. He shifted again.

Elizabeth, too, sat back, tucking her knees up and angling toward him. "Yes, Catherine told me. I cannot blame her, but I will miss her dear companionship."

He nodded in both agreement and sympathy, for he would miss Walford's company. And his sensible guidance. If the Home Office followed through on their threat, Richard had the legal background to pursue them, but Walford had the field experience and knew how best to approach them. He only hoped a resolution was found before the Walfords left London.

"Richard?"

Doubt hovered in her eyes, and he cursed himself for it. He'd promised her this day. "My apologies," he said, taking her hand in his. "You were saying?"

"I'd like to visit Woodfield after the baby has arrived. I remember how important it was to see caring faces."

Richard's stomach contracted as though he'd been kicked. He had not been among the caring faces. Once he'd known all would be well, he'd run. He was overwhelmed with the urge to withdraw his hand from hers and his person from the room, and keep on going until there was ample distance between them once again.

But her eyes held no accusation, only hope. The muscles in his abdomen slowly released. *This day*, he said to himself, *this day.*

A mantra to be repeated as necessary so he stayed by her side and made things as right as they could be between them.

"I wager it would be a far better visit to Woodfield than our last," he said, glancing toward the door one last time, deciding to stay firmly put.

She smiled. "They are proof you can overcome great adversity in a marriage."

He contemplated the truth of that as he sipped his brandy, watching her enjoy her champagne. It had always been a favorite of hers. Her tongue dipped tentatively into the glass, her eyes creasing with pleasure as the bubbles teased her tongue. After what seemed an agonizing hour of watching her tongue playfully bobbing about the glass, she finally tipped its contents into her mouth. He observed the muscles in her pale throat working to swallow the liquid. He stifled a groan. He'd like to swallow her.

"Richard."

It would seem he had not successfully stifled the groan. Her voice was gruff and thick with need. He set his brandy on the table and held out a hand for her glass, which she willingly surrendered. He tugged her hand, pulling her close, and rested his forehead against hers.

"Elizabeth," he said, ready to tell her it was impossible to go further.

She drew back and put a finger on his lips. "Shh," she said. "I don't want to hear…" She ran a finger under the fabric at her shoulder and pulled it down, revealing her breast cradled in her stays. "But I'd like," she continued as she slipped out of her left sleeve, "to feel…"

Her full breasts glowed alabaster in the lantern light, her nipples discreetly cresting the cotton, a temptation he had no strength to resist. He groaned loudly, and she smiled seductively. He must forfeit his own, but there was nothing to prevent him from giving her pleasure. He leaned in and freed a breast, taking it in his mouth. Her moan was his reward. Lord give him strength.

CHAPTER TWENTY-SIX

*You have absorb'd me. I have a sensation at the present moment
as though I was dissolving.*

—Keats, Love Letter to Fanny Brawne

ELIZABETH HAD RECOGNIZED Richard's hesitancy and had been afraid he'd withdraw. Slipping her dress off had been an audacious move, but she knew she must do something to regain his attention. All calculation disappeared when Richard took her nipple into his mouth. The sensation stimulated a need for more. Much more.

She pulled the ribbon from Richard's hair, freeing it and running her fingers through the long strands. He moaned appreciatively, and she continued, alternately massaging his scalp and clasping him tight to her breast as sensation built between her legs. She fell back upon the sofa, pulling Richard with her, pleased by his hard length pressed against her leg. She wiggled, sliding down, trying to position herself so she might feel him pressed against the spot that longed for him. When she had succeeded, she arched her hips, hoping no words would be needed to tell him what she wanted.

He pulled back abruptly, balancing on his elbows, a sliver of distance between his body and hers. The gold flecks in his eyes danced in the firelight, and his face looked grim, almost pained.

Elizabeth sucked in her bottom lip, tears stinging her eyes. Was this all so distasteful to him?

"My God, Elizabeth, you are beautiful in your need," he said gruffly.

He shifted downward, raising her dress as he did so until she was fully bared for his viewing. His breath was warm and as rapid and haggard as her own. He inhaled deeply, then rested his forehead against her mound, the rise and fall of his chest adding to her growing excitement. A shudder ran through her body at his proximity, and when he gently forced her legs open, she did not fight it.

His tongue warmed a delightful caress through her nether regions, and she rolled her head to the side, biting back a moan. His fingers parted her, and he did it again. This time, a small sound escaped.

"I would hear it all, my love," Richard cooed soothingly as he spread her further. He took her nub into his mouth and suckled as he had her breasts.

But the sensation tonight was like none she'd ever known. She both wanted to arch against him and withdraw from its force. She alternately tried to do both, but his hand under her buttocks held her firm. His momentum grew, and he was relentless, offering her no calm from the storm that was quickly brewing. When he inserted a finger, she gasped at the sensation. But when it assumed the rhythm of his delightfully wicked tongue, she was convinced she would truly lose her mind.

"Let go, my love. Let go," he said and resumed his administrations.

And she did. It was not a gasp. It was not a moan. It bordered on a scream. Of pain. Of pleasure. Of absolute release. When the last ripple had slowly rolled through, she relaxed back upon the cushion on the sofa, her hand cradling Richard's head, who lay with his cheek pressed against her inner thigh.

Once the overpowering sensations had subsided, sanity returned. As incredible as the experience was, she'd not fully reclaimed their relationship. Making love was a mutual experience, a shared pleasure, not a worker bee providing for the queen. Although, she'd not discourage her bee from that particular line of work in the future. It had been divine.

She tugged on his head, encouraging him to inch up her body. His eyes were glazed with the same need that burned deep inside her. She pulled at his cravat and yanked at the front of his jacket.

"I want more," she said. "I want it all."

HE SAT UP. *More? All?* Careening with the satisfaction of the heights of pleasure he'd brought Elizabeth, Richard could not think straight. His cock twitched, reminding him it was alive and well and would thoroughly enjoy the *all* she was suggesting.

"Elizabeth," he started, not wanting to ruin such an intimate moment but not knowing how to explain this was as far as it could go. He stared at his lap, running his hands through his hair and shaking his head, trying to dislodge the desire ripping through his mind and body.

"Yes," she said softly, and he made the mistake of looking at her. She was shimmying out of her dress, her eyes holding fast to his.

Before he could speak, she lifted her hips and pulled the dress fully off. He should look away, but he could not. She tugged at her stays until she could wiggle out of that too. She lingered for a moment, her pale body resplendent in the lamplight, then she lay back on the cushion. Richard swallowed, trying to find his voice, mesmerized as she ran a hand sensually along her side, leaving her fingers dangling tantalizingly close to the spot he had just pleasured. The firelight flickered, dancing over her body, the entire scene surreal and tempting as hell itself.

"Elizabeth," he said again. This time, his voice was a warning, although he still could not bring himself to look away.

"Yes," she said, drawing up her legs and dropping her knees to each side. "I have missed you, Richard." Her voice was low and rough as she reached between her legs and ran a finger over her flesh. She visibly shivered, and Richard's balls tightened. He sat rigid, willing his traitorous body under control.

He should get up and leave. Go to his bedroom and relieve his need. He fumbled for the decanter and shakily topped his brandy, sipping it while watching her fingers work the magic his tongue had enjoyed. When she inserted a finger, he growled in frustration. The minx laughed and got to her knees.

"We need to get rid of this," Elizabeth said, tugging at his half-untied neck scarf. "And this." She fully undid his jacket, and he obligingly shrugged out of it as though he had no will of his own. "This," she said, removing his waistcoat. "Yes, this," she said, unfastening the buttons of his shirt. He lifted his arms so she could tug it off, knowing full well he should have stopped her at his jacket.

She sat back on her heels, her magnificent body on full display. "Oh yes, I much prefer this," she said, running a finger down his chest and stopping at his waistline. "Wait," she said playfully, smiling with feigned innocence. "What light through yonder window breaks?" She trailed her finger lightly over the tip of his cock, which was straining to get out of his trousers. She undid his placard and let it drop, and his member sprang free.

Elizabeth ran two fingers, one on either side, up his length, gently smoothing the crest before grabbing it firmly and pumping several times. Richard was ready to spend right there, but she unexpectedly released it and lay back on the cushion.

"It is the east, and I am the sun," she said, spreading her legs and smiling in sensual invitation.

Richard lost all self-control. His every fantasy centered on Elizabeth, and she was teasing and taunting him and willing him to do what he so wanted to. He growled, pushing his trousers below his hips and towering over her, glaring, wanting her to push him off, to refuse him. But she did not.

"Come home to me, husband of mine," she said, arching against him. "I have missed you."

There was love and desire in her eyes. A mirror to his heart. And her need echoed his. "Yes," she said on a sigh as he plunged, her warm flesh embracing him as snug as the arms that were pulling him closer. He lost himself in the feel of her. The rhythm both familiar and foreign after the long drought, he could not get enough of it.

He shifted her, moving her legs nearer his shoulders. He wanted to bury himself deep inside her, make her his once again. His nerves were pinging, and he longed for completion, but he methodically entered her until he could sense her rising pleasure. He reached between them and pressed the precious bud, rolling it gently until Elizabeth was panting. Seconds later, she arched, pushing and withdrawing in frantic increments.

He grabbed her buttocks and pulled her close and began an attack of his own, pummeling mindlessly. Blood rushed to his head, creating a hazy, roaring landscape. Their first time, tender and awkward. The day in the woods at Thornwood Manor when she'd daringly tasted him. The night they were convinced she'd conceived.

Mentally, it was cold water splashed on a dog in heat, but physically he was too far gone. The pressure of completion was upon him. And Elizabeth. She sighed a scream, and he withdrew as quickly as he could and finished by spending on her stomach.

He lay upon her, weary from exquisite release. Her heart beat against his, and her hands ran up and down his back. Eventually, both their hearts and her hands calmed. Elizabeth brushed at the strands of hair draping over his face and pulled him in for a kiss.

"I love you, husband," she said on a whisper, her voice filled with fatigue.

In the time it took him to formulate a response, she was asleep. He rolled off her and removed his shoes and trousers. He carefully crawled over her and wedged his back against the sofa, pulling her backside snug to his body. He should be berating himself for his actions but found he could not regret enjoying their joining one last time. He only prayed he had pulled out in time.

He lay there through the night, holding her, relishing her warmth, the weight of her on his arm a familiar comfort. When shades of dawn lightened the room, he eased his arm out and shifted, fighting an overwhelming melancholy at their separation. He traced the lines etched across her ivory skin. She'd grown so round with child. He kissed the marks lightly and pressed his ear against her midriff as though he could hear Sebastian's heartbeat once again. He paused, ensuring he could hear hers. *May it never stop.*

He gently eased away and stood, stretching as he went into her bedroom and pulled off the top blanket. He returned and stood there for a few minutes, drinking her in. As she gracefully lay on her side, one knee pulled up, a hand tucked under her cheek, he took in every inch of her. God, she was beautiful. He took a deep breath, committed her to memory, and covered her before he turned away.

This could never happen again.

CHAPTER TWENTY-SEVEN

Enjoyed no sooner but despisèd straight,
Past reason hunted; and, no sooner had
Past reason hated as a swallowed bait
On purpose laid to make the taker mad;
Mad in pursuit and in possession so,
Had, having, and in quest to have, extreme;
A bliss in proof and proved, a very woe.

—Shakespeare, "Sonnet 129"

ELIZABETH STRETCHED LANGUIDLY and opened her eyes. She knew instantly Richard was not in the room. She wished she were not such a sound sleeper, as she would have enjoyed picking up where they'd left off. She clutched the blanket to her chest and stared at the ceiling, grinning like a fool, picturing the delicious wickedness that had occurred in the very spot she lay. It had been a sublime night, the first of many to come. She lay there planning on what she would do to Richard the next time she got him undressed.

The sun was well risen when she awoke again, the light tap on the door between the sitting room and her bedroom pulling her from sleep. She hoped it was Richard, but in case it was not, she ensured she was well covered by the blanket before bidding entry. Lucy poked her head in, and Elizabeth swallowed her disappointment.

"Lord Thornwood has ordered some chocolate and bread," Lucy said. "Would you like it in your room or out here, my lady?"

Lucy did an excellent job of not reacting to Elizabeth's state of undress, although she was certain the woman was biting back a smile. Her maid had not been unaware of the lonely state of her marriage bed nor of her unhappiness about it.

"I best not have it anywhere until I am dressed in something more elegant than this," Elizabeth said, glancing at the blanket and back at Lucy. She grinned, and Lucy's smile broke through in response. Elizabeth stood, pulling the blanket around her, and made her way awkwardly to her bedroom. She looked around the room, hoping soon she could once again think of it as their bedroom.

Later, after she'd enjoyed her small breakfast, she bathed and dressed for church. From the top of the stairwell, she could see Richard pacing in the entranceway. He always behaved as a caged tiger when he was waiting. She glanced at the longcase clock. She was only a quarter of an hour late. Not too bad considering the state she'd been in.

He walked out of sight, and she could hear his low voice as she descended the stairs.

"Mama!" William said excitedly, running to her side. "Papa says I can sit with you today in the big box!"

"Is that right, dearest?" she said, leaning down and kissing his cheek before glancing up and catching Richard staring at her. "What a lovely treat," she said, straightening, holding his gaze. She could not read his expression at all, yet familiar unease rippled through her. A feeling she immediately dismissed. Their reunion was simply so fresh and new, and it would take some time to adjust.

"Yes," William said, taking her hand. "Sebastian has to go with Hannah and the others, but I have proven myself to be very grown-up, haven't I, Papa?"

Richard cleared his throat. "Indeed you have, William. Hastings, Lady Thornwood's wrap, please."

William chattered happily as they piled into the carriage, sitting beside her while Richard took the bench opposite and stared out the window. Was he embarrassed about last night? Impossible. Could it be, with his son by his side, any show of their newfound closeness made him uncomfortable? His mood was far too solemn, but they were off to church, not a ball.

Greetings and conversation, when they arrived at the church, distracted her from her worry. They finally managed to get seated in their box pew, William between them, shortly before the vicar appeared. When he ascended to the pulpit and bellowed his sermon, she tried to focus, but his relentless speech on the value of virtue crawled under her skin. Was her seduction last night immoral? But she'd led a virtuous life, waiting for Richard to return to her, and where had it gotten her? Rambling around a lonely house was where. She glanced over at Richard, his jaw rigid as he stared up at the vicar. She could not regret coercing him back to her bed. Surely it was not a sin to want her husband?

Richard remained unapproachable, so she continued her internal debate on the ride back to the town house. Even William was subdued. It all seemed particularly grave in contrast to the joyous freedom that had lightened the night. This was not how she'd imagined the day would go. She sighed heavily, and Richard looked at her, a myriad of emotions moving so quickly across his face she could not name them. Except for the final resting expression. She feared it was regret. Or worse, pity. Had that been what last night had been to him?

"A stroll in the park on this sunny day?" he asked quietly.

Her heart beat rapidly, all dark dissipating immediately. She'd been overreacting. The result of too many hours lost and alone. She was simply having a difficult time believing she had finally found her way. That was what all this uncertainty was about. "That would be lovely."

"But, Papa, you said—"

"Manners, young William, manners," Richard chided. "I did, and I am a man of my word, as you must always be."

William nodded solemnly, and Richard looked at her. "I promised him I'd take him out on his pony. His yet to be named pony," he said, pointedly staring at William before returning to his attention to her. "It will be a family outing. I will lead William. Hannah can follow with the pram. I'm sure Sebastian could do with some air as well."

"Of course," Elizabeth said and turned to look out the window.

Had she not dreamed they would once again be a functioning family? Why did her body vibrate with frustration? No, not frustration. Something else. It was on high alert as though it was trying to warn her. Of what, she wasn't sure, but she couldn't shake the feeling. Not during their promenade when he was every bit the attentive father as William rode proudly alongside. Nor during their dinner, where he was the consummate gentleman making polite conversation. And certainly not when Richard left her with a chaste peck on the cheek at her bedroom door before going to his.

CHAPTER TWENTY-EIGHT

Ay me! for aught that I could ever read,
Could ever hear by tale or history,
The course of true love never did run smooth.

—Shakespeare, *A Midsummer Night's Dream*

RICHARD HAD SEEN the optimism in her eyes when she'd joined him and William in the entryway, and it hurt his heart to know he would have to watch it fade. In the cold light of the day, his fervor abated, he'd become overwhelmed by the small possibility he may have planted a child. He could not bear it.

He must find a way to navigate their relationship, make her feel wanted but not fall to temptation. He would not take his desires elsewhere, therefore he must learn to manage them. Yesterday, he was ashamed to admit to himself, he'd blatantly used his children as a shield. Today he removed himself from the town house long before Elizabeth got up. He needed a strategy, but until then, he'd no recourse but to fall back on his avoidance techniques, cowardly though they might be.

He went for a ride, even considered stopping by Walford's for some marital advice. But he found he could not share such personal information. Instead, Richard continued to ride, oblivious of his surroundings. He didn't know what to say to

Elizabeth. The other night, he'd misled her through deed, offering a promise he could not honor. If he could bring himself to speak to her of his endless sense of foreboding, they might find a middle road. He'd enjoyed the pleasure he'd given her. It would be enough for him. But would it for her? She pursued lovemaking as though there were no issues. And *devil it all*, she knew the danger. She knew it and still persisted. He'd admire her courage if it did not make him feel all the more a coward about his fears.

He'd finally wound up at White's, ordered some food, and sat brooding, staring at the book on the far left of the shelf as though it was the root of all his problems. Well, he could not solve his domestic issues, but it was time to finish with espionage business. There had been no word from Patricia, and time was running out. He was left with no choice but to seek her out and bluntly tell her the fate that awaited should she not share her source.

He penned a note indicating his plan and discreetly slid it in the book, assuming someone from the Home Office checked it regularly. He'd go home, attend to some business, and head out to Mrs. Tate's at a more suitable hour. He did not want to raise her suspicion. He decided to walk back to the town house, hoping the fresh air might help him think things through, but there was no clearer a path for what to do about Elizabeth's happiness. There was only one road forward for her safety, though, and he would not veer from it again.

Richard surprised Mrs. Fernsby as he entered through the back door, and he placed a finger to his mouth to shush her. She nodded, and he walked quietly through the hall and into his study, closing the door behind him. He'd prefer Elizabeth not know he'd returned. He eyed the pile of correspondence he'd been neglecting, hoping it would provide much-needed distraction.

A short time later, there was a rap at the door, and Richard braced himself for Elizabeth's disappointment. Instead, it was Hastings, looking more severe than normal.

"My lord, there is a…" He cleared his throat. "A woman at

the back door who wishes to speak with you. I informed her you were not in and sent her on her way, but she has refused to leave."

Richard's heart leaped into his throat. He dismissed his panic immediately. Patricia would not come to his home. "Who is it?"

"A Miss Paisley," Hastings said, archly biting out her name.

He jumped to his feet. *Damn and blast the woman.* Her audacity boiled his blood. He was ready to stampede through the hall but caught himself before doing something so foolish. The less attention drawn to her and her business, the better. Plus, it would save him having to go to the brothel, a small gift he should appreciate. He would end this thing here and now.

"Where is Lady Thornwood?"

"She has gone shopping with Lady Tessaro and Lady Walford."

Richard blew out a relieved breath. "Show Miss Paisley in," he said, surprised by Hastings's astonished look but choosing to ignore it. The man had been with him since Richard was a child, and rarely did the butler let his emotions show. He'd not chastise him for this slip, for it truly was an anomaly to have anyone come to the back door and demand to see Richard, never mind a woman, a prostitute. And he had no doubt Patricia had been less than gracious.

He was particularly grateful Elizabeth was not home when he heard Patricia chirping as she neared the study.

"I do not need a lesson in proper etiquette, you buffoon," she said as she stepped into the doorway. "Thornwood." Patricia did not wait for an introduction or invitation. She walked into the room and unceremoniously threw herself into the chair across from his desk.

Hastings was red with fury but somehow managed to ask if he could get anything. Richard dismissed him and asked him to close the door. Poor Hastings was not used to being the brunt of a sharp tongue.

"It was not wise of you to come to my home," Richard said,

leaning back in his chair and studying her. "It had better be important."

"What will you do if it's not? Beat me? Smack my backside? I didn't know that was your proclivity, but I can raise my skirts if you'd like to have a go with a paddle." She scanned him, her eyes lingering where they shouldn't, as though she could see his crotch through the desk. "Or you can have a go at me with anything else you'd like," she said seductively.

"Enough, Patricia," he said, irritated that she continued to play these flirtatious games when he'd made it clear he didn't have, nor would he ever have, any interest in a dalliance.

Patricia smirked unbecomingly. "A girl can try, right?" Inelegantly, she stuck her hand into her bosom, pulled out a sheath of paper, and shoved it across the desk toward him. When he reached for it, she yanked it back, looking around the study. "You have payment available for me here?"

"Patricia," he growled, losing patience, but it had no impact on her. She tucked it back into her gown. "Of course you will get your coin," he said irritably, holding out a hand.

She studied him for a moment and handed it over.

Richard glanced at the sheet, but it was coded and held no meaning for him. He had to trust it carried the same value as her earlier missives.

"I do apologize for coming to your home," Patricia said, her tone changed, now seeming genuinely contrite. "But it does not go well with Mrs. Tate."

A tinge of bruising was evident beneath her makeup, but it did not look fresh. "Has she raised a hand to you again?" he asked, anger beginning to grow once more.

"No. She's limiting my freedom and searching the rooms. She suspects I am holding out on her. Which, of course, I am." Her smile was not reflected in her eyes. "And I'm being watched. I climbed out a window and snuck through the side lane early this morning."

Richard weighed telling her those men who watched her

were with the Home Office but decided against it. The less she knew, the better until he drew from her the information he needed to keep her out of prison and end his involvement in this little spy ring.

He waved the paper at her. "Patricia, where are you getting this information?"

She threw her hands, palms up, into the air as though she had no idea what he was talking about.

He wanted to throttle her for her dismissiveness. Did she take none of this seriously? "I'll have his name or you will be at Bridewell before week's end." It was all he could do to refrain from raising his voice at her.

"You wouldn't dare," she said, unruffled, brushing at her skirts. "I know you too well to believe you'd do anything of the sort."

"I wouldn't dare, but those receiving the information have promised to see it done if I do not provide your source." He softened his voice. "I cannot stop them from following through with their threat."

Her face crumbled, all bravado dropped. He could once again see the young woman who had brought such light into his life when there had only been darkness. She had comforted him as he'd come to grips with the loss of his mother. He'd felt less alone in the world. He could not let her go to prison.

He got down on one knee, in front of her, and took her hands in his. "Please, Patricia, let us end this now. Who is he?"

"I don't know," she said, her eyes brimming with tears. "Truly. I have seen him clearly only once, when he came to Mrs. Tate's. Tall, dark-haired. Dark eyes, I think. French. His accent was thick...yes, French, I'm sure of it."

"He came to Mrs. Tate's?"

"Once. Never again. But like you, he didn't want what I was offering. Only wanted me to pass on information."

"Why you?"

"He didn't say. I didn't ask. It seemed easy money." Patricia shrugged, obviously unconcerned about why he'd chosen her. "He said to pass it on to a lord, suggested considering one of my old protectors. I thought of you immediately."

"If he doesn't come to Mrs. Tate's, where do you meet?"

"Nowhere. Everywhere. The market. A side street. A tavern. He finds me. Always."

"But you must know where to find him. How do you give him the money?"

"I don't. He told me to charge for it. But he doesn't collect. Ever."

Richard stood. He believed she was telling the truth. He rubbed his forehead. What to do now? Would the Home Office accept her explanation? He doubted it. Which meant she remained in jeopardy.

"Think, Patricia. There must be something more you know. Something I can give these people so they don't put you in Bridewell."

She shook her head. "I wish there were. I've no idea who or where he is." A single tear ran down her cheek, and Richard knew he must do something. He could not throw her to the wolves, even if the wolves believed they were doing it for a higher cause.

"You cannot go back to Mrs. Tate's. It is my people watching you, and they'll not let you slip by them again. Do you have somewhere safe you can go? Somewhere, hopefully far away, not connected to you?"

"Yes. I have long planned for such an eventuality. And I have my money, the money you gave me."

"I will get you more."

He walked over to the safe and opened it. The charity money remained uncounted. It had been next on his list. He reached beyond it and grabbed the servants' wages and Elizabeth's pin money, making note of the amount. He'd replace it later this week when he went to the bank. He turned and handed it to Patricia, who dropped it in her reticule and got to her feet.

"Thornwood, I'm sorry to have dragged you into this, but…"

She wiped at her eyes. "It seemed a way to dig myself out of the life I had buried myself in." She threw herself at him, wrapping her arms around his waist. "Thank you. I've never forgotten you. I never will."

He stepped back and took her hands in his. Her red hair escaping her bonnet, her powdered cheeks streaked with tears, she was still a beautiful woman, and a likable one despite her attempts at tough bravado. He wished her well in life. "Reinvent yourself. Far away." He leaned down to look directly in her eyes. "I mean it. Far."

Patricia touched his cheek with her gloved hand, and he covered it with his own. "Stay safe, Patricia," he said quietly.

"Richard?"

Both their heads swung toward the doorway. Elizabeth stood there, paler than he'd ever seen her, rigid as a statue. She looked at the two of them and at the safe beyond before returning her shocked stare back at them. Then she turned and left.

He could only imagine what she thought of their little tableau. *Damn and blast.* What the devil was he to do now?

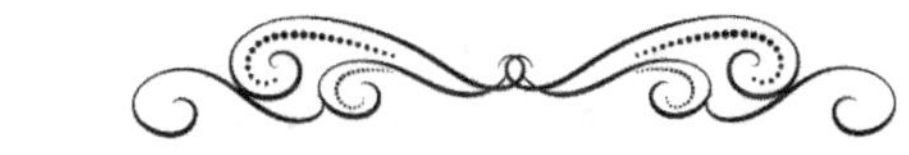

CHAPTER TWENTY-NINE

Past cure I am, now reason is past care,

And frantic-mad with evermore unrest;

My thoughts and my discourse as madmen's are,

At random from the truth vainly expressed:

For I have sworn thee fair, and thought thee bright,

Who art as black as hell, as dark as night.

—Shakespeare, "Sonnet 147"

ELIZABETH REFUSED TO accept a chaste relationship, not after the night they'd shared. And rather than wait for Richard to return from wherever he'd run off to—according to Hastings, not even returning for his breakfast—she had penned a note to Sophia and Catherine.

"You truly are the best of friends," Elizabeth said as Madame Moreau slipped into the back room to gather some fabric. "I want something daring and enticing, and I'm not sure I am a good judge of that."

"I'm here for the company," Catherine said, wiggling in her chair, trying to get comfortable. She rubbed her growing belly absently. "I won't be much help. The only daring nightgown I've ever owned Sophia picked out."

"And it worked, no?" Sophia said, not looking up from the fashion plates she was sifting through.

Elizabeth wondered at the series of emotions that played across Catherine's face before she said it had, most definitely, worked. It was not so long ago Catherine had struggled in her own relationship. Elizabeth remembered well the hurt haunting Catherine's face on her wedding day and the discomfort at their celebration dinner. Nicholas had been blatantly angry and Catherine far too subdued. It had not been her place to ask how Catherine and Nicholas had moved from such antagonism to the state of comradery and open affection they now shared. Still, it gave Elizabeth hope that she and Richard, too, could find such happiness together once again.

Madame Moreau entered, and their attention turned to the fabric she'd selected. "The sheer pink will look best," Sophia pronounced. "Do you have black? It might make her too *bianca*, too pale and delicate, or she might look deliciously ominous, like the *vedova nera*…" She scrunched her delicate nose, then she snapped her fingers. "…the black widow spider."

"I will see what I have," Madame Moreau said and disappeared again.

Sophia set aside the fashion plates and eyed Elizabeth. "I believe in collecting beautiful things, *mia amica*, and in keeping *amore* interesting, but I must confess I was surprised by your unexpected request this morning. You are letting gossip under your skin and…" Sophia pursed her lips, looking for the words. She shook her head in irritation and lifted her arm, scratching it in demonstration. "The itch?" she asked.

Elizabeth's cheeks burned recalling the ladies who'd called her a broodmare. "I am not scratching anything. Those two ladies did not get under my skin."

Catherine and Sophia looked at each other, then back at her. Sophia tilted her head and knitted her eyebrows, her lips pressed tightly together, and Catherine looked genuinely distressed.

"What?" Elizabeth's skin now crawled with more than an itchy feeling. The trepidation that had been percolating since Sunday threatened to boil over.

"You did not read this morning's paper?" Sophia asked, watching her closely.

"Richard was not home for breakfast, so I ate in my room. I usually read it when he is through with it." She shook her head. "No, I have not read the paper."

"Oh dear," Catherine said quietly.

"I have this," Madame Moreau said, holding a bolt of midnight-black silk out for them to see.

"Do you have the *Morning Chronicle?*" Sophia asked Madame Moreau.

"*Non, madame*, but I can send *une fille* to find it."

"Do," Sophia said, waving the woman out of the room. "Sit, *bella*. Catherine, Madame keeps cognac in the cabinet in the other room. If you would, *mia cara.*"

Elizabeth watched Catherine leave the room. "What is this about?"

"I will let you see for yourself. Perhaps I am too dramatic. It is in my blood," Sophia said, shrugging unapologetically.

"*Le voici*," Madame Moreau said, raising the paper in triumph. "They had a copy in *le magasin* next door." She handed it to Sophia.

"*Merci, Madame. Ce sera tout*," Sophia said as Catherine returned with a tray of glasses and the decanter of cognac. Madame Moreau arched an eyebrow at Sophia but said nothing before leaving, closing the door behind her.

"Page three, halfway down," Sophia said, passing the paper to Elizabeth.

Elizabeth's hands trembled slightly as she flipped the sheets.

A picnic in winter. What could be more delightful? Dare I say, many things. The company could have been much improved upon. A distinguished duke was noticeably absent by the side of a certain lady, who nevertheless found many a gentleman upon whom to bestow her attentions.

"That is not true," Elizabeth said. "You spent little time with the men. You were with Catherine and me much of the picnic." As for poor company, she cared not what anyone thought of her friends or her other guests. It was a petty statement, and she'd never had any patience for such nonsense.

Sophia flapped her hand at Elizabeth's concern. "It does not concern me. Read."

Gentlemen more interested in children's games than our fresh crop of debutantes, Lord B attentive to a girl not yet out of the schoolroom, and food as gray and bland as the day were not the lowest points of the event. No, the depths of bad manners were plumbed by the blatant affection displayed by married couples, the worst offenders the host and hostess themselves! Were they trying to lay to rest rumors that Lord T is plowing more fertile fields?

Elizabeth read the last line over and over until the words blurred as her eyes brimmed with tears. Catherine pressed a glass into her hand and quietly told her to drink. Which she did and choked, then began to cry. As Catherine rubbed her back, Elizabeth's mind was a maelstrom, searching for the truth in the accusation, wanting not to find it. When her tears subsided, she was no further ahead in her thoughts, but her stomach churned with dread. Had this been the cause of his distance? She had never doubted his faithfulness. Until now.

She took a slower sip of the cognac, letting it warm her from within. She inhaled slowly and blew out a long breath, calming her racing mind. She should not question it now. Not based on gossip from someone who must be bitter about something. Elizabeth raised her eyes and met Sophia's sympathetic stare.

"You don't believe…this?" She grasped the paper and shook it at Sophia. "This rag? Do you?"

Catherine's hand stilled, and she sat back on the sofa, her hand rubbing her stomach. Elizabeth did not miss the look she exchanged with Sophia. She looked from one to the other. "You do believe it!" Elizabeth stood, fury overwhelming her good manners. "How could you?" She turned to Catherine. "Richard was there for you when you needed him." She swung on Sophia. "And you have known him for years. Years! You should know better."

Sophia held up her hands. "Your anger is misplaced, *bella*," she said calmly. "You slay the messenger."

All the wind went out of her anger, and she deflated instantly, sitting back on the sofa and putting her head in her hands, shaking it back and forth, trying to dislodge the traitorous imaginings that were tumbling around.

"For what it is worth," Catherine said, "I find the reference concerning, but I don't believe it. And Nicholas called it a pile of rubbish when I showed it to him this morning. I should think he would know."

"And you?" Elizabeth asked, her heart sinking, for she saw the truth in Sophia's dark gaze. "You do." She sucked in her bottom lip, trying to stop a fresh bout of tears.

Sophia leaned forward and touched her knee. "I do not know. Where there is *fumo*, sometimes there is also fire." She lifted her shoulders, and dropped them with a heavy sigh. "You must ask the man who knows the truth. It is the only way."

"I agree," Catherine said. "Avoiding an issue solves nothing. Nicholas and I are living proof of that. It was only when we talked honestly with each other that we were able to move forward."

"And look how that turned out, *mia amica*." Sophia patted Elizabeth's knee and sat back. "This may be a good thing. You will talk. You will make amends with each other. And you will have your happy ending too."

Elizabeth had no spirit left to pursue her seductive nightgown and apologized profusely to Madame Moreau before getting into Sophia's coach. When they pulled in front of the town house, she took a deep breath as though it could brace her for the confrontation she knew was coming. She still could not believe Richard would be unfaithful, but one thing she knew for certain: he would not like that she questioned the fact. Which she must do, if only so they could put their heads together and decide how best to counter the vile rumors that were sure to come from that nasty bit of gossip.

"*Grande coraggio*," Sophia said, squeezing Elizabeth's hand before her man closed the door. Catherine waved sadly through the window. Elizabeth watched the coach pull away, hoping she could find the great courage Sophia had wished for her.

Clarkson let her in as Hastings came rushing down the hall. Richard's study door was closed, which meant he was in. Good. She wanted no time to second-guess whether to confront him.

"Lord Thornwood is in his study, I presume?" Elizabeth asked as Clarkson took her cloak.

"He is, my lady, but has asked not to be disturbed." Hastings's eyes shifted to the study door, then back to her.

A subtle move, but those warning bells sounded again, ringing through Elizabeth's body. She pulled at the ribbon under her chin and yanked her bonnet off, shoving it into Hastings's hands. "Indeed? Well, I shan't be more than a moment." She strode quickly to the door and opened it without knocking, and the air left her lungs.

Richard was leaning intimately toward a shapely redhead, the woman's hand placed familiarly on his cheek. The safe behind him was open, the moneys collected from the picnic strewn about inside. *Patricia.* He'd said her Christian name. She saw all this at once but could make no sense of any of it.

"Richard?"

They turned toward her, and his face betrayed his guilt. She had seen enough. She turned and flew up the stairs. Too angry to cry, too hurt to even feel, she dismissed Lucy and lay fully clothed on the bed, staring at the ceiling. She was finished. The battles were behind them. The war was over. And she had lost.

CHAPTER THIRTY

Gone—glimmering through the dream of things that were.

—Byron, *Childe Harold's Pilgrimage*

RICHARD PACED HIS study. He'd arranged for Patricia to be dropped at a coaching house and instructed Simon to wait until she'd made arrangements. He didn't know where she was going, and he didn't care to. He could do no more for her. Nor could he assist the Home Office any longer. He regretted the loss of information to help the war effort, but the line of communication had gone dry, and putting Patricia at Bridewell would be of no benefit to anyone.

How to handle Elizabeth was not so clear. He wanted to rush upstairs and explain what she had seen. But how could he? He'd sworn an oath of confidentiality. Even if he did demand the same discretion of Elizabeth, how would she accept that he'd been regularly visiting a brothel and meeting his ex-mistress? A mistress she'd never known existed. He ran both hands through his hair and shook his head in frustration. He should never have agreed to enter into this intrigue. Deception was an endless loop.

He wrote a note to the Home Office and grabbed the final missive from Patricia, tucking them both safely into his pocket. He'd finish this business and take time to decide how best to deal with Elizabeth. He needed to tread carefully. Richard did not want to hurt her more than he already had.

Hastings was the consummate professional as he assisted Richard with his greatcoat, but Richard could sense his censure. He didn't blame the man. He'd had to escort Patricia into the town house and witness the distress of his mistress when she'd found her husband enclosed in his study with a prostitute. Richard was grateful for the man's discretion. Both Hastings and Mrs. Fernsby would ensure this little escapade was not whispered about beyond these walls.

"Shall I find a hackney, my lord?" Hastings said, obviously aware the coach was elsewhere, and equally clearly, he did not approve of its current use.

"I shall walk," Richard said, putting on his hat.

"And what will I tell Lady Thornwood should she ask about your whereabouts?"

Damned if he knew. "Whatever you want," he snapped and left Hastings and his astonished expression behind. But he could not leave the memory of Elizabeth's expression behind. It haunted him as he made his way to White's. Wiggled under his skin as he slipped the sheets in the allocated book. Danced before him as he sipped his third sherry, the roaring fireplace doing nothing to chase the chill from his bones or her face from his mind.

"I thought I'd find you here." Walford sunk into the chair beside Richard.

Richard lolled his head to look at Walford, hating the pity he saw in his friend's eyes. He returned his stare to the fire. "It is over. This business. For me, anyway. I've told them that." He thrust his chin in the direction of the book. "It's the last missive. And Patricia is gone."

"What do you mean, *gone*?"

"Out of it. She had no idea who was feeding her the information. And she had no way to contact him. He always sought her out. The bloody man never even collected payment."

"And you believed her?"

Richard nodded, saying nothing further as the server handed Walford a brandy and refreshed Richard's sherry. When the server was well out of earshot, Richard continued, "I did. I do."

"But the Home Office will not have your faith," Walford said, swirling the brandy in his glass, watching him.

"I know. Which is why she's gone," Richard said, taking a large sip of his sherry. "I am assured we will not see her again, and I hope to God they are unable to find her."

Walford did not look entirely surprised by this turn of events. "You once encouraged my compassion. I would expect you to demand no less from yourself." He clasped Richard's shoulder. "I'm glad for it. For her. For you. Let your conscience be at ease on that front. They'll find other sources."

Richard took another drink, thankful for Walford's understanding. He'd proven to be as true a friend as Richard hoped he'd proven to be to Walford last summer. He was grateful Walford had come by the club. Unusual for him to drop in without preplanning it. Richard's brow creased as he turned to Walford. "What brings you here?"

"More like who."

Richard shook his head slowly from side to side. He did not want to hear anything more from the Home Office. He was good and truly done.

"Catherine," Walford said, eyeing him over his glass. "It seems she received a note from Elizabeth. They have grown closer these last weeks."

Richard stared into the fire, not responding. What was there to say? He could not blame Elizabeth for seeking her friend's support. No doubt Countess Tessaro was already aware of what happened as well.

"She has requested to return with us to the country at week's end."

Richard's head snapped around. He had not expected such quick action.

"She and Sophia had been helping your wife choose seductive

nightwear." Walford held up a hand before Richard could respond. "Catherine's words, not mine. But apparently there was some gossip. About you. A suggestion of an affair. Catherine was shocked it had progressed so quickly to Elizabeth wanting to leave the city. I assumed it had something to do with your business here. Figured I'd come see if I could help sort it." Walford sat back in his chair and waited.

Richard relayed all that had happened while his head spun. Elizabeth had hoped for more nights with him. Nights he could not give. He detested that she wanted to leave him, but he also debated if it would not be for the best.

"Tell her," Walford said quietly, when Richard was through giving his accounting.

"Tell her what? That I have been spying? I gave my word, Nicholas."

"And is your word worth the price of your marriage?"

There was a time the answer to that question would have come easily. Nothing was worth destroying his marriage. But now? He had proven he could not keep her safe. This was the only way.

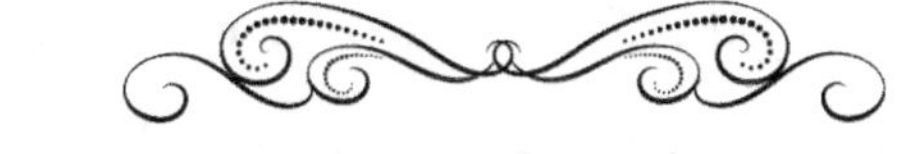

CHAPTER THIRTY-ONE

The silence that is in the starry sky,
The sleep that is among the lonely hills.

—Wordsworth, "Song at the Feast of Brougham Castle
upon the Restoration of Lord Clifford, the Shepherd, to
the Estates and Honours of his Ancestors"

S OPHIA HAD EXPEDITED Elizabeth's departure, declaring she, too, would like to return to the country and insisting she needed to put some distance between the duke and his persistent intentions. Elizabeth suspected Sophia exaggerated for her sake, but she was grateful for the offer to leave London quickly. It was also a much better solution, as the Walfords would have had to go far out of their way to bring her to Thornwood Manor, whereas Sophia lived on a neighboring estate. Richard could keep his coach. He could keep everything for all she cared. She could not get far enough away, nor accomplish it fast enough.

In truth, she'd wanted her departure to wound him, but he'd seemed impervious. He'd dispassionately insisted the entire staff return to the manor and, as if she could not be gone soon enough, had piled them into carriages and sent them off early in the morning. With the exception of Hannah, Lucy, and Gordon, who had taken Sebastian out to the Thornwood carriage and were waiting for William. It would follow Sophia's. Her composure brittle, Elizabeth stood with William in the entrance-way as Richard gave final instructions to Simon.

"You are the man of the house when I am not there," Richard said, kneeling to look William in the eye. "You must be good and take care of your brother." He paused and cleared his throat. "And your mother."

William nodded sagely, as Elizabeth bit her lip and stared at the wall, refusing to let him see how this departure pained her.

"Papa, will you come soon?"

Richard stood. "I'm afraid parliament will keep me here for some time. I will write to you."

"But I can't read," William said, tears brimming in his eyes.

"Hannah will read it to you. Or your mother will."

Elizabeth knew Richard was staring at her, but she did not look directly back at him. Anger and anguish clashed within her, but she refused to speak about either. If he could so coldly let them leave, then she would remain equally impassive. Let him feel the full import of her chilly demeanor.

He sighed heavily. "Safe journey," he said, and Clarkson, who was remaining behind to take up Hastings's role, opened the door for them. Richard put his hand on William's shoulder. "I hope to see you in late spring."

The sun hurt her already stinging eyes as they stepped out-side. Sophia's coach was loaded with chests, followed by the Thornwood carriage, which was also fully stacked. William's pony, tethered to the back of the carriage, whinnied. William waved at it and paused. He yanked free of her hand, spun around, and ran up the steps.

"Papa!" he shouted, and Richard stepped into the doorway. "I have a name for my pony! Hope. Her name is Hope. I will think of you coming in spring every time I say her name."

He threw his arms around Richard's legs, and Elizabeth could watch no more. Richard would see William into Hannah's capable hands. She climbed into the coach beside Sophia and sat stiffly as they pulled away. She did not peer out the window. She could not look at Sophia. Any sympathy, and she would break. Crumble. Shatter into a million jagged pieces like her heart had already done.

"ARE YOU SURE you would not prefer to stay with me?" Sophia asked for what must have been the tenth time. "You will be lonely, no?"

The servants' coaches had managed a half day advantage on them, and the courtyard was alive with movement. The house towered imposingly, its dark exterior a reflection of her mood. But she knew these walls well and hoped to find some comfort within them. At least here she would not have to daily face gossip or pity. Or Richard.

"I am used to lonely," Elizabeth said and hugged Sophia. "Thank you for listening to me these past days. Thank you for being my friend."

"Always, *mia amica*." She kissed each of Elizabeth's cheeks and stepped back. "In times of need, we must be there for one another, no?" She turned and got back into her coach, leaning out before her man had a chance to close the door. "I will give you a few days to lick your wounds. But no more. We will come together and find a way for you to heal."

Elizabeth nodded, although she knew there was no healing in her future. She waved as Sophia's coach pulled out. After it had passed through the courtyard arch, she turned to the manor. Once her haven, it had become a prison in the last few years. One she'd believed she'd been freed from. It would seem she'd been wrong.

Exhausted from travel, William had gone to bed early, so she took her meal alone in the dining room, Richard's ancestors staring morosely at her from the paintings on the wall. Afterward she went to Richard's study and poured herself a sherry before heading to her room. She'd dismissed Lucy earlier, not only to let the poor girl get settled and organized for life at the manor but because she wanted no idle chatter this night.

Tomorrow she would throw her shoulders back and soldier forward as she had always done. The boys, and the orphanage, would fill her days. She stared out at the lake in the distance, the moon shimmering across its surface, its invitational magic a mockery of her reality. What would now fill her nights?

CHAPTER THIRTY-TWO

Before, a joy proposed; behind, a dream.
All this the world well knows; yet none knows well
To shun the heaven that leads men to this hell.

—Shakespeare, "Sonnet 129"

"CHAFING COLD OUT there." Walford threw himself into the neighboring chair, rubbing his hands together and holding them toward the fire. He looked across at Richard. "The Home Office is not impressed with you."

Richard raised his glass. "Well, tell them I said, 'Welcome. I'm not impressed with me either.'" He took a sip and stared at the fire. Nor was Elizabeth. Hell, even William had inadvertently made him feel like a swine. Which, of course, he was.

"They were, however, impressed with the latest information. French troop movements along the main road from Lisbon into Spain. And indications of heavily defended bridges and fords. This knowledge may save many men."

"At least some good has come from it all," Richard said, and he meant it. He could not lament the saving of lives regardless of how it had turned his own personal world upside down.

"They've asked me to press you about Patricia's whereabouts. I told them you didn't know, but they're still furious that their own agents let her slip out. Your aiding and abetting her escape is fuel on the fire. I'm not sure they're going to let it go. Especially after seeing the value of her last piece of information. Operations are desperate for such insight." Walford's brow wrinkled. "Miller in particular seemed especially keen to know Miss Paisley's whereabouts. I suspect he's one of the ones under fire for letting her get away. He cornered me privately, insisting you reveal where she'd gone."

Richard shrugged. "You cannot get blood from a stone."

"That may be so, but it might not prevent them from trying. Consider yourself warned. They can be tenacious. And they remain concerned that the source is playing both sides. They've not resolved how he came to have the letter from Wellesley." Walford stood.

"Not staying for a drink?"

"No. We are off tomorrow morning. It's fresh air and country living for me for the foreseeable future. For the first time in my life, I am looking forward to seeing Woodfield and my father. It's all so much easier with Catherine by my side."

Richard winced. If Walford had meant to wound, he had hit his target.

Walford stared at him for a moment. "Our lives are richer for our wives' companionship. Talk to yours, man. I learned the hard way that silence only increases the void." He thrust out his hand, and Richard shook it. "You know where to find me if you need me."

Richard sat for a long time, pondering Walford's advice. If only it were so easy. Finally, he got up, ready to head home. He shook his head. Not home. Without Elizabeth and the boys, it was solely a house. He sighed. It was nobody's fault but his own.

CHAPTER THIRTY-THREE

Who, moving others, are themselves as stone,
Unmoved, cold, and to temptation slow.

—Shakespeare, "Sonnet 94"

WILLIAM PARADED PAST them, the two boys, Patrick and Jonathon, following in line behind. The three of them had become fast friends over the last two weeks. The children weren't certain of their ages. As far as Elizabeth could discern, Patrick was a year older than William, and Jonathon a few months younger. One thing Elizabeth was sure of—they were little balls of energy. Parson Brown was exhausted trying to keep up with them and was hinting she should consider making other arrangements.

"They begin framing next week, if the weather remains clear," Elizabeth said. "I will soon need to look for staff."

Sophia twirled her parasol as she studied the spot where the orphanage would go. "It is a big undertaking," she said.

"It is, but it keeps me busy."

"And you can avoid thinking about your marriage."

Elizabeth ignored Sophia's pointed statement. "I may take the boys in until the orphanage is built. Parson Brown is weary of them underfoot, and Mrs. Elder is a beast with them. Says she was hired to cook and clean, not chase vermin all day."

"You are changing the subject, *bella*, but I shall let you. Are you sure it is wise to take these two into your home? There will be more children. You cannot take them all in, *mia amica*, no matter how big your heart."

"Would that I could, but you are, of course, correct. I cannot take them all. But these two are before me now, and I can make a difference for them. At least temporarily. Nurture them and let them know someone cares. Look how happy William is. Look at the joy on their faces. And all three are so patient when Sebastian tries to join in their merriment."

Her courses had started. Elizabeth had been both relieved and devastated. There was a time she and Richard had dreamed of filling the manor with children. That was never going to happen, but for a while, she could enjoy the sound of these boys bouncing off the walls. The orphanage would likely not be ready for months.

Sophia scooped Elizabeth's elbow, and they walked back toward her coach. "Catherine tells me you have declined her invitation for a stay at Woodfield."

"This is the last month she will have Nicholas all to herself. I'll not rob her of it." She didn't add that she was in no mood to bear witness to a happy marriage. "Everything changes when a child arrives."

"Then I am glad I have never had children," Sophia said. "For had I love like theirs, I'd not want it to ever change."

Emotion brewed, unexpected and harsh, bubbling up and clogging Elizabeth's throat. She blinked back tears.

"Oh, *bella*, I have upset you." She leaned in closer. "But I think maybe I do it deliberately."

Elizabeth pulled her arm free and turned to her friend. Why would Sophia want to upset her?

"You cannot hide here forever."

Elizabeth swiped at her eyes. "Two weeks is hardly forever."

"It has been an eternity to me," Sophia said dramatically. "After so much activity, I am finding country life horribly dull.

And I am not hurting, like you. The nights are endless, no?"

She could not argue, for they were. Yet she had no desire for company except for Sophia's.

"I have some business in London. Why don't you come with me? You can stay at my house, if you'd like. Although, you must face Richard sooner or later."

Elizabeth shook her head. Yes, she must, but she preferred later to sooner. She was too raw right now to hear his truth. Or worse, his lies. "I am not ready," she said quietly.

Sophia studied her for a moment before speaking. "I will not push you...today. While I am in London, I will investigate this gossip and see if I can find out who this woman is, the one you think you caught in a compromising position."

"Not think. I did. I know what I saw." Anger surfaced again but was quickly smothered by grief.

"Ah, *mia amica*, of course. I am sorry." Sophia leaned in and kissed each cheek. "I want only to make things better."

"You do," Elizabeth said, grateful to have a friend to trust with the full truth of her situation. "I do hope you won't stay long in town. I will miss you."

"Only as long as I need to. When I get back, I will expect more of you. I will throw a *festa*, and you will come. Yes, that is exactly what I will do."

"Oh, Sophia, I don't know when I will want to show my face in public again."

"Mama, look at us. We are lions." The boys roared, yellowed strands of grass sticking from their collars like manes. They clawed at one another and tumbled to the ground, laughing.

Sophia looked at them, her eyes narrowing thoughtfully. Her face lit up. "Yes! We will do like them and pretend. A masquerade. You will not need to show your face. It is brilliant, no?" Sophia hugged her quickly. "I will send out invitations before I leave."

Elizabeth could not mirror Sophia's excitement, nor could she slight her when she was working so hard to cheer Elizabeth up. She forced a smile and promised she would consider it. Which, of course, she would not. She'd find a suitable excuse when the time arrived.

The boys' giggling subsided, and they all piled into the carriage, Sophia smiling triumphantly. Elizabeth would let her have this moment, but sooner or later, Sophia would have to accept that everything had changed for Elizabeth. She would never be the same. She looked at her sons, the heir and the spare. Those two women were right. She *was* a mare put out to pasture.

CHAPTER THIRTY-FOUR

Suffering is permanent, obscure and dark,
And shares the nature of infinity.

—Wordsworth, *The Borderers*

RICHARD STARED VACANTLY at the empty nursery. He sat at the small desk in the corner, feeling completely ridiculous and absolutely lost. He came here every few days to write a letter to William. At least on that, he could keep his word. He'd not much to say so often relied on giving him advice on how to care for his pony and how to help out around the manor.

He'd been working on a treatise about social conditions and street urchins and their connection to crime, trying to draft a proposal for housing and education in the poorer areas of London. He doubted he would get a chance to present it at parliament this season. The war effort came first, the lords pounded the floor with their questions and concerns, and the government solicited their support. His proposition was something positive to come from the affair with Patricia, he supposed. Regardless, it was good to have a purpose. As Elizabeth had with the orphanage.

Elizabeth. He could push her to the back of his mind during the business of the day, but she did not leave him at night. He saw, over and again, her joyous smile at the picnic announcement regarding the orphanage, her ashen face in the doorway of his study, her stiff posture and pained expression as William said goodbye. Even knowing she could hold nothing but contempt for him now, he tossed at night, longing for her. Her laughter, the warmth in her eyes, her touch. He repeatedly dreamed about their night together, reliving it, spending himself in the empty bed. His endless desire for her only confirmed he must stay the course and remain in London. Alone.

"My lord?" Clarkson's tall frame darkened the doorway. "A note has come for you. I would have left it in your study, but it is marked urgent."

"Give it here," Richard said, folding his letter and handing it to Clarkson in exchange for the note. "See that it goes out today."

Clarkson bowed and turned to leave.

"Who delivered this?" Richard asked, noting the neat printing but nondescript seal.

"A young boy, my lord. I asked him to await a response, but he said he wasn't supposed to and ran off before I could grab his collar."

"Thank you," Richard said, dismissing him and walking over to the window. He looked out at the street below but could see no sign of the child. Not that he'd really expected to. The ragamuffins used for delivery moved like mice in the night, darting quickly and blending into their surroundings.

Richard unfolded the note, his heart rate accelerating as he read it.

I have news of your woman. Meet me, as before, at three. M.

His pulse slowed when he realized it was not about Elizabeth. M. Miller had referred to Patricia as his woman. It could only be him. Richard tore the note in two. He was done with this business. It had wreaked enough havoc in his life. He stomped downstairs and tossed it onto the fire before throwing himself in a chair. The clock struck two, and Richard cursed and got to his feet. *Hell and devil confound it!* He could not ignore the command.

He must ensure Patricia was safe.

He got to the pond before Miller, considered dismounting but decided against it. This was not a social call. He'd let the man speak, then be on his way. Horatio shifted restlessly. Richard was in a foul mood, and it was not surprising the horse would pick up on it. He tugged at his collar as a cold breeze drifted across the pond, swirling the light drizzle around his neck. Miserable afternoon to be out.

Richard heard Miller's footfalls, but he continued to stare at the water. Let the man come to him. He'd show him who had the power in this relationship. He harrumphed to himself. *Relationship*. There was no relationship, and he'd make it clear there would be none in the future.

"Lord Thornwood," Miller said, stepping beside the horse and moving a few paces forward to face him.

Richard did not greet him. He waited silently for him to explain why he had the audacity to summon him.

Miller eyed him as he took off his hat and ran a hand through his thinning hair. "Miss Paisley has been taken."

"What do you mean, 'taken'?" Richard asked tersely, although all his haughty anger was quickly deflating as he chased the concept through his mind.

"Kidnapped. She was on her way to York and was plucked."

"I thought you'd already lost her. Was that not the point of your anger with me?"

"I picked up her trail in Leeds. She'd gotten on the coach to York, but she didn't arrive. According to the driver, they'd stopped for some food and she didn't return to the coach."

"Have you considered she was onto you and slipped away? It wouldn't be the first time," Richard said bitterly. Their inability to keep Patricia in their sights, never mind deduce the spy, was what had led to the scene in his study. "It is also possible she'd never intended to go all the way to York. I see nothing nefarious in any of this, nor do I see a need to have dragged me out to tell me about it."

"I assumed since you turned your back on the Home Office to help her on her way, you cared something of what became of her. It would seem I was wrong." He jammed his hat on his head. "Good day, my lord."

Miller walked past him, toward the walnut grove. Something was off, but Richard couldn't put his finger on it. He turned Horatio and faced the departing figure. "Why do *you* believe she's been taken?" he shouted.

Miller turned around. "Because they've asked for a ransom," he said and turned and walked away.

Devil it! Richard heeled Horatio and trotted after Miller. It would seem he was not done with this business after all.

CHAPTER THIRTY-FIVE

The day drags through though storms keep out the sun;
And thus the heart will break, yet brokenly live on.

—Byron, "There Was a Sound of Revelry by Night"

WILLIAM HAD HIS own room at Thornwood, adjacent to the nursery. Elizabeth had gotten into the habit of sitting with Sebastian before his bedtime. Afterward, she'd leave him under Hannah's supervision and spend some time with William.

"Papa says I should reward Hope," William said as Elizabeth tucked him in.

She flinched, although she knew the child did not understand the irony of what he'd said. Reward hope? She'd surrendered hope. Her days were filled with alternating emotions of suffocating grief and burning anger, and more and more, familiar numbness was championing both those emotions. None of it was healthy for her body or mind, and she knew she needed to let it go. It was not as though she would ever leave Thornwood Manor and the boys.

"He says Hope is doing a great service for me and I must respect her for it. And reward her. Did I say that already?"

"You did, my dearest." She leaned in and kissed his cheek. "Sleep well."

She left William to his dreams and wandered down the hall

toward her bedroom. Thornwood Manor's halls were narrow and dark, with rich wooden paneling. Built two hundred years ago, the home did not have the glamour of Sophia's newer manse, or even the open expanse of light of Catherine's Woodfield Hall, but despite its rambling size, the manor had felt cozy in the early years of her marriage. Now it seemed the walls were closing in on her.

"My lady," Lucy said when Elizabeth entered her bedroom. "Your tea is set in the other room."

"I would have it in here tonight, Lucy."

Lucy bobbed a quick curtsy and disappeared into the sitting room, which lay between her and Richard's room. She'd spent too many nights contemplating his closed door and had no wish to stare at it this evening. Lucy quickly returned and set a tray on the side table near the fireplace, and Elizabeth sat beside it.

"Do you know what frock you wish for the morning?"

Elizabeth did not look away from the fire. "It truly doesn't matter, does it? You pick one. That will be all this evening. Thank you."

She waited until Lucy left before pouring her tea and sitting back in the plush chair. Still young, Lucy was far more enthusiastic than Elizabeth and had been thrilled to go to London for the season. Poor girl had been so happy when Elizabeth had returned to society, ecstatic to unpack the new gowns and shoes, to dress Elizabeth, and to artfully fashion her hair. Of course, so had Elizabeth been, and she was not so naive. Yet she'd been filled with hope.

Hope. Reward Hope. Was that what Richard had been doing the night she'd thought they'd found their footing again? Had he been merely rewarding her attempt, her optimism that all could be right again between them? But what about respect? He'd also told William he must respect hope. Richard's dalliance made a lie of that little piece of advice.

She set her teacup down. It had been a month since they'd left London, and she'd not heard a word directly from Richard.

Bosley received financial instructions regarding the orphanage and shared those with her, but that was it. Other than the letters to William, which arrived faithfully twice a week. He was a good father, and she must hold on to that. Many men weren't. Of course, she'd believed he was a good husband once upon a time too.

Returning to rusticate in the country was no one's fault but her own. She'd chosen her path. She hadn't wanted to stay and suffer the gossip. She also hadn't wanted to live in the house with Richard while he…while he did whatever it was he'd been doing. She'd hoped that after she left, he'd follow and beg her forgiveness. But hope alone had not made it happen. Nor would she demand it of him. If he could not find it within himself to make amends, they were well and truly finished.

The wood snapped, sparks flew into the air, and the logs settled back into a steady burn again. She had once hoped her marriage would be like the fire. Sudden passion followed by warming comfort. Her sorrow and longing clung together, rolling in her stomach, and she willed them into submission, inviting in numbness. She must detach herself from him and create a life of her own. She would not throw away any more years waiting for him.

Resolute, Elizabeth pushed from her chair, went to her writing desk, and sat again. She pulled out a sheaf of paper and wrote her list of things to do. Time for a governess for William. He was far too bright for his own good and might find himself in trouble if she did not channel his energies into something that would feed his mind. Patrick and Jonathon could join him so he'd not be alone in his studies.

The framework had begun on the orphanage. It was time to seek staff. And furnishings. She had not finished selecting everything. She had ordered paper hangings for the dining room when shopping with Catherine, and they had long ago arrived, but she'd not had the heart to care. Tomorrow she would consult with Mrs. Fernsby and get those renovations underway.

Elizabeth tapped the tip of her quill lightly, making small dots. She must commit her plans to paper if she was ever going to commit to deed. She wrote, *Reenter the world*. She stared at those words. Elizabeth was done with hiding and licking at her wounds like a scared cub. She would begin to make calls and accept visitors. And she would attend socials. She knew exactly where to start. Sophia was going to be so happy.

Later, when she tossed and turned, she reviewed her list in her mind over and over. It calmed the turmoil that rolled in each night with the darkness, when she'd once again revisit the lovemaking she'd believed had reset their relationship. His gaze, his touch, the promise she'd thought it implied. The hope she'd felt.

Elizabeth shook her head and ran her hands down her face. She must accept reality. Hope was dead. But determination was standing in its stead, and she must…she would…return to the land of the living.

CHAPTER THIRTY-SIX

He spake of love, such love as Spirits feel
In worlds whose course is equable and pure;
No fears to beat away—no strife to heal—
The past unsighed for, and the future sure.

—Wordsworth, "Laodamia"

RICHARD BURIED HIMSELF in building arguments for his treatise and daily attended speeches on the war effort, constantly analyzing them to see if any of the information Patricia had provided had truly helped at all. Each evening, he went to White's, waiting for word from Miller. The man said he'd be in contact when he knew more, but Richard had not heard a word.

A week of worrying and fretting, compounded with the aching absence of Elizabeth and the boys, had brought on the worst of headaches. Clarkson had brought him a tonic, but it had not lessened his throbbing pulse. He looked at the pile of paperwork awaiting his attention. He shoved it to the side, put his elbows on the table, and rubbed his temples. There'd been a time Elizabeth would do that for him, and it had always worked. But his fingers held no soothing magic. God, he missed her.

He should never have allowed her to stay with him in London. He'd grown accustomed to their distance, not happy about it but used to it. Having her and the boys here had changed everything. Not to mention making love once again. He groaned into his hands. Now the town house was a mausoleum for those memories.

A rap at the door drew his attention. "Enter," he said, sitting upright.

"My lord, Lady Tessaro—"

"Is here to see you," Sophia said, pushing past Clarkson, whose eyes grew wide. "I'll have some tea," she tossed over her shoulder before dropping elegantly into the chair across from him.

Richard nodded to Clarkson, who bowed slightly and left the room. Sophia set her reticule on the table and took a seat, brushing at her dress, shifting on the chair so that the folds fell perfectly. Her melodramatic beauty deserving of the talented stroke of Jean-Baptiste Greuze, she sat as though posing for such a painting, her face expectant.

"I thought you were in the country," Richard said.

"I was, but I am now not," she said but did not elaborate.

He sighed heavily, resisting the urge to return to massaging his temples again. He had no patience for games today. "To what do I owe the pleasure of your company?"

Sophia casually glanced around the room, her gaze landing on his stack of paperwork before she looked back at him. "How have you been?" she asked, avoiding his question.

"How do you think I've been?" he snapped, instantly regretting it. She didn't deserve his anger. "My apologies. I find myself much ill-mannered these days."

She tilted her head and looked at him. "You are unhappy, no?"

He didn't answer. He had no doubt she knew the whole sordid situation with Elizabeth. What was there to say?

"Elizabeth is miserable too," she said quietly. "Only you can fix what is broken."

He'd thought so too. Thought they could live together in loving companionship. He'd underestimated the strength of his desire. And his fear. "You don't understand."

"Then explain it to me, Richard. What happened to separate two people who have much *amore* for one another?" She threw her hand up as he began to deny it. "Don't tell me it's not true. I have seen it with my own eyes."

Richard hesitated. It was a bloody awkward subject. He'd not talked about it with anyone. Not Bentley. Not Walford. Definitely not Elizabeth. She would dismiss it. He debated the wisdom of telling Sophia. She had been there through those awful days and nights, when Elizabeth lay cold as marble, her lifeblood staining the sheets until he wondered if she had any left.

"I will not risk losing her," he said, choking on the words. "I will not put her life in jeopardy ever again."

Sophia's eyes darkened with sympathy. He saw the moment they lit up, comprehending what he was trying to say. She reached across the table and covered his hand with her gloved one. "You did not put her life in danger, *mio amico*. Those decisions are in hands bigger than yours."

She squeezed his hand and sat back, and he swallowed the lump in his throat. "Perhaps the decision to let her live was," he said, "but it is I who put her in that cursed state in the first place."

"I believe Elizabeth would not describe it so. More a blessed state. Would you regret your boys?"

"Of course not. But I know better now. And have vowed to do better."

She nodded in understanding, but he wasn't sure she truly grasped it. Nonetheless, it felt damn good to tell someone. To share the anxiety that infiltrated his every moment with Elizabeth.

"I know your loyalty lies with Elizabeth, but I'd have this conversation stay between us. It would be of no benefit for Elizabeth to know," he said. Clarkson interrupted with tea service before Sophia could answer, and they both remained quiet while he served. When he'd left the room, Sophia watched Richard over the rim of her cup, as though weighing his measure.

"I have the answer I needed," she said, setting her cup on his desk. "*La femmina*, the woman you were found with, she is not *un affare di cuore*…an affair of the heart."

"Dear God, no," Richard said, running a hand through his hair and letting it drop clumsily back to the table. "She is not an affair at all. She is—" He cut himself off. He couldn't believe he'd almost told Sophia.

"She is…?" she prompted, one eyebrow raised.

"She is nobody," he said, his bloody head pounding harder than before. He should not have shared his fears with Sophia. She would not keep it to herself. She would also continue to probe about Patricia, and he could give no satisfactory answer.

Sophia slowly put her cup on the table and sighed heavily. "You can say it to me." Her eyes narrowed, sympathy and consideration now absent from her face. "She is a prostitute, Richard, and a spy, no?"

CHAPTER THIRTY-SEVEN

Make not your thoughts your prisons.

—Shakespeare, *Antony and Cleopatra*

ELIZABETH HELD SEBASTIAN on her lap and rocked him while Dr. Redding examined the boys. Patrick and Jonathan were remarkably mannerly, but even with her attempts at stern looks in his direction, William giggled every time Dr. Redding touched him. When he opened his mouth and made the sound of a trumpet instead of a simple "ah," she had to bury her smile in Sebastian's head, pretending she was pressing kisses. William's unfettered joy in all things was a delight to watch, and it was thanks to the boys. He'd been born solemn, and they had brought him a sense of freedom and playfulness.

Dr. Redding was neither young nor old, with dark hair graying at the temples and a face of soft lines that deepened when he smiled, which he did along with the boys. He'd been the Thornwoods' doctor since she'd been there, and his father had been their doctor prior to that. He'd seen her through both births and been attentive during her recovery after Sebastian's painful entry into the world. He was kindness personified, and she was grateful to have his steady presence in her life over the years.

When he was done with the boys, he handed each a lemon drop and gave them permission to leave. Which they did with great haste. He took Sebastian from her arms, brought him over to his crib, and set him on his back. Sebastian kicked playfully, grabbing Dr. Redding's hands and trying to swing them. From the day he'd arrived, he'd been a cheerful baby. He babbled happily as Dr. Redding examined him, but very few words were discernible. It continued to worry Elizabeth. William had had an extensive vocabulary by Sebastian's age. She voiced her concerns to Dr. Redding when he was through with his examination.

"I see no issue at all," Dr. Redding said. "He is thriving. You must remember he came into this world early and with a good deal of struggle. It is a marvel he survived. Give him a few months to catch up to William's pace and he'll be out the gate like that new pony William can't stop talking about."

Hannah stayed with Sebastian, and Elizabeth and Dr. Redding left the nursery.

"You have done wonders for those two waifs, although I can hardly call them that now, can I? They are hale and healthy, with exquisite manners. It bodes well for your orphanage that you can perform such wonders. But it seems miracles are your forte, aren't they?"

"I don't understand."

"Well," he said, smiling kindly. "Sebastian's life is not the only miracle of survival in this house, now is it?"

Elizabeth cheeks warmed with a blush. She'd never considered her recovery a miracle. It was an experience endured, a mountain climbed. "Do you truly think I might never conceive again?" she asked as they entered the great hall. He'd told her that when she'd grown healthier, but she'd never told Richard, hoping to prove the doctor wrong.

He paused and studied her for a moment. "I am not God, so I cannot say for certain. But if I were a betting man, I would say no, it is extremely unlikely. And forgive me for speaking so boldly, but since it has been almost two years since Sebastian made his debut, the proof is in the pudding. Or lack of pudding," he said, chuckling at his own joke.

She smiled indulgently. Although the subject did not sit humorously with her, she could not begrudge the levity he always tried to bring to situations.

"As I told Lord Thornwood, it is not just a matter that you can't get with child. You *should* not get with child. Be happy with those two boys of yours. They are more than enough."

Elizabeth thanked Dr. Redding and watched him descend into the courtyard. She waved to him as he guided the horse drawing the gig toward the west gate and the drive that led to the main road. She listened to the clopping of hooves until she could hear it no more, standing dazed as though he'd taken her energy with him.

As I told Lord Thornwood. Richard *knew* she could not conceive. Had known all along. His dreams of a house full of children had long been crushed. It explained his distance, his disappointment in their marriage. His aversion to physical intimacy. What need did he have of an empty vessel? There was no hope for them. None at all. She could not fulfill the promise she'd made. She was not simply a broodmare put out to pasture. She was a mare who would never have foal again.

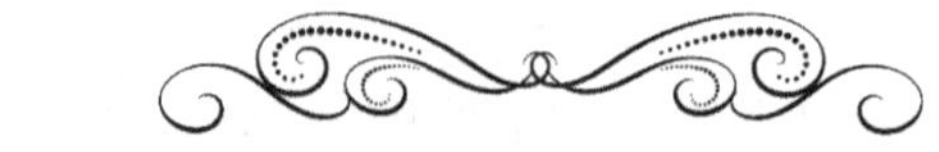

CHAPTER THIRTY-EIGHT

But since the affairs of men rest still incertain,
Let's reason with the worst that may befall.

—William Shakespeare, *Julius Caesar*

"I BEG YOUR pardon?" Richard asked, although he did not need to hear Sophia repeat her statement. He'd heard it loud and clear, but his aching head was wrestling with the fact that she was spot on.

"There is no need to pretend with me. Patricia Paisley." Sophia held up a finger. "Works for Mrs. Tate." Up went another finger. "Has been passing information to you." Rather than raising a third finger, she pointed at him. "What I don't know is her relationship to you and the depth of your involvement with her."

Richard pushed his tea aside and got up. "I need a drink."

He strode to the side table and uncorked the crystal decanter. He needed a few minutes to gather his wits. How could Sophia possibly know all those things? He poured a cognac and hesitated. He might not be the only one in need of a bracer. He looked over his shoulder. "And you?"

Sophia nodded but didn't say anything. Her demeanor demanded a response to her question, but he'd given her enough of his secrets today. He wasn't going to share the reason Patricia had solicited his assistance. Elizabeth would never believe his innocence if she knew of their prior relationship. Not that he wanted her to be convinced of his innocence. Did he? Wouldn't a clear conscience bring some peace? *Devil confound it*, he wasn't thinking straight. He needed Elizabeth to believe in his culpability, not grant him clemency.

He strode back to the table, placed the brandy in front of Sophia, and took his seat. "I don't know why I was the chosen one," he said, holding her stare.

Although it would ensure Elizabeth never came near him again, he could not bring himself to tell her Patricia had once been his mistress. If Elizabeth had to know that information, it would come from him. He hoped he could avoid causing her unnecessary pain.

"May I ask how you know about all this?" He circled his hand in the air as though he was harnessing the events of the past two months and pulling them down for her to see.

"I know much about many things," she said cryptically. "And about many people." She took a delicate sip of the cognac before going on. "I also know the woman has been kidnapped."

Richard almost spit out his brandy. Instead, he swallowed it roughly and studied Sophia as he choked. She remained impassive. As the coughing subsided, he continued to stare at her, his pulse pounding from more than his headache. "How the devil do you know that?" he finally asked.

"You forget the broad company I keep. It is easy to find out what I need to know. Men are...how do you say?" She looked to the ceiling as though the answer was there. She shook her head, wrinkling her nose. "They are naive. Easily convinced to give their secrets away."

Like he had done. He'd spilled his heartache at the first sign of a sympathetic ear. He was a fool, but his pain was hardly on the level of government secrets.

"And what are you going to do about her, this...this...*la prostituta*?" she asked before he could pursue who these men were who so easily divulged such information.

"Why should I do anything about her disappearance?"

"I have known you for almost ten years, and I know you to be a man of honor. If you have had dealings with this woman, you would see her safe, no?"

"How do I know she has not vanished of her own free will?" He rubbed his temples. That was what had been bothering him as he waited for instructions on how best to approach the situation. He had no way of knowing if anything untoward had truly happened to her. It was one man's word. He wished Walford were in the city. He had access to more information than Richard.

"You doubt she has?"

"I encouraged her to disappear," he said. "I gave her money to ensure she would."

She arched an eyebrow but didn't comment about the payment. "There has been a note," she said instead.

He leaned forward in his chair. "Have you seen it?"

Sophia shook her head. "But I have no reason to doubt its authenticity. Do you?"

There was the rub. He didn't, but he was wary. He told Sophia as much.

"It is good to be cautious, but if it is true, she is in grave danger, no?"

His skin prickled. Patricia had seemed genuine in her desire for a fresh start. He'd not like to see any ill befall her. "I've heard nothing from the man who told me of this. I've been waiting for his instructions," he told her truthfully.

"I know," Sophia said. "It is why I am here. Mr. Miller has asked me to help out. Since it involves you, I have agreed."

"Miller? How do you know Miller?" There was no way the man ran in Sophia's social circle, of that he was certain.

Sophia smiled slightly. "Ah, a man may explain himself to you, but I will not. Women are far better at keeping secrets." She grew serious again. "Besides, it is irrelevant. You need a plan, and I have one. I am hosting a masquerade at Château Nouveau. Mr.

Miller will arrange for the exchange to happen there."

"Why not somewhere in London?"

"Too easy for the culprit to slip away. It is much harder in the country. Mr. Miller assures me the Home Office will have men stationed, and the costumes will hide them. It is a good plan, no?"

Richard pinched the bridge of his nose, trying to process everything. Sophia's knowledge, her participation as intermediary, Patricia's jeopardy, his role in all of it. Lord, but he wanted to be free of the mess. But he knew he could not walk away.

"What do they want me to do?" he asked.

Sophia set her glass on the table and sat back. "They want you to bring the money. To be the person who does the exchange."

"Why me?"

"Because the woman may be double-crossing you and will trust you to follow through. She might run if it were someone else. Because whether you are aware of it or not, the spy she has been working with has come to know you too. It might be him and not the woman. Even if it is not, they assume he has been watching you to see if you know where the woman is. And he will follow you to the masquerade. It is not the woman they care about. They are trying to smoke out the real spy."

"*Bloody hell*," he said and immediately apologized. "So you want me to bring money. How much?"

"No," she said, shaking her head. "That is what *they* said. *I* want you to come to the masquerade. No money. It will only cause trouble."

"But what about Patricia?"

"They will have their men there. The girl will be safe." She waved her hand dismissively. "There is no need to bring money. We keep it simple. *Non complicato*. We will, how you say, make a show as though you do."

"I will not risk a woman's life over money," Richard said. He was weary of conspiring, but he'd not be the cause of harm to Patricia or anyone.

Sophia smiled. "*Mio amico*, you truly are the man I knew you were. And I remain the woman you know. I would not risk her either. She would not be in danger at my masquerade, but I will admit that I, too, am wary. Something is…eh…*non proprio giusto.*"

Richard's skin tingled. If Sophia sensed something was not quite right, then his instincts might be correct. But what was he to do? He was damned if he did and damned if he didn't.

"It is why I offered Château Nouveau. I, too, will have men there. And so will you. I have asked Nicholas to be your second in this. He will be by your side."

They discussed the details, and Richard tried again to probe Sophia for answers. She stubbornly refused to explain how she'd come to be involved in this affair in the first place. Could it be her situation was no different from his and she'd been solicited? Regardless, her planning was thorough, and he had no choice but to go along with it.

"I will see you in two weeks," Sophia said, getting to her feet.

Richard stood too.

"Maybe we will be lucky and end this quickly. Then you could have a little fun, no?"

Richard's heart rate accelerated, pounding relentlessly in his head. He'd momentarily forgotten about Elizabeth. "Sophia, tell me you did not invite Elizabeth to the masquerade."

"If I did, I would be lying," she said. "Don't look so distressed. She declined." Her eyes narrowed, and she pursed her lips before speaking again. "I would see her there, happy and dancing, but it seems she prefers to pine for you."

She shrugged as though she could not comprehend why Elizabeth would long for him. Of course, he could not fault Sophia for it. He couldn't understand why Elizabeth did either, if indeed that was the truth.

"It is in your power to make things right. But that is an argument for another day." Sophia picked up her reticule and slipped it on her arm.

Richard walked around the table and took her hand. "Please

don't tell her I will be there. I'll not have her in danger, and I'll not see her hurt, knowing I have come so close to Thornwood Manor and not come home."

Sophia leaned forward and kissed each of his cheeks. "I will keep all your secrets, *mio amico*." She stepped back. "For now."

He saw her out and returned to the study, pouring another brandy and dropping into the more comfortable chair by the fire. He could not fathom how Sophia had become embroiled in this mess, but he was oddly grateful. There was comfort in knowing if something happened, someone knew the truth of it all. And that someone was a trusted confidante of Elizabeth's. Sophia would make sure Elizabeth knew he had not abandoned her in his heart. That he'd never been unfaithful. That he'd never meant to hurt her. That he had never stopped loving her.

CHAPTER THIRTY-NINE

My drops of tears
I'll turn to sparks of fire.

—Shakespeare, *Henry VIII*

ELIZABETH WATCHED HANNAH as she led the boys down the road toward the general store. They'd been such bright lights in her days Elizabeth had decided they deserved a treat. She would join them, but first she must speak with Parson Brown about the orphanage. There had been several respondents to her posting at the servant registry office, and she'd like him to participate in choosing the best candidates.

Mrs. Elder opened the door when Elizabeth arrived, looking none too happy to see her. "Lady Thornwood." Her polite tone was in utter contrast to her expression. "We were not expecting you. I'm afraid I am on my way out."

"That's fine. I won't be staying long," Elizabeth said and waited expectantly.

Mrs. Elder sighed audibly and invited Elizabeth in. "I will let the parson know you are here."

Elizabeth could not comprehend why Parson Brown suffered the woman's insolence. There must be others who would have a more suitable disposition for the job.

"Lady Thornwood," Parson Brown said as he entered the

hallway. "What a pleasure it is to see you. My apologies for keeping you waiting. Come, come."

She followed him to the front parlor, where he had evidently been at work. Papers were scattered on the table, and a pen freshly dipped in ink bled onto the corner of one of them.

"It is I who should apologize for not letting you know I'd come by," she said, thrusting her chin toward the table.

"Nonsense and stuff," he said affably. "You are always welcome." He waved toward the table. "Working on a sermon. Nothing I cannot set aside. Let us sit."

Elizabeth sat on the chair he indicated, and the parson sat across from her. "I would offer you tea, but…" He let the sentence drift and scrunched his lips ruefully.

"Mrs. Elder made it clear she was on her way out. I'll be but a minute."

"I must apologize once again." He shook his head. "Mrs. Elder can be far too blunt sometimes."

"May I ask why you keep her on?" Elizabeth knew it was far too personal a question, but she was genuinely curious.

"Loyalty, I suppose. And faith. The subjects of the sermon I'm working on. Her husband was a childhood friend. Sadly he left this world too soon. Unfortunately, he was remiss and did not provide for her. For both their sakes, I took her in. For him I keep her on." He grinned.

"Where does faith come into it?"

"Faith? Well, does that not come into every relationship? One must have faith that people will eventually come around to be the best humans they can be. That everyone is good at heart. Even when behavior does not match my expectations, faith compels me to continue to look deeper into every individual to see the world as they see it, to nurture and nourish their better side. Faith is not the sole realm of God. Maintaining it is part of man's work on earth. And woman's," he added with a smile. "I believe you have helped me find direction with my sermon. I do hope I remember it when you've left." He chuckled. "Now, what can I do for you this fine day, Lady Thornwood?"

Parson Brown promised to review the applicants and deemed it would be a pleasure to help with any interviews. He assured her of his assistance in all things. Elizabeth left, grateful to have such a stalwart man anchoring their small corner of the world. His words tumbled around in her head as she strolled to the store. Loyalty and faith. Should she not show both to her husband? Was it not the duty of a wife? Was duty all there was to a marriage?

Mrs. Elder stepped from the doorway of the store, followed closely by Mrs. Reeves and Mrs. Neal. Mrs. Elder dipped her chin curtly and moved aside on the veranda. The other two women were more polite, greeting her and welcoming her back before sidling over to Mrs. Elder.

The boys were in the far corner, sitting on some barrels, sucking on sticks of candy. There were no other customers in the store, and Mr. Morton was nowhere in sight.

"I don't know how that woman can hold her head so high," Mrs. Elder said as the door closed behind Elizabeth. "The mighty hath fallen, yet she dares to look down her nose at me."

Elizabeth stood rooted to the spot. Another woman muttered something, but Elizabeth could not make out the words. Mrs. Elder's voice, on the other hand, was perfectly clear.

"I have it on good authority he keeps a woman in the city. And since he is never here, it is clear which woman he prefers, isn't it?"

Her words cut through the glass and landed, as intended, like a knife in Elizabeth's heart. Hurt and anger churned in her stomach, and she took several calming breaths. She could go out there and put the woman in her place, shame her publicly, but what good would it do? She would make a scene, and a fool of herself, since the woman only spoke the truth. A truth she had run from but that apparently had followed her. If Mrs. Elder knew about Richard's activities, the whole village did.

"Can I help you, Lady Thornwood?" Mr. Morton's jovial voice boomed through the room as he stepped to the counter.

"No, thank you," she said quietly, wishing he could. Wishing someone could turn her world upright again. "I'm here to collect the boys."

Elizabeth called the boys to her, and they merrily bounced over, with Hannah carrying Sebastian. She stiffened her shoulders before turning and exiting the store. She'd not let Mrs. Elder see she had caused any hurt. Elizabeth was relieved to see Simon waiting with the carriage. Without a glance in the women's direction, they piled into the carriage.

She usually enjoyed the boys' boisterous conversations, but she found them exhausting on the way home. Her face was stiff from her attempts to smile, and as they rode along the drive, she counted the minutes to when Hannah would take them to the nursery. They pulled into the courtyard, and the boys leaped out, with Hannah and Sebastian following them a little more slowly. Elizabeth was tempted to tap the roof and ride away, to tell Simon to keep going until the horses could go no further.

She slid across the seat, took Gordon's hand, and stepped into the courtyard, and her heart immediately lightened.

"Has she been here long?" she asked Gordon.

"About a quarter of an hour, my lady."

Elizabeth rushed past Sophia's carriage and up the steps, where Hastings was waiting for her in the entranceway. She tugged at the ribbon of her bonnet. "Where is she?"

"I have taken the liberty of ordering tea for the small drawing room, my lady." He took her hat. "Far away from the boys," he added with a slight smile.

"Thank you, Hastings. You are a wonder." She left him in the entranceway and scooted through the corridor, past the breakfast room, to the small drawing room. She paused in the doorway and smiled. Sophia, looking voluptuous in a daring green silk gown, was far too overdressed for an afternoon call. Elizabeth adored her audacious confidence.

"*Bella*," Sophia said, looking up and meeting Elizabeth's gaze. "I feared you were never coming home."

Elizabeth laughed. "Gordon told me how long you've been here, you fraud."

Sophia shrugged innocently. "It seemed so very long," she said, smiling.

"As has your absence, my friend. I missed you dearly." Elizabeth walked to Sophia and kissed each cheek before taking a seat beside her on the settee. "How was London?"

"It is dark and dreary and no place for me right now. It is getting busier. All the mamas coming with their babies." Sophia shuddered theatrically. "I do not enjoy watching them shop their daughters around like a peddler's wares." She leaned in closer. "And I do not like how old I look beside them."

"There is no one who can compete with you," Elizabeth said, although she knew Sophia was not remotely interested in competing in the marriage market. "Your beauty is timeless." It was no exaggeration. Sophia was stunning. Eyes as dark as her hair, a smile so white it seemed impossible, she had a body that was a siren song calling all men. More importantly, a warm vitality radiated from within, making Sophia the most beautiful woman Elizabeth had ever met.

"Ah, *mia cara donna*, this is why you are my best friend." She leaned back against the settee. "You are blind to my faults."

They both laughed but grew quiet as the tea service was brought in and prepared. "Did you accomplish what you needed to do in London?" Elizabeth asked when the door closed behind Hastings.

"I did. Everything is in order, so now it is time for fun." Sophia frowned. "I did not see a response from you on my list. You will come to my masquerade, no?"

Elizabeth was about to decline. *It is clear which woman he prefers, isn't it?* Mrs. Elder's biting remarks still stung. She considered telling Sophia about the encounter but quickly decided against it. She would get sympathy and comfort, but she'd had more than enough of commiserations. No, it was time to stop wallowing in her grief and accept the things she could not change.

"I would love to come to your masquerade."

Sophia squealed and hugged her tight. She released Elizabeth and clapped her hands. "You have made me very happy. I think you will be made very happy too. Find some *amore*."

"How can you even suggest such a thing?" Elizabeth asked, although she was certain Sophia was teasing.

"But if you are…what is it you say? A horse in a field, *mia amica*. If it is true, you have some rights. You have given two heirs. You need not rob yourself of attention."

Sophia wasn't teasing. Elizabeth shook her head in disbelief. "Are you suggesting I seek another man's company?"

Sophia sipped her tea, wagging her eyebrows up and down. It would be comical if it were not attached to such a shocking proposition.

"You know I would not, could not, do that."

"Why, *bella*? What is good for the gander is good for the goose, no?"

Leave it to Sophia to put Richard's perfidy out on the table for discussion. "Well, let's skip all the moral reasons, since you are correct: Richard seems to have done that. But he does not risk getting with child."

"Ah, a practical woman. It is a fair argument. But there are ways to ensure it does not happen. You have not seen me grow round, *mia amica*."

"You have…you stop…you?" Elizabeth could not formulate a question. She knew Sophia entertained men—it was a luxury of widowhood—but she'd never contemplated her lack of conception.

Sophia put her cup on the table and sat back. "I have never wanted children. I never will. I make no apologies for it."

"Of course not," Elizabeth said, finally coming to her senses. "You owe me no explanations."

"No, I do not. And I won't give one, because I have none to give. It is not something I crave. Although, I do enjoy your boys, the thought of any of my own…" Sophia scrunched her face in disgust, visibly shivering, and Elizabeth laughed.

"So, *bella*, you can have your *amore*."

"I don't want—"

Sophia held up her hand. "One does not always choose if the arrow strikes the heart," she said. "Or when. To be prepared will bring no harm. To not be prepared…" She let the sentence drift.

They switched to sherry as Sophia divulged her secrets, talking of barrier devices and pessaries.

"If you soak the sponge in brandy, it is even better. You become a tasty snack," Sophia said, smiling wickedly.

Elizabeth could hold her laughter back no longer, and Sophia joined in.

"It is valuable information, Sophia, but it is wasted on me," Elizabeth said when their laughter subsided, wiping at the tears in her eyes.

"But you will come to the masquerade?"

"I will if I can come up with a costume," Elizabeth said, putting another obstacle in the way despite her promise to attend.

"Ah, but I have already thought of everything and have brought you the material to make it so. You will be virtue. Lady Virtue," she said triumphantly.

"Considering our conversation the past hour, you would have me be Virtue Fallen," Elizabeth said.

"*Perfetta!*" Sophia clapped her hands excitedly.

Elizabeth couldn't, could she? Be so daring? So bold? Invite a liaison? *It is clear which woman he prefers, isn't it?* Even with that reminder ringing in her head, she didn't think she could, but she was going to the masquerade. She would dance and enjoy some company, at least for one evening. If somewhere down the road she changed her mind and did find another, it would only be her body engaged. Her heart was forever closed.

CHAPTER FORTY

*I have heard it
said, the fittest time to corrupt a man's wife is
when she's fallen out with her husband.*

—Shakespeare, *Coriolanus*

RICHARD TOOK HIS breakfast in a private room at the coaching inn. He'd spent a restless night upstairs. Knowing how close he was to Elizabeth had not helped matters. It seemed ridiculous not to sleep in his own home, which was near Sophia's, but he'd not wanted to alert Elizabeth to his presence. How could he possibly explain it even were she willing to listen?

He looked forward to Walford joining him, which should be sometime early afternoon. He'd had no contact from Miller, nor had Richard attempted to reach out to the man. As far as he was concerned, the burden was on the Home Office and Miller to work out their part of this operation. Walford and Richard would go along with Sophia's plan, one that would, hopefully, finally end this insanity and let him get back to his life.

His life. What would it look like now? He'd tasted the life he wanted and let it slip from his grasp. Sophia had dismissed his concerns, but he could not. Knowing Elizabeth remained on this earth must be enough. He hoped, with time, he could manage his hunger for her. It was said as a man grew older, his interest waned. Richard ran a hand through his hair. He was not yet thirty. It was going to be a long wait.

Richard headed to the stables and took Horatio out for a ride. He rode the hour to the edge of his estate, staring at the drive, wishing he could take it. Return home to the life that had ended two years ago. He thought ruefully of the proverb, *If wishes were horses, beggars would ride.* Richard turned Horatio, urging him into a gallop.

Horatio seemed as anxious as Richard to run from Thornwood Manor, and they covered the return to the inn far more quickly than he would have considered possible. He left the stallion with the groom and crossed the courtyard back to the inn. There was a definite increase in traffic, with an equal number of marked and unmarked carriages. It was far too early in the year for an exodus from the city. The social season was only beginning to get into full swing. Sophia's masquerade was obviously a not-to-be-missed event. Not for the first time, he questioned her magnetic draw and the extent of her influence.

"Lord Walford awaits you in your rooms, my lord." Mr. Bolton thrust his chin toward the stairs. "He insisted it would be fine with you."

Richard took the stairs two at a time and threw open the door to the small sitting room. Walford turned from the window and grinned, a glass of sherry in hand. "It's a bit like the old days back in Eton, don't you agree?"

"The room or the impending deed?" Richard asked, tossing his hat on a table and shrugging out of his coat.

"Well, the room is as appealing as the one at school, but it is the adventure ahead I reference. We had our share, didn't we?"

"We did," Richard said, pouring himself a glass. He dropped onto an overly worn but comfortable chair. "But I do wish to be done with this particular adventure."

"I thought you were through with it," Walford said, taking the chair across from him. "Tell me about it. Sophia's note was cryptic. Out of necessity, I assume."

Richard shared his meetings with both Miller and Sophia, and Walford expressed the same surprise about Sophia's involvement.

"She wouldn't divulge how she came to her knowledge about Patricia or why she felt compelled to help out. But she's not convinced everything is at it seems, and that is where you come in. She didn't want me to be on my own."

"Smart woman," Walford said and leaned forward in his chair. "We must resolve this tonight, Thornwood. Catherine is too close to delivery, and I'll not leave her again."

Images flashed quickly through Richard's mind. The night they'd snuck away from the party and Elizabeth had told him she was finally with child. The morning he'd watched as William had suckled for the first time. He'd been moved to tears. Her clever announcement of Sebastian's impending arrival—a note tucked under his morning eggs. Dark memories quickly rushed in, blacking out the good, and Richard cleared his throat as he shoved them far back into a corner of his mind.

"And I'll not ask you to. You must be at her side. Besides," Richard said, running a hand through his hair, "regardless of what happens tonight, I must be done with it all. My business, parliament, the estate, they've all been neglected for too long." He did not explain it was not solely the fault of the espionage but also his continued preoccupation with Elizabeth. He needed to put everything firmly aside and attend to business.

A tap at the door drew their attention, and Richard bade the person come in.

Mr. Bolton opened the door. "Packages for you, my lord." He stood aside, and several footmen entered, depositing the paper-wrapped goods onto the settee. "The coach driver is having his dinner downstairs and has asked me to inform you he will be leaving at eight o'clock."

Walford cocked an eyebrow at Richard as the door closed.

"An unmarked carriage and"—Richard gestured toward the settee—"our costumes. Sophia has always been a master at detail." Richard chuckled humorlessly. "Now, Walford. To our plans." Richard refreshed their sherries, and they reviewed their strategy.

Afterward, when Walford went to arrange for his horse to be brought later to Sophia's so he might return directly to Woodfield Park, Richard stood at the window and watched him cross the courtyard. A small part of him fought envy. There was such joy ahead for Walford. But the larger part of him felt concern and an overwhelming sense of melancholy. The concern was for his friends, that it might not turn out as they dreamed. And the oppressive sadness? For himself. For Elizabeth. For the boys. That he could not be the man she needed, that they needed. He sighed heavily. Time enough to dwell on it all. Tonight he needed his wits about him.

"YOU CANNOT BE serious!" Elizabeth backed away from the dress. Well, she could hardly call it a dress, since those consisted of actual material.

"*Bella*, you will make the men froth at the mouth like stallions." Sophia held the dress in front of herself and swayed her hips back and forth, the strips of black silk swinging freely, exposing the deliberate, strategically placed rents in the white silk gown.

"My stockings will show if I move too quickly," Elizabeth pointed out.

"If you move too quickly, more than your stockings may show." Sophia smiled naughtily and held the dress out toward Elizabeth. "Come. Take it. Be brave, *mia amica*."

Sophia had gleefully designed Elizabeth's costume, enjoying taunting her by disguising her as Lady Virtue. The white mask, now blankly staring at her from her bed, was tailored to cover her entire face. The track of a single black tear contradicted its set smile. Her distinctive hair was to be cloaked by a cap of black-

and-white plumes.

Elizabeth reluctantly slipped off her robe and took the dress. Sophia stepped forward and helped tug it down, the bodice snug against her torso. She took a few steps, and the ribbons fluttered, exposing her legs. "I cannot wear this. It is indecent."

"Ah, *bella*, it is mild compared to some of the costumes you shall see."

Elizabeth turned to Sophia and narrowed her eyes. "What kind of a ball are you hosting, Sophia?"

"It's a masquerade. It is meant to be risqué. You are meant to be daring." She scooped Elizabeth's arm with her own and leaned in close. "You will have your mask. No one will know who you are. Have some fun, *mia amica*. Be free." She pulled Elizabeth to the mirror. "You are beautiful, no?"

Elizabeth gasped and stared at herself. She'd thought some of her new dresses were too bold. This one was beyond audacious, the white silk cut so low she wasn't sure it would contain her breasts.

"Ooh la la!" Sophia exclaimed as Elizabeth pulled at the fabric, trying to cover herself more fully.

"I cannot…," she sputtered, tugging to no avail.

Sophia tsk-tsked, walked over to the pile of cloth on the bed, and pulled out a swatch of sheer black fabric before returning to Elizabeth's side.

"You English are such prudes." Sophia softened her chastisement with a smile. "It is a masquerade, *bella*, not a debutante's ball. You could wear it. You *could* wear anything you want…or not wear anything you want," she said teasingly. "But you will not." She sighed dramatically and tucked the delicate gauze around Elizabeth's neckline, creating a skimpy fichu. "There, my prim English friend. Keep your secrets hidden."

Sophia leaned in and kissed Elizabeth's cheek, making her feel very young and inexperienced.

"Now I must go and see that everything is as it should be. I will see you tonight. You will not disappoint me, Elizabeth."

Sophia rarely used her Christian name, and the gentleness in her eyes as she made her demand made Elizabeth's eyes tear. She shook her head.

"*Mia dolce innocente*," Sophia said quietly. "You will be safe. I will see to it." She sashayed across the room. "I have left a special package for you. *Addio bellezza*."

Elizabeth stared at herself in the mirror. Was she truly the innocent Sophia called her? How could that be at her age? Only three years until she was thirty. How long before she was no longer attractive? She'd had curves like Sophia when she'd been pregnant, but she'd lost them with illness. Would she become a gaunt matron, watching from the sidelines as the children grew into men? When would wisps of gray mute the spun gold? Would her eyes grow milky blue with age? If Richard did not care for her now, what possible hope was there of gaining his esteem as the years slipped by?

She groaned and turned from the mirror. He'd made clear his lack of interest in her. When would she stop wanting him? She stared at the mask. A single tear. Elizabeth was tired of crying. She would not disappoint Sophia. She would not let herself down.

She grabbed the package Sophia had left on the side table and sat on the bed. She tugged at the string on the bundle, unfolded the paper, and stared at the contents. Sponges and vials of liquids. Elizabeth knew instantly what they were for. Dear Lord, was this what Sophia meant by keeping her safe? What had she gotten herself into?

CHAPTER FORTY-ONE

I stood
Among them, but not of them; in a shroud
Of thoughts which were not their thoughts.

—Byron, *Childe Harold's Pilgrimage*

ELIZABETH HAD BEEN sitting in the line of carriages for almost half an hour. She was tempted to peek out, but she was afraid she might see a familiar face. And it seemed silly to wear her mask while sitting here all alone. Sophia had arranged for an unmarked carriage so Elizabeth might remain anonymous—and nameless she definitely wanted to be. She would be a fly upon the wall this evening, despite Sophia's ludicrous encouragement toward an affair. Elizabeth wanted only the amusement of watching one of Sophia's wild gatherings in action.

She tapped on the seat, then consciously stilled her fingers. She must find patience to sit and wait. It was a virtue, after all. Of course, Sophia wished her to be Virtue Fallen tonight. It seemed she was already melding into the role, since she had little tolerance for the wait.

Elizabeth smoothed her far-too-revealing gown. The single lantern shone on the folds of silk, shimmering white in the darkened coach. She poked at the sheer ebony, ensuring it was firmly tucked into the neckline. She had no desire to spill out unexpectedly. Sudden panic surged. What was she doing here?

Sophia was widowed, was indecently wealthy, and cared not a whit what anyone thought of her. She could do as she pleased. Doubt filled the cabin, almost a visible entity swirling around, threatening to smother her. Who was Elizabeth to think she could be here, should be here tonight? She was a married woman. A countess. Her sigh filled the space, and her spirit sank further. A singularly lonely countess. Without her earl. Still, she could not do this. It was, perhaps, no coincidence this was All Fools' Day. For she was behaving like one. She should get Simon to pull out of line and turn the coach around. Go home. Accept her lot in life.

The door opened unexpectedly, and Elizabeth bit back a gasp.

"My lady?" Simon's voice was quiet, questioning.

He was a loyal servant, insisting he drive the carriage, not the man Sophia had sent. He'd not balked at her attire. Although he'd not seen it fully, as she'd covered herself with a cape when she'd left the house, it must have been evident this was not her usual state of dress. While waiting, she'd slipped off the cape, and he was getting a good look at it now. Her cheeks warmed with embarrassment.

"My lady," he repeated, holding out his hand. He did not reference her by name, and she was thankful for his discretion.

She should ask him to take her home. Return to Thornwood Manor. Walk the halls for another night. Stare into the fire until she was weary. Go to bed. Alone. Elizabeth took a deep breath, placed her hand in his, and put her satin-slippered foot on the step.

"My lady," he hissed emphatically, "your mask!"

Elizabeth withdrew instantly, falling back on the seat, her heart beating ferociously. She truly was a fool! How pathetically unseasoned. She'd almost revealed herself. She muttered to herself, trying to calm her already edgy nerves. She could do this. Before her hesitation could drive her to return home, she grabbed her mask and tied it under the plumes. She checked to ensure it was secure, tilting her head this way and that. When she was through, she flew out of the coach, barely touching Simon's waiting hand as she set foot upon the ground.

Simon's brow furrowed in concern, but he said nothing.

"I know I am quite out of my waters, Simon, but Lady Tessaro will ensure I am not left alone." She turned to join the stream of people flowing to the mansion.

"My lady?"

She turned back toward him.

"At the risk of being too forward, may I suggest I have the coach ready before midnight?"

"But, Simon, I do not know when I might tire of this evening's festivities. I'd not have you waiting at the ready for hours. I'll have one of Sophia's men inform you of when I am ready to return."

She made to move again, but his expression was so pained she couldn't lift a foot. He looked to the ground.

"Simon? What is it?"

"Midnight, my lady," he said, too quiet for any passerby to hear him. "They reveal themselves at midnight."

She stiffened. *Reveal themselves?* If she stayed to midnight, she would have to remove her mask? Simon had known, and she had not. What else did she not know about the evening ahead? Why had she not asked Sophia about all the intricacies of a masquerade?

"Simon, you are correct as usual. I forget myself. Please be ready well before twelve." She turned away before Simon could somehow see the trepidation racing through her mind.

Elizabeth joined the crowd, adrift in the crush that flowed up the steps. The lack of an escort was equal parts disconcerting and liberating, the thrill of the latter buoying her spirit. She wondered if it was what Sophia enjoyed about widowhood. The heady power of independence.

The grand foyer was much brighter than outside, and Elizabeth felt uncomfortably exposed. She looked around at the paintings lining the walls, at the carved detail of the ornate cornice, anywhere but at the people who surrounded her. There was a shout to her left. She turned toward it but was jostled unexpectedly from the other side. She lost her footing, squeaked, and fell backward. It was mere seconds, but it seemed like a moment frozen in time, when strong hands clasped her arms and pulled her tight.

Elizabeth registered the solid wall of a man's chest at the same time embarrassment infused her face. Her countenance must be splotched with the heat. She pulled one arm free to touch her burning cheek and connected awkwardly with the mask. She tried to fully pull away only to find her rescuer was now her captor. His grip on her arms was gentle but firm.

"My lady." His voice was a husky whisper. "No need to fear me."

His breath caressed her ear, and goose bumps raced across her skin in response. The man's heat enveloped her. She'd grown chilled in the cool April air, and his warmth was almost welcome. A shiver ran a path down her spine. She tried to turn to see him.

"No." It was a command, not a request. "Let me hold you until you are fully recovered." He inhaled slowly as he traced a path from her earlobe to the base of her neck. Her skin tingled along the trail.

Elizabeth did not like her response to this man at all. "Sir!" She pulled away and rotated to face him.

He was dressed as a domino, cloaked in black. His face was covered with a mask, its beak almost striking her nose as she turned. He didn't say a word as she stared at him. Between his mask and the dark cavern created by his hood, she could not see his eyes. She sensed his returning gaze. Did he think her rude? Ungrateful for saving her from a fall?

"I would be your protector this evening, should you wish it." His voice was quiet behind the mask, and with the noise of the crowd, she wasn't sure she'd heard him correctly. He repeated himself and was clearly waiting for a response.

"I've no need of a protector," she stated with a calm that was pure facade. She took a deep, steadying breath. The man smelled like…Sophia! He must be one of her *amanti*. Had Sophia assigned him the task of taking care of her?

He tilted his head as though he was considering her. "An escort, then. To see you safely onto the dance floor."

Safely. Surely his use of that word was not a coincidence? This was what Sophia meant when she'd said she would see her safe. Elizabeth should have known Sophia would not leave her floundering alone. She was too good and caring a friend.

Elizabeth decided it could do no harm for the domino to escort her into the ballroom. It was not as though he would be ushering her into a dark hall or a back room. As unsteady as she was feeling, a firm arm ensuring she did not trip again would not go amiss. "Yes. That is fine. An escort to the ballroom."

"As you wish," he said, bowing. He clasped her gloved hand in his and pressed a faux kiss above it.

Those words. Such a simple conditioned response on his part. If life had unfolded as she wished, she would not be here tonight.

He presented his arm, and she placed her hand upon it. Together they waited in line to enter the ballroom. Neither of them spoke. Sophia stood regally at the far side of the foyer, greeting her guests. Even from a distance, her costume made Elizabeth's seem tame. Dressed as a man, with her hair down in a queue draped over one shoulder and only a corset under her jacket—supporting and displaying her ample breasts—Sophia was anything but masculine. Her shapely hips and legs were outlined in her snug knee-length trousers, and her stockings were the sheerest Elizabeth had ever seen. And no mask for Sophia. Elizabeth envied her boldness, her lack of care for society's esteem.

Eventually they stood before Sophia. Elizabeth smirked beneath her mask at the surprise on her face. It was clear Sophia believed Elizabeth would have forfeited the masquerade. That she had no courage whatsoever. Well, it was a pleasure to prove her wrong. She'd have to tease her about it tomorrow.

"My Lady Virtue." Sophia's voice was neutral and void of recognition. "And?" She looked pointedly at the man by Elizabeth's side.

"Monsieur Réclamation." He bowed, taking Sophia's hand and miming a kiss over her glove.

Sophia laughed at his introduction, and Elizabeth felt as though she had missed a joke. Sophia looked from Elizabeth to the domino and back again, several times. Elizabeth did not doubt Sophia was as taken aback by the fact that Elizabeth had accepted the man's offer of accompaniment as much as she was surprised by Elizabeth following through and attending the masquerade. Sophia would assume Elizabeth wouldn't know she'd put the man up to it and would be too cowardly to allow him to escort her. Well, she had proven Sophia wrong. Twice. She could hardly wait to rub it in tomorrow.

"My Lady Virtue. Monsieur Réclamation. Please." Sophia gestured toward the ballroom behind her. "Enjoy the evening." Her small smile blossomed to a full grin before she turned to the next guests.

Elizabeth hesitated. Sophia's grin had been unmistakably lecherous. After she teased her in the morning, Elizabeth would need to explain that she'd quickly surmised Sophia was behind the domino's offer. She'd not leave Sophia believing he had caught her interest. The man placed her hand on his arm, turning them to face the ballroom. He patted her hand paternally, and it allayed any unease she had that he, too, might misconstrue her reasons for letting him lead her to the floor.

Slowly, in unison, they entered a carousel of the spectacular.

"*Hell and the devil.*"

"What is it?" Walford asked, leaning over to look out the

coach window.

Richard did not realize he'd said it out loud, but he might as well explain himself. Walford would find out anyway. "Elizabeth," he said, panic, frustration, and desire rolling into a single ball and spinning in his already too full mind. "Sophia assured me she would not be here tonight."

He'd recognized Simon first, but even had he not, he'd know Elizabeth anywhere. By God, she looked exquisite, even after she put the mask on. He pulled out his fob and checked the time. It was over two hours before their assignation. He grabbed his ridiculous mask and tied it on. "I'll meet you at the summerhouse at midnight. It's not as though I will not recognize you."

"You'll smell me first," Walford said and sniffed his cloak, which was identical to Richard's. "Did the countess wash these in her perfume?"

Sophia's scent had filled the coach, and Richard had also speculated about it.

"Catherine will wonder what I've been up to tonight." Walford chuckled, then grew serious. "I may need to tell her. I'll not have her suffering from misunderstandings."

Richard did not miss the accusation, and it irritated him. "Do what you must," he barked, pushing at the door and hopping out, tempted to slam it shut. He caught himself before doing it, recognizing he was behaving like a horse's ass. None of this was Walford's fault. He'd been a true friend throughout. He leaned back in, almost catching his beak on the frame. "My apologies." His voice was oddly muffled behind the mask.

"None needed," Walford assured him, grabbing his mask, an exact match to Richard's, except the black-and-white coloring was reversed. "Let's see this done, my friend." He offered his hand, and Richard shook it before closing the door.

In a few strides, he was at the carriage. Simon had already climbed back onto the box seat. Richard hailed him before he could pull out from the lineup.

"Simon, have the carriage ready for eleven."

Simon eyed him suspiciously, and it struck Richard that his driver didn't know who he was. Richard threw back his hood so Simon could glimpse his hair. He tugged it quickly back on, not wanting to risk being spotted. For this to work, there must be confusion as to which one was Richard and which was Walford. The culprit knew he would be cloaked in a beaked mask. Sophia's differentiation in color was a stroke of genius. Her men would know who was who. As would Miller's, he assumed.

"Oh, my lord," Simon said, his relief clear. "Eleven."

"Turned and ready to go at a moment's notice."

"Yes, my lord."

Richard walked away. He didn't know what this night held, but he knew he would not allow Elizabeth to be in the middle of it. He would see her gone well before the designated hour. But first, he must find her.

He pushed his way through the crowd, spotting her at the entrance to the foyer. Squeezing past what must be a Robin Hood, he stepped in beside a monk. "Excuse me," he said, and walked in front of the man as a ripple of movement occurred to Elizabeth's left. He leaned in, clasping her arms, preventing her from hitting the floor. Her warm flesh beneath his hands so familiar, he almost groaned in pleasure. She struggled, but he held her firm.

"My lady," he said. "No need to fear me." He released a long breath, thankful for the two air holes in his beak, and she tried to turn in his arms. "No." He wasn't ready to let her go. "Let me hold you until you are fully recovered."

He breathed in, wanting to inhale her scent, following a path from her earlobe to her neck. Damn Sophia's infernal perfume. He could not smell his Elizabeth. *His* Elizabeth? His stomach tightened, and he loosened his grip.

"Sir!" Elizabeth spun around, her indignation clear even if he could not see her face.

Feathers hiding her hair and a mask covering her features could not disguise her beauty nor the guilelessness in her eyes. He scanned her dress, and his body responded. Her eyes might say innocence, but her body screamed sin. He should be distressed that she would show herself in public like this, but instead he wanted to shout to the world that this was his wife. *His?* There it was again, and he liked the thought.

"I would be your protector this evening, should you wish it." He was not going to let her out of his sight until he'd seen her into the carriage. And then what? *His.* It echoed in his mind and settled in his heart. He was decided. He was going to sort everything out. God only knew how, but Richard knew one thing was for certain—he could not go on with this distance between them. Determined, he repeated his offer.

"I've no need of a protector," she said calmly, looking past him toward the ballroom.

She seemed so composed. Richard wished he could see her face, wished he could get a sense of what was running through that beautiful mind of hers. What did she need from this night? Why had she come to such a gathering? He knew the answers before the questions were fully formed. Guilt and hurt tangled. He had no one to blame but himself. But he could not leave her to her own devices. He would not. Yet he could not reveal himself here.

He tilted his head and considered her. "An escort, then. To see you safely onto the dance floor."

She paused for a moment, and he thought she was going to decline his offer. "Yes. That is fine. An escort to the ballroom," she finally said, the tremble in her voice belying the confident thrust of her shoulders.

"As you wish," he said, bowing, grateful she had acquiesced. He clasped her gloved hand in his. He hesitated, wanting to turn her hand and press a kiss to her pulse. To feel her heart beating. How many nights had he listened for the faint strains of her heart? He passed a faux kiss over her hand.

He lifted his arm, and she placed her hand upon it. She did not speak, so he followed her lead. The silence was not uncomfortable. Sophia was her usual dramatic self. Dressed as a voluptuous man, she'd not be lost easily in a room full of costumes. She looked surprised to see him. Or was it Elizabeth? She'd assured him Elizabeth was not coming to the masquerade, but she had invited her. Richard wondered what had changed Elizabeth's mind.

"My Lady Virtue." Sophia showed no sign she recognized Elizabeth, although she must have had a hand in her costume. He could not believe Elizabeth would have designed such a thing herself. "And?" She looked pointedly at Richard.

She was good at this game. Too good.

"Monsieur Réclamation." He bowed, taking Sophia's hand and miming a kiss over her glove. The name had popped into his head out of nowhere. No, that was incorrect. It had come from somewhere. From the depths of his desire. From the truth he'd been refusing to acknowledge but would no longer run from. *His.* He wanted Elizabeth in his life every day. Every night. When this was over, he would go home and reclaim his life. Their lives.

Sophia laughed and arched one eyebrow at him. "My Lady Virtue. Monsieur Réclamation. Please." Sophia gestured toward the ballroom behind her. "Enjoy the evening."

She grinned, looking far too smug, and turned her back to them. Had she planned this too? In the middle of trying to take down a criminal? What was she thinking?

Richard placed Elizabeth's hand on his arm and turned to face the ballroom. A tremor ran through her body, and he patted her hand, hoping to reassure her. He had an hour or two to indulge Elizabeth, to allow her this fantastical experience. He didn't know for sure what she was seeking, but he knew what he wanted.

After the culprit was nabbed, he would come clean. About tonight. About everything.

CHAPTER FORTY-TWO

And then my heart with pleasure fills,
And dances with the daffodils.

—Wordsworth, "I Wandered Lonely as a Cloud"

ELIZABETH'S HEARTBEAT ACCELERATED as she watched the medley of colors swirling around the dance floor. She thrilled at the contrast to her bland life, unexpectedly happy she had decided to come to the masquerade. She turned to the man beside her.

"It is dazzling, is it not?" she asked.

"You are far more breathtaking."

Her heart fluttered in reply, her being partly uncomfortable with a stranger's praise and partly pleased by his compliment. Was it so wrong to be warmed by his admiration? Was tonight not all about deluding herself? About escaping her reality?

"You flatter me, sir," she responded, glad her blushing remained well hidden.

"Au contraire, I do not do you justice with my words, Lady Virtue."

"I fear tonight I feel more like Virtue Fallen," she said honestly, glancing at her dress, her heart pounding, not knowing what else to add to the blunt revelation.

His muscles tensed beneath her hand. Was he shocked? Repulsed? She'd not meant to mislead him into thinking she was looking for anything, and her mind scrambled for something to correct any misinterpretation. Her nerves tightened like the strings of a violin, each second a peg turning, adding tension.

"Well, Virtue Fallen. I am concerned you may hurt yourself. I respectfully request to remain by your side to catch you as you fall."

Elizabeth scanned the room, noting the many scantily clad women and the men who were lewdly vying for their attention. It was overwhelming, and she wanted no part of it. She looked at the man beside her, wishing she could see his eyes, for they would tell her more about him than his words. She glanced at the crowd again. Sophia had picked well, as he'd been kind and considerate so far. She would do far better staying by his side than on her own out there.

"Monsieur Réclamation," she finally said. "I would be honored to have a *gentleman* by my side." She hoped he caught her emphasis.

He turned to her, removed her hand from his arm, and raised it to where his lips must lie beneath the mask. "My Lady Virtue Fallen, I am honored. I vow I shall be here should you need me."

She would swear there was sincerity in his voice, and it sent an uncomfortable tremor through her body.

"Would you care to dance?" he asked when the music for the current set came to an end.

Elizabeth agreed, and he bowed, sweeping his arm toward the dancers. They walked to the outskirts of the dance floor as the first strands of a waltz floated through the room. They joined the promenade, side by side, marching along with the other revelers. She looked straight ahead, anxious to sneak a peek at her partner, but her mask blocked the opportunity for a sideways glance.

Ahead of her was a woman with a wig of golden curls, her shoulders draped in a luxurious red velvet hooded cape. Beside her a man was swathed in black, the snout on his mask entirely wolfish. She grinned. She was following Little Red Riding Hood and her wolf. Oh, that could lead to nowhere but trouble.

Abruptly, the music changed. The wolf turned, planting his hip beside Little Red Riding Hood's, one arm across the front of her cape, the other clutching her hand and holding it over their heads. Little Red Riding Hood looked to the wolf, and the smile she bestowed on him made Elizabeth blush. There was no disguising the heat emanating between the two.

"Lady Virtue?"

She turned to look at her masked man as he pivoted to face her. Monsieur Réclamation extended his arm across her midriff, clasped her waist, and pulled their hips close together. He took her right hand in his left and pulled her tight to his side, looking down at her.

"Are you afraid?"

His muffled voice seemed an odd mix of concern and challenge. She hesitated. Was she afraid of him? She should be, but oddly, she was not. Elizabeth glanced around at the circle of dancers immersed in their own illusions. On the other hand, she was not at all comfortable with the likes of them. She would allow herself this dance, then go home. It would be adventure enough.

"*Non*, monsieur," she said. "I am not afraid of you."

They slowly turned. It was an odd sensation to stare at a mask, to sense the intensity of a man's gaze but not see his eyes. There was a connection nonetheless. Elizabeth was acutely aware of his hand at her waist, of the press of his hip, and of the security of his grip on her hand. Mesmerized, she felt fluid, pirouetting in perfect synchronization to his direction. Their dancing seemed endless, and lost in the movement, she did not notice the increase in tempo until he leaned in and whispered, "It is regrettable, but my favorite part of the waltz has finished. I find myself overheated. Could I interest you in a stroll in the gardens to refresh before a more energetic quadrille begins?"

Her heart beat a staccato, echoing in the chambers of her head as she heard her voice from a distance agree. He pressed a hand to the base of her back as he steered her toward the open doors to the veranda. He leaned in closer as the cool night air awakened her from her stupor. What was she doing?

"Monsieur…" Where to start? How did she explain to him that she should not have accompanied him outside? That she was not, nor ever would be, Virtue Fallen? That regardless of how neglectful Richard was, she loved him with all her heart and could never be with another?

He cocked his head to the side, waiting for her to finish.

"I would like to go home." And lest he misconstrue her meaning, "Alone."

RICHARD ALMOST GROANED in relief. He'd scanned the crowd, trying to discern who were Sophia's men, who were Miller's. If Miller himself was in the room, Richard did not spot him. As the waltz progressed, he'd forgotten the plan and enjoyed the pleasure of holding Elizabeth…far too much. She'd distracted him from his purpose and, he did not doubt, clouded his judgment. Like a fool, he'd led her out to the veranda, an invitation if there ever was one. At least she had some sense, for apparently he didn't have a grain of it.

"I will see you to your carriage," he said, taking a step back.

"I am capable on my own," she said, her delicate shoulders stiffening, the sensual woman of moments ago now gone.

"I am certain you are, but I'd see you safely to your carriage. As promised." He held out his arm.

She hesitated but then muttered, "Of course. Sophia." She placed her hand in the crook of his elbow.

He didn't know what Sophia had to do with him walking her to the carriage, but he was happy he didn't have to argue with her. They slipped down the veranda steps and took the walkway that led toward the front. Lanterns were lit, but shadows loomed imposingly. Elizabeth's hand tensed on his arm.

"I mean you no harm," he said and could feel her relax again.

"You are a good friend of the countess?" she asked quietly.

"She is a good friend to me," he said. He was not pleased to see Elizabeth here tonight, yet the time with her had shifted everything for him. He must remember to thank Sophia.

They came around the corner of the manse, and the drive threw off more light. He glanced at Elizabeth, but she seemed distracted, looking for her coach. Simon was exactly where he'd asked him to be, so Richard led her between carriages, directly to him.

Simon hopped off his box and opened the door.

"Thank you, Monsieur. You have been very kind. Perhaps our paths will cross again."

He took her hand and whispered a kiss, his beak almost scraping across it. He wished he could whip his mask off and let his lips touch the heat of her beneath her gloves. "It was my pleasure," he said as he straightened.

He assisted her into the coach and closed the door before she was fully seated. He ached to follow her and was afraid he'd give in to the temptation to do so.

"Straight home."

"Yes, my lord," Simon said and hopped up on the seat box.

Richard watched until the coach was out of sight. His heart was both heavy and light. He pulled out his fob. It would soon be time to face the culprit. Let this night be the end to the chaos of espionage. He glanced in the direction the coach had taken. And the beginning of something far better.

CHAPTER FORTY-THREE

The time approaches
That will with due decision make us know
What we shall say we have and what we owe.

—Shakespeare, *Macbeth*

RICHARD TOOK THE path back around the house, but instead of returning to the ballroom, he veered left through the formal gardens. At the sound of rustling from the rose arbor, he stopped and listened. Giggling and a low moan of frustration assured him it was someone enjoying the pleasures a masquerade often offered and not one of Sophia's men, nor the kidnapper.

He stepped through the gate at the far side of the gardens and continued along the path to Sophia's summerhouse by the lake. Nestled in a copse of trees near the shoreline, it was an extensive house with a wraparound veranda. No light shone through its many windows, and the moon was behind the clouds, but Richard knew the place well enough. He and Elizabeth had picnicked here in private a few times. He smiled at the memory and made a mental note to ask Sophia if they could do so again. Maybe with the boys? Or maybe not. Anticipation trickled down his spine. He swung toward a noise in the woods, anticipation quickly replaced by trepidation. He wished this night over for many reasons, not the least being so he could return to Thornwood Manor.

Nothing further sounded, and he decided it must be an animal or bird startled by his presence. He took the stairs two at a time and opened the paneled glass double doors. He stepped inside, stopped, and listened, his breathing echoing back at him in the mask.

"Thought you'd never get here," Walford said from the corner of the room. "Have fun with your wife?"

Richard could hear the smirk in his voice. "I did indeed," he said and smiled to himself. He could still feel the warmth of her hand in his. But this was no time to linger on the memory. "She is safely away."

"I assumed you would see her gone. I've seen no sign of anyone. Truth told, it's been bloody boring. Although, it's a far more comfortable assignment than watching the comings and goings at Tate's privy." Walford chuckled. "Here's your satchel."

As Richard's eyes adjusted to the darkened interior, Walford was becoming more visible. Richard stepped forward and picked up the bag, slinging it over his shoulder. Walford had an identical one. "What's in it?"

"Sophia's doing. Nothing of value, I'm sure." Walford stood and stretched. "Any idea how many men Miller has here tonight?"

"No. I've not heard from him at all. It's all been funneled through Sophia. Lord knows how she became involved in this mess. I hope she knows what she's doing." Richard had not been able to tell who was who in the ballroom, other than Sophia, who had made no attempt to disguise her identity.

"It is an unexpected twist in this adventure of yours, but have no doubt, Sophia always knows what she's doing." Walford tied his mask on, grabbed his satchel, and slung it over his shoulder. "Ready?"

"As one can be, I guess."

"Give me a few minutes to disappear into the woods, then go to the designated area." Walford clasped Richard's shoulder.

"Don't worry, my friend. Regardless of who is on standby to assist, we've got it in hand. You and me. Like we did last summer." He walked toward the door, stopped, and turned around. "If you hear me warn him, get out of the way. The last bloody thing I want to do is rob Elizabeth of her husband. Catherine would never forgive me," he said and chuckled again before turning and slipping out the door.

Of course Walford would bring a gun. Richard had considered it, too, but he doubted he could use it on a man. Some grouse or pheasant was one thing, but to aim at a human? It was not in him. He'd more likely find it used against himself. Nevertheless, while Richard hoped Walford would have no need to use it, there was some comfort in knowing he had one.

Richard waited until he was certain Walford was well into the woods. He headed out, walking cautiously along the path, pausing periodically to ensure no one was behind him. His nerves tingled, but they did not vibrate with warning. He rolled his shoulders and adjusted the satchel. It would be good to be done with this intrigue.

They were to meet the scoundrel outside the garden gate. Men would be in the woods and stationed around the grounds, so the culprit would be trapped on both sides. Walford was guarding the far side of the path, and if anything seemed untoward in the exchange, he would show himself and confuse the situation by pretending to be Richard. The idea was to provide an opportunity to solicit information while giving everyone involved a chance to get closer to ensure Patricia's safety as well as nab the scoundrel. Richard had been adamant she be the priority, and Sophia had agreed.

The gate area was empty when Richard rounded the curve in the path. The clouds shifted, and a dusky light fell on the trail. He stepped into the shadows of the trees and waited. He could not see his fob but knew it could not be long until midnight. Thoughts of Elizabeth crept in. What had she come for tonight? Was she truly seeking pleasure in another man's arms? It did not sit well, but it was his own fault if she was. He had driven her to it.

The gate squeaked, scattering all thoughts of Elizabeth. A dark shadow stepped through. Cloaked in black and carrying a scythe, he glanced in Walford's direction, then looked toward where Richard stood. Wearing a solid black mask, the man looked like Death come to claim a soul. Richard was sure he'd not seen Death in the ballroom. He waited a few minutes, but there was no sign of Patricia, or anyone else for that matter. It must be their man, for who else would come and stand idly outside the gardens? And the man continued to scan the area, his tension evident even from where Richard stood.

Richard counted to three to calm his nerves and then stepped from the shadows. Death swung fully around to face him and pointed the scythe menacingly. Richard could have done without the added dramatic effect, never mind the potential danger of it all. "Put that damn thing down, or I'll not come closer."

Death hesitated, but slowly he set the scythe against the gate. Richard noted that it remained within arm's reach. He'd need to get the man to move farther afield. Richard walked toward him but stopped at a safe distance. "Where's the girl?"

"You'll get the girl when I get the money." The voice was unrecognizable under the mask, as was Richard's, he hoped.

"That was not the plan." In the scenarios he and Walford had worked through, they did not anticipate the villain would not bring Patricia with him.

"Plans change," Death said calmly.

Richard's nerves had now entered the vibrating stage. Something was off. "No girl, no money," he said with a bravado he did not feel. What of Patricia? Could he actually walk away from this?

Death shrugged, grabbed his scythe again, and turned to the garden gate. Richard heard movement in the woods, but he did not want anyone nabbing the man until Richard knew where Patricia was. The man might not be forthcoming in the hands of the police. No victim, no proof. One thing Richard knew was the law and how easy it was to circumvent it.

"No, wait!" he shouted as much to stop whoever was in the woods as to stop Death. "Tell me what you want."

"The money," he said, holding out one gloved hand, the other one gripping the scythe.

"And the girl?" Richard asked, taking one step closer as though he intended on cooperating.

"I'll send word of where you can find her. When I'm safely away."

"How do I know I can trust you?" Richard asked, trying to buy some time. He could not let the man leave even if it was the safest course of action. There was no money in the bag. The culprit might harm Patricia in retaliation.

Death shrugged again. "You don't."

There was nothing for it but to hand over the satchel and hope Walford had been following the conversation and would proceed as planned. Richard pulled the bag off his shoulder and held it dangling by the strap. It was the agreed-upon cue.

"Stop!" Walford shouted, running up the path, panting as though he'd traversed a great distance. "That man's a fraud. I'm Thornwood. Here. Take the bag." Walford slowed but continued forward with the satchel held out.

Death had swung around, and Richard took advantage of the momentary distraction and leaped. His foot caught on his cloak as he landed, and he stumbled forward. He fell to one knee, momentarily taking his eyes off Death. When he looked again, Death towered over him, the scythe raised high.

The next few seconds were a blur of movement as the gate crashed into Death and a harlequin, in a swirl of color, wrestled for the scythe. Another figure, a domino like Richard but masked in plain white, charged from the woods, knocking Death to the ground as Walford yelled, "Stop, or I'll shoot!" Richard heard the warning loud and clear and rolled to the far side of the path, out of line of the shot.

Another man flew from the woods and fell upon the two men

wrestling on the ground. It was clear Walford could not shoot even if he wanted to, so Richard stood slowly. The two men subdued Death, and the harlequin dropped the scythe he'd freed from Death's grip. He looked from Richard to Walford and back at the three on the ground, turned to the gate, and slammed directly into Sophia, knocking her to the ground.

What the devil was she doing here? Before Richard could get up, the harlequin pulled her to her feet.

"*Mon Dieu!*" she said, her face in shock, taking a step back.

The harlequin bowed to her, then sprinted down the garden path. Walford, now without a mask, approached the pile of men, his gun raised and ready. Richard pushed himself to a standing position and circumvented the men. Walford abruptly came to a halt, but Richard did not stop to see what was happening. He ran through the gate, to Sophia.

"Are you hurt?" Richard asked, as he, too, removed his mask and tossed it into a shrub.

Sophia shook her head, her hair in disarray, her very exposed bosom heaving with labored breathing. "Winded," she said as he helped her sit back onto the ground, the quake of her body obvious even in the dim light.

He hesitated.

"I am fine. Go," she said, waving back toward the men.

It was an odd tableau. Walford stood rooted to the same spot, but his gun was lowered and his face ashen, and he was staring at the domino. The domino stared back, keeping Death's back pinned beneath his knee while the other man held Death's arms.

"You," Nicholas said quietly.

The domino shook his head and picked up the mask that had fallen off in the struggle. Walford studied the domino as the man put his mask back on. Then Walford seemed to return to the issue at hand. He glanced at Richard before turning his attention to Death.

"Unmask him," Walford commanded, and Richard stepped forward as the domino grabbed the back of Death's head and jerked it off the ground. Richard leaned in and yanked off the black mask, stepping back in disbelief.

"Miller!" he said at the same time as Walford, who had come around to see.

"You bloody bastard," Walford growled, grabbing Miller's shoulder and wrenching him to his feet. The other men scrambled to theirs and took hold of Miller again before he'd even had a chance to register they'd let go.

Miller glared back and spit on the ground.

"I trusted you. Led my friend to you. A traitor." Walford ground out the words.

Miller's nostrils flared. "Not all of us get handed an easy way out of the war, Captain Sinclair. Oh, my mistake, Lord Walford."

"You bloody little—"

Richard grabbed Walford's arm before the punch landed. "Patricia?" he asked Miller.

Miller smirked. "Your whore? How would I know?"

Richard pulled back his hand, and before he could reason himself out of it, his fist landed in Miller's face. The crunch of bone and the trickle of blood were a satisfying balm to the instant pain in his hand. "I asked you where she was," he said with a calm he did not feel.

"Wherever you sent her, I imagine." Miller sniffed in the blood and coughed as he tried to free an arm.

The two men tightly held him in place. Walford growled and raised his arm, and Miller flinched.

"I didn't need her to get the money. You're an easy mark," Miller said, turning his attention to Richard before looking back to Walford. "I knew you would be more of a challenge. You were supposed to be holed up at your *new* estate." He struggled, but the men did not loosen their grips.

"Was the Home Office in on this?" Walford asked, staring past Miller, at the domino, who shook his head.

"You don't want your good name sullied, now do you?" Miller asked, returning his attention to Richard. "Mrs. Tate keeps records of payment. She was kind enough to share them with me. Clever woman also ensured there were gentlemen witnesses to your presence. It would seem she's not particularly fond of you." He tsk-tsked, then licked the blood off his lips. "I'm sure Lady Thornwood would enjoy seeing and hearing your name linked with a common whore's."

This time, it was Walford who stopped Richard from landing another punch. The more Miller talked, the more Richard's anger grew. The blood was pounding in his temple, and for the first time in his life, he understood what drove a man to kill.

"There's the small detail of sharing information from the Crown," Walford said.

"You can't prove I had anything to do with it. No trail. None at all." Miller smiled.

"Is that true?" Walford once again directed his question at the domino, who shook his head.

"So you can call off your dogs now." Miller looked far too confident for a man who'd just tried to extort a lord, never mind one who was on the hook for spying on his own government.

"They're not my dogs," Richard said quietly, and Miller struggled to look at the two men. It struck Richard that Miller had not arranged for backup. The scoundrel thought the men holding him were hired by either him or Walford. It was clear Walford knew exactly who they were, although Richard still hadn't figured it out.

There was a commotion by the gate, and Richard turned in time to see Sophia shake her head at the two pirates who'd arrived. Sophia stood and walked toward them, her breathing now returned to normal. "My men will take him." She scanned Miller from head to toe and back up again very slowly. "They will travel the long way to the Home Office."

Her composure was magnificent, and Richard marveled at it. He'd always known her as daring and determined, but she was tough as old boots too. She was unmoved by Miller's blanched and bleeding face and the panic that was clear in his eyes. More surprising was how the men readily handed Miller over to the pirates without question.

"I must see to my guests," Sophia said. *"Fino a domani."* She turned and followed her men. The domino thrust his chin in the direction of the departing trio, and the other man nodded and disappeared after them.

The domino raised a finger to the lips on his mask as Walford was about to speak. He turned and headed toward the lake. Richard and Walford walked behind him, neither saying a word. Richard had many questions, but he kept them to himself for now. It was enough the culprit had been caught and, it appeared, Patricia had never been in jeopardy.

They mounted the stairs and entered the summerhouse. Richard and Walford stood silently as the domino walked to the fireplace and grabbed the tinderbox off the mantelpiece. A minute later, he lit a candle, walked over to a side table, and lit the lantern. He turned to the two of them and slowly untied his mask before dropping it on the table.

"By God, it really is you." Walford's voice was hoarse as he stepped toward the domino and pulled him into an embrace. The domino hugged him tightly back.

Richard had no idea what was going on, but he'd had enough adventure for one night. His legs were unsteady, and his hand ached. He sat on an overstuffed chair and put his head back. Whatever this back pounding was about, it wasn't his business. He was finally done with all the cloak-and-dagger. Done with hiding. From Elizabeth. From himself. He smiled at the ceiling. *I'll be home soon.*

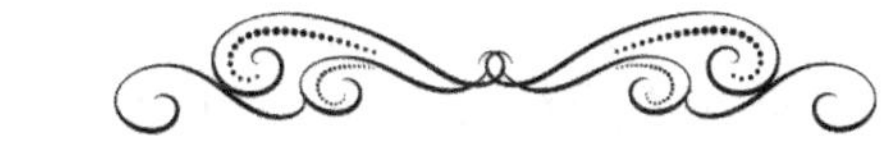

CHAPTER FORTY-FOUR

The earth is all before me. With a heart
Joyous, nor scared at its own liberty,
I look about; and should the chosen guide
Be nothing better than a wandering cloud,
I cannot miss my way.

—Wordsworth, *The Prelude*

"THORNWOOD, STRATTON'S SON, Laurence Baring," Walford said before adding, "My brother-in-law," as though he could not quite grasp that fact. "Bloody cold in here." His voice was gruff as he turned abruptly, grabbed the candle, and walked to the fireplace before squatting in front of it.

"Good to finally meet you, my lord," Laurence said, walking toward Richard, holding out his hand. "I understand I owe you a great debt."

Richard was too weary to stand but gladly shook the man's hand. "No debt at all," Richard said, trying to process everything from the night and figure out how Walford's brother-in-law fit into it all. "Do sit," he said, motioning to the sofa across from him.

"I thought you were in the colonies?" Richard asked once Laurence was settled.

"You were meant to. Everyone was to believe that. It is far

easier to hide in plain sight if you are thought to be half a world away." Laurence glanced at Walford, who was taking far too long with the fire.

"You rubbing sticks together over there?" Richard teased, knowing full well Walford was composing himself and gathering his wits. It was not every day someone you believed lost appeared in the flesh.

"Horse's ass," Walford grumbled. He stood and rolled his shoulders before turning to the room, the fire highlighting him from behind.

Richard smiled. His friend had clearly finished processing. Walford sat beside Laurence and patted the man's back again.

"It's happy I am to see you, but I do have some questions," Walford said, his face clearer in the growing light from the fire. Richard could see the play of emotions on Walford's face. He remembered that overwrought look well from last summer when he and Walford had been bonded in another effort to catch a culprit. A culprit who'd held Laurence's future in his hands.

"I knew you would," Laurence said good-naturedly. "I need a drink though. I suspect you two could as well." He walked into the shadows, and Richard heard the clink of glasses. "Sophia keeps a fine cognac in stock."

Walford raised his eyebrow at Richard. It did seem odd Laurence knew that, but again, there was nothing normal about anything that had happened these past few months, never mind tonight. Laurence returned, and Richard took a cognac from him. When he was seated once again, Laurence raised his glass. "To a successful ending."

"Hear, hear, I'll drink to that," Richard said and let the mellow liquid warm his throat.

Walford watched Laurence throw back his cognac, but he didn't have any himself. He sat forward on the settee, his hands cradling the glass between his knees, not taking his eyes off Laurence. "My questions?"

Richard would have laughed were he not so tired. The old

impatient Walford, whom Richard knew so well, had finally surfaced.

"I will answer as best I can." Laurence set his glass on the side table and held up his hand as Walford was about to speak. "Let me start at the beginning. Tonight was long in the making. Lord Sidmouth." He paused. "The home secretary…"

Laurence addressed his explanation to Richard as though he needed it. Did the man think he lived under a rock? He spent his days in parliament. He could list the entire bloody roster of lords along with their roles. But Richard was too tired to roll his eyes or make a sarcastic quip, so he merely nodded.

Laurence returned his attention to Walford. "Lord Sidmouth knew there was a traitor in the Home Office. I was put on the case months before you came into town, but had made little headway. Then they received the letter from Miss Paisley and the Home Office was in turmoil. Only one of their own could have replicated that letter from Wellesley. I had my own suspicions about Miller, but I could find nothing on him. Until he arranged this little exchange."

"I'm not following the logic here," Richard said. "If you knew he had arranged it, why not take him in? Why put us through this bloody night?" Richard knew he'd agreed to participate in the transfer of information, but it was beyond the pale if they could have prevented this little caper and did not.

"A fair question," Walford said quietly.

"It is. Miller wasn't our main target tonight. We wanted the informant. But I digress. If I can ask for your patience, I'll return to that." Laurence picked up his glass and took a sip.

"Go on," Richard said, and Walford grunted in agreement.

"Miller did not inform the Home Office of this kidnapping. That was when we knew we had him. Lord Sidmouth suspects there's another traitor somewhere in either the Home or Foreign Office working with Miller, so he decided against using his own men to apprehend him. There were no men from the Home Office here tonight."

"You're not with Home Office?"

Both Walford and Richard sat forward, staring keenly at Laurence.

"Then what were you doing here? Who the hell do you work for?" Walford asked.

"I am a member of a small elite squad. We work outside the parameters of what the Home Office is allowed to do. There are only a handful of us. Even the prince regent does not know of our existence."

"Well, I'll be damned," Walford said, finally taking a swig of his cognac.

"As I said, Miller was not our primary target, although we were pleased he'd finally exposed himself and we could apprehend him. We've been trying to find the man who's been feeding Miss Paisley the information. My partner and I watched Mrs. Tate's house, but everyone checked out. I began following her, but none of her activity seemed out of line or suspicious."

"It wasn't," Richard chimed in. "He found her when she was out and slipped it to her, sometimes without her even being aware it had happened."

"We figured it must be going on before our eyes. Whoever he is, he's good. Exceptionally good. Which is one of the reasons we want him. The information he has divulged has been solid, but the big question remains: Why did he share the Wellesley letter? Was he demonstrating he could play both sides of the fence, or was he trying to expose the traitor among us? If it is the former, he is a dangerous man to the security of our operations. If it is the latter, he could prove invaluable."

"Why bring Thornwood into it again?" Walford asked.

"We didn't. Miller did. We were watching him the day he met you in the park." Laurence turned his attention to Richard. "If you hadn't followed him into the grove, we wouldn't have been able to overhear your conversation."

"You were there? How did I not notice?" Richard asked, his mind racing back to the day, trying to recreate the scene. He was certain no one had been around.

"You are not trained to notice, my lord. Besides, I would not be very good at my job had you, now would I?" Laurence smiled.

Although Laurence's looks favored his father more than his sister, Richard could see Lady Walford in that smile. It was oddly reassuring.

"And for the record, the Home Office never threatened you. That was all from Miller. Originally we presumed he knew the spy he'd shared the letter with, but it seems he didn't. He would not have gone to these great lengths to draw him out if he did. Imagine Miller's surprise when the information he'd given the man returned to the Home Office via Miss Paisley. We assume the spy misled Miller, in some way, to garner the letter in the first place. Which is why Miller was as anxious to find him as we were. Of course, our main concern is the man may not be loyal to the Crown, whereas Miller's concern would be that the man could identify him as a traitor.

"We figured the spy would be watching you after Patricia disappeared. Which, by the way, taking that pawn out was a stroke of genius," Laurence said to Richard.

"There was no great thought behind it other than to set her on a better path," Richard said, his head spinning with the tale Laurence was weaving. He'd been a part of much more than he knew.

"Well, you have." Laurence raised his glass in a cheer. "She's bought a small tea shop in Hull. I might have had a friend there to help her invest wisely." Laurence smiled sadly. "I know what it is like to have your life in shambles and become an outcast."

Walford cleared his throat and clasped Laurence's shoulder. "You are not an outcast in my home."

Richard watched the interplay between the two as he relaxed back in his chair, trying to digest all the information. He was relieved to hear of Patricia, but there were many missing pieces to this whole game. "You did not get your spy," he said, not wanting to intrude but anxious to have his answers and head home.

"It would seem not. Nor, however, did Miller. Although, our guess that he was watching you and would follow you here seems to have been on the mark."

"How? I didn't see anyone," Walford interjected, his personal feelings set aside again and his focus back on the events of the evening.

"I believe it was the harlequin. I assumed he was one of the countess's men until he fled unexpectedly. From what I saw of her interaction with her pirates, they did not succeed in capturing him." Laurence shrugged. "A loss, but I'm optimistic he is on our side. At the very least, I'm certain he's not against us."

"Why?" Richard asked. The man had dealings with Miller. How could he be trusted?

"Because he saved your life tonight, Lord Thornwood. That scythe was ready to swing at you, and I was too far away to stop it. So was Nic."

Walford's stern expression confirmed Laurence's assessment of the situation. *Damn and blast.* Richard blew out a breath, trying to steady himself. Those minutes had unfurled so quickly he'd had no idea he'd come so close to being slain. He finished the last of his cognac in one swallow.

"Why did Miller choose out here for the exchange?" Walford asked. "He had to know it would be harder to escape here than in London, where he could slip away like the rat he is."

"He didn't," Laurence said. He looked at Richard. "You did. We sent the directions to him from your stationery with your seal. He would not think you capable of any trickery, and as far as he knew, the Home Office was unaware of his extortion attempt."

"My stationery? My seal?" Richard asked, shaking his head.

"The countess is a good friend, is she not? She can come and go freely in your home?"

Laurence raised both eyebrows in question, but Richard knew he was not waiting for an answer. Richard's head was beginning to ache with fatigue and confusion. "I don't understand. Sophia is…?"

"The countess is a woman who loves her adopted country and is well connected. She helps out when she can."

"Well, I'll be damned," Richard said, echoing Walford's earlier words. "I need another drink. Anyone?"

"A tall one," Walford said. Laurence shook his head, declining.

Richard took Walford's glass and his own and headed into the shadows where the cognac sat. He could hear the conversation behind him, hear the wonder and confusion in Walford's voice.

"How did you come to be part of this…this…?"

"Squad," Laurence replied, filling in the word. "My father. He knew I must leave Stratton Hall but would not have me across the world. I've always been good at ciphering, and he had connections at the Home Office. That's why I could not let Miller see me tonight. He might recognize me from my short-lived time there, and I'd be no good to the squad anymore."

"Why could Lord Stratton not tell us? Tell Catherine?" Walford asked, and Richard stopped, standing in the shadows, letting the two men work through Laurence's deception.

"Originally the lie about going to the colonies was for *your* father's benefit. My father did not trust him, was afraid he'd punish me for your brother's…for Daniel's death." Laurence choked on the name, and the room grew silent for a moment. "But Lord Sidmouth recruited me when he discovered I had other skills."

"What other skills?" Walford asked.

"A daring that comes with not caring if you live or die," Laurence said so quietly Richard strained to hear him.

"Good God, man, you know the truth now. My brother would not want that to be his legacy. And Catherine. What about her? You have to care," Walford sputtered, the emotion clear in his voice.

"I'm beginning to, Nic. I'm beginning to."

Walford pulled Laurence into a bear of a hug. Richard waited until he let him go and sat back before entering the pool of light and handing Walford his drink. Richard resumed his seat.

"Catherine will be thrilled to see you," Walford said after taking a drink of the cognac.

"She can't know."

Walford's head snapped toward Laurence. "I don't keep secrets from your sister, Laurence. And I'll certainly not keep this. She has been worried sick. She believes you are over in the middle of a bloody war right now."

"But you must. It's a dangerous game I play, and there are people who would hurt me by hurting those I love. They don't know who I am, and I pray they never find out."

"But Catherine—"

"Is better off believing me to be in the colonies," Laurence said, running a hand through his hair. "Father has agreed. He knows the peril she could be in were the connection to be made. There can be no slipups on her part if she does not know."

"But you are asking me to lie when I can ease her worry. What am I to tell her when she shares her fears?"

"Tell her you can't find me in the rosters. Tell her you'd know if something had happened to me. Tell her whatever you want, but for the love of God, don't tell her I'm nearby. If not for the sake of her, for the sake of that little niece or nephew of mine she's carrying."

Walford looked kicked as emotion washed over his face. Richard bled for his friend's worried confusion but recognized it was time for him to depart. He'd learned enough for the night, and neither man needed him standing witness to their pain any more than he already had.

"If you'll excuse me, I believe I'll head home," he said, standing.

Walford cleared his throat. "Take my horse, if you'd like, Thornwood. I'll be staying for a while, I hope?" He looked at Laurence, who nodded. "I'll take the carriage when I'm done."

Laurence stood and held out his hand. "Thank you, my lord. I know you stepped into this arrangement unwillingly, but you stayed the course. I'll do my best to keep you from it from here on."

"I'd appreciate it," Richard said, shaking Laurence's hand and then Walford's before turning to the door.

"On your word, Nic, promise you will not tell Catherine I am here. I'll not bring any more pain to my family…or yours."

Richard closed the door on Laurence's words, their voices reduced to murmurs as he stepped off the veranda. The cool night air refreshed his senses and reawakened his mind to thoughts of Elizabeth. He was grateful for Walford's offer of his horse. He couldn't get home fast enough.

CHAPTER FORTY-FIVE

Away! away! for I will fly to thee.

—Keats, "Ode to a Nightingale"

BY THE TIME he'd mounted and was on his way, the clouds had parted and the moon easily lit his way. He was thankful to be able to keep a steady pace. It felt good to put some distance between him and the events of the night, and he was glad for his friend to have some time alone with his brother-in-law. It was going to be a burden for Walford to keep Laurence's secret, but Richard did not doubt he'd manage. Walford would do anything for his family, and knowing it was for their safety would ease the guilt of not sharing the good news with his wife.

He paused at the entrance to the drive, the trees, on both sides of the road, standing somberly in the dark, sentinels for Thornwood Manor. Richard knew he, too, would do anything for his family. How had his thinking become so skewed that he'd believed his absence would be a benefit to anyone, never mind Elizabeth? He'd been so worried Elizabeth would see him as less of a man for not being willing to perform his duty, so sure she would dismiss his dread and he'd surrender and put her in an unpardonable situation. He could have lost his life tonight. Surely if he could face Death, he could tell her everything and face down his own fears. Then together they would find a way to move forward. He nudged the horse, and it trotted along the drive. At the end of the lane lay his world, and he vowed never to neglect it again.

There would be no one in the main courtyard at this time, so he guided the horse to the left and into the stable yard before dismounting and hooking the reins to a post. His own horse would not move, but Walford's was not familiar with Thornwood Manor, and Richard did not want it to bolt. He stepped into the dark stables. The smell of hay and dung hovered warmly in the air.

"Simon!" he shouted as he walked between the stalls, the path to Simon's room as familiar as the halls of the manor house. A light flickered, and Simon stepped out at the far end of the stable.

"My lord?" His hair disheveled, standing in his nightshirt, Simon held the lamp higher to better see Richard.

"My apologies for pulling you from your bed. I have Walford's stallion in need of care."

"Yes, my lord. I'll see to it."

"And have someone ride it to Woodfield. Later in the day, when it is rested." Richard turned and walked through the side yard and in through the servants' door. Warmth spilled from the kitchen fire, and he could hear movement in the scullery, but he didn't stop to see who was already up and about. He took the hallway leading to the main house, pausing at Hastings's rooms. A light shone under his door. Richard tapped lightly.

"My lord!" Hastings said, pulling at his waistcoat and touching his bare neck as though embarrassed to be caught without his jacket and neck cloth.

"Have you not gone to bed?" Richard asked, surprised by the man's state of dress. It was a stark contrast to Simon's nightshirt.

"Yes, my lord. I went to bed after Lady Thornwood retired. I was reviewing accounts before heading out into a new day." Hastings stopped fidgeting and stood straighter, and Richard admired the pride in his voice.

"Well, my apologies for interrupting at such an hour. I ask

you that not disturb myself or Lady Thornwood this morning. We will ring when we are in need of anything."

"Yes, my lord. Shall I send up a bath?"

"It's far too late. Or too early?" Richard had no idea what time it was, only that he was growing tired. "I've disturbed enough people for now."

"It would be my pleasure, my lord. The footmen will be happy you are home. Everyone will be," Hastings added, uncharacteristically forthcoming with his opinion.

"A hot jug of water will be fine, thank you."

Richard left Hastings and entered the main house. He'd not missed Hastings's point that the entire staff was aware of his absence. Well, they were all about to see changes around here.

The moon provided enough light to navigate the hall and take the stairs. He stopped at the top and glanced to the left. She was so close, but he could not go to her as he was. He smelled of dirt and horse—and Sophia. Now *there* was a mystery woman if he'd ever met one. He wondered if she was simply one of those people who had a nose for adventure. Or trouble.

Richard turned to the front of the house and entered his room, shedding the cloak and walking to the window. It had been far too long since he'd stood here without planning how to quickly leave again. Now all he could think of was how to manage it so he could stay. What if Elizabeth did not want him?

He bade the person enter when there was a tap at the door. Gordon came in and knelt before the fireplace. In minutes, the flames roared to life. Hastings arrived with a jug of water and set it on the stand. He dismissed Gordon and turned to Richard.

"Can I be of assistance?" Hastings asked.

"I'm fine," Richard said. "I believe I'm more than fine, Hastings. That will be all."

Hastings bowed and exited the room. Richard had left Marcus in London. He'd had no intention of coming to Thornwood Manor, and he'd not been able to bring his valet along to the coaching house. He could not risk their plans being overheard.

He'd send for him in the morning. He looked outside at the gray fraying the edges of darkness. Or in the afternoon. He ran a hand through his hair. *Devil it*, he was tired.

He stripped off his clothing and grabbed a piece of linen and a cake of lightly scented soap. His head dense with fog, he soaped and rinsed and dried himself off. He walked into his dressing room, grabbed a silk banyan, and slipped it on. He stepped back into the hall and headed to the rear of the house.

Richard tapped lightly on Elizabeth's door and pressed his ear against it. There was no sound. When she slept, she slept deeply, something he'd always envied. He tended to rest on the verge of wakening, the least sound pulling him from slumber. He eased open the door.

Between the moon and the dying embers, there was enough light to see she was snug and fast asleep, both hands tucked under her cheek like an innocent. His heartbeat slowed, and his mind mellowed, the building fatigue finally overwhelming him. He would not disturb her sleep. There was nothing that could not wait for a few more hours.

He turned to leave but changed his mind. He was tired of an empty bed. Tired of the distance between them. Richard wanted to be near her, to hold her. He walked to the bed and stood staring at her. Her beautiful blonde hair, braided, swirled in a halo above her head. Elizabeth. His angel.

Richard carefully pulled back the coverlet. The bed dipped with his weight as he eased in behind her and snugged into her warmth. He inhaled slowly, deeply, smiling in memory of trying to find her scent through that damned beaked mask. Well, he could smell her now, a luxury he had missed.

He gently put his arm around her waist, resting one hand on her breast. The gentle rise and fall of her chest, the short breathy exhales across his knuckles, and the slight pulsating of her heart against the palm of his hand combined to create a sweet lullaby. Richard drifted quickly toward sleep.

CHAPTER FORTY-SIX

Doubt thou the stars are fire;
Doubt that the sun doth move;
Doubt truth to be a liar;
But never doubt I love.

—Shakespeare, *Hamlet*

L IGHT TEASED THE edges of sleep as Elizabeth stirred but fought fully awakening. She'd arrived home, checked on the boys (both fast asleep), and come straight to her chambers. She'd undressed and sat numbly staring at herself in the mirror as Lucy had braided her hair. It was not that she was disappointed in herself, for she'd never truly thought it was in her to dally as so many lonely wives did. She'd only been drawn to one man in her life, and she'd believed it would always be that way. But she could not deny to herself that she'd been drawn to the domino, and it made her sad. Another wedge between her dreams and her reality.

She stirred, almost ready to greet another lonely day. Her night had been filled with imagery. Wolves devouring Red Riding Hood in the most lascivious of ways. Bosoms and long legs twirling to music and laughter. And a long-beaked domino holding her close, his breath on her neck so real she'd trembled as if she'd been touched.

Elizabeth shifted, registering the weight of the arm draped around her waist. She opened her eyes, her heartbeat racing, pounding in her chest, as she thought for a second that she had somehow made good on Sophia's daring challenge. She risked a glance downward and frowned, the hammering of her heart slowly receding. The hand lying idly on her stomach was nothing to fear. She'd recognize it anywhere. Now that she was pulled completely from sleep, she also knew the breath upon her neck was not the fabrication of a dream.

"Richard?" she whispered, but the only response was his deep breathing, bordering on a snore. She carefully rolled until she faced him, edging farther away from him so she could see him more fully. The haze of sleep still hovering like a thick fog, she was both amazed and confused by his presence. Joy threatened, but she quickly squashed it. It could only lead to regret.

Elizabeth loved Richard's face. All angles and edges, it was very patrician, quite Romanesque. She'd always thought he looked like a pirate when his hair was queued and had imagined their early days of lovemaking as unleashed plundering. For he had been so much freer in those days. When had that changed? She knew the answer. When he'd become a father. She sighed heavily. Everything had changed with the arrival of their children.

His hair was not tied back now. It was free and as disheveled as any woman's. She wanted to run her fingers through those dark strands, but she did not desire to wake him, did not wish to lose the moment. For surely she was dreaming. Richard could not be in her bed.

His green silk robe had slipped, revealing his sharp shoulders and his chest, his flesh pale beneath the dark patch of hair. She wondered if it was all he wore, and the thought of him almost naked pulled at her womanly parts. She vividly recalled the evening of the picnic where she had successfully seduced him. Memories of the fallout of that plan were like a splash of cold water, and she moved further away from him.

Elizabeth rolled onto her back and stared at the ceiling, light flitting around the room as the sun shone through the branches dancing outside the window. Why was Richard here? Back at Thornwood Manor? In her bed? She could not do this anymore. The expectation. The anticipation. The agonizing disappointment. It all hurt too much. It was like being on the teeter-totter they'd made for the picnic. It was as though each time she was sitting high on the one end, Richard leaped off and let her slam to the ground.

She would get up and let Richard explain his presence in a less intimate setting. She put her hand to the mattress to gently ease away, but his hand covered hers. Her heart pounded as she glanced at him. He was watching her, the gold flecks in his eyes highlighted in the early-morning sun.

He softly stroked her wrist with his thumb. "Your heart races, Elizabeth." He continued the gentle caress. "Do I make you nervous?"

She shook her head, unable to voice what she *was* feeling, not sure she even understood this visceral reaction warring with caution. Richard lifted her hand to his mouth, pressed a kiss to her palm, and returned it to the mattress. He continued his gentle stroking. It was such a simple gesture, but after all that had happened, it was everything. The need to bolt from the bed lessened. Instead, she shimmied to a sitting position.

"Why are you here?" she asked, adjusting her cotton nightgown with her free hand.

His caresses, slow and light as a feather, swept the sensitive flesh of her inner arm.

"You are a beautiful woman, Elizabeth," he said, ignoring her question. "That has not changed despite the years and the fact that you have given me two sons." He looked up at her face. "If anything, you are more so now than when I first saw you across the dance floor. The purity of your heart mingling with your womanly experience has deepened your beauty. You are both otherworldly and firmly rooted in this one."

Elizabeth flushed with the compliment, but wariness continued to prickle beneath her skin. She searched his face for some sign of what he was about but could see nothing but sincerity. Richard was not one for artifice, but why this sudden change of heart?

He sighed heavily. "I see you are unsure." He moved to a sitting position beside her. "You do not believe me. Or perhaps you do not believe in your own power." He turned so his shoulder rested against the headboard and he was facing her. "Either way, it is my fault, and I owe you an apology for that amid the long list of my many sins."

Elizabeth's heart stalled. Was Richard about to confess his infidelity? Could she bear to hear him talk about another woman? She didn't think so. "Richard—"

"Hush. Hear me out, for I have much to say. And much to apologize for."

She sat back and stared at the fireplace. The chill running down her spine had nothing to do with its empty grate. She pulled the coverlet under her chin and turned to face him, bracing for his confession.

"I have been lying to you for months." He ran a hand through his hair and shook his head. "I don't even know where to begin." Richard pursed his lips as though coming to a decision. "I do know where to start. As much as I would like to avoid sharing this part with you, I must. I did have a mistress."

Elizabeth's heart sank, and her eyes stung with tears. As much as she'd known it, the truth was hard to hear. He grasped her covered shoulder, and she pulled away. She'd not have him touch her while he spoke of another woman.

Richard dropped his hand and sighed. "I met her when I was eighteen, fresh from Eton and new to London. I was achingly lonely, wallowing in dark misery after the loss of my mother. Patricia…"

He glanced at Elizabeth. He flinched at what he must have seen in her face at the use of another woman's Christian name, for he apologized before continuing.

"Miss Paisley was as young as I but filled with light and laughter and knowledge of physical pleasure I had never known. I tell you this only so you know why I was drawn to have a mistress at all. Can you appreciate the appeal to a lad of eighteen?"

Elizabeth nodded, although she had no idea why he was sharing ancient history with her, unless it was the same woman? Dear God, had he kept her all through their marriage? Had even the early years been a lie? She wiped at her eyes, willing her tears to stay put. She'd not cry for such a betrayal.

"Oh, my dearest, I can see your thoughts play out across your face. I said goodbye to her the day I spied you across the ballroom. Before I'd even met you. Before I knew I stood a chance to become part of your life. I wanted you the first moment I laid eyes on you, and I cleared the path of any and all obstacles that might stand in my way."

Elizabeth blew out a long breath, biting at her lip to fight the emotions flowing through her and threatening to spill out. At least their first few years together had not been a fallacy.

"It is that same woman you saw in my study." He grabbed her arm as she pushed from the headboard, ready to leave. "No, Elizabeth, you are wrong, although I understand why you're thinking what you're thinking. Since I have known you, I have not, nor will I ever, be with another woman."

Elizabeth stilled as those words sunk in. *Have not. Will not.* It did not explain his neglect, but he had not betrayed her. Her heartbeat returned to normal, and she turned to him, resting her shoulder back against the headboard, ready to hear him out. "Then what? Why?"

"What was Miss Paisley doing in my study?" He rubbed his forehead and looked at the ceiling before returning his gaze to her. "It is a fantastical tale, but I assure you it is the truth."

Elizabeth listened to Richard talk of brothels and madams, of clubs and secrets hidden in a leather-bound book, of spies and allies, and of trying to help the woman move on to a better life. It was a lot to take in and make sense of, and she was overwhelmed and a bit confused.

"And why can you tell me of it now?" she asked when he finally paused.

"Because I am finished with it all. Last night we caught the culprit. He had threatened Miss Paisley's well-being. Demanded a ransom for her return."

"Oh no!" She sat up straight. Elizabeth did not know the woman but wished her no harm, especially knowing she had pulled Richard out of some dark days.

Richard smiled and touched her cheek. "There is my Elizabeth. Worried about a stranger. I assure you she is alive and well. In fact, she had never been kidnapped. I can't share all the details, but last night we caught a traitor to the Crown at Sophia's masquerade."

Elizabeth felt the blood drain from her face as her stomach churned. Richard had been at the masquerade? Could he have seen her with the domino? It would seem she also had a confession to make.

"Richard," she started, not knowing what to say. She had done no wrong, yet she now felt she had. Especially in light of his revelations. He'd been working for the government, trying to uncover a traitor, whereas she'd been wallowing in self-pity. "I was there last night," she whispered.

"Were you?" He cocked his head to one side and studied her for a minute before speaking. "And did you enjoy yourself?" he finally asked.

"I did," she answered honestly. "Until I didn't. But I considered…" What could she say? That the domino had been alluring? That she'd liked the feel of his hands on her waist as they'd danced? That for a few heady moments she'd once again dreamed of possibilities?

"Oh, my sweet Elizabeth." Richard pulled her to his chest. "You did no wrong. It is me and me only who has confessions to make. I pulled in a few carriages behind yours, and I saw you alight. You silly woman," he said, kissing the top of her head, still holding her snug. "No mask. I would have known you anywhere, but to step out at a masquerade, unaccompanied and undisguised?" He chuckled softly. "I love that you do not know how to behave at such events."

She adjusted her position so she could see him better. She wanted to trace his lips, to taste him once again, but none of what had been shared tonight changed the fact that he did not, would not spend time with her as her husband. So she stuck with the masquerade, too afraid to ask about them. About their future. Too afraid to destroy this new fragile bond.

"I did not see you."

"Au contraire, my love, you did." He gently ran his fingers along her braid and moved it so it draped over her left shoulder. "I would be your protector this evening, should you wish it."

It took a few seconds for his words to sink in. When they did, she shoved his chest, frantic to get away from him. "You! You were the domino?" Her face burned. "You have made a fool of me!"

He let her go, and she fell back on her bottom. He looked pained, and she could see hurt darken his eyes. "No," he said quietly. "I am the fool. In truth, I should have been dressed as a court jester, as I have made a mockery of our marriage. I'm not sure I can ever make you understand why."

"Try," she said, his contrition extinguishing her ire.

He took both her hands in his and raised them, pressing a kiss to each. "First, may I ask a question? You don't have to answer it if you don't wish to."

"Yes." She watched as he seemed to search for his words.

"The masquerade. It is not the type of gathering you attend. Last night I sensed your draw to me. Well, not to me—to the domino. Did you seek revenge for my neglect?" He quickly raised her hands and kissed them again. "I would not blame you."

"No," she said, swallowing emotion. She had never considered revenge. She'd gone because she was lonely. So damnably lonely. "I could not sit here another night, imagining you in

London with that…with…" She shook her head. She could no longer think hatefully of the woman. "I wanted to feel." Feel what? Feel anything except the pain he'd created. It was the raw truth, but she could not wound him with it now. Not when it seemed she was closer to discovering his truth. "I wanted to feel free of melancholy, if only for the night."

He dropped his head to her chest. She held him tightly, agonizing over the pain she was now causing him. She had not set out to hurt him. She'd believed he wouldn't care. She would never hurt him. She ran her fingers through his hair and massaged his scalp. They sat that way for some time, each lost in their thoughts.

Eventually he raised his head, his eyes glazed, his gaze regretful. "We may not be able to fix us at all."

She stiffened in response. What was he saying?

"My apologies may not be enough. That you would even entertain the idea of another tells me how low I have come, how dreadfully lonely I have made you." His eyes seemed washed in pain, not anger.

He took her hands in his. "Please forgive my behavior. My thoughtlessness. My neglectfulness."

He kissed her hands, holding them tightly, looking directly into her eyes.

"When you delivered William, I believed our lives would never be happier or richer. Until you grew round with Sebastian, and I knew we were going to fill this old manor with children. Then Dr. Redding sent you to your bed in your last month, insisting you not get out of it for more than minutes at a time. And despite my love for William, I knew that without you, my world would be a dark place. I fully accepted the new baby would be the last one we'd have. I was quite reconciled to it. What I hadn't anticipated, had not prepared myself for, was Sebastian's birth."

"But how could you, when—"

"Hush," Richard said, pressing a finger to her lips. "Let me finish."

She nodded, her heart pounding, her stomach roiling as his eyes darkened with emotion and glazed with tears.

"The night Sebastian arrived, we almost lost you. Sophia held me that night, and we both cried. We were sure you would be gone by morning. But you hung on." He cupped her cheek. "You are such a fighter, dearest. I don't know if you battled for me or the boys, but I am so grateful you did not give up."

Elizabeth turned her head and kissed the palm of his hand, then covered it with her own, her eyes burning with tears.

"But you kept on bleeding. By the next evening, you were fading. Dr. Redding didn't think you'd make the night. I curled in behind you and held you close as your life force slowly ebbed, your heart becoming fainter beneath my hands. I wanted to go with you."

He choked and cleared his throat, and Elizabeth swiped a tear from his cheek as her own slowly shed.

"I swore," he continued, his voice rough with emotion, "that should you live, I would do everything in my power to keep you safe."

His words began to sink in, and Elizabeth shook her head slowly. "You don't come to my bed because...?"

"Because I am not just a fool. I am a coward. A weak-willed one at that. I am petrified to make love to you for fear it will put you in jeopardy again. Yet when I am near you, it is all I want to do."

She had no memory of those days, but it all became so obvious to her—his distance, his absence, this constant push and pull. Her heart soared, and she swept her tears away. These were the words she had longed to hear.

"Richard, my love…" She could not finish. He had laid bare his soul, and the longed-for revelation was a bubbling brook of angst and happiness, regret and joy. It was freeing.

"Elizabeth, you are my life."

She tugged him close, pressing her nose against his cheek and tracing a path to his ear. "I love you, Richard Arlington, Earl of Thornwood, father to my children and keeper of my heart." She continued a leisurely path along his neck and nestled close to his chest, relishing his scent. Elizabeth looked up at him. "I love you," she repeated.

"I love you. Only you. It has only ever been you." He ran his thumb down her cheek. "I burn to make love to you, but…"

Elizabeth straightened abruptly. "Do you think Sophia knew it was you with me at the masquerade?"

"I know it for a fact. She provided my costume. I am convinced she orchestrated the nabbing of the culprit at her place to manipulate it so that we would come together." His eyes narrowed. "Why?"

Elizabeth laughed, hopped off the bed, and walked into her dressing room. Now she understood what Sophia meant when she'd said she would keep her safe. How could she have possibly known about Richard's fears? She'd have to ask her next time she saw her. Elizabeth returned to the bedroom and dropped the package on the bed.

"Sophia has been schooling me, and now I know why."

Richard opened the package and stared at the contents for a minute. Finally, he looked at her and grinned.

"I'm not entirely certain what to do," Elizabeth said, pulling her nightgown over her head, pleased with both her boldness and the look on Richard's face.

"Me either," he said, "but I believe I will enjoy figuring it out."

Elizabeth laughed, her newfound power and her love for Richard making her feel attractive and invincible.

Afterward, they lay together, his weight a blanket of comfort. She was certain they had become one, that they'd melted one into each other and become a singular entity. When he rolled off her body, she whimpered at the loss. He chuckled that wonderful laugh of his—oh, how she'd missed it—and he rolled onto his side. He pulled her closer. Facing each other, his leg wrapped around her thigh, he kissed her temple.

"I never knew…" She didn't know how to explain it. The energetic lovemaking of their early days had given over to a comfortable release before their separation. But this had reached a height she'd not been privy to before, like youthful enthusiasm colliding with familiarity and creating a whole new experience.

"Neither did I, my love. Neither did I." He traced her jawline with his finger.

"What will we tell the children?" she asked jokingly, although there was some truth to her worry. The boys weren't used to their parents spending time together.

"We'll tell William his pony was aptly named and that he can name all the horses from now on. The child obviously has some power with the gods."

She smiled. William would be over the moon.

"And our friends?" She was struggling to reconcile the new with the old. "We let down the facade, I'm afraid, and they saw the disaster we'd become. What will we tell them?"

"We will tell them nothing. They will see for themselves and draw their own conclusions." He cleared a few stray strands from her cheek. "There will still be gossip, my love. There is nothing I can do to prevent it, as I cannot make anything I have told you public."

Elizabeth rose onto her elbow and kissed him. "I don't care. I know the truth. They'll not be able to keep it interesting for long if…"

"If?" he prompted, running a finger between her breasts and looking back at her, his eyes warm with affection.

"If we return to society behaving as a couple…in love." She pulled her lip in and scrunched her nose. It was hard to believe her world had unexpectedly tipped upright in one morning.

"In love," he repeated. He lifted his head and kissed her nose before resting back. "You can say it with ease, for it's true."

She put her hand against his chest. His heart beat firm and steady.

"Our friends. The children. And the gossips. That only leaves Sophia." The corner of Richard's lips quirked.

"Sophia? What do you mean?"

Richard shifted unexpectedly and rolled her onto her back, covering her body with his.

"I owe Sophia a great deal," he said, his gaze dark with need.

She smiled. "I will be sure to tell her," she replied, teasing him. "Beware. She might cash in on that debt someday."

"Thanks to her, tonight I reclaimed my life. Our lives. She can name her price. You are worth it."

Elizabeth grinned. "I do believe I would like you to prove that."

Richard did.

Again.

And again.

And again.

EPILOGUE

We have within ourselves
Enough to fill the present day with joy,
And overspread the future years with hope.

—Wordsworth, *The Recluse*

"CAN THE NEW baby ride Hope?" William asked optimistically.

He'd been as excited by the picnic today as Elizabeth. Actually, she'd probably been more excited. Their last picnic, she had worked so hard to contrive an atmosphere to seduce Richard. She looked over at where he stood talking to Sophia. There was no manipulation this time. Richard was firmly back in her bed and, more importantly, by her side.

"It will be a few more years before Daniel will be able to sit on a pony." She looked over at Sebastian, who was chattering away with Jonathon and Patrick. She knew half of it was still gibberish, but as Dr. Redding had predicted, his vocabulary had increased tenfold. And he was now solid on his feet. "But it won't be long before you can walk Sebastian on a pony."

William clapped his hands happily. "I *hope* Sebastian likes Hope," he said, laughing at his cleverness.

"I do too, my dearest. Why don't you go play with the boys?"

William scampered off, and Elizabeth moved toward Richard

and Sophia. It was to be an intimate picnic, nothing as extravagant as the London one, especially with Catherine so newly a mother. Sophia was the first to arrive. Richard held out a welcoming arm as Elizabeth approached, and he wrapped it around her waist, pulling her close.

"I was telling Richard he can stop thanking me," Sophia said with a wink. "Some souls, they are destined for one another." She glanced past their shoulders. "Ah, *miei amici*, here are two more such souls. Catherine," Sophia said, walking away from them, toward the Walfords, "you are a *bella mamma*, no?"

Elizabeth watched as Sophia cooed over little Daniel. Born late on the same day she and Richard had reconciled, Elizabeth would forever think of April 2 as a day of birth. Catherine's little boy and her relationship. She supposed hers was more of a rebirth, but she liked the connection. From life came life.

"What were you two really talking about?" Elizabeth asked, turning to Richard.

He smiled. "You know us too well. We were talking about Miller."

"And what of Miller?" Walford asked as he joined them.

"The Home Office is ready to put him before a magistrate. They have exhausted attempts at questioning him. It seems greed was his primary motivation," Richard said, shaking his head. "The consequences will not be mild. He might face death."

"Money over fellow man and country?" Walford shrugged. "I have little pity for him." He shifted and looked at Catherine before returning his attention to them. "A good friend"—he glanced quickly at Elizabeth before returning his gaze to Richard—"assures me Miss Paisley is thriving and has no need of your attention or worry."

Elizabeth smiled. She'd no idea who the good friend was, but it had been her idea to reach out and ensure the woman was truly doing well. She'd asked Richard to find out and to provide for Miss Paisley if she was in need. While Elizabeth never wanted to set eyes on Miss Paisley again, she was grateful she'd been there in Richard's hour of need. Perhaps he would not be the whole man he was had he not met her.

"Look at that handsome lad," someone boomed, and Lord Stratton, Catherine's father, stepped from the shelter of the doorway. "So anxious to meet his grandfather he tumbled into this world a little early." He held out his arms, and Catherine handed him the baby.

"Of course, your beauty," he said to Catherine, "and yours," he added, looking at Sophia, "are second only to the looks of this angel."

Elizabeth smiled, a little ache in her heart. She wished they had parents alive to thrill in their boys. "Wouldn't it be wonderful if our parents were here too?"

"We are enough," Richard said quietly, kissing the top of her head as Walford strode over to join the trio. Quartet, if one counted little Daniel, who was not at all visible beneath his swaddling.

"Are we?" she asked, looking up. Her heart would never stop leaping at the sight of him. She would never get enough of him.

"Well, if we're not, I have no doubt you'll find more," he said teasingly, looking toward where the boys played in the corner.

The orphanage was nearing completion, but Jonathon and Patrick would not be moving there. She had suggested they continue, at least for a time, to live at Thornwood Manor. Richard had taken it one step further, adamantly insisting they foster them permanently. He was also looking into the possibility of formal guardianship.

She turned into him and wrapped her arms around his waist, her cheek pressed to his chest, hugging him tight. The boys' laughter rang out behind her. Richard had embraced the abandoned boys as his own as fervently as he had reclaimed the love he'd abandoned. The boys ran by, bumping her skirts and shouting, and Richard reprimanded them. They stopped within Elizabeth's eyesight, looking contrite.

Elizabeth peered up at Richard. "You wanted Thornwood to

ring with the sound of children's voices," she said and grinned.

He tilted his head to see her better and smiled. "It would seem my every dream has come true." He leaned down for a breath-stealing kiss.

She pulled back and looked at him, all the promise of their early years lighting his eyes. "It would seem my every dream has come true too." She tilted her head up. "I love you, Lord Thornwood."

Richard stared at her for a second, his eyes growing darker, his passion always flitting beneath the surface. "And I you, Lady Thornwood."

"Lord Stratton, I feel we must fall madly in love and produce a child or we'll not be fit for this company." Sophia's lovely laugh drifted through the air, mingling with Lord Stratton's chuckle.

Elizabeth turned and looked at her friends, at her children as Patrick hoisted Sebastian on his back and galloped like a horse, and at Richard, who had not left her side these past few weeks. Thornwood Manor loomed in the background. The long shadows it cast upon the lawn were simply reprieves from the warm spring sun rather than reminders of the darkness within it. For those halls were now lit with joy and happiness.

The End

About the Author

Rose Phillips has a BA, BEd, and an Advanced Degree in Educational Leadership—none of which led to her dream of being a romance writer, but they did help pay the bills. As an educator, she worked with at-risk adolescents, so writing young adult novels seemed a natural place to start. She has three novels published in that category. While she thoroughly enjoys writing for young adults, her true love has always been adult romance, especially historical.

Rose grew up in eastern Canada, on the island of Newfoundland. She now resides on the opposite side of the country, on Vancouver Island. She enjoys kayaking, hiking, playing pickleball, and visiting the many local wineries. She long ago found the love of her life, and he continues to be the reason she believes in happy ever afters.

Twitter: @roserambles1
Instagram: rosephillipsrambles
Blog: rosephillipsrambles.blogspot.com
Amazon: amazon.com/Rose-Phillips/e/B06XB1374P
Goodreads: goodreads.com/author/show/5976526.Rose_Phillips
Bookbub: bookbub.com/authors/rose-phillips